Burglars & Blintzes
Moorehaven Mysteries #2
Morgan C. Talbot

Burglars & Blintzes
Moorehaven Mysteries™
Red Adept Publishing, LLC
104 Bugenfield Court
Garner, NC 27529
http://RedAdeptPublishing.com/

This book is dedicated to Peter Cheeseman, who taught me freshman English. He let me write a time-traveling murder mystery play about King Tut, and he praised the "Scarlet Ibis" chalk art I worked so hard on, even though I'm objectively bad at drawing.

1

"LADIES AND GENTLEMEN, it's a fine day for a tsunami." I lifted my mimosa in a toast. The crisp summer breeze, freshly woken by the morning sun, flowed off the Pacific fifty feet behind me and ruffled my summer-blond hair as I faced my friends and guests on Moorehaven's widow's walk, three stories above the ground. They raised their glasses, and a couple of them raised plates, returning my salute. The summer had been long, hot, and busy, but here at the burnt and dusty end of yet another profitable tourist season, with a packed bed-and-breakfast below my feet and a small sea of content faces before me, I could not have loved my job more.

Moorehaven graced the corner lot with its green-and-gray glory. Its three turrets gleamed in the morning light, while its lush landscaping gathered around the B&B like a green velvet gown. To the west and the south, the cliff dropped away to the Pacific. My business, my home, was a Victorian lady resting on a carven throne, and the sea itself was coming to pay homage. *I must've earned some really good karma somewhere.*

"Ooh, Pippa, how long until it arrives?" Abby was the curly-haired half of Abby-Gabby, an inseparable pair of author friends who strongly resembled each other, despite not being related: a cross between Paula Deen and Miss Marple. They even dressed alike. To-day's outfits were pink seersucker shorts and camisole for Abby and a mint-green one for Gabby. The pair came to Moorehaven the same week every summer to get their writing kicks before returning to sep-arate sides of the country.

I checked my phone. The earthquake in the Aleutian Islands had occurred several hours before then, but its small tsunami waves had crossed the Pacific Ocean and were bearing down on the Pacific Northwest. "Seventeen minutes."

Along the north side of the widow walk, my BFF, Jordan, and our fellow gossip-group member, Emily, served my delectable fruit-topped blintzes to everyone in line. Jordan's dramatic pomegranate-red hair stood out in the small crowd. Despite her only being a cou-ple inches taller than me, she even managed to loom. The color fit her personality well, and I was glad to see her even at the early hour. Early for her, anyway—Jordan had opted to work the night shift at Seven Vistas' concierge desk during the tail end of summer. Emily, on the other hand, was shorter with cotton-candy-pink highlights in her hair, and she was still wearing her yoga pants from her early-morning workout. Her pastry shop was just around the corner from Moorehaven, on the main drag. Emily was as sweet as her confec-tions, and she'd freely offered to help out.

The enormous batch of crepes and sweet, cheesy fillings Uncle Hilt and I whipped up the night before had taken us quite a while, but my assistant, Chloe, and my neighbor Tyleen had helped prepare a delectable variety of toppings this morning. In no time at all, we had transformed dozens of crepes into enticing blintzes that kept warm in Emily's pans. The aromas reached me on a swirl in the breeze, and I breathed deeply of cinnamon, vanilla, coconut, peach-es, cherries, strawberries, blueberries, and oodles of sweet gooey fill-ing. Jordan caught me sniffing appreciatively, and she shot me a com-ically big wink followed by a nod of her bright pomegranate hair, inviting me over for another helping. I waved her off. Though I'd normally try to fit in just one more delectable blintz, I was too excited to see my first tsunami. The next time someone asked me how I was doing, I'd much rather say, "I just survived a cute little natural disaster" than "Just the usual: cooking, cleaning, and murder plotting."

Three of my authors had opted not to join us on the roof, but a couple watched from the second-floor sunroom right below us, which had almost as good a view. Nearly everyone from the Glaze and Gossip group was here too. My great-uncle Hilt, with his fear of water, had wisely decided to tackle the wiring in the second-floor sunroom instead of watching the ocean try to murder us. Everyone who knew him understood his absence.

I frowned at the sight of my slim, curly-haired little sister, Trudie, at the front of the line for the third time. I'd invited her and her boyfriend, Gabe, to join us, but I'd done it so she could enjoy the historic view, not so she could eat the food meant for my paying customers and local contacts. No one else seemed to notice how many times she'd been through the line, though, so I smoothed my expression and let her be.

Her animated kite-surfing conversation with the two people behind her in line—my guest Ashley Potts and Fallon Vanderveer, owner of the large hotel across the street—was so engaging that most people were blatantly eavesdropping with smiles. *Why did Fallon ask to watch the tsunami with us? He could get a better vantage point atop Seven Vistas—it's nine stories taller.* But Seacrest was a small community, and I couldn't say no to an influential town council member, not even when my BFF, Jordan, kept warning me that he seemed interested in me. The fact that I had a boyfriend didn't seem to dim his enthusiasm, especially since Lake had a way more dramatic spot to experience the incoming wave—out at sea, saving his tour boat, the *Mazu II*, from being crushed against the marina's stone cliffs.

The only person who didn't seem engaged by the kite-surfing discussion was Tyleen. For some reason, she'd taken a dislike to Ashley from the first moment they'd met the previous week. Tyleen was a fifty-something overzealous neighborhood-watch lady who dressed like she lived in the 40s, suspected half the town of murder, and cooked like a goddess. I was just glad that my nosy, nearsighted, excellent cook of a neighbor only had occasional interaction with the aging blond-bombshell author.

To my right, fellow Glaze and Gossip member Naoma Jassley, exquisitely dressed in a periwinkle suit and matching pumps, ran her light-brown fingers over the settings on one of her three cameras. Though she served as the head editor of Seacrest's weekly newspaper, the *Beacon Weekly*, she was also an accomplished photographer and well respected among her local tribe and others along the coast. I suspected that Naoma would end up with a few exquisite photos of the tsunami even if it wiped half of Seacrest off the map.

Such an outcome would probably please Wallis Callendine, fellow G&G member and Seacrest's funereal florist, who stood at the corner of the railing and gazed solemnly out to sea. Wallis looked like the farm girl next door, but her demeanor was perma-stuck on "my condolences." Despite the summer crush, Wallis's florist business was struggling. She'd had an embarrassing mix-up where she'd delivered a new mother's *Congratulations* bouquet to a local fisherman who'd just had two toes amputated. Besides, tourists bought ice cream, not flowers. Wallis's business and her demeanor flourished best when death visited Seacrest, rather than sticky, sunburnt tourists.

I stepped in Naoma's direction, curious what kind of shots she was looking for, but another of my authors, the self-titled Ranch Hand Writer, Zach Finney, intercepted me. The appellation worked both ways, since he was an actual ranch hand who wrote about a sleuthing ranch hand. He introduced himself to every author in Moorehaven using that nickname and followed it up with "And I'm allergic to science. Good old-fashioned hard work is the best cure for everything." He'd pulled the line from his book, thinking it made him sound clever, but he'd had to explain every time that he only meant he had a latex allergy and tended to avoid doctors. He leaned an elbow onto the black wrought-iron railing and gazed soulfully out to sea. The morning sun caught his bluff features at an angle and highlighted his cheek and square jaw. "You really think we'll notice this thing when it gets here? Three feet ain't nothing. That's just like all them other waves."

I gazed out across the Pacific. "A tsunami is a little more than a wave, Zach." *It's a force of Nature.* Somewhere out there, safely beyond the crash of the waves, all of Seacrest's boats floated, waiting out the tsunami waves. Lake was out there, piloting his new boat, the *Mazu II.* Chloe was out there, too, keeping her father's boat out of harm's way. I had asked Lake to keep an eye on her. "A three-foot wave will wash in and out," I continued. "A three-foot tsunami is more like a three-foot rise in sea level. It washes in, and it keeps getting pushed farther in by all the water behind it. Seacrest sits atop a thirty-foot cliff, so the water shouldn't reach the town. But it will run up the Silver River and swirl around in the marina. All our boats and the floating dock are way out there somewhere." I pointed. "They'll come back when it's safe."

Zach looked down across the green, landscaped stretch of Moorehaven's property, occupying the corner of the block. To the west and the south, the cliff dropped away to the sea. "Well, if it's so safe, why have all of them sandbags piled up?"

I smiled fondly at the sandbags. "You just got in last night, so you didn't see it, but some of my friends organized a sandbagging event to make extra sure that the buildings in Seacrest that are most vulnerable to the ocean are protected."

Zach's thick eyebrows drew down in puzzlement. "You got more sandbags here than the big hotel on the next block. Why'd they pick this place to protect the most?"

There was no simple way to explain to a first-time guest that Moorehaven was the soul of Seacrest, that when a young man named Raymond Moore made his way to this town a century before, he'd left his mark on it and everyone who'd lived here since, that his books would be read the world over, and that his house, Moorehaven, would become a literary mecca for mystery writers. "It's been here a long time," I simply said, "and they don't want to lose it."

My eyes found the old lighthouse across the river's narrow gorge. Its tower remained broken, its light darkened, but the base that remained was in the midst of receiving a fresh coat of white paint. The basement levels had been renovated to the point where Lake had been able to move in a few weeks back, though the upper floor, with its guest room, was still in process. No longer underfoot at Moorehaven, Lake was swamped with his tourist-laden boat tours. Even though we'd been dating seriously for four months, I barely saw him anymore, and I didn't want to lose him.

Butch Thorsen, a towering, wiry older gentleman with a gallantly receding hairline and a string of Vietnam-era military thrillers to his name, approached us, perhaps thinking he needed to save me from Zach. "Everything squared away, ma'am?" he asked. "If that soo-nammy out there tries to throw its weight around, you just hang on to me." He pointed his thumbs at his own chest. "Navy man. I float like a cork, see. Haven't met anything yet that could sink me, aside from my wife, Rosetta's, smile."

His love for his wife radiated from him. I couldn't help it; I made the *aww* face. "That's so sweet. She couldn't join you on this trip?"

He hid an old sadness under a cough—a technique I'd seen Hilt perform from time to time. "I lost her a few years back. Cancer. But she did see me get published. Hell of a gal, Rosetta."

My heart warmed at the love Butch still cherished for Rosetta, but Zach seemed to be feeling left out. "Hey, Butch," he said with an eager smile, "you should write a tsunami into your next book. Have it sink a Japanese destroyer or something."

Butch's expression morphed into bafflement. "Son, I write *Vietnam* thrillers because I served during the Vietnam War. Not World War II."

"What?"

The older author sighed patiently. "The Japanese weren't fighting in Vietnam—no destroyers, no soldiers, no nothing. They put a 'no-war' clause in their constitution after World War II. In fact, they were very *anti*-war during 'Nam, at least on a citizen level. Don't get me started on their government's economic profits."

Zach's thick eyebrows dropped down, and he wrinkled his nose in confusion for a second, but then he shrugged one shoulder. "Have it your way." He wandered off.

Butch frowned, drawing deeply shadowed lines in a face that had seen many a dark day, and gazed off toward the west. "I'd be willin' to handle a little more o' that guy's silence. Every time he opens his mouth, seems some half-cocked idea comes shootin' out. Can't believe that's the very thing that makes his books so popular."

I rested a hand on his forearm in sympathy. "It's a good thing readers come in a nearly infinite variety. Authors can't control readers' desires, but there's always someone who wants to read what you write."

"And thank God for that. Those zany war enthusiasts put food on my table. I love my readers, even if—no, *because*—they're mostly aging, grumpy people who worry that history might be repeated someday unless we find a way to remember our mistakes. My readers," he said with pride, "are me."

I grinned. "And that's groovy."

Butch barked a laugh. "Yes, ma'am. It's groovy."

Someone bustled through the small crowd in my direction, and it parted to reveal Sarah, the new-mom author who was staying in the Cobalt Suite with her young family and who had developed a friendly rivalry with Butch, despite the difference in their ages. Her face carried hints of Asian ancestry, and her long, dark hair hung in a simple ponytail. She moved like a dancer or a martial artist as she carried an object protectively against her chest. As she reached me, she halted abruptly, out of breath. "I'm so sorry to interrupt, Pippa, but might I possibly store something in your refrigerator?"

I mentally inventoried the ingredients and leftovers jammed in my fridge at that moment—the perils of a full bed-and-breakfast included a dangerous lack of perishable storage space. I'd been using the root cellar in the basement all summer for the overflow. "Maybe so. How big is it?"

Sarah opened her hand to show me what she held. "Just until Jackson's next feeding at ten."

Butch stiffened at the sight of the small bottle of freshly pumped breast milk as if someone had shoved a metal rod along his spinal column, and his face reddened. The way his mouth stuttered soundlessly, he seemed to want to excuse himself from the conversation without actually speaking aloud.

I politely ignored his discomfort. "Sure thing. Tuck it anywhere it'll fit, and just zip in to retrieve it whenever Jackson's hungry for as long as you're here. I hereby bestow fridge privileges upon you."

Jordan zoomed in behind me and gave me a giant squeeze from behind. "Lucky kiddo," she murmured. When I gave her a chiding look, she added, "What? Moorehaven fridge privileges are the bomb. And I get hungry after bedtime. I'd much rather raid your fridge than mine."

Sarah smiled at Jordan, gave Butch an appraising glance, and headed back inside.

Butch gave me a gentlemanly nod and excused himself toward the far corner of the railing with Wallis. I was soon swarmed by several people at once: Abby and Gabby in their gumball-colored seersuckers; Trudie and Gabe; Fallon, tall and intense, whose eyes smiled at me every time I caught his gaze, and my Glaze and Gossip friends.

"When does the apocalypse arrive?" Tru asked in a squealy fangirl voice, grabbing my arm excitedly.

The others laughed, but I had to hide a flash of irritation at my little sister. I managed to free my arm so I could check the time again. "Two minutes." I raised my voice so everyone could hear me. "Two minutes, everyone." Whoops and clapping filled the widow walk.

"This is *so exciting*," Tru said to her sturdy boyfriend, who hugged her and kissed her dark hair. He seemed to be growing his dark, buzzed hair out. The small scar over his left ear, the one the rumors said was from the fight that sent him to jail, was barely visible anymore. "There weren't any tsunamis in Philly or Chicago or anywhere else. They had other natural disasters, like Snowmageddon, the search for the *Nathaniel Browne*, and until recently, the Cubs." Everyone laughed at that, and Fallon abandoned his decorum and let out an undignified bray.

"What's the *Nathaniel Browne*?" Naoma asked.

"Oh, it's nothing special." Tru gave a wave of dismissal. "Just a ship that went down in Lake Michigan during a freak storm in 1913 and hasn't been found since. But just before I moved out here, a salvage crew tried to find it for a Chicago museum. And their brand-new ship also sank in a freak storm. Talk about bad luck!" Again, everyone laughed at Trudie's remarks.

Everyone, locals and guests alike, had been reacting to Tru this way since she'd arrived in Seacrest three months prior. They saw her wacky side, all right, but they didn't know her the way I did. Her seaglass art and jewelry, while gorgeous, couldn't be bringing in a lot of money, and Gabe did residential fence art when he could get work.

She doesn't have a practical bone in her body. If only she'd grow up and take some responsibility!

I'd been horrified to hear that Tru's idea of settling down in Seacrest had involved hooking up with an underemployed ex-con and moving into his trailer after two weeks—so horrified that I'd actually approached my boyfriend's ex-wife, Seacrest's Acting Chief of Police Mallory Tavish, for help. "Please," I'd begged her. "Keep an eye on Trudie. I don't want her to get hurt, but she won't listen to me."

Mallory, all proper posture and tight brown bun, had taken my request seriously—*what* doesn't *she take seriously?*—once she saw Gabe's rap sheet, even though she wouldn't tell me what exactly he'd been in jail for. But Mallory had also made a few assumptions about my sister's moral fiber and taste in men. "I suppose it's too much to ask that you set a better example for her, Winterbourne." Mal had taken to addressing me by my last name, and hearing her judgy comment in that cool, professional tone she always used was profoundly irksome.

I fumed at the very memory of that conversation. *She's just jealous that I'm dating her ex-husband. There are* miles *of difference between my stable relationship with Lake and Tru's reckless fling with Gabe. And how dare she impugn my sister's character? No one insults my sister! Except maybe me.* I had to admit, on some level, I agreed with Mallory. But I'd die and rot before I ever told her that.

Anticipatory conversation swirled around me, and soon, everyone on the roof pressed against the old iron railing, blintzes and mimosas forgotten. I was glad I'd asked Uncle Hilt to reinforce it the previous week. No one had ever died in Moorehaven, and I didn't want to break tradition by letting an overexcited mystery author topple to their death on such an exciting day.

Emily wormed her way through the crowd and pushed a radio into my hand. "It's Lake," she said over the babble. "He says it's coming."

My eyes stared westward as if able to see Lake and the *Mazu II* in the blue distance. I made sure my voice sounded calm, even though my stomach offered up a worried little hiccup. "Lake, it's Pippa. Has the first wave passed you yet? Over."

"That's affirm, Pippa." Lake's voice crackled over the airwaves, and my guests quieted to hear his report. "It flashed by with barely a flicker. Harry says he didn't even notice it," he added, mentioning his latest hire—an extra pilot for the summer season. "We're all safe and sound. And Chloe's waving at me to tell you hello. Over."

I felt my shoulder muscles release some of their tension at the sound of his relaxed tone. As much as my boyfriend loved all things water related, I knew the sea was under no obligation to love him back. It wasn't every day that a natural disaster struck across the street from my house, and the man I loved was out riding atop it. *And having the time of his life, no doubt. I can't believe we each nearly drowned this spring. Yet there he is, on top of the world. I should change my name to Brandy, like the girl from the song.*

In my nearly seven years living in Seacrest, I had never felt like an insignificant organism perched on the edge of a giant flat rock next to an enormous pool of water. But knowing that even a little slosh in that enormous basin would wipe my town off the face of the earth made me—and civilization in general—feel arrogantly insignificant. "We're looking for the wave now. Any word on how many waves we can expect? Over."

"Latest word is six or seven noticeable waves. And by noticeable, I mean that scientists with highly specialized equipment can tell which waves are a little higher than the others. But we'll stay out here for the next few hours, just to be safe. We don't want the marina's floating dock reinstalled one wave too early. Over."

"Thanks, Lake. You all stay safe. We'll see you in a few hours. Over and out." I had a moment of concern that we wouldn't even be able to tell when the little waves reached us. *I hope I didn't carry all this food up here for nothing.*

"Is that it?" Abby gestured with a peach-colored nail.

"I think that's it." Gabby pointed with a fingernail lacquered in lime-green. They squealed together like teenagers—or single middle-aged women who'd drunk a few too many mimosas.

I gazed out toward the foot of the cliff that supported Moorehaven, which stretched out into the sea in a ragged, rocky line. The whole edge of the ocean dipped low, exposing dark, wet basalt that hadn't been visible since low tide, and then a smooth, unassuming bump of water charged the coastline, stretching north and south as far as I could see. Its edges ripped into foam along the cliff's foot, and the tsunami struck.

I thought I felt the floor shake underfoot with a slight vibration, but I couldn't be sure. The cliff face across from Moorehaven seemed unaffected, but then a bright-white spray of foam shot up into the air, glinting in the sun. My breath caught in my throat at its magnificent, wild beauty, and everyone around me *ooh*ed and *aah*ed. Naoma's cameras whirred busily, recording still shots and video. The white water landed harmlessly on the boardwalk that lined the cliff top. I let out a relieved sigh. "Well, that was—"

A metal-on-metal crash caught my ears, and I jerked my gaze to the street on the left side of the property. Some tourist hadn't gotten the memo about the tsunami—or maybe they had—and was driving along the southern cliff just above the beach. Foam had lightly splattered the roadway, and the driver had apparently panicked and veered inland—right into an illegally parked car on our side of the street. As I watched helplessly, the crash forced the parked car up and over the kindly stacked sandbags and into the top edge of my pretty white-picket fence. The poor wooden posts were no match for the weight of the car. The two nearest the point of impact cracked and collapsed inward onto my lawn.

"Oh no!" I cried.

Then physics—that cruel mistress—took over, and the rest of the fence, trying its best to hold together under the strain, did so at the cost of its uprightness. Several more posts in both directions snapped off and fell like dramatically collapsing damsels onto my grass. I stared down, gripping the iron railing with clenched hands. Gasps rose around me. *Crap on a cracker! Of all the Rube Goldbergs, I get the one that means insurance paperwork.*

"Oh, look, Gabe," Tru's voice rang out happily in the sudden silence. "You've got work!"

I glared at my sister before I could stop myself. *Hundreds of dollars out of* my *pocket, but she only cares that it's gonna land in* his! I squeezed the metal railing, begging for patience.

Instead, I saw the wiry figure of my great-uncle striding down the front steps, camera in hand, headed right for the damaged fence. The car's driver opened his door and stood leaning on the roof, yelling into his phone. I wasn't worried, though. Hilt could handle anything. Knowing he was already taking care of the problem eased the knot in my tummy.

Someone's phone rang, and after a few moments, Naoma pushed through the tsunami watchers and grabbed me by the wrist. "It's Lori. You're going to want to hear this."

Her intense tone dragged me out of my burgeoning frustrations, and I let her tow me over to the abandoned breakfast corner, curious as to what our missing G&G member had to report. *Lori works at the Urgent Care clinic. Did someone get hurt by the tsunami?* In the corner of the widow walk, Emily had succumbed to eating one of the last blueberry-peach blintzes. The rest of my fellow Glaze and Gossip girls homed in on us like torpedoes.

Naoma held her phone out on her palm. "Say that again, Lori. I've got the whole crew here now."

Emily gulped down her bite and looked from Naoma to me with wide-eyed innocence then stabbed the last bite on her plate and stuffed it in her mouth. Jordan made a disappointed noise that she hadn't gotten some, too, and Wallis put on her best mourning face for the loss of the blintz.

On the phone, Lori spoke in her efficient-nurse voice as if she were asking after a patient's sprained ankle. "Morning, Pippa. How's the tsunami?"

Worried that someone had been injured, I replied with a gloss-over. "It broke my fence. What's going on, Lori?"

"It broke your—? They said it was only three feet high. I thought we had better forecasting than this."

Impatient worry tightened my chest until I felt like I was wearing a corset. "Lori, is someone hurt?"

"Oh, no. I'm sorry. As far as I know, everyone's fine. But you know that new overlook they're building north of town? They were clearing the land out there this morning, and they found a skeleton."

"A skeleton?" I repeated.

Naoma's eyes went wide with interest. Her reporter side was itching to get on the case. Wallis cocked her ear toward the phone, no doubt hoping for a floral funeral boon from the grisly discovery.

"Doesn't finding a skeleton mean that everyone is *not* fine?"

"That's the kicker, Pippa," Lori said. Her voice lowered to a mysterious hush. "The skeleton they uncovered had some gold coins with it—and not any modern Sacajawea dollars. I'm talking actual treasure! They dug up a body that's buried with Spanish pieces of eight!"

2

LORI PROMISED TO CALL the second she had any more news on the skeleton, since we Gossips were all so morbidly fascinated by the idea of a new death—or rather, an old one—all except Wallis, who seemed mournful that she wouldn't be able to sell anyone grave-side flowers.

Naoma left two of her cameras in my care and headed up the highway to take photos of the discovery for the *Beacon*. Gabby helped me fold up the tripods and pack everything away. After I stashed Naoma's expensive equipment in the pantry for safekeeping, I took a minute to breathe. My insurance agent's card sat in a drawer at the hostess station, and I'd have to call her for the second time in a month, this time to report the damaged fence. My head was starting to hurt even thinking about dealing with this sudden mess.

Uncle Hilt came in through the side hall and handed me his small digital camera. "I got the fence damage and the license plates of both the cars. The guy who panicked about the wave is yelling at his insurance company over the phone—wouldn't give me the time of day—so I just took my pictures and came back in."

I squeezed my great-uncle's hand. "Thanks. Those'll be a big help for Rhonda. I'm about to call her. Again."

"Oh, then I better get crackin'. If I remember right, her favorite muffins are lemon poppy seed. I'll just whip up a batch, make sure Rhonda's in a good mood."

I waggled a finger at him and smiled. "You sly dog. Go on, then. And save me at least one muffin."

His departing cackle down the hallway toward the kitchen made no promises.

I called Rhonda, who said she'd be right over. My guests were gradually getting back to whatever they had to do that day. Several had gone upstairs to get in some writing or to change for a trip to the antiques mall up by the highway. As their hubbub died down, I heard Jennifer and Ogden in the small parlor right across from my hostess station. I stepped to the door to listen for a moment, in case they needed something, but I didn't open it and interrupt.

Ogden Kemp was a bestselling author who lived with social anxiety. He loved Moorehaven, but his anxiety didn't. He compromised by lurking in empty rooms and wandering the halls in the middle of the night, pretending he had the place to himself. He communicated with me exclusively by text, preferring the simple clarity of the written word. He'd been visiting Moorehaven since before I'd arrived in Seacrest, but I'd never seen him connect with another author until this visit, when he met Jennifer.

The young, aspiring author had just graduated from high school in June, and she'd worked all summer to save for a trip to Moorehaven as part of her ambitious quest to become a world-famous mystery author before she hit thirty. She'd waltzed through my door a few days prior, as bold as brass and just as bright, and impressed everyone with her eagerness and determination, that was, until a writerly discussion with a full complement of veteran authors at her first breakfast at Moorehaven.

I'd just served everyone a giant peach-cinnamon roll and refilled their coffee cups when the conversation moved to the topic of pen names. Ashley had said, "I've always liked the sound of Ashlen Potachev. It's got that exotic flair, you know?"

Butch added, "Y'know, 'Butch' ain't my real name, but I've had it long as I can remember, so I figured I'd just publish under it. Lucky for me, my publisher agreed."

"I'm writing as Gennessee Quois," Jennifer added proudly.

Everyone laughed. Jennifer had been so embarrassed she'd fled the table and hid in her room on the third floor. I'd followed her immediately, and I explained that the other authors were only laughing in appreciation of her witty pun. Her hurt expression made me realize she hadn't expected anyone else to figure out that she'd based her pseudonym on the French phrase *je ne sais quoi*. Further embarrassed by her overestimation of her own cleverness, she refused to come back down, and despite our repeated encouragement and invitations, she'd basically hidden in her room or lurked in doorways, eavesdropping, ever since.

On the upside, she and Ogden had begun running across each other in Moorehaven's rare moments of emptiness, and their mutual silence had been taken for nonjudgment on both sides, resulting in one of the most comfortable and pure companionships I'd ever seen under my roof.

Jennifer shifted in the green wingback chair and smoothed a finger across the nap of its velvety arm. "Demetria Graves is basically me. I mean, write what you know, right?"

"I bet you know about more than simply yourself, though," Ogden said with a smile in his voice. "You're asking more of Demetria than you do of yourself. She's gonna need extra layers to survive your plot. Ynez, my Deadly Damsel, has a lot of layers to her."

Jennifer chuckled. "I can't believe a guy as nice as you writes such a fearless, scheming badass like Ynez."

"Just balancing everything out. I have all the anxiety, so Ynez doesn't get any. We're a great match."

"Hey, I like that idea. Can I write that down?" she asked.

"Uh, oh, s-sure. I mean, do whatever you like, just—no, never mind. Sure. Argh. I'm talking too much."

Concerned that his anxiety was flaring up, I peeked through the crack in the door. But Jennifer didn't laugh at him. She just grinned like he'd given her an unexpected gift and scribbled some notes. "You're the best, Ogden."

Ogden glanced at her like he didn't believe her, but she kept writing, and eventually, he nodded with an eyebrow-lift of acceptance. I was so thrilled for their friendship that I had to press an excited fist against my lips to keep quiet and not interrupt.

I left them to their quiet discussion on layering character traits and made my way into the back corner of Moorehaven, where an isolated spiral staircase led up to the single room on the third floor: the Oubliette. The Oubliette's repair crew wasn't in yet. No doubt they were taking their time on account of the tsunami. But I could check on their progress, anyway.

I reached the door—well, the door*way*. The door itself rested against the wall at the very top of the stairwell. Inside, fresh white drywall covered the hundred-twenty-year-old wall studs.

How refreshing to see proper walls again! It finally looks like a room now, complete with cats, even. Pure-white Svetlana and gray-tabby Rex lay sprawled on the floor, forming a yin-yang of feline grace. The excitement surrounding the impending tsunami had driven Moorehaven's cats from their usual haunts, but they'd be lazing in the sunroom by afternoon, as usual. The vast majority of Moorehaven's guests got along with our cats. Ashley had nearly tripped over Svetlana on her first day in town, though, and they had settled on a mutual dislike. Unfortunately, Tyleen insisted that the cats' mistrust was a sign, and she too had been standoffish to Ashley ever since. I kept my comments to myself, but it seemed pretty clear that Tyleen was taking a leaf out of the wrong chapter of her pet-psychic son's book.

Svetlana had begun treating Rex more as an equal over the summer, rather than a dim sort of intern, and he'd paid her back by bathing her ears with his rough tongue every chance he got.

"Hey, you guys. Comfy?"

Svetlana blinked slowly at me. Rex rolled up onto his front paws and began licking her ear. She folded it down but began purring.

As soon as we paint, we can move the furniture back in. I shuddered at the thought of carrying the bed, small dresser, writing table, and Tiffany lamps up two flights of stairs, even with Hilt and Chloe's help. I'd pulled a muscle in my back getting that bed's metal frame down the stairs in the first place. *A room half complete... A map half drawn... A story half told... I wonder who will be the first guest to use this room once it's good to go? Hmm. I wonder how much I should raise the price for this "newly updated" room.*

The last time I'd seen the furniture in its rightful place had been a month prior, during an intolerable heat wave. The bed's footboard had been kicked so hard it had snapped in two. One of my Tiffany lamps was shattered on the floor, and over a hundred stab marks marred the circular room's walls. And then there was the fake blood. I still didn't know where that thriller author had gotten it or if he'd made it himself, but whatever was in it had stained everything it touched. In the end, he'd splashed a couple gallons of the stuff around the room, and most of it ended up soaking into my floorboards. I'd asked Doc Stevens to double-check its origin for me because even though I adore my mystery authors, I'm very aware that they all have a penchant for murder. I was relieved to hear her assure me the blood wasn't real. But all the repair work was. *Unfortunately.*

I stood in the clean, mostly repaired room, wrapped in the memory of what had been done there in the name of storytelling, and I found myself hunching defensively. I hadn't been myself for a couple of days after discovering that horrible disaster and kicking its perpetrator to the curb, never to be welcome under Moorehaven's roof again. Fake blood was one thing, but damaging my property? His stabby, smashy "research" told me he had some deeper issues that Moorehaven couldn't help him with. The other two guests I'd had at the time had been morbidly thrilled with my disaster. And they hadn't missed the author or his habit of dissecting his meals like an autopsy one bit. I just wanted my cozy life in Moorehaven to continue as it always had. *It'll get better once the furniture is back in place—and after my fence gets fixed. Keep calm and carry on, Pippa.*

I heard a car door slam through the open window. Below, in the Moorehaven parking lot, the repair crew's van had arrived. I met them in the foyer. Tim and his teenage nephews slipped in through the stained-glass front door, bearing paint cans and equipment.

He nodded and smiled at me. "Morning, Pippa. We'll get started right away, but if you don't hear from us by suppertime, don't *forget* to come looking. Heh, heh."

"You got it. Thanks, Tim." I appreciated his daily joke about being forgotten in the Oubliette since it had let me explain to his nephews the meaning of the French term for a dungeon where one put people in order to forget them. The boys had found it creepily fascinating. Moore must've as well; he named the room, after all.

They traipsed through the parlor and the library door. Then Hilt approached from the side hall, camera in hand. "Word's gotten round about the treasure skeleton. Tyleen came over with a huge pot roast for supper, and her gossip caught the ears of a couple of guests. Now they're all spinning theories so fast it seems like they're tryin' to power the town grid with 'em. Let me handle Rhonda and the fence. You go chat." He waved a hand toward the dining room.

I squeezed his forearm. "Thanks, Hilt."

On my way to the dining room at the other end of the mansion, I thanked my lucky stars for my wise, understanding great-uncle. He'd been a police officer then the chief of police here in Seacrest for twenty years. He'd retired at forty and became an unlikely best friend to the local famous author, A. Raymond Moore, whom he met in the local bar. And when Moore died a year later, full of years and scotch, he'd willed his Victorian home to Hilt, who oversaw its transition into a bed-and-breakfast for mystery authors.

Ever since Hilt had signed Moorehaven over to me a year and a half before then, he'd gracefully stepped aside and supported me. I'd never once had to fight him for control of my business. The man talked like an extra in *Grease* and dressed like a hipster lumberjack without the bushy beard, but to me, he was perfect.

In the dining room, I found several of my guests talking animatedly over each other. Butch waved me over. "Whaddaya think, Miss Winterbourne? That skeleton gonna be a Spanish conquistador, or a lucky Injun who found some hidden treasure?"

"Or someone else?" Gabby nudged Abby in the ribs. The pair wore matching velour active wear. Gabby's was mint green, and her hair curled around her ears, setting off her delightfully square jaw.

"What's your theory, Abby?" I took a seat at the head of the table.

"I want the skeleton to be an informant for the mob, and the gold coins are a red herring," she replied. Her velour suit was bubblegum pink, and she sported a straight bob and a rounder face.

Zach gave a noncommittal grunt. "Naw, he's a Chinaman who got washed out to sea in his fishing boat and then got picked up by a Spanish galleon. And then they dumped him off as bad luck, but he stole the coins first, and then the Indians killed him."

"I think those 'Chinamen' go by 'Asian' now," I suggested, hoping to smooth one of Zach's rough edges. He really hadn't been around other authors much—or anyone outside his small town—and it showed. I worried for his experience—or lack there-of—if his brother and sister-in-law ever ponied up for him to attend a writer's con. Zach shrugged off my comment, so I turned to another of the authors. "What're you thinking, Ashley?"

The fiftyish blonde with the aging bombshell looks seemed surprised that I'd called on her. "Oh, I hadn't really settled on just one idea yet," she said with a self-conscious wave of her hand. "But you know what they say: follow the money."

A chorus of agreement ringed the table. Zach reasserted himself. "Money makes the world go 'round. Everyone knows that rich people pull all the strings in the background."

Butch tipped his head in reluctant agreement. Ashley gave a soft chuckle that seemed to concur.

I nodded at their reasoning. "Good plan. But if the coins are genuine, why was the body buried with them?"

"Ooh." Ashley offered a significant look around the room. "I know I'd take them." She giggled.

"Maybe it was cursed?" Gabby asked.

Zach said, "Maybe the guy wouldn't tell anyone where the rest of the treasure is."

"If there is one," Butch said.

I took over. "What do you all think? Is there really buried treasure in these here parts?"

Abby, who hailed from Michigan, asked, "Did the Spanish even explore the West Coast? I mean, is there actually a chance the coins are real?"

"I bet they're fake," Zach said. "And someone killed that guy for it."

Butch gave him a frown. "You just got through saying they were real, and stolen."

"Ladies have skeletons too, you know," Gabby said with a sharp glance.

Zach shrugged again. "Yeah, but how many ladies run around with fake gold treasure?"

The Ranch Hand Writer was getting unruly again. I leaned forward and placed a calm hand on the table. "I'm sure we can all agree that the number of ladies' skeletons with fake gold treasure is not zero, so there is at least a really slim chance that each of your guesses is correct. And there's gotta be a slim chance my guess is right, and the skeleton is a time-traveling Amelia Earhart," I said cheekily. That got a chuckle out of everyone. "You know, I'm about ready to take lunch orders, but Sarah isn't here. Is she napping with her kids? I'd hate to bother her."

Gabby spoke up. "Oh, no. I saw her writing in the second-floor sunroom. I think her husband's napping with the kids. That's usually why she writes out there."

I whipped a notepad from my pocket, along with a pen. "So, what do you guys feel like today? Mozzie's sandwiches? Tacos? Chinese?"

The group settled on Mozzie's, and I wrote down their orders. On my way to the stairs to get orders from the others, I ran across Hilt.

As the guests streamed past me toward their rooms, he said, "Rhonda's come and gone. She says she'll get everything taken care of. And I told her I already know a great fence guy."

"Look at you go, Hilt." I remembered Tru's excitement over her boyfriend possibly getting paid to work on my fence. If Gabe *didn't* get the work, perhaps it would be karma repaying my sister for her glee at my misfortune. "Who's the fence guy?"

"A really old friend, lived here all his life: Ernie Ross." Hilt hesitated then took another breath. "Gabe is his assistant. Does the decoratin' and such. You know that old pioneer wagon on Highway 101, out front of the fire station? With the seascape painted on its weathered side, and all the glass floats? Gabe did that."

"Well, what if I don't want decorating?" I blurted.

Hilt's eyebrows judged me for a moment but not harshly. "We both know you do."

Prime real estate location, right on the boardwalk, historic house, good for tourism... All those unspoken reasons flitted through my head. Hilt was right. I *did* want a pretty fence for my Victorian bed-and-breakfast. And I wanted a *very good* pretty fence. I sighed, annoyed at myself. "Yes. I do. Will you call your friend and arrange everything?"

Hilt gave me his snaggletooth grin. "You got it, doll."

The walkie-talkie, which rested on the counter at the hostess station, crackled to life. "Pippa? You there? Over." Chloe's voice was tinny but clear.

I strode over and grabbed the walkie. "I'm here, Chloe. Everything okay? Over."

"We've gotten the all-clear to come in. Guess we survived the tsunami." The laconic tone in her voice reassured me that everything had gone just fine. My black-haired assistant loved drama, as long as she could pretend she didn't. "Lake let me be the one to tell you. The floating dock is being towed in now, and once they've locked that puppy down, I can park this thing and get back to Moorehaven. Maybe a couple of hours? Over."

"Roger that." My heart did a flip, anticipating Lake being back with me on dry land. "Has anyone told you guys about the skeleton that got dug up yet? Over."

"The *what*?"

I chortled to myself at her sudden interest.

"Pippa? What skeleton? What's going on? Don't make me say, 'Over.'"

I decided to wait until she got back to fill her in. She'd enjoy being held in suspense, even if she never admitted it. "I'll tell you in person. You need to focus on piloting safely. Over."

"You're an evil boss, you know that? Good thing you pay me well. I want to know about the details the second I get back. Over."

"Deal. Over and out."

Feeling evil and proud of myself, I headed upstairs to get lunch orders before I forgot. I texted Ogden on the stairs, and by the time I'd jotted down Jennifer's order, I had his as well. I knew where to find Sarah.

The second-floor sunroom faced west next to the southwestern turret, its broad windows drinking in the flood of summer sunlight. Sarah sat at a table in the far corner, her laptop open, but she seemed to be putting something away in a bag at her feet rather than typing. Outside the sunroom's open double doors, Hilt was engaged in a muttered conversation with Butch.

They looked up at me with a mix of emotions on their faces: guilt and embarrassment. I stopped short of the door. "Can I help?"

Butch got a little red in the face. "I don't see why that has to be done out here, is all I'm saying," he said, as if concluding some discussion with Hilt.

"Why what has to be—" Out of the corner of my eye, I caught sight of Sarah standing up with the bag that held her pumping kit in one hand and a bottle of freshly pumped milk in the other. *Ah.* "Her family is asleep right now. She's writing out here so she doesn't disturb them. She can't help when she needs to pump. The girls get sore if you don't empty them regularly."

Hilt looked at me strangely, but I just grinned at him—the longer I hung out with mystery authors, the fewer subjects remained taboo. "You know the kinds of weird and interesting facts I pick up in this job, Hilt. It's biology. Mother produces milk; baby drinks it. But with this new-fangled technology we have," I said to Butch, keeping my grin in place, "a woman can feed her baby and pursue her career at the very same time. It's a brave new world."

Butch went beet red. "That's not what I—you know what I—"

I was bracing for the rest of his narrow-minded comment when Hilt gently took me by the arm.

"Why don't you get Sarah's lunch order?" he asked with just a hint of insistence. Then he whispered, "I'll finish up this conversation. I think your youthful attractiveness is making it hard for Ol' Ironsides here to hold a coherent discussion on this particular topic right now."

Ah. Just as the ladies told me Woman things, Hilt spoke Man with the men. "Are you saying you don't think you're youthful and attractive?" I teased.

Hilt merely made a brief exasperated face.

I let myself into the sunroom, while Hilt guided Butch toward the stairs. He'd handled the fence accident with aplomb, and I had faith that he'd soothe Butch's rumpled feelings in no time. Sarah was sitting on the overstuffed russet couch nearest the door, holding her pump bag and the milk bottle.

She lifted her chin with a welcoming smile as I came in. "I didn't want to disrupt whatever discussion you were having, so I waited here for a second. I wasn't eavesdropping."

Embarrassed that I'd made a new mom wait with her own milk while I was trying to defend her to an old guy, I simply nodded. "They've headed off, so go right ahead. I hope we didn't keep Jackson from his lunch."

Sarah rose from the couch, dismissing my concerns with an easy shake of her head. "No, not at all. He's out like a light. I have another hour or so before he wakes up. He sleeps hard, but he eats like a little monster."

"Speaking of eating, what kind of sandwich can I get you from Mozzie's?"

"Oh, gosh, I'm starving," she said, as if she'd only now realized it. "Does he do a BLT? Hold the cheese, no mayo, on white."

I scribbled her particulars. "You got it."

Sarah smiled her thanks and slipped past me and entered the Cobalt Suite as quietly as a thief. *Or the Milk Fairy.*

I called in the sandwich orders to Mozzie, who said he'd have them ready by the time I biked to his shop. After I hung up, I peered through a blue panel of stained glass at the sea. The boats were coming in.

On a romantic whim, I rushed up to the widow walk again. With the breeze whipping through my summer-blond hair, I leaned on the rail and waved madly at Seacrest's boats spread out over the blue waters. The floating dock was making its way up the river's mouth, nearly out of sight behind the cliff at the sea's edge. I spotted the *Mazu II* in the far distance, close to the *Darwin.* The vessel Chloe was piloting for her dad was right behind them. My heart filled with the wild romance of a bygone era.

I'm actually on a widow's walk, waiting for my sailor to come in from the sea, I thought, tearing up from a combination of emotion and wind. *And he survived, so no widows here.* Awkward feelings about the fresh new relationship I had with Lake fluttered around in my mind. We'd gotten together despite his ex-wife, Mallory, being transferred to the Seacrest police station. But then summer came upon us both, and though our love wouldn't cave to Mal's possessiveness, it had no choice but to bend to tourism. Lake ran boat tours, and I ran a bed-and-breakfast. We were slaves to our businesses, and we wouldn't have it any other way—except when we desperately wanted to have any time alone.

Entire days passed when the only communication I had with my boyfriend was a series of quick texts because we were both run off our feet or tired to the bone. Our face-to-face conversations were often short and filled with affirmations of our love, which always thrilled my heart. I loved Lake more than I'd ever loved anyone. But there was never time for deeper conversation, never time to take it slowly. Our relationship was basically stolen trysts and good-night texts. It had yet to progress out of the horny teenager stage, which was basically what my last relationship had been from start to finish, almost seven years before. I wasn't really sure how to take the next step, but I knew I wanted to, with Lake by my side.

The precarious nature of my relationship with Lake was threatened further by Mallory's bullheadedness. I sent authors to work on the lighthouse restoration for first-hand research whenever I could. Mallory assigned the same duties to wayward teens to keep them out of trouble—and out of jail. Both of us tried to outdo the other with our helpfulness. But Mallory took an extra step I couldn't. Technically, she owned the lighthouse and rented to Lake.

Early in the summer, he'd mentioned that she'd casually brought up the idea of crashing in the lighthouse's guest room some nights, once it was complete. To my utter dismay, Lake had brushed her suggestion aside, based solely on the notion that "It's silly to talk about a situation that hasn't happened yet." *If only he'd been firmer with her!* But he didn't really seem capable of telling her no. As summer progressed, Mallory kept mentioning—to Lake, and even to me—how nice it would be to have a place to relax by the sea now and then, in the company of a man she knew so very well. Though she always kept her tone casual, I couldn't ignore her obvious power play. I took to asking Lake on a weekly basis how the renovation was coming. The situation upset us both, but neither of us was in a position to fight Mallory's oppressive intent.

As the wind tried to push me back from the rail, I gazed down at the *Mazu II*. Its pilot was a man I knew to be capable of deep thought, a caring, open-minded person who knew better than to judge anyone on first glance or even second. More than one part of me ached for him, but the biggest ache lay in my heart. I needed to know him better. Summer was nearly over—the tourists would soon trickle away. Then I could spend much more time delving into the deep mysteries of Lake Ivens. *All I have to do is not royally screw up until then. I think I can manage that.*

Lake saw me. He stuck his arm out one of the cabin windows and waved, and my heart overflowed. I pressed my fingers to my lips and blew him a kiss. *I have a sailor. I love my sailor.*

From the depths of my emotions, a quiet question arose. *Why did Moore's aunt Felicity build this widow walk? Was she in love with a sailor too? Or did she just love the view? Either way, I'm glad it's here. Moorehaven has plenty of secrets, just like Aunt Felicity.* My mind shifted to Lori's alert about the skeleton and its gold coins. *And one way or the other, secrets eventually have a way of coming out.*

3

"Cheese fuels my imagination. A blintz in the morning helps me write all day long. I've sworn off of grilled cheese sandwiches right before I sleep, though. I don't write horror."
Raymond Moore, 1939

TWO DAYS LATER, THE tsunami had almost disappeared from casual conversation, and the civic preservation crew had removed all the sandbags that surrounded Moorehaven during the tsunami, but my fence was still broken. Apparently, Hilt had ordered something special, and Ernie and Gabe had to wait for delivery after the weekend before he could begin. I had to admit that I was a little bit pleased not to have my little sister's boyfriend tromping around my grass quite yet. And I'd found a couple of hours to begin rereading one of my favorite Moore books: *The Brass Artifice*. Following Moore's sleuth, Hilton Gray, as he tried to solve the murder of a reclusive historian and the theft of some priceless Spanish artifacts was a treat for my overworked brain.

My kitchen hummed as we cranked out blintzes left and right, per a collective request from my guests, who hadn't gotten nearly enough of the sweet, warm delights on Tsunami Day. Rex and Svetlana watched intently from their kitchen windowsill. Hilt manned two skillets, and Tyleen—my culinary guardian angel—was filling crepes and folding them for Hilt's expert attention. My neighbor's professional cooking skills were a welcome addition to Moorehaven's kitchen during peak tourism, and her sandy-haired son, Sebastian, used to his mother's bustling kitchen routines, made himself useful by helping the rest of us coordinate. Today, Tyleen had pinned up her bright, bottle-blond hair in an Old World do that would've made Moore sit up and pay attention. I could almost feel the world-famous author's presence in the hot, busy room.

The summer was nearly over, and my counters and pantry were bursting with crates, canning jars, and cartons of delicious fruit from the fertile Willamette Valley across the hills. Blueberries, peaches, strawberries, raspberries, cherries, apricots, and more made my kitchen smell like a fruit-laden paradise. Chloe kept bringing more requests for strawberry-blueberry blintzes, so I took up a station at a chopping board and did my best to keep up with demand.

"Anything more on that skeleton?" she asked me for the fiftieth time in two days.

"When I know, you'll know," I assured her.

"Gah, this is driving me crazy!"

I grinned. "Relax. He's not going anywhere."

Sebastian returned from delivering heavily laden breakfast trays to Jennifer and Ogden and immediately held out his hand for the knife. Gentle kindness radiated from behind his generous smattering of cinnamon freckles. "You should be with your guests, Pippa. I can handle those strawberries for you."

My tummy rumbled. It reminded me that I had yet to eat anything other than a few stolen pieces of fresh strawberry. With a smile of thanks, I handed the knife to my pet-psychic friend.

But as I headed to the door, Hilt called after me. "Wait, you haven't ordered. What do you want me to bring you?"

I paused at the doorway, where I could smell the delectable aroma of blintzes from the dining room. "I've been chopping all those strawberries. I think it's only fair that I start with a strawberry blintz."

"Coming right up."

I stepped across the hallway and took my seat at the head of the long dining table, where my authors greeted me enthusiastically—well, most of them. Ogden, with his social anxiety, texted me his breakfast orders each morning, and Jennifer, still smarting from her embarrassing humiliation in front of the "grown-up" authors, had followed suit, claiming she just wanted to focus on her writing. I'd let her know several times that she was very welcome to come down, but after she refused for the fourth time, I figured I'd give her space. I wasn't her mom, after all.

"Good morning, everyone." I poured myself a big glass of orange-mango juice. "Did you all sleep well last night?"

Amid a chorus of affirmatives, Gabby raised a hand. "I had the strangest dream last night, and now all I can remember is walking down a darkened hallway with tattered wallpaper and feeling like something terrible was about to happen."

A quiver of alarm resonated in my belly, and I hoped nothing sinister would happen in Seacrest. Again. The spring had been full of danger and adventure, and I felt lucky to get out of it with my friends and family intact. And Lake. We'd fallen in love surrounded by murder and mayhem. *What does that say about me? About us?*

Gabby continued, "The feeling sat so strongly in my mind even after I woke up that I think I want to incorporate it into my book somehow."

Butch paused, his bite of gooey blintz halfway to his mouth. "Must be nice to write a book that lets you use dream sequences. All I really get to explore in my thrillers is traumatic flashback stuff, like that one time I made Captain McReynolds relive walking through the jungle without his boots." He glanced at Sarah, who sat beside her husband and daughter, and offered her a sheepish grin that told me he and Sarah had ironed out any differences between them. "Let's just say you don't want the particulars while you're eatin' breakfast."

"Sounds rather gruesome." Ashley swirled the last bite of her blintz around in the sweet, fruity sauce left on her plate. "But then, I confess that I have been known to use the occasional prophetic dream in my work."

Butch's boots story distracted me for a moment. I was sure I'd heard Hilt mention the same terrible situation on one of the rare occasions when he spoke about his time in Vietnam. But my authors were expecting one of my famous pop quizzes over breakfast, so I focused on Ashley's comment to get my mind in gear. "Remind me, Ashley, what genre you write in."

"Supernatural mystery, the kind with demons and prophets and such. Your uncle Hilton was kind enough to read a chapter for me earlier." She smiled at him over in the kitchen, and he gave her a nod.

"That's right." It tickled me how Ashley insisted on using Hilt's full name. The day she'd arrived, she'd said it reminded her of the fancy hotel chain. Hilt sure didn't mind, although he was actually named after Raymond Moore's main character, Hilton Gray.

Chloe came out bearing two plates of blintzes and handed them to Abby and then to Sarah's husband, Thad, who held their toddler, Penelope, on his lap. I used the distraction to finalize my quiz idea.

"The next two blintzes are for Ashley and Pippa." Chloe took Ashley's plate for her before disappearing back into the kitchen.

"All right, then," I said. "Before I stuff my face with blintz, let's begin our morning quiz. If the main character of the book you're writing here at Moorehaven had a nightmare at the point in the story you're writing right now, what would it be about, and what would that say about your character? Let's start here on the left with Butch."

"Oh, okay. If Vin had a nightmare." Butch shrugged thoughtfully and twitched his mouth to the left in a small, unshaven pucker. "Captain Kelvin McReynolds is the savior type. His nightmare would be standing helplessly by while the bad guy killed McReynolds's ally or escaped, especially if it was his fault because he had failed to anticipate properly or missed a clue."

"Sometimes, it's our deepest fears that motivate us the hardest," I said. A tiny shudder deep in my chest triggered memories of sudden death, my own helplessness, and paralyzing fear. In my mind, I shoved the memories down into a box, tied it with a big red bow, then set it on fire. *Motivated to stay as far away from all of that as I can.* I pasted on a smile. "How about you, Zach?"

Zach stretched and leaned back in his chair as if we all hung on his next word. "Well, now, as you know, my main character, Chuck, is an ordinary, hardworking ranch hand. He's at one with the land, but he's got a special sort of intuition because he stays calm and listens to his own heart. It's what lets him solve impossible mysteries that happen all around him in the ranching community."

I could sense the interest in the room waning at Zach's long-winded preamble, so I directed Zach back on target. "And what sort of nightmares would Chuck have?"

Zach indulged another stretch before replying. "Oh, probably the usual stuff, coyotes getting into the chickens, cattle rustlers, maybe even a flash flood."

I nodded. "So a similar idea to what Butch's Vin goes through."

Zach's bushy brows lowered, and he leaned forward, putting his elbows on the table. "No, no, nothing like that. Chuck would never dream about people dying."

Butch spoke up beside Zach, and his tone carried a thread of exasperation. "What she's saying is, your guy and my guy both worry about doing their job right."

Zach turned his gaze on the older author next to him. He pointed a fork that speared a piece of sausage toward Butch. "Chuck doesn't worry about his *job*. He's great at his job. If you'd read my book, you'd know that." Zach stuffed the bite of sausage in his mouth, dropped the fork on his plate, and stood. "Thanks for breakfast," he said in my direction. He nudged his chair back and strode from the room.

Everyone watched in surprised silence at his sudden departure. Butch, still visibly disgruntled, said, "I mighta read it, if he hadn't introduced himself with one breath and tried to charge me full price for his book with the next."

I took in a slow breath and eased it back out again. Moorehaven hosted mystery authors of all subgenres and skill levels, published or not. Some, like Zach, hadn't gained much social experience in their professional capacity. In such situations, I did what I could to steer everyone toward the nearest positive, which, in this case, was back to nightmares. *Nightmares as a positive thing—how 'bout that?*

"Sarah, what about you? What kind of nightmares would your main character have?"

Sarah shot a quick glance at her husband, who lifted one eyebrow and tipped his head in a knock-yourself-out gesture. Her daughter, Penelope, was busy stuffing her face with raspberries. Sarah said with an apologetic hint to her voice, "I write gritty psychological thrillers, where my FBI agent, Zinnia Lao, goes up against all kinds of horrible, crazy bad guys. Thing is, she's kind of an antihero. She's not catching them because she thinks they deserve to be put away or that the world is safer without them roaming around. She puts them away because she's smarter than they are, smart enough to join the FBI instead of becoming a villain, smart enough to work within the system. If she has nightmares, they involve being bested by someone she thought she could outwit. But she's not really the kind of person who is afraid of things."

"Ooh, she sounds like she might be a psychopath or something," Abby commented. "Oh, and it looks like I'm next. Lady Lisbet is a consort to the king of Germany, and she's currently embroiled in international politics and about to make a shady deal with English privateers. She's in love with her king, and she'd do anything to keep his kingdom safe, so her nightmare would involve not being able to talk—or kiss—her way out of a tight spot in time to save the day."

"Now, that's a woman with serious skills." I had a habit of drawing on my guests' main characters for inspiration in times of need, and it sounded like Lady Lisbet would be a shoo-in.

"I'll say." Sebastian shook his head in an I'll-never-be-that-awesome way. But he was already being comforted by Rex and Svetlana, who rubbed against his ankles appreciatively. He handed me my strawberry blintz, and Ashley got her peaches-and-cream. I hid a frown when I saw that her blintz was a little underfilled. *I hope Tyleen isn't punishing her for tripping over my cat.* But my breakfast called to me, and I let the thought go, inhaling the delectable aroma of the sweet cheese filling. The strawberries I'd chopped up pooled atop the blintz in a sweet red sauce. After just one bite, I was in heaven.

Abby nudged Gabby to go next. Unlike her friend, Gabby hesitated before speaking, and she shredded her napkin with small twists. "I suppose Dinah would have nightmares about her grandchildren. Maybe they'd get lost in a natural disaster like a tsunami."

Abby leaned forward. "Gabby based Dinah off of Miss Marple, but with no sense of her own limitations. Remember that scene, Gabby, when you had Dinah try to scale a fence in order to peek over into someone's daylight basement, and she got halfway up the fence and got stuck there?" Abby giggled. "Didn't have the strength to climb over, didn't dare jump off and break a hip! Dinah was fine, but that scene had me in stitches!"

Gabby flushed prettily at her friend's enthusiasm. I chuckled appreciatively, along with everyone else, and then I turned to Ashley. "Your main character is a prophet, right?"

Ashley's smile had a wicked glint. "Scarlen Fate only *claims* to be a prophet. Deep down, he's pure trickster." Appreciative murmurs ringed the table, even from Abby. "Scarlen likes to be in charge without anyone realizing how powerful he really is. So his nightmare would probably be the angels really speaking to him. He wouldn't want to share power, and he wouldn't want to admit that someone had more power than him." She smiled and shrugged. "That would ruin all of his amusing little plans."

The phone rang down the hallway, and I rose to get it, knowing my Phone Queen, Chloe, was beginning cleanup in the kitchen. But Tyleen breezed out of the kitchen, drying her hands, and said she'd get it. Butch was in the middle of a joke his main character, Captain McReynolds, had made about how many GI's it took to screw in an Army-regulation light bulb when Tyleen returned to the kitchen doorway. Her thin lips were nearly invisible as she pressed them together. "Hilt, it's Mallory. She says it's important."

Hilt slipped away down the hall to take the acting police chief's call. I stifled a grumble about Mallory interrupting a perfectly good morning—and Butch's joke.

Ashley leaned forward, having just polished off her last blintz. "Mallory's your police chief, right, Pippa? Does she allow ride-alongs or interviews? Scarlen's antagonist in my book is the police chief, and I'm hoping to pick up some pointers while I'm here."

I took a deep breath and shared a *not likely* glance with Sebastian. "Acting Chief Tavish is..." I searched for a neutral adjective and came up empty. "She's really swamped with the summer rush right now. You can fill out a request form at the hostess station here and walk it over to the station. But I don't want to get your hopes up that she'll say yes." *Chief Craig was very helpful to my authors. I know Mallory's busy, but if only she were more accommodating. Or friendly. Or respectful of Lake's personal boundaries. The woman stalks him like a psychopath sometimes. At least tourist season has cut back on her free time to park her cruiser on the Cedar Street bridge and stare at him while he works on one of his boats.*

"I understand. Maybe I'll just come back in a few—"

Ashley broke off at a sudden, clattering sound. I recognized it as the coat tree by the front door falling over. Everyone seemed to hang their windbreakers on the same side of the tree when they came in, and a strong gust of wind through the open door could easily topple the poor thing. I'd lost track of the number of times I had set it back on its feet over the summer. Frowning, I excused myself to see what was going on.

But no one had arrived, and Hilt was gone. I righted the coat tree and hung all the coats back on its arms. Hilt's blue windbreaker was missing.

"Whatever Mallory had to tell him," Tyleen said as she joined me in the foyer, "it doesn't seem like it's good news."

"I know what Mal's like. Did she offer any kind of clue what she was calling about?"

Tyleen adjusted her thick 40s-style glasses, and her thoughtful frown brought her pointed chin to a nearly Disney-villain sharpness. "Not really, no. Oh, well, I mean, she was calling about an old case of his, and she said something about a breakthrough, and did he have time to meet her at the coroner's office to go over some details. But other than that, I'm so sorry, but I can't remember a single thing." She gave me a bright, airy smile and returned to the kitchen.

I stood in the foyer, digesting Tyleen's words. Hilt never talked much about his years as a Seacrest cop. I'd kind of assumed he'd been a Sheriff Andy Taylor policeman, genially strolling down Seacrest's old streets and waving to all of its happy citizens, with the occasional stern talking-to for boys who snatched candy bars from the general store. I wasn't sure what kind of old case Hilt would follow this long after he'd switched careers, but the fact that it had a breakthrough made me intensely curious. I made a mental note to pester the truth out of him when he came back.

My front door opened, and for a moment, I thought Hilt was coming back. But it was Officer Vic Nuncio instead, wearing wraparound sunglasses and the tailored shorts and short sleeves of Seacrest's dark-blue summer police uniform. He stepped inside and raised the glasses until they rested on his shaved head. His bright hazel eyes twinkled at me out of a bluff, tanned face. "Hope I'm not interrupting anything, Pippa. I was hoping to snap up the latest G. Hopewell thriller. Do you have any copies?"

"You bet I do." I waved Mallory's deputy over to the Shelf, Moorehaven's bookstore. He grinned like a kid in a candy store, and in three big strides, the beefy man vanished inside the converted closet, which was lined with shelves of books that had been written under Moorehaven's roof. I had been leery of the big-city cop Mallory hired after she became acting chief of police, expecting him to follow in her robotic footsteps. But Vic was a diehard thriller-lover, and he had fallen in love with several series that had been penned by my guests, becoming a Shelf regular in record time.

Vic emerged from the bookstore, clasping his prize, and I rang him up. "You let me know when G. Hopewell stays with you again, okay? I want her to sign this for me."

"I'll do that." I jotted myself a note. "Hey, Vic, you hear an update on that skeleton?" I asked, hoping for a clue regarding Hilt's sudden departure.

But the deputy only shrugged his massive shoulders. "Sorry, haven't heard anything on the skeleton. The coins, though... Funny thing..."

My curiosity lunged forward, and my elbows landed on the counter. "Do tell."

Vic thoughtfully scratched his chin. "I took one up to the pawn shop to see if Mr. Axelrod could authenticate it—or prove it was a fake. Every time I walk in there, he starts sweating and dry-washing his hands, but when I showed him that gold coin... I could've thrown a bucket of white paint at his face, and it wouldn't have turned him pale as fast as that coin did."

"Wow. Did he say why?"

Vic *tsked*. "Blew me off with some smokescreen about how rare the coins are, historical value, a privilege just to hold one, that sort of thing. He was talking a mile a minute. Guy's up to something. Probably smells a scam he can use. I'll keep an eye on him."

"Good idea. But did he authenticate the coin?"

"He called a historian buddy from up the highway who came down and did it. While we waited, I didn't let that coin out of the evidence bag. No way I'm letting him get his greasy paws on it. The historian did authenticate the coin. It's legit."

I blew out my breath. Somehow, I'd been expecting the treasure to be fake. "Holy cow. Actual treasure."

"Exciting, right? Other than that interesting bit, I've been keeping tourists from blocking local driveways, and I did get to rescue a little girl's stuffed animal from past a safety fence on a cliff."

"We're lucky to have such a heroic officer serving here in Seacrest."

His eyes twinkled. "Just doing my job, ma'am."

My customer left happy, and I remembered that I had a mouthwatering strawberry blintz to polish off. I had another, and one more with apricot-cheese filling. I'd just started loading the dishwasher with plates that Chloe rinsed and handed to me when the phone rang again.

Tyleen left her cleaning cloth on the dining room table and called that she'd get it. I hoped it was Hilt, so I'd finally understand why he dashed off. In a moment, she returned, saying it was for me. "It's Trudie," Tyleen added in an ominous tone.

I dried my hands and picked up the phone. "Tru? What's up?"

My sister sounded breathlessly urgent. "Your phone is off. Or dead. And every time I called the B&B, the line was busy. I've been trying to reach you for half an hour."

"Sorry about that. I turn it off during breakfast, and I forgot to turn it back on. It's been busy here this morning—"

"Pippa, something terrible has happened."

I blinked. She sounded stressed but not distraught. I hoped she hadn't just taken a positive pregnancy test or anything. "What is it?"

"Gabe just got a call from his grandma, who got a call from Mallory."

"Oh no, is he in trouble?" *What's gonna happen to Trudie if her boyfriend gets arrested again? Can I find a way to let her stay at Moorehaven?*

"God, Pippa! No! You're not *listening* to me. Mallory called Grandma Maggie because Doc Stevens has identified that skeleton they found a couple days ago, the one with the pieces of eight?"

"Y-Yeah, I remember." I tried in vain to connect my sister's boyfriend to Mal's call to Hilt. My world seemed to bend and connect in places it shouldn't, like in *Inception* or *Doctor Strange*. "Who is it? Who did they dig up out there?"

Tru sighed heavily and paused. "It's Grandma Maggie's brother, Ramòn. He... he went missing in 1964. Or so everyone thought. He was wearing a watch she'd given him for his twenty-first birthday. Their names were engraved on the back."

"Oh my God. He's been right outside of town this whole time." A weird sense of sinking backward in time made my tummy cold. Hilt had only been a policeman for a couple of years in 1964. He'd told me a couple of stories of his early days, when he'd hang out with his friends, Ritchy, Ernie, and Ramòn. He'd never told me, not once, that he'd had to look into his friend's disappearance. He definitely hadn't mentioned that he'd never figured out what happened to Ramòn. *No wonder he dashed out of here so fast.* "I'm so sorry, Tru. How is Maggie taking it?"

"Well, um, that's kinda why I'm calling. Mallory said that... She told us his skeleton bore clear signs of violence."

4

"VIOLENCE?" MY VOICE was higher and unsteadier than I intended. "Are you saying Ramòn was murdered?"

"All Doc Stevens is willing to confirm is that Ramòn's skull is badly cracked. Mallory said that Doc Stevens's brother, *also* a Dr. Stevens, is coming down from Portland to help her examine the skeleton. He's one of those what-do-you-call-ems, forensic somethings that look at bones."

"Forensic anthropologist." I pursed my lips, though my sister couldn't see my expression over the phone. "But Ramòn didn't bury himself in that shallow grave."

Trudie paused. "You may be able to think that way, but I can't. Right now, I need your help. Gabe wants to go see Grandma Maggie, but Pippa, I have no idea how to comfort a grandma who just learned that her brother's not living happily in Mesa, Arizona, or wherever. No, he's been dead a couple miles up the road for the last half a century. I-I just, what do I say?"

I flailed around for an answer for my little sister. I barely knew Gabe, and I'd never met Maggie. Tru had charitably described her with that line from the *Titanic* movie: "an indoor girl." "Well, she should know that it's okay to be sad, even for something that happened so long ago. She just heard about it. She'll be in shock. You can tell her how sorry you are for her loss, and you can stay if she wants, but you can leave if she needs to be alone."

"That hardly sounds like anything. Shouldn't I say something else? I mean, your authors probably have funerals all the time in their books, right? What do people say then?" Her tone was oddly insistent.

Knowing I probably sounded pedantic, I said, "Funerals only happen in mystery novels when the dead person is important to the main character, Tru, or maybe if there's going to be a clue given at the funeral, or the killer shows up and says something that gives him away once the sleuth recalls it—"

"Okay, I get it. Never mind about the funerals." Tru's voice sounded strained. Handling grown-up emotions was clearly an unfamiliar task for my vagabond, artsy kid sister.

Although my answer was way too technical for her question. Feeling a little guilty, I said, "You know what? How about I come with you to visit Maggie?" *Maybe I can pick up a little of what's going on, since Hilt's gone.*

The pause that followed was longer than I'd expected. "Yeah," Tru finally said. "Yeah, thanks."

She gave me Maggie's address, and I said I could be there in twenty minutes. I called Tyleen and asked her to keep an eye on Moorehaven and my guests for a short while, and she very kindly agreed.

Something didn't feel right about Ramòn's disappearance, though. Something felt very wrong, indeed. I called Naoma and filled her in on what Trudie had told me.

"Oh my God. That's terrible news," she said sadly. "Poor Maggie. How can I help?"

"Trudie and I are on our way to see her now. But the whole situation feels wrong to me. If Ramòn died in an accident, who buried him? And if he was murdered, why didn't Hilt solve the case? Why wasn't Ramòn found for more than fifty years?"

"Ah, of course. You want me to nose around in the newspaper archives, see what I can find?"

"Please. You're the best."

Just before I was ready to leave to meet Tru and Gabe, Hilt returned. He slipped in the front door and stood there, lost, with the bright summer light streaming through the stained glass behind him. He was a tarnished saint in a blue windbreaker, his halo dulled, his face downcast.

He'd heard the news. I approached him gently. "Hilt?"

He kept his eyes on the floor. "Looks like I botched it, Whip."

Uncle Hilt only called me "Whip," short for "Whippersnapper," when he felt old, and the term tugged at my heart. "You were young, and everyone makes mistakes."

"You don't understand." His voice fell to a murmur.

My great-uncle had never looked older and more defeated than he did in that moment. I was used to guiding my little sister in the right direction, but Hilt had always been my road sign. I hesitated, unsure how to help.

But he rallied, trying valiantly to be his old self. "You were already heading for the door. Don't let me get in your way."

"Actually..." I hesitated before continuing. *Maybe he won't want to know what I'm about to do. Maybe he's not ready to see Maggie's grief when his own is so freshly unearthed.* But he was still Uncle Hilt. I'd let him decide. "I'm headed over to Maggie's to meet Tru and Gabe. He wants to be with his grandmother."

Hilt's reaction couldn't have been more pained if I'd stabbed him in the chest, but then he closed his eyes and smoothed his expression. With a tip of his head, he said, "No, I should go with you. I need to see her too."

Something about his last sentence sounded deeply incongruous with his body language, but I let it be. Hilt was entitled to deal with his grief and shock like everyone else.

I grabbed my coat, and we slipped out the front door.

We unlocked our bikes from the bike rack down by the parking lot and rode, side by side, through town, up the gentle hill that rose away from the sea. The sidewalks were packed with tourists and treasure hunters, and cars circled blocks fruitlessly, hoping for free parking opportunities. Brightly painted storefronts gleamed in the strong sunlight and offered the very best of small-seaside-town wares laid out on tables and in windowsills. Kites and wind-spinners twirled from reinforced garden arbors and fences. Blown-glass ornaments and bowls gleamed with jewel tones. The smells of cottage fries, waffle cones, and cotton candy swirled down the street on the brisk breeze. *Do I really get to live in this magical town? I guess even magic towns have dark days, though. And Seacrest's no exception.*

With the insistent wind at our backs, carrying the raucous cries of tourist-fed gulls, we made good time up to Highway 101. The constant flow of summer travelers slowed to a vehicular conga line as it wended through Seacrest's commercial district, and Hilt and I waited patiently for the only stoplight in town to turn green for us.

Hilt gazed up the hill toward the north, where cars, motor homes, and bicyclists with wheel-bags continually crested the low rise, visible in the sharp cut through the low, thick forest. "This highway used to be so quiet," he said wistfully. "Back in the day, you didn't even need to wait to cross in the summer. And most of these buildings weren't here. This was the edge of town. The town council insisted, when the highway came to town, that it should be outside the town boundary. And back then, this was it." He pointed. "Ritchy's pawn shop, there, didn't get built for fifteen years. Ritchy bought it in the sixties. He used to be a good friend. Back in the day."

Ritchy Axelrod, who freaked out at seeing the treasure coin Vic brought in. The light turned green, and the flood of automobiles reluctantly paused for us to dismount and cross the highway. "What happened?"

Hilt focused on pushing his bike across four lanes of traffic. "A lot happened. Maybe too much."

We mounted again and continued up the hill. The grade steepened, and the houses grew smaller, products of 1940s bungalow-type expansion after World War II. Neatly kept lawns landscaped with clusters of shrubby bushes, bright flowers, and maritime decorations lined both sides of the road. The fences drew my eye, since I had a broken one. Many were short and white, while others were natural brown. Several bore cute seaside décor, whether painted seashells, tiny shelves holding glass floats, or swooping reclaimed fishing nets in blues and greens. *I wonder how many of these fences Gabe decorated.*

Hilt and I turned left at the last intersection before the road dead-ended at an alpaca farm. Trudie and Gabe were waiting restlessly on the road next to the drainage ditch that ran along Maggie's side of the street. Our arrival brought a relieved smile to my sister's face, but Gabe didn't react beyond giving us a quick wave.

Maggie's house was once a bright sunshine yellow, but even in the strong summer light, it appeared to have greened and faded with age. In contrast, her lawn was in perfect condition, weed free and gloriously healthy. A border of decorative shrubbery and beautiful flowers ringed the grass, and in its center, a small flowering tree shaded another small flower bed. A low fence surrounded the grass, painted white and bearing inlaid blue anchors interspersed with tiny glass fishing floats that curved out of the wood in 3-D. Hand-painted detail brought the motif together. I bit the inside of my lip with chagrin, wishing I had thought more kindly of Gabe. He clearly adored his grandmother.

"Hey, you made it." Tru gave a nervous wave. "Oh, Uncle Hilt, you came too." She gave him a quick hug, as if consoling him at a funeral. I wondered how much she knew about Ramòn. *Probably more than me.*

We walked our bikes to the single-lane, rough-pebble driveway and left them there. Gabe guided Tru to the front door with an arm around her waist. I found myself staring at it with distaste. *Oh, come on, I'm not jealous or anything. I have a boyfriend. Whom I never see, but that's not the point. The point is, well... I don't need a point. I'm her older sister. I can disapprove of anything I want to.*

Gabe knocked before he opened the front door. Hilt and I followed him and Tru inside. I gave the strawberry pot a sympathetic glance as I passed it. Inside, the house smelled of fresh earth and herbs, with a faint aroma of cigarettes. The front room held two dark-gold rocking chairs and a matching sofa. Their color and rough texture proclaimed their 70s origins.

"Gram?" Gabe called, loudly enough to be heard throughout the small home.

"I'm here, Gabriel." Her flat, quiet voice rose from nearly right under my nose. She'd been sitting so still in a mustard-colored dress in the rocking chair near the door that I hadn't registered her presence. Everyone else jumped too.

"Gram." Gabe walked around the sofa and squatted by Maggie's knee. "Gram, I am so sorry." He took her wrinkled hand in his and squeezed it then laid his cheek against the back of it. "I am so sorry," he repeated. "You need me to stay today? I can stay."

Tru looked at me, uncertain. I gave her a nod of sisterly concern, and she said to Maggie, "Me too. We can both stay if you need us."

I nodded at my sister again, approving and just a little smug. *See how well things go when you listen to me?*

Hilt dropped a gentle hand on Maggie's shoulder and squeezed. "You have my deepest sympathies, Maggie, and my deepest apolog—"

I'd never seen a septuagenarian move so fast in my life. Maggie shrugged out from under Hilt's condoling hand, shot to her feet, spun around, and slapped him hard across the face. As she struck

him, a breathy cry slipped from between her lips, not shrill, but bur-
dened with decades of fruitless desperation.

The room went dead silent. Gabe, unbalanced by Maggie's swift
movement, fell onto his butt and gaped up at her. I felt rooted to the
threadbare brown carpet in shock, all my self-satisfaction blown out
of the room by Hurricane Maggie. Patently, I was missing about fifty
years of information. But Hilt wasn't. He accepted the slap, rocking
back on his heels in silence. He even seemed to be waiting for another blow, but it didn't come.

Maggie stared at him, wide eyes brimming with tears, but her
hands remained clenched at her sides. She couldn't seem to find any
words, so her breath hissed angrily through her teeth.

"Gram, don't, come on." Gabe picked himself up off the floor.
"This ain't the way." His eyes were as wide as hers, and he didn't
sound confident that he was right.

"No, she's fine." Hilt's cheek glowed pink. "I deserved that and
much more."

"What? Why?" I blurted.

Tru looked as shocked as I felt. She backed against the wall,
seemingly unwilling to walk all the way around the sofa to get to
Gabe and possibly draw Maggie's ire upon herself.

"Before Ramòn disappeared," Maggie finally said, "I used to
think I was the luckiest girl ever. A doting brother, good friends, and
a man who loved me. A man who deserved far better than me. But
then my brother went missing, and the love of my life backed away
from me like I was a walking curse. And I started to think I was
too—that he deserved far better than me. My rebound marriage was
a total disaster. My daughter's a drug addict in Austin, and my grand-
son, bless his sweet heart," she said, sparing a less severe glance for
Gabe, "spent time in jail because he stood up for family. My whole
adult life, Hilton, has been a downward spiral. I thought if I learned
the rules, I could get out from under this curse, and then I'd be okay.

But my whole life blurred by in a fog of superstition and painkillers, and now—*now*—you come to me and tell me that my brother was never missing. That he was killed and buried like a dirty secret. That someone has spent the last fifty years getting away with a murder *you—couldn't—solve*." She poked Hilt in the chest with each of her last three words.

Hilt spread his hands helplessly, at her mercy—and I hoped she'd have some. "I'm so very sorry, Maggie. I knew I'd failed you. I just didn't know how to make it right. I could never close the case. I had a couple decent leads, sightings in other states, but they never panned out. I didn't know what else to do."

Maggie stepped around the chair and stood nearly nose to nose with Hilt, though she was a good six inches shorter than he was. "You could have visited. You could have called. You left me alone, Hilt, you and Ritchy and Eddie. You were all Ramòn's friends, not mine, and when he left me, so did you. You all abandoned me! Is it any wonder that I turned to psychics and tarot readings to get through the day? To get through my *life*?"

Hilt seemed battered by her tirade, but still, he took it. *He's plagued with guilt. He thinks he deserves this verbal beating.* Had he really left a young woman alone to grieve her brother—for fifty years?

"I... I just didn't know how... I never knew what to say..." Hilt stammered.

Another ringing slap echoed through her living room, catching Hilt on the cheek and making me flinch. When Maggie spoke again, it was with an icy calm that chilled my spine. "You didn't have to *say* anything, Hilton. I just needed someone to *be* there for me. And you never were. None of you were." She drew herself up. "Get out of my house."

Hilt humbly nodded and turned to go.

I probably looked like a shell-shocked war victim as I hastily muttered, "I'm so sorry." I hurried after my uncle, leaving Tru and Gabe behind. I'd seen—and been in—my share of fights, but nothing I'd experienced could compare to the sheer depth of desperate rage that shook Maggie to her core. My hands shook, and I couldn't quite catch my breath.

Out in the bright sunshine, we mounted our bicycles. Words failed me, and I couldn't bring myself to meet Hilt's eyes.

Trudie darted out after us. "Pippa, wait a minute. Gabe's decided to stay, so I'll stay with him, at least for a little while. Are you okay, Uncle Hilt? That was..." She turned to me. "I thought you said mourning people need comfort. Grandma Maggie looks more like she needs a sacrificial victim. And she picked Uncle Hilt."

"I'll be all right, girlie-pie," he told her. "I deserved every word of that. You girls are lucky to live in a world where you can talk about failure and how it makes you feel. We didn't have any of that stuff back in my day. I thought it best to tough it out, to wait until I could solve Ramòn's disappearance. I thought I'd fix everything if I could go back to Maggie one day and bring Ramòn through the door with me. But I never could, and now I know why. I kept telling myself, *Just a little longer, and you'll figure it out, Hilt.* I never wanted to think about what she was going through. I just wanted to fix things. I wanted to make everything right."

I was alarmed to see tears welling in his eyes. I'd never seen my uncle cry, not once in all the years I'd lived at Moorehaven. But this pain was deep and old, and hauling it up from the murky waters of his own history was bound to rip him open. I laid a hand on his arm. "Come on. We'd better get back to Moorehaven. God knows what Tyleen's gotten up to."

My practical concern got him back on track. He nodded, sniffed hard, and put a foot on his pedal.

I hadn't felt this close to Trudie since she moved to Seacrest. "Let me know how it goes. I really didn't know how bad things were for Maggie. If I can help, I'm there for you."

She gave me a quick hug. "Thanks. I'll see you around."

As Hilt and I biked back down the hill with the broad blue of the Pacific Ocean spreading out along the edge of the North American continent, my mind turned over the little I knew about Hilt's complex relationship with Maggie, and the murder case he didn't know he had to solve. A certainty drilled itself into my consciousness: *Hilt is going to try to solve Ramón's murder. He believes he owes it to Maggie. And after what I just saw, he probably does. I hope the search for the truth doesn't tear them both apart. And I'll do whatever I can to see that it doesn't.*

5

"I can't imagine living anywhere besides Seacrest. Nothing ever happens here, and nobody comes to visit. It's perfect."
Raymond Moore, 1942

HILT AND I HAD CROSSED Highway 101 and biked halfway back to Moorehaven before he spoke. We paused at a stop sign, and he muttered, "How could I get this so wrong?"

I felt absolutely terrible for him. One of his best friends had been murdered, and he hadn't even seemed to suspect it. Hilt prided himself on his incisive mind. I'd learned some of the basics of investigative thought by spending most of my time with mystery authors, so I had an inkling how foolish he must've felt. I remembered the self-anger of sleuths from Doyle's Sherlock to Christie's Poirot and TV's Mr. Monk when they realized something they felt they should've known much earlier. Hilt must've felt even worse, though. He hadn't belatedly discovered whodunit, he'd missed the entire crime.

"Let's go see Jimmy," I suggested. Several reasons that Hilt might want to see his old partner crowded my tongue. But I didn't need to say any of them.

"Yeah." He wheeled out into the intersection and hung a left.

Of course. He's already thought of all those reasons too. They were partners for years, and Jimmy's lived here since the 70s. No one else in town understands my uncle like Jimmy. Definitely not some upper-crust city cop like Mallory.

I followed Hilt out of the main section of town and south along the coastline, taking the winding, narrow beach-access road. A dozen cars had pulled into sandy pullouts, and families cavorted on the broad swath of sand and in the foamy water beyond it. Clusters of scrubby trees leaned away from the constant Pacific wind and offered shelter and shade as we passed beneath them. We coasted down a long, gentle hill from the cliff that Seacrest was built on, until we rode a few feet above sea level, cruising beside a pale, sandy beach edged with sea grass. A handful of bleached driftwood logs had been pushed by the recent tsunami right up against the steep five-foot drop-off at the edge of the road. A couple of the smaller logs had even been lifted across the road by the water and rested on the far side against the rise of the hill. The salt air pressed itself against me like a physical being, warm and adventurous. For a moment, I ached for Lake, for his touch, the sweet-salty taste of his lips.

We reached a side road that led to a neighborhood of summer cottages and beach houses. Hilt made a sharp left then a right, and I reluctantly let Lake fade from my thoughts so I wouldn't crash into a decorative rock or a blue-painted anchor set a little too close to the edge of the pavement.

Former police chief Jimmy Craig had lived in a 1960s summer cottage since it was built. Since he'd been forced into medical retirement the previous spring, he rarely left its boxy walls except to fish. A squared-off structure with giant windows facing the sea and cedar shakes all over its two-story walls, the home resembled a DIY shaggy wooden hunting blind more than a seaside getaway. The lawn was immaculate. Its only decoration was a miniature dinghy surrounded by sea grass and filled with hen-and-chicks succulents. A lone glass fishing float nestled among the spiky leaves, gleaming with a reflection of the cloudless sky. Jimmy was a little rough around the edges, but even one cloud added character to a plain blue sky. I missed seeing him in uniform, especially considering that Mallory was his re-placement.

We parked our bikes, and Hilt walked up the narrow gravel path ahead of me. He and Jimmy had a secret knock—more than one, actually, like a series of codes, and I'd never been able to crack them. Hilt paused at the navy-blue door and took a deep, heavy breath before he raised his hand and tapped a series of knocks with his index knuckle.

I looked into the wind as we waited. One street sat between Jimmy's house and the rocky coastline. The waves were kicking up foamy water in the distance, and I shivered, feeling equally unsettled. Maggie's rage had really thrown me for a loop.

The door swung open, and our portly former police chief stared out at us. His hairline might have been marching in an even retreat, but the wavy gray army massed behind it ruffled in the breeze, intending to put up quite the fight. And despite his pink face—from high blood pressure as opposed to sunburn—the chief looked like he'd dropped a solid thirty pounds since he quit the force. I was impressed.

"To what do I owe this honor, you old so-and-so?" He extended a hand to my uncle.

Hilt grasped it with the aggressive firmness of his generation, and his smile broke out like the sun coming out from behind the clouds. "Just wanted to make sure you hadn't tripped into the Pacific."

I suddenly felt like a third wheel. "I should get back, Hilt. You stay as long as you want. We'll find a way to survive without you."

"No, no, come in for at least a lemonade or something." Jimmy waved us inside. "Gotta make the neighbors stop pitying me for my total lack of social life. In fact, head on up to the viewing deck around the side. That way, Mrs. Norris can see you." His eyes drifted to a pale-green beach house whose balcony faced his at an angle.

"She ask you out this week too?" Hilt asked. I trailed him along the hardwood floor toward the narrow spiral staircase to the second floor. Jimmy's floor plan was so open, I felt like an action figure waiting to be discovered in someone's Happy Meal box.

"Once on Tuesday and again yesterday," Jimmy said with pride. He fetched some glasses from a glass-fronted cupboard. "I still got it."

"But you won't let her have any, you selfish son of a biscuit," Hilt called down from the staircase.

I grinned at the older men's romantic antics. *They're all talk, but they still love to dream.*

On the upper floor, we crossed Jimmy's small sunroom and stepped through his sliding glass door onto a narrow deck. His beach furniture consisted of mismatched folding chairs with nylon webbing, along with a weighted glass-topped table. I grabbed the chair with green webbing and set it with my back to the sun.

Hilt took another chair and glanced up at the folded awning. "Yeah, too windy," he muttered before sitting with the sunshine full on his face.

Jimmy came out onto the deck and expertly slid the glass door shut with his foot as he held a tray of lemonades. He handed them around, and I admired the display they made: frozen cubes of lemonade so the drink wouldn't dilute, a slice of lemon on the rim, and yellow-and-white crazy straws.

"It's worse than I thought," Hilt stage-whispered to me. "He's gone full Martha Stewart."

I giggled, and Jimmy gave us a mock frown. "I need a break from watching sport fishing now and then. 'Sides," he added as he drew up a chair and sat, "Mrs. Norris is watching us. No, don't look over. I saw her red housecoat in an upstairs window."

"You know an awful lot about a woman you're not interested in dating, Jimmy," I said.

Hilt hooted with laughter and slapped the glass tabletop. "She tells it like it is, Jim."

"Pippa knows better'n most that the best fiction springs from grains o' truth." Jimmy sipped his lemonade then sat back and rested his folded hands atop his rotund belly. "That new guy working out okay for Mallory? I don't get into town much."

"Vic? Yeah, he's pretty decent, for a city cop," Hilt said. "And I'll say this for him: he's comfortable with crowds. This summer rush doesn't seem to faze him one bit."

Jimmy chuckled. "Hope he doesn't go stir-crazy come winter."

"He's a good fit at Moorehaven too," I said. "Comes by every couple of weeks to buy a new book from the Shelf. At first, I thought he was just paying his respects to Moore, but he genuinely likes to read."

"That's a good sign," Jimmy said. "What's he like to read?"

I heard the import in Jimmy's tone. Everyone in Seacrest read mysteries, but what one liked mattered a great deal to some of our residents, and Jimmy was one of them. Since I read every kind of mystery, I wasn't in any position to judge anyone else. "Don't worry, Chief," I said, "he's into international spy thrillers and political stuff, just like you."

Jimmy preened for a second. "I should ask him what he's reading next time I bump into him, then." We sipped our lemonade for a while, enveloped in the warm breeze and drenched in sunshine.

I didn't feel I could speak for Hilt, but he hadn't yet told Jimmy what he'd just learned. So I nudged his foot under the table and gave him a meaningful stare. Hilt's reluctant frown dissolved into sad acceptance.

"You hear about Ramòn?" he asked quietly.

Jimmy hadn't. I sat back and let Hilt explain the facts, followed by a recap of his background with Ramòn and Maggie. The look on Jimmy's face told me that Hilt hadn't spoken to him about them much, either. Ramòn had been missing for years by the time Jimmy came to town. The more he said, the more often Jimmy interrupted with sympathetic noises. When Hilt finished relating our recent visit to Maggie's house, he stared into his lemonade, ashamed.

Jimmy blinked several times then looked at me as if for confirmation. I shrugged and nodded. It was all true.

"Pardon my French, Hilt," he said, "but holy *cats*! Dead all this time and just outside town? I ain't never heard of anything like this before."

Hilt didn't look up. "I never meant for it to get like this, Jim. I gotta make this right."

Jimmy nodded in a concerned fashion. "But you *know* this ain't your fault."

"It is," Hilt protested.

"No, sir. You know what that night was. You told me about it a few times, and though I wasn't there, your experience never left me."

Hilt looked puzzled. "It didn't?"

"Well, you were kinda haunted by it all," Jimmy said apologetically. "I took that lesson to heart. Some things were never meant to be controlled, just to be dealt with as best we can. And you did the best you could, that night and afterward."

I was missing something. "You guys are talking about more than just Ramòn's murder, aren't you?"

Jimmy's blue eyes cut from me to Hilt. "You didn't tell her?"

Hilt hunched his shoulders just a little. "Got tired of rememberin'." He sighed and tipped his head toward me, giving Jimmy the go-ahead.

Jimmy pursed his full lips and nodded thoughtfully. "March twenty-seventh, 1964. You know it?"

I shook my head. "Not particularly. That's the night Ramòn vanished?"

He nodded and shifted on his chair, which squeaked in protest beneath his large frame. "It's also the night of the Great Alaska Earthquake."

I dragged together the few things I could recall about that historical event: Alaska's largest quake—landslides and tilting ground—and it *created a tsunami*. Over a hundred people had died. Chills stiffened my spine. "Did it hit here, the tsunami?"

Hilt spoke first. "It did. Washed right over the cliff, even flooded Moorehaven's basement a couple feet. Most of the town was okay up the hill, but we had minor flooding right in the downtown area. Whole houses got washed away down along the beaches. The wave hit late, way after dark. Some people didn't make it. We all thought it was a miracle no one died here in Seacrest, until the next day. No one could find Ramòn."

I gripped his hand. "I understand."

His eyes held on to their pain. "You don't, Whip. I didn't want him to be dead, so I told myself he'd left town. He was having some issues, see? He really coulda left. I scoured everything from wanted posters to John Doe morgue photos to guys walking behind TV reporters covering the disaster, hoping to be right."

My chest ached. I felt torn between sympathy for my uncle's need to hope for the best, and Maggie's need to learn the truth.

"The town's power was out for days," he went on. "I tried to be everywhere at once, helping dig people and cars out of debris piles, getting the roads cleared, setting up emergency shelters, and getting the injured to medical care. I..." He spread his hands helplessly. "Everyone needed me at the same time. I didn't feel I should put Ramòn above everyone else in Seacrest. I kept hoping he'd wander in one day with that cocky grin of his."

Hilt took a deep breath, and his eyes stared toward the distant horizon. "We got the power restored, and he didn't come home. We repaired the roads, and he didn't come home. We finally found Rick

Hollister's dapple mare—she'd wandered to the whole other side of the ridge and was living amiably with a small herd of cows—and Ramòn still hadn't come home. I did what I had to do, but I couldn't do everything for everyone. I started my investigation late—at least a month after the tsunami. All the clues had washed away. So I suspected everyone I could. Even thought Ernie Ross—a mutual friend—might've done it because his car mysteriously went missing soon after the tsunami. Or Ritchy Axelrod, because he had such a crush on Maggie despite Ramòn's disapproval." Hilt stared into his nearly empty lemonade glass. "Feels like I had to let someone down. And I chose Ramòn. And Maggie."

Hilt thought the fence guy or the pawnshop owner might've killed their friend? I blinked, trying to imagine myself suspecting Jordan and Tyleen of murdering Wallis or something. I couldn't do it.

I shared a concerned glance with Jimmy, who said, "You did what you had to do, just like you said. You got your town through a natural disaster, Hilt. It was just bigger than all of you put together. Nothing anyone can do about that, except their best, which is what you did. I probably never told you this, but you getting Seacrest through that tsunami, with your fear of water and all, made you a hero in my eyes. You were a legend up and down the coast and practically a deity here in town. I practiced over and over what I was gonna say to you during my first interview for deputy. I was so nervous that morning, knowing I was going to meet the Savior of Seacrest, that I put my underwear on inside out. Beg pardon, Pippa."

I waved off his apology. I put my underwear on inside out more often than I cared to admit.

"I can't see myself that way, Jimmy," Hilt said.

"That's okay, though," I said before Jimmy had to start repeating his encouragements. "As long as you let us see you the way we want to see you, Uncle Hilt."

Hilt had many more years of dealing with authors and their characters than I did. I knew he'd understand my point. He took a heavy breath. "Objectivity."

I smiled. "Yup. If your point of view counts, then so do ours."

He let a half smile cross his face, as if he were tired of keeping it at bay. "All right, think what you want. Still ain't gonna change my mind. I gotta put this right."

"And I'll help you however I can, Uncle Hilt," I said. "But I probably need to get back to Moorehaven soon. Is it okay if I leave him with you, Jimmy?"

Jimmy nodded. "My mom won't mind one bit, Pippa. Although the surfperch might, if I can convince him to come out to my secret fishing spot and make a few casts with me. Go on, now. I'll see he gets home eventually."

Jimmy's "secret" spot wasn't secret at all. It sat in plain sight of everyone in the neighborhood, but no one poached from his spot out of respect. That made it more of a conspiracy than a secret. "Thanks. You two play nicely. I mean it." I finished off my lemonade and gave each man a peck on the cheek for Mrs. Norris's sake and showed myself out.

I rode back toward the beach road with the wind in my face. As the sandy expanse came into view, I saw that a couple dozen more cars had parked along the edges of the lane in the short time I'd been in Jimmy's house. The beach wasn't exactly crowded, but there were lots of people beachcombing with metal detectors who hadn't been there before.

Some were also flinging sand around with clam shovels. I veered to the side of the road and counted at least three dozen people who were speed-clamming as if their lives depended on it. "What in the Sam Hill?" I muttered, quoting my uncle. It took a second for me to shake off the melancholy story Hilt told about the 1964 tsunami and recall that Ramòn had been found with gold coins in his pocket. *Of course. They're looking for treasure. In all the wrong places.*

Something Vic said during one of his visits to the Shelf came to mind: "I have a second cousin who works at a Fish and Wildlife. He's dating one of my exes now. I know, it's weird, but if you ever see something legitimately fishy, he's my guy, so let me know."

I whipped out my phone and called Vic, but I had to leave a message. "Vic, it's Pippa. I'm seeing way too many people doing a terrible job of clamming on the beach south of my place. This beach is closed for clamming until September thirtieth, so something crazy's going on. Can you talk to your cousin for me? I'd hate for these folks to disturb the clam larvae and ruin the harvest later on. Thanks."

Feeling only halfway satisfied, I biked onward. The whole beachfront area of Seacrest seemed far more overcrowded than it had twenty minutes before. Before I reached the top of the rise, I had to veer into a driveway to avoid a speeding maniac in a bright-blue Toyota truck, and before I could get back into the street, another driver followed, seemingly eager to ride the Toyota's bumper. They screeched down toward the beach I'd just passed.

"Might just wanna walk, Pippa," Sebastian called from across the street. His sandy hair gleamed copper in the sun, and his freckles had faded under a light tan. He held the leashes of over a dozen dogs that sat patiently, even adoringly, around his feet. "This is supposed to be a therapy walk, but the traffic is even crazier than usual. I was just about to head back to the promenade when I saw you zip off the road. You okay?"

"I am, thanks. And I'll take your advice and just walk from here. It's only a few blocks. Can I walk with all of you?"

Sebastian consulted his canine clients. "Whaddaya think, guys? Can Pippa come with us?" Several tongues lolled out in happy agreement.

I pushed my bike across the street to join Sebastian and his pack, and we turned back toward Moorehaven. I knew a few of his companions, and he introduced me to the rest. Each dog lit up at the sound of its name. They clearly adored Sebastian.

"You certainly have a way with animals. How do you get my cats to pay so much attention to you?" I asked.

Sebastian stared at the sky with a smile, as if debating with himself. He seemed to come to a decision. "Catnip. I put it in the cuffs of my pants."

I frowned with mock outrage. "You cheater!"

But Sebastian only smiled. "Rex and Svetlana don't think I'm cheating."

"The way everyone's speeding for the beach, you'd think they all had an app to alert them for rumors of buried treasure," I commented wryly.

"Oh, is that it?" Sebastian asked. "I do remember my mom mentioning a skeleton and some coins. It's a good thing none of these very good dogs were there when he was found. Bones are very tempting." Several of the dogs looked at him expectantly at the sound of the word "bones."

I giggled at Sebastian's innocent comment. After several minutes, we'd reached the corner of Moorehaven and its broken fence.

"That's some crazy luck, getting your fence broken because of a three-foot tsunami." The dogs gathered around one of the broken posts and intently sniffed the grass nearby.

"Don't worry. Hilt's getting someone to fix it."

"That's great. Well, I'll leave you here. Gotta get these boys and girls a little more leg time."

I wished him a good day and used Moorehaven's southern entrance. As I approached the main hall, I overheard Chloe on the hostess station's phone. Her usual gospel-singer phone voice sounded worn and stressed.

"I'm sorry, but—yes, I underst—I'm very sorry, but there's nothing—" Then she sighed heavily, hung up the phone with an abrupt *click*, and swore under her breath.

I peeked around the corner and was surprised to see her hunched over, face crumpled as if she were about to cry. "Chloe? Was that a bad call?"

My assistant stood straight and took a deep breath, smoothing the stress off her face. Her black hair hung over one eye, but she tossed her head to swish it aside. "The phone's been ringing off the hook for the past couple of hours, and everyone's been way crazier than usual."

"I'm sorry. I had no idea. I had to go with Hilt—"

"No, it's fine." She gestured to the peacock-pane chandelier in the foyer. "Every time I get a rude caller, I assign them a pane up there, starting with the inner ring. There's only eight panes of glass up there, but most weeks, I don't get enough rough calls to fill them. Today, I did, and then I filled the other five rings too. The whole thing."

I stared at the art nouveau chandelier. I'd dusted it so often, I should've known how many panes it had, but I didn't. "There must be, what, a hundred panes there?"

"A hundred and eight," Chloe said miserably. "I started a hash mark collection on a piece of scratch paper for the extra ones."

"What do they all want?"

"Rooms, of course. But none of them are authors. And they get furious with me when I tell them I can't give them a room here unless they're writing a book. They try to lie, but when I start giving them the email for the ten-thousand-word submission as proof, most of them hang up. And those that don't, they start yelling like it's my fault they got caught in a lie."

I stared at her. "You've had a hundred and eight people calling for rooms in the past couple hours?"

She shrugged. "Yeah. Weird. A couple of them asked about beach access. A couple dozen offered to pay me double."

"If we weren't fully booked, I'd be tempted to take them up on that. Sounds like word has gotten out of town regarding those gold coins found with the skeleton. Tell you what, Chloe. Take a break from the phones. I'll answer them, and you can field any questions from our guests and tidy up around the place for a while. Deal?"

"That's *so* a deal." Chloe was already bailing out of the hostess station's chair.

The near-constant ringing of the phone kept me occupied for a couple of hours. In keeping with Chloe's system, I added a hash mark to her paper every time someone called, looking for a place to stay but unfamiliar with Moorehaven's reputation. One irate man even threatened to sue me for discrimination when I wouldn't book him a room. I lost count of the times I said, "Oh, you don't have a novel in progress? Well, I'm sorry to hear that. Please keep us in mind when you start your next manuscript." I really hoped I wasn't starting to sound snarky.

Chloe and my guests circulated through my peripheral vision several times, and she handled their needs swimmingly, including explaining why I couldn't even leave the phones long enough for a potty break. She thoughtfully ordered my favorite sandwich from Mozzie's for lunch, and I answered the phone between bites. News of the gold coins found with Ramòn's body was definitely spreading, and treasure fever was hot on its heels. Everyone wanted a front-row shot at finding their very own buried treasure, and Moorehaven was located in the closest town to Ramòn's crime scene. *First a real tsunami, then a tsunami of phone calls.* I rubbed my forehead in a vain attempt to smooth away an oncoming stress headache.

When I found a free second, I called Jordan at work. "Are you getting as hammered as I am?"

Jordan's reply was wry. "Are you drunk on the job, Pippa?"

I had my first laugh in hours, a deep belly jiggler. "Thank you for that. I needed a chuckle. Do you have any rooms left over there?"

"Nope. I just came on shift an hour ago, and I've been apologizing on the phone ever since. The last available room for tonight got filled just before lunchtime. Mr. Vanderveer is thrilled—all two hundred sixty rooms are fully booked, including the suites! It's like the solar eclipse all over again. Is this treasure thing real? If this is all happening over some overblown story, heads will roll. Or at least eyes."

"The coins are real. Vic had them tested. This is crazy, right? I've had calls from all over the country and even Canada."

"Me too. I even had a lady call from Thailand. I'm usually pretty good with accents, but she was talking really fast, so it's entirely possible that she's sending someone to assassinate me for not being able to book her a room."

I smirked. "But where is the assassin going to find a place to stay?"

It was Jordan's turn to laugh. "I've got more calls piling up, so I should go. Talk soon. Good luck."

"You too." I hung up, and the phone rang right away. After half an hour, the phone finally gave me a short break, and I snatched the opportunity to call Lake at the marina. "Hey, you," I said when he answered. "I thought you might be out at sea. What luck!"

"Hey there, beautiful." His voice was soft and warm, a caress in my ear. "I'm headed out for a tour in about ten minutes. I was just getting my stuff. You need something?"

Do I ever. "Ivana Kamanova." Our code phrase, a silly version of "I wanna come on over." Lake and I hadn't been together, alone, in nearly two weeks. And we'd only been intimate once since he'd moved out of his emergency quarters here in Moorehaven into his lighthouse basement apartment the previous month. He'd been understanding of Moorehaven's summer crush and agreed to take a comfy cot in the basement's laundry room. Hilt had offered it so eagerly that I knew my uncle was trying to create the least romantic sleeping arrangements he could think of. So I sneaked Lake up to my room like a horny teenager. I'd also mentally stuck my uncle in a broom closet for his old-fashioned, inconvenient, and probably selfish motives.

Lake hesitated before replying. "I'd love that, Pippa. I really would, but I've got Mal's snapback-wearing delinquents painting my guest room this evening. They're usually here in the mornings, but she's trying to occupy their time so much that they can't break into anyone else's houses, and she had some kind of hunch they'd be up to something today, so she switched up their schedule."

I stuck Mal in the same freedom-crushing broom closet I'd stuffed Hilt into, and then I had to stifle a snort of rude amusement at the thought of them both squished in there, blinking awkwardly in the dark.

"And I'll be working until after eight again tonight," he added. "Sunset cruise again. And even though I'm not Raymond Moore, I've also got the curse of eternal paperwork. I probably won't get out of here till after midnight. Rain check?"

I forced a smile into my voice. "Of course. I understand. It's a madhouse around here too. I miss you, though." One time, I'd been desperate enough for his company that I'd gone over when the Snapback Crew was working, but their constant immature sniggering from the other room made it impossible for Lake and I to hold a conversation, let alone have any fun. I promised myself I'd never again try to get romantic within earshot of teenage boys.

"You too, beautiful. I gotta head out. My guests are here. See ya." He hung up, and I cradled the phone to my chest, aching for more of a connection. *Is it my imagination, or am I the only one in this relationship who wants more?*

I hung up the phone, and it immediately rang again. "Moorehaven Bed-and-Breakfast Inn, how may I help you?"

After fielding nine calls from treasure-mad enthusiasts, I was approached by a few of my authors.

"We hate to bother you when you're so busy, Pippa," Abby began.

"But the power strip we were all sharing in the second-floor sunroom just fried," Gabby finished.

"Oh no! I'm sorry about that." I envisioned soot smudging the outlet panel. *I thought Hilt had finished repairing the wiring up there. He must be really distracted. I really don't need this right now.*

Ashley and Sarah nodded, and Ashley said, "We were doing speed trials, trying to get more words on the page for our rough drafts, and it started shooting sparks." She winced and massaged her hands, which bore stretchy fingerless compression gloves.

"We unplugged it." Abby reassured me that my bed-and-breakfast was not on fire.

"But my computer's battery is pretty old," Gabby said. "And we're not ready to stop doing speed trials yet. Do you have an extra power strip we could borrow, just for a while?"

"Of course I do," I said. "Did Chloe not remember where our extra supplies are?"

The ladies looked amongst themselves. "We couldn't find Chloe," Sarah said.

I'll need to talk to Chloe about remaining visible in case guests have questions like this. "It's okay. I'll get a power strip for you right now." I darted back to one of the supply closets down the side hall and returned with the strip. As the authors thumped their way back upstairs, I popped down to the parlor, checked the library and sunroom, and peeked in the Shelf. No Chloe. After fielding several more calls, I managed to get away to the kitchen, where I found Tyleen and Sebastian cooking up a huge pot of clam chowder as well as a tossed salad and breadsticks.

"I'm so glad to see you here again, Tyleen. You're a treasure. You guys seen Chloe?"

Mother and son exchanged a thoughtful glance.

Sebastian said, "Not for a while."

"But Hilt's outside, talking with the fence guy. Ernie, right?" she asked her son.

He nodded.

Relieved that the fence repair was underway, but still baffled about Chloe, I merely thanked them and headed back to face the Phoning Squad.

6

CHLOE CAME INTO WORK Monday morning like she hadn't ditched us at all, but I never found a good moment to ask her what had happened. Abby, Gabby, and Butch roped her into some sleuthing role-play up on the third floor right after they finished eating, leaving me to clean up. As I bustled around the kitchen, I kept coming back to old questions like *Why was Ramón killed? For the treasure? Then why was he buried with it?* Such questions were impossible to answer without more information, and I was determined to get it.

Moorehaven's doorbell rang, scaring the cats from their sunroom perches. They scampered toward the kitchen, where I was wiping down the counters. "Dogs don't ring doorbells, guys. And Ashley's up in her room, so she can't trip over either of you. Relax. It'll be fine." I left my rag on the edge of the sink. Moorehaven had a doorbell, but locals just ignored it and knocked. Whoever was at my door was from out of town, and I intended to give them a great first impression.

I opened the door to find a man and woman a little younger than me standing on my porch. "Good morning. How can I help you?" I asked brightly.

"Are you Pippa? Our concierge, Jordan, recommended your bookstore." The woman stood an inch or two taller than me with athletic grace and a gorgeous poof of natural hair that rose taller than her companion's head.

You're such a good friend, Jordan. "I am, indeed. Come on in and look around." I indicated the Shelf with one hand as I backed up to let them enter.

"Oh yeah, that's the stuff." The sturdy blond man grinned greedily and walked, zombie style, into the small bookstore.

His companion sighed and tipped her head. "I apologize for Connor. He loves mysteries, but"—she glared at his back—"his social skills could use some work." She looked back at me. "I'm Patrice. It's great to meet you."

Her light-brown hand was warm and dry when I shook it. "You too. You're lucky you got a room at Seven Vistas. I hear it's all booked up."

Patrice laughed. "Oh, no. We're not together." The smiling glance she shot after Connor hinted that she might prefer they were, though. "But I think we did get the last few rooms in the hotel. We're here for work."

My curiosity was piqued. "Are you reporting on the treasure craze?"

Patrice tipped her head with a secretive smile that revealed one crooked incisor. "Not exactly. Connor and I are graduate students. Different fields, but this endeavor was put together pretty quickly, and if we hadn't been studying right over in Eugene, Mandy would have picked someone else."

Patrice was playing it close to the vest with specifics, so I probed in a different direction. "So what's your field of study?"

Patrice's whole stance shifted, and she adopted a relaxed, confident manner. "In a nutshell, I'm studying the history of the west coast of North America as it pertains to Spanish-Filipino trade routes from the sixteenth to the nineteenth century."

Impressed, I said, "Wow, I'm not sure I knew that was a thing."

Patrice grinned and clasped her hands together. "A lot of people don't. You don't know how excited I am that my obscure field of study has landed me this amazing opportunity. Don't tell Connor, but I kind of feel like Indiana Jones right now."

She slipped into the Shelf, and I contemplated what she had said between the lines. *Jordan must've known I'd be interested to meet these two. Patrice sounds like she's got what it takes to identify lost treasure, unlike Tibbsy and Marco.*

Tibbsy and Marco, the two bumbling burglars in Moore's *Brass Artifice*, had overheard Ichabod Bellwether, the historian, refer to a pair of bronze cannons as "worth their weight in gold." After their complex but successful burglary, the dimwitted men had melted down the cannons, expecting literal gold—and destroyed the bronze artifacts' historical value. I hoped to find some time to read the part where Hilton Gray caught them. I couldn't remember exactly how he did it.

Connor seemed to know what he was looking for and picked out his book before Patrice did. He stood next to the rack of books hanging on the Shelf's open door and examined his choice, blond head bowed in interest. He was built like a football player, but he had the fingers of a pianist, and his hands were gentle as he held his new book.

He might have been overeager at seeing Moorehaven's boutique bookstore, but he insisted on buying Patrice's book for her, and the lingering look he gave her while she was reading its back cover told me why.

She hugged it to her chest and thanked him. "You found a mystery novel set in Pompeii? Of course you did." She turned to me. "Connor is a geologist. He thinks everything rocks."

I chuckled at her pun, but Connor laughed wholeheartedly. Patrice saw the cute little handmade sign Chloe had designed, letting people know they could sign up for the Moorehaven newsletter to stay abreast of current events and new releases, and asked to sign up. I took down her particulars, including her phone number in case I ran a sale while she was still in town, and then I wished them good fortune with their venture. The way their eyes shifted at my word choice was another clue that fell into place. *Definitely treasure hunters.*

Jordan called my cell while I was vacuuming the hallway on the third floor. "Glaze and Gossip, ten minutes," she said before hanging up on me. Her voice was hushed and breathy, so I imagined her crouched out of sight behind her concierge desk at Seven Vistas like a secret agent.

Meetings of our not-very-secret local insiders group, Glaze and Gossip, occurred whenever one of us had a blazing-hot story to share, and we'd all gather in the back of Emily's pastry shop, Glazin' West, between Seven Vistas and Moorehaven, to hear it. Something must've happened at the resort hotel for Jordan to call the meeting. *Unless she's just calling me for another member who has a secret. It's not like we have a shortage right now, what with Ramòn's murder, Hilt's obsession with his old case, whatever's happened to Maggie, and God knows what-all the treasure hunters are dragging into town. I know what I'm going to ask them to help me with.* I wheeled the vacuum back to its closet.

Downstairs, I found Hilt flipping through a recipe book. "Penelope really liked that leftover blintz I gave her after the tsunami. She asked me to make her some more, so I'm looking for somethin' she'd like." He seemed calmer and more himself since talking with Jimmy, for which I was eternally grateful.

"Put a little of the strawberry sauce in with the cheese as well as on top," I suggested. "She's really into red foods. And she likes the crepes open, not folded, so use some that I fried on both sides. Listen, I gotta pop out for a minute. Can you handle everyone while I'm gone?"

Hilt leaned an elbow on the kitchen counter and gazed up through the ceiling as if he could pierce the tiles with his gaze and see the guests in their rooms. "Pretty quiet right now. Most of 'em are writing for a spell before lunch. Authors generally bein' introverts and all, they aren't too partial to claustrophobia-inducin' crowds. 'Course, Butch and Zach are out stompin' around out there somewhere."

I grinned. "Of course they are. I'll be back in a little while." The bright, breezy day welcomed me with a salty gust. From Moorehaven's porch, I glanced at the curve of the promenade, which wrapped around the cliff top across the street. I could barely see the boards because of the ambling crowds. The stairs down to the beach just south of Moorehaven were crammed as well with people and their treasure-hunting gear. Several cars were illegally parked along the promenade too. Three extra cars had also jammed themselves into my parking lot, blocking in any author who might want to leave. "Nope," I muttered out loud. *No one blocks my authors in. And I know just the woman to sic on them.*

Phone in hand, I was dialing Acting Chief of Police Mallory Tavish when a familiar figure in an official green-and-white SUV eased into view around the next corner. I darted to the curb and waved him down.

Sheriff Kettleman rolled down his window and let out a waft of arctic air conditioning. "Miss Winterbourne? How are you this fine day?" The wiry sheriff's even teeth beamed out of his tanned, leathery face.

"I'm just peachy, Sheriff. Thanks for asking. But I can't help noticing that a few cars have blocked in my guests." I pointed to the stationary traffic jam in my tiny lot.

Kettleman leaned over his steering wheel and studied the problem. "I'll call it in. This place is the busiest spot in the whole county right now, so I figured I'd amble on over and help Tavish out. That's a towing offense. Okay if the tow company leaves their info with Hilt? This could happen again."

"He's got Ben's number," I said, referring to the local tow truck owner.

"Ben and half a dozen other companies are fighting over Seacrest territory. This part of town belongs to Speedy's, out of Florence."

Seacrest suddenly seemed like a fragile cake threatened by ruthless butcher knives. "They're carving up my town?"

Kettleman offered a creaky shrug. "Treasure fever. Not much we can do, except what we can do. Gotta keep the streets as safe as we can. I'll let a lotta things go before I let that go. I have an actual list, in case of a run on the bank, a zombie apocalypse, or the sudden knowledge that we're actually living in the Matrix."

His perspective wasn't comforting, exactly, but it helped. "I understand. Thanks, Sheriff."

He nodded acknowledgement and plucked his radio handset from the car's dashboard to call in the parking violations. I took a deep breath and shed my worries, trusting in the old law enforcement officer to do his best for my guests the way I always tried to do.

At Glazin' West, Emily's pastry shop around the corner from Moorehaven, I slipped between a couple of waiting customers, weaved among the cute little round tables, and passed the register toward the kitchen. Emily's pastries had a well-deserved reputation for excellence, and tourist season was usually as big a draw for her as it was for the ice cream shops and stands. But today, the place was half-empty, despite its cute pastel decorations and choose-your-own K-cups. Grant, Emily's assistant, was busy ringing up a customer who'd ordered a dozen raspberry-filled doughnuts, so I smiled and nodded a greeting on my way past.

In the kitchen, Emily sat at the head of a folding table. Baking ingredients clustered on her countertops, and Emily still wore a flour-dusted cornflower-blue apron. On her left sat Wallis the florist, Lori the nurse, and my BFF, Jordan. On her right, newspaper editor Naoma sat by my neighborhood-watch neighbor, Tyleen. Everyone smiled and called greetings as I stepped in. *Can't be too dire. But then again, these ladies have helped solve actual murders before.*

The seat next to Tyleen was empty, so I slid on in. "You guys are fast. Jordan just called me."

But the time for pleasantries was already over. Naoma leaned around Tyleen and pinned me with an urgent stare. "Is it true? Is Hilt trying to solve Ramòn's murder?"

Oh. I guess I don't need to ask for their help, after all. I took a deep breath and took in all my friends' intent gazes. "Yes, it's true. He's obsessed with solving it, and even though I don't know much about the case, I don't blame him." I decided I wouldn't mention Hilt's personal connection to Ramòn or how guilty he felt. But my friends could definitely do their best to help figure out what actually happened that long-ago night.

"Oh, I don't, either." The way Naoma sat back in her chair fairly reeked of inside knowledge, and I wasn't about to let her keep it to herself.

"What did you find in the paper's archives, Naoma?"

Naoma sat up straight and aimed her mulberry frown and retro '50s bob at every one of us before she spoke. "The articles I've managed to find are very tight-lipped with their information. The big story was the tsunami that struck the night Ramòn went missing. I found one article that mentioned Hilt, though. Ramòn's disappearance was the first missing persons case Hilt ever handled."

"How perfectly awful." Wallis's tone was, as always, a gentle cross between Alexa and Eeyore. "To have the first missing person be a friend—I'd be devastated."

"He couldn't have had an easy time of the investigation." Lori shook her chin-length blond hair. "Not in the middle of a wrecked town, and certainly not with his fear of water."

The other ladies all nodded solemnly, but I felt a pang of embarrassment for my great-uncle. He couldn't help that he'd become terrified of all bodies of water after his younger sister drowned in a river right in front of him any more than he could help wanting to be a policeman. But Lori was right. Dealing with one of his worst nightmares while trying to help a whole town recover couldn't have left much time for Hilt to focus on Ramòn's disappearance.

"I think I know who killed Ramòn," Tyleen intoned.

We all leaned in, though with Tyleen's reputation, I had doubts the size of fifty-pound flour sacks.

"Those Baker Twins. They're always skulking around, looking shifty."

Naoma and Jordan exchanged a worried glance.

"Tyleen," Naoma said, "I know those two live a little rough up in the hills, but they can't be a day over forty. When Ramòn died, the Baker boys weren't even born."

Tyleen shifted, uncomfortable with this new truth. "Well, if you're sure. But I still don't trust them."

"Doc Stevens and her forensic anthropologist brother have finished the autopsy by now, right?" Jordan asked. "Or whatever you call it when you examine a skeleton. So how did Ramòn die?"

Lori shook her head with regret. "Blunt-force trauma. His skull was cracked right about here." She pointed to her own head, halfway between her ear and the back of her head. "And he had a freshly broken nose."

"A fight, then," Tyleen pronounced.

"Likely, but it's hard to tell for sure without the soft tissue," Lori said.

I nodded, having talked with Sarah and Butch on the same topic a few days back.

"We should call in Bones," Tyleen said.

"The Star Trek doctor?" Wallis rested a hand on her chest. "He's so angrily handsome."

"He'd probably solve it too," Naoma said, "but I think Tyleen meant the one from that forensic TV show."

"You do know she's fictional, right?" Emily asked Tyleen.

"No, not her, the *real* one, who wrote all the books." Tyleen gave a knowing wink. "Then I could get her autograph."

"Maybe one forensic anthropologist is enough for now. Why don't we try to take it from here ourselves?" I suggested. "We have to be able to help Hilt somehow."

"Right." Tyleen nodded firmly. "Any other clues, Lori?"

The nurse shook her head. "Sorry, guys. There's no clear impression in the skull. From what the Doctors Stevens could determine, the murder weapon was probably just a nearby rock."

Wallis leaned forward. "I've had a rush of orders on sympathy and condolence bouquets and vases for Maggie or deliveries out to Ramòn's empty grave. Do you think they'll bury him in it, now that they've found him?"

"I expect so," Naoma said.

"Ernie the fence man bought Maggie a huge bouquet," Wallis continued, "and he also bought my most expensive funeral wreath for the graveside." Her voice dipped into pure tragedy. "You remember Millicent, who sold me the flower shop? When I was just her assistant, she told me how those two used to be an item back in the day. So, so tragic."

"What, Maggie and Ernie the fence guy?" Emily asked.

"Yes." Wallis's breath was an ethereal whisper. "Ramòn and Ernie were best friends, and Ernie was sweet on Maggie. But then Ramòn disappeared, and the tragedy, well... It drove Maggie and Ernie apart.

They lived the rest of their days locked into their solitary mourning, never able to reach out and connect again." Wallis reached across the table toward Naoma with a trembling hand and an agonized expression.

Naoma tilted her head and let out a longsuffering sigh at Wallis's dramatics.

I raised an eyebrow. "Wallis, they're both still alive."

She nodded solemnly. "But for how long?"

"So Ernie still carries a torch for Maggie," Jordan said.

"Or he just feels guilty that the two of them could never overcome their mutual pain," I said. "That really is a sad story." *He must know something from back then about Ramón, about who wasn't getting along with him. I wonder if he'll talk to me about it. That might be weird, since I'm employing him for a job. Maybe Trudie, though, since she's Gabe's girlfriend. My sister is nothing if not chatty.* I made a mental note to ask her for help.

Wallis didn't quite smile, but then she hardly ever did. Her shoulders rose, and her eyes widened with my validation, though.

"I have it on good authority," Naoma said, "and by 'good authority,' I mean I cornered Mercer Braxton in the dairy aisle at Safeway this morning—did you know they're carrying drinkable yogurt now?"

"Oh, that stuff is good." Tyleen nodded.

"What do you have on good authority, Naoma?" I prompted.

"Right." Naoma pointed at the ceiling for emphasis. "The town council is putting on a street fair to take advantage of this treasure craze."

"What? When?" several of us asked at the same time. It was clear none of us had heard this news yet. I was thrilled, though. *Maybe they'll stop calling Moorehaven and go enjoy themselves there.*

Naoma's mulberry smile was smug. She'd truly gotten the scoop on this one. "It's scheduled for Tuesday night. And if any of you want to volunteer, the Hall on the Green is being used to repurpose the usual Fourth of July decorations and anything else we've got lying around. Downtown Seacrest is going to be glittering like a golden treasure hoard by tomorrow night."

Tyleen leaned forward. "Ladies, that is my jam. I'm going to head right over after we're done here."

"It's going to be a traffic jam too," Wallis said. "No one is going to be able to find my flower shop at this rate."

"On a lighter note," Jordan said, "there's an honest-to-God treasure-hunting team checked in at Seven Vistas. Oh, pardon me. A *marine-salvage* team."

"So the treasure is underwater?" Lori asked.

"It could've been at first," I said. "But we all know how stuff washes ashore. That's probably how Ramòn found it. But these guys will want to locate the original site. It'll have historical value and…" I trailed off as everyone stared at me. "What? I watched a Discovery show about it once. And do you know how many historical mysteries I've read that involve lost treasure? More than my fingers and toes." I waggled my fingers at everyone.

"Well, I hope they find it quick, so we can all get back to normal around here," Emily said. "What are they like?" she asked Jordan.

She brushed her bright-pomegranate hair back from her shoulders. "There are four of them—two veterans and two new hires from Eugene."

"Oh, I met the U of O masters students this morning," I said. "Connor and Patrice. Really nice. I think he likes her."

"The Bayside Buccaneers," Jordan said, claiming the conversation from me with a *don't-hijack-my-topic* look. "Wade is a certified diver, and Mandy's a spelunker. They're from the Great Lakes area. Connor's a geologist, and Patrice—"

"Studies how Spanish galleons trading between New Hispaniola and the Philippines ended up on the Oregon Coast," I blurted, wrinkling my nose with laughter at Jordan's exaggerated pout.

Emily, ever the peacemaker, waded into our silly rivalry with a calm tone. "The Philippines are a long way from here. And I've never even heard of New Hispaniola. How in the world did some Spanish gold coins end up in Ramòn's pocket?"

"I think we all want to know the answer to that question," Jordan said. "And from the way Mandy shushed Connor and Patrice, it seemed clear that she didn't want anyone else to overhear what little information they were sharing."

I picked up on Jordan's vibe. "Folks with a lot to lose tend to be pretty tight-lipped. I think we should let them do their thing. We're here to solve Ramòn's murder. This marine-salvage team can't help us with that. We don't need to risk our necks pestering people who might defend their expert knowledge with force. If we want to know what they're up to, we'll need to keep an eye on them from a distance."

"Treasure hunting can be pretty cutthroat," Tyleen said. "I saw this one movie with Matthew McConaughey, and everyone there had guns and bombs and stuff."

"I'm sure our local law enforcement will be able to handle any bomb threats, now that Vic Nuncio has joined the force," Wallis said.

"Do they have a lot of bomb threats in Chicago?" Naoma asked.

"I thought he was from Atlanta," Jordan said.

"Pretty sure he's from Dallas," Lori added.

"Anyway, somewhere urban, where they probably have bombs," Emily said.

"*And*," Jordan wrested the geographic guessing game away from everyone, "Mandy also asked about boat rentals, so I gave them a brochure for Lake's charters. Not sure what they're looking for, but they'll be doing something out on the water."

"Diving, probably," Naoma said.

"Is there anything else you can do from a boat when you're looking for treasure?" Tyleen seemed to expect a *no*.

"Well," I said, "there's only one way to find out. I'll have to pump Lake for information after he takes them on a tour."

Jordan's eyes twinkled at my implication. "And I'll keep an eye out for nocturnal shenanigans over at Seven Vistas, since I'm on the night shift right now."

"I'll keep digging through the archives for more information on Ramòn's disappearance," Naoma offered. "And if I find anything I can share with Hilt, I'll let him know. He's been asking."

"Thanks, Naoma," I said. "I'm not sure if Hilt will want to talk about the old case with me, but I'm worried how the discovery of Ramòn's body is affecting him. If we can all keep an eye out for him, help him with little things..."

Jordan reached across the table and squeezed my hand. "Of course, Pippa. Anything you guys need."

"I'll see if Hilt will open up to me," I said. "There's so much we don't know, and I'm not sure if he knows, either."

"If there are any further developments from the autopsy," Lori added, "I'll loop you guys in. Or..." She nodded at Tyleen. "If any world-famous forensic anthropologists show up."

"And Tyleen and I will keep an eye out for treasure hunters and anything else of note," Emily said.

Tyleen brightened. "There's only another week of summer vacation, guys. We can survive this."

"And we can solve it too," I said.

Emily cocked an ear toward the front of the shop. "Sounds like the line is getting unruly. I'd better get back out there. Everyone, take a lemon bar on your way out. They're fresh."

We filed out, obediently picking up lemon bars. I took a bite as I stepped outside with Jordan right behind me, and my mouth melted with heavenly tartness.

"You take care of yourself, and Hilt." Jordan spoke around a bite of lemon bar and gave me a quick side hug.

"You too. Let's try to do coffee sometime this week."

"You, my dear B&B hostess, are on." She pointed a brightly painted nail at me.

As I returned to Moorehaven, I felt better knowing my friends had my back. It was what stood in front of me that worried me.

7

"Why don't I go out more? Well, I never liked fishbowls."
Raymond Moore, 1968

FIVE MINUTES AFTER I'd placed the lunch order at Fancy Francie's Foodie Fiesta, a very young voice called to me from the top of the stairs. "Spill." Penelope drew out the word. "Is a spill. I wanna tell you."

"Okay, Penelope. Stay right there. I'm coming right now." I hurried upstairs, unsure how safe she was at the top of them by herself. *Cats, I can handle. Toddlers, not so much.* As I ran down my mental list of things a toddler could spill—*please don't let it be chocolate*—I swung by the second-floor supply closet for cleaning spray and rags. But when Penelope led me to the reading nook that faced the ocean, I found her father, Thad, looking embarrassed.

"Here I am telling Penelope not to spill her sippy cup, and then I knock over my orange juice," he said apologetically. "I don't suppose you have a sippy-cup lid for my big-boy cup?"

Penelope giggled as if her father had said the funniest thing ever, and Thad insisted on cleaning up his own mess to set a proper example for his daughter. I was happy to let him. I hadn't taken five steps back down the hall when my phone rang.

"Get down to the marina." The voice on the phone was growly and gravelly, as if its owner was trying to disguise it. I couldn't even be sure if it was male or female.

"What? Who is this? Tyleen?" I glanced involuntarily toward my nosy neighbor's house, though the second-story wall blocked my view of her peaches-and-cream home. "What's at the marina? Is one of my authors getting too nosy down there?" A memory surfaced. "Is it about Ashley? Tyleen, I know you don't like—"

"Get down to the marina. Now." The line disconnected.

I stared at my cell phone with a frown. *That's not like Tyleen. Maybe it's just an old local. Some of these guys can be pretty crusty.* I slipped the phone into the pocket of my pleated shorts. As I reached the main floor, I heard Chloe coming up the stairs from the basement, so I said, "I just got a call. Something's up at the marina. I'm gonna go check it out."

Chloe shifted her armload of folded towels and flipped her dark hair out of her eye. Svetlana curled around one of her ankles. "Which author this time?" she asked resignedly.

"Not sure yet. And I'm not gonna limit myself to just one, not with this group. Hopefully, I'll be back shortly."

She jerked her chin down once in acknowledgement. "I'll call if anything comes up." She passed me with her load of towels.

"Thanks, Chloe." *Maybe she's wandering off because she's feeling underappreciated.* I paused. "You okay yesterday? You left without telling anyone."

"Oh. Yeah... My dad needed me."

"Oh, I see. Just let someone know if you need to step out, so someone's always watching the place, okay?" She nodded, and I added, "I appreciate all your hard work this summer. I'm honestly not sure how we did this without you."

A faint tinge of pink reached her cheeks, and she tried to hide her face behind her long hair. "Thanks. I guess I really like working here. It's kinda fun. Some days."

High praise from the thrash-metal enthusiast. "Glad to hear it. If I get hospitalized from a street brawl or arrested, remember to—"

"Get the lunch order. I know."

"I leave Moorehaven in your capable hands." With a smile, I headed out.

I spotted the gathering crowd at the upper rim of the marina from two blocks away. Hundreds of people ringed the low cliff that surrounded our small inlet, despite the hot afternoon sunshine beating down on their shoulders. The marina rested in a squarish bowl of rock a few blocks from the river's exit to the sea. I had to push my way toward Blade and Boom through jabbering rows of tourists with their cameras out.

Finally, I reached the door to Lake's tour boat company and let myself in. The din instantly hushed as the door shut behind me, and I leaned on it with relief. I peeked around the corner toward the office, hoping to see Lake, but his desk sat empty. His assistant was in, though, at a smaller desk tucked into a corner.

Harry had been born in Sri Lanka, but he'd grown up in Los Angeles. He was a slight man in his early forties with smooth cinnamon skin and a thick mop of black hair that made him appear much younger. His brown eyes were always smiling, and his charming confidence usually won customers over quickly. Because he wasn't Caucasian, people always assumed his name was short for something more ethnic. Harry found their guesses amusing, and he hadn't even told Lake what it was short for. He also found teasing me about my name hilarious. "Hey, hey, it's Pippa Longstocking," Harry joked.

"You know her name is Pippi." I grinned.

He tilted his head. "Are you sure? I'm pretty sure it's Pippa."

I shook my head at his good-natured persistence. "I guess Lake's out on a tour."

"Yep. Taking the marine-salvage team up the coast, actually." His voice betrayed his intense interest, and it piqued mine.

"They really think there's treasure close by, huh?" I wished I'd gotten the chance to talk with Lake before his tour, so I could've asked him to spy on the down low for the Gossip group.

"Close enough to book a bunch of tours, yeah."

"Hey, I just got a call about something going on down here. Please tell me one of my authors isn't at the center of that media frenzy outside."

Harry gazed out the front windows. "Actually, no. No authors this time."

My shoulders sagged in relief. "So you didn't call me?"

"I called the cops," Harry replied, "after some tourists told me what was going on. But I didn't call you. Wanna go see?"

I didn't have to worry that one or more of my authors, and by extension Moorehaven, would be publicly embarrassed, but since someone had wanted me to see something down here, I found myself morbidly curious. "Sure."

Harry checked his pockets and clasped something in his hand. "Then follow me."

He opened the door, and the roar of myriad voices surrounded me as I followed him outside. Amusement, cynicism, eagerness, and jealousy—I heard nearly every tone of voice as we pressed toward the lip of the marina, with Harry holding his boat pilot's license up as a right-of-way. I held onto Harry's arm so I didn't lose him, and the crowd reluctantly parted for him and closed firmly behind me. Soon, we squeezed into a tiny spot near the top of the marina stairs.

The marina cliffs were sheer on three sides, dropping thirty feet to the still waters inside the floating jetty that bordered the edge of the river current. A smattering of watercraft sat moored below, and the broad metal staircase descended the cliff face, connecting with a wooden dock at the water's edge. The staircase's usual rain cover had been taken down for the summer, and we all had a clear view of the shenanigans below. Halfway down the stairs, a pair of maniac miners seemed determined to dig a tunnel straight into the cliff face. They had pickaxes and headlamps, and they were whacking away at the hard, dark basalt as if their lives depended on it. One of them briefly glanced up, and I recognized him by his long nose and straggly blond ponytail.

Of course it's the Baker Twins. Who else would be this reckless? Tyleen will be pleased that she was right about them being up to something, even if it's not murdering Ramòn before they were born. A piece of stone flew free and arced out toward the nearest boat below. "Oh my God. They're gonna damage someone's boat."

Harry nodded laconically. "They better hope the cops get here first. If Mr. Milligan knew they were raining ancient lava rocks onto his Fly 40..."

I winced. "Ouch, yeah."

Boop-boop! A police siren cut through the press of voices, and the cruiser eased through the crowd. Officer Vic Nuncio stepped from his vehicle, wearing his summer uniform and a pair of wraparound sunglasses and carrying a bullhorn. His shaved head showed the barest of dark stubble. The crowd, sensing his inherent authority, actually parted ahead of him, seemingly eager to see—and film—whatever happened next. I was certainly happy to see my favorite—out of two—Seacrest police officer on the scene.

To my surprise, he headed straight for me. His head glistened with a sheen of sweat by the time he reached me, and his face gave no hint at his mood. "Miss Winterbourne, Mr. Shamsi. These are the infamous Baker Twins I've heard so much about?"

"Well, they're not actually twins," I said. "They're stepbrothers who look so much alike that people confuse them."

"And confusing them isn't very hard to do," Harry added. "I don't know how those two goofballs come up with so many harebrained schemes. Their wits are dimmer than my uncle Mahesh's, and that's saying something."

Vic took Harry's description in stride with a judicious nod. "Pippa, could I have a quick word with you when I'm finished here?"

"Uh, sure, Vic." Before I could ask what was up, he'd given me an efficient nod and started making his way to the railing at the edge of the cliff. Once there, he pointed his bullhorn down over the edge. "Attention, staircase miners," he boomed. "You are blocking access to a public area and endangering private property. If you will take a moment to look up, you will notice you are on the brink of becoming internet famous. What you're famous for will be determined by your actions in the next sixty seconds."

Vic paused, and the two frantic diggers did indeed stop and glance around, seemingly surprised to be surrounded by so many onlookers and their phones.

"If you stop digging and enter my custody willingly," Vic continued through his horn, "I will ensure your safety out of town, and any fines assessed will be minimal. If you make me come down there..." The officer paused for several seconds, and the marina rim was dead silent. "I will have no choice but to inform the owners of the boats you may be damaging, and they will no doubt press charges. You'll be held here in town, and all these videos these helpful citizens are taking can be used as evidence against you. Your choice. You have thirty more seconds until I come down there to get you."

The hot sun beat down on the waiting crowd. Hundreds of phones recorded the scene. *They have to realize how much trouble they'll get in if they stay down there. C'mon, guys!* I glanced at Harry, who gave me a brief, knowing smile.

"The power of the Other," he murmured.

I wasn't sure what he meant, but after about twenty seconds of hasty murmuring on the staircase, the two would-be miners held their pickaxes up in surrender and headed up the stairs. Vic walked behind us and met them at the top, where he confiscated their axes. From this close, I was pretty sure the Baker Twins were at least a little tipsy. With an efficient lack of fanfare, Vic escorted them into the back seat of his car.

I love small-town entertainment as much as the next girl, but what does this have to do with me? Why did someone want me down here to see this?

After Vic locked their axes in his trunk—all the while completely ignoring the mass interest focused on him—he approached me again.

I gulped. Vic was a pro, a big-city cop transferred to a tiny tourist town. His look shouted *faceless authoritarian robot*, which might have helped him do his job in a busy urban environment, but it made him stand out in Seacrest like the sorest and most dangerous of thumbs. Even though he'd been nothing but polite, and despite his regular visits to Moorehaven's Shelf for the latest thriller novels, having him walk up to me in his professional capacity was a little intimidating.

"What can I do for you, Officer?" I asked in my best hostess voice.

Vic's professional façade cracked a little as he twisted his lips in indecision. Then he leaned in and murmured for my ears only, "I don't want to go on the record with this out of respect, but I feel you need to know. I haven't even told Chief Tavish. Our archives room was broken into last night, and I'm pretty sure Hilt was involved."

My eyes widened in shock. The police archives shared space with a few other institutions, like the *Seacrest Register* and Seacrest's historical records, in a pink postage stamp of a house situated kitty-corner across the intersection from the police station. If not for the official sign out front—and the high-end locks on the door—anyone would believe the tiny home belonged to a cat lady who baked cookies for charity. Anyone who'd dare break into it would need to be very sure they weren't seen—or didn't seem suspicious if they were.

"You're sure?" I searched for some semblance of humanity in his wraparound shades.

He lowered them and met my gaze with his hazel eyes. The fine wrinkles around them told me he was concerned. "None of the locks were forced, but I found smudges in the dust on the door frame. Someone's got skills. The file drawer containing the info for 1964 was ajar. It's old. It sticks."

A cold realization sank into my bones. "Thanks, Vic," I managed. "You're the one who called me, then." At his puzzled look, I added, "Just now, someone called me at Moorehaven and told me to get down to the marina. That wasn't you?"

His cue-ball head shook in a brief *no*. "Not me. Glad I ran into you, though." He nodded and drove off in his cruiser.

I was more confused than ever about that odd phone call. "Sorry, Harry, I need to get back."

"You don't wanna wait to say hi to—oh." He broke off, a little embarrassed.

Harry was staring down into the marina, and I followed his gaze. Lake had been piloting the thirty-foot *Mazu II* back into its mooring at the far end of the marina during all the crazy miner drama, and I hadn't even noticed. But even at this distance, I could see what had caused Harry to break off suddenly.

Lake tied off the boat while a group of four guests disembarked. *The marine-salvage team,* I surmised. Mandy, the tall, slender woman with shoulder-length blond hair, was paying very close attention to Lake—close, personal, touchy-feely attention. And he was letting her. One of her hands rested on his bicep. The other was fiddling with the open collar of his blue shirt.

I'm losing him was the thought that rocketed through my mind. *I'm not spending enough time with him, and he's forgetting me.*

"I need to get back," I repeated, blundering my way through the crowd, blindly leaving Harry behind.

8

WHEN MOOREHAVEN CAME into view around the corner, my heart lifted. Its three octagonal towers brushed the bright-blue sky and stood firm against the unending salty breeze. The afternoon sun brilliantly lit its face. The building's fog-gray paint fairly glowed, and its green trim glimmered like emeralds. Moorehaven was the one constant in my life, and I needed it right then.

Even better, my fence repairs were finally underway. Hilt's old friend Ernie and Trudie's boyfriend, Gabe, examined a brand-new fence post along the far edge of the property. Their bikes rested against one of my sturdy fir trees. Gabe's posture was tense, and he glanced distractedly at me as I mounted the stairs to the front door. I hoped the repairs hadn't hit a snag already. *Or maybe Gabe's hoping for Tru to pop out and distract him from work. No, silly,* I told myself. *He's just having a hard time focusing on the ordinary task of working after he found out that his great-uncle was murdered before Gabe was even born.*

A shudder shivered up my spine as I stepped into the cool interior of the bed-and-breakfast. I didn't know what I'd do if Hilt died. He was my rock.

Voices reached my ears from the parlor to my left. Trudie said, "Just blow it off. It doesn't matter."

Chloe responded, "Kinda hard when my job is to help the guests."

"No, your job is to help Pippa," Tru said. "The customer isn't always right."

"Well, Zach certainly wasn't right about where a woman's place is. I just wish I'd said something."

"Say whatever you think he deserves next time. If there is a next time."

"Yeah, maybe."

"And that goes for the other thing you told me about too," Trudie added. "You get to have a voice."

"'Kay, thanks. I'll see you later. I gotta go hand Hilt a bunch of tools I don't know the names of."

Appalled at Trudie's bad customer service advice, I slipped behind the row of coats by the door until Chloe stepped out and walked away down the hall. Then I swung around the doorway into the parlor.

Trudie sat on the red couch, sipping coffee while Rex perched in the windowsill behind her, watching seagulls. Tru's dark, shoulder-length hair always managed to look like she had just woken up and hadn't yet smoothed out her unruly curls. She was a little shorter than me, but her hazel eyes seemed bigger than they should be, giving her face a childlike, anime appeal. "Hey," she said nonchalantly, as if she hadn't just been encouraging my intern to be rude to my guests. "How was the marina? Anyone fall in?"

Vic's news about Hilt breaking into the records office, followed by the memory of Lake and the treasure hunter lady flirting, flickered through my mind's eye. I didn't want to talk about any of that. "What do you think you're doing?" I demanded.

"Uhh..." Tru checked her cup. "Having coffee? Is that not okay?"

"I meant with Chloe." I gestured after the girl. "Encouraging her to lash out at a guest is not exactly Dear Abby-level advice, Tru."

Tru's eyes slid to the side, and she quirked her lips into a moue. "I'm just trying to help."

"Well, maybe consider that Chloe doesn't need the kind of help you have to offer." I crossed my arms.

To my surprise, Tru sat up straighter and met my eyes directly. She'd never been much of a confrontational kid. "Maybe you should consider that Chloe needs *exactly* the kind of help I have to offer, Pippa. She's on the fringe, just like me. She has to make her way through life, out there. You never had that problem."

I rocked back at her assumption. "What do you mean, I 'never had that problem'? You think my life has been easy?" A cascade of bad memories marched in quick-time past my mind's eye: a fifth-grade bully, those knee surgeries, learning to avoid my half-brothers, a skeevy landlord from hell, my college roommate's suicide, my depression.

"No." Tru backed down and slumped. "Your life wasn't easy. But mine... I had different challenges and more of them."

"Oh yeah? Like what?"

Tru let out a long-suffering sigh and rested her head on the back of the couch, staring at the ceiling. "If I'd had bigger boobs, my life would've been so much more normal."

I burst out laughing. "What?"

She sat up again and set her coffee on the lamp table beside her. "You had those double-Ds by the time you were fourteen, Pips. You had everyone's attention: the boys, the girls, our parents. Everyone had a reason for watching you. No one cared what I was up to. My little A-cups never attracted anyone's attention." She gave her girls a small bounce with her hands, and they didn't jiggle. Mine had always jiggled. She had a point. Everyone had noticed my chest. They still did.

I packed up my defensiveness. I had been crazy popular, starting my freshman year in high school. Most of the attention I drew had

been negative in one way or another, and it had brought conse-
quences—some I still lived with—but I'd never really stopped to
think about what my early, busty fame had done to my little sister.

Tru continued, "I started locking myself in my room to hide
from everyone. So I was ignoring *them* instead of the other way
around, you know? And I started drawing. Painting, sculpting, all of
it."

"Yeah, I remember the time you got all that clay in your carpet.
Mom was so mad."

"And I painted my own room, like, half a dozen times over the
next couple years."

"And you did mine that one time. With *High School Musical*
stuff. It was pretty good."

"Thanks. I did a ton of sketches and stuff I never showed anyone.
Sometimes, I'd wake up at three in the morning with an idea and
sketch it out right then. I had to. I grew a muse while you were growing boobs. And I might never have done that—gotten into art—if it
hadn't been for the difference in our bra cups."

I squinted at her logic. "Wait, you're really serious about that?"

She gave me a look of mild frustration. "Yes, I legit became an
artist because of your boobs. My art showed me that it was okay to
be myself. I didn't *have* to be you. I could be me. And Chloe doesn't
have to be you, either. She can be herself. And you need to let her."

I blinked and realized I'd been looming over my sister like a dis-
approving parent. I took a deep breath and stood back a step. "Well,
that's something to think about." Then I recalled my plan. "Tru, I
need you to do me a favor. Can you talk to Ernie for me? I think he
likes you."

"Of course he likes me. I'm very likeable." Her hair shifted brass-
ily. "But you're using your Master Plan voice, and that doesn't always
go well. Talk to him about what?"

I sighed patiently. "I'm curious about what he might know about Ramòn's life right before he went missing. Maybe he can help Uncle Hilt figure out what happened."

Trudie went still. "No. No, that sounds like a terrible idea."

"What? I'm trying to help Uncle Hilt solve his friend's murder here!"

"I know, but pestering an old man while he's working for my sister? And while he's paying my boyfriend our mac-and-cheese money for the month? I'm not doing it, Pip. It's not worth it. Sorry."

Disturbed by our argument, Rex hopped from the windowsill and trotted back into the library. I shut up, mad at myself for upsetting both cat and sister, and then I heard raised voices outside. Trudie met my eyes, her own full of concern. "That's Gabe."

With a mental sigh, I added, "And Zach."

Out on the porch, I saw Zach and Gabe up in each other's grills, with Ernie standing prudently a step or two back while he ineffectually waved his arms to calm them down.

Tru grabbed my arm. "You have to make him stop." Her eyes remained locked on Gabe.

"He's your boyfriend. You make him stop."

"Not *Gabe*," she said. "Your jerk of an author."

I bristled, even though I knew that Zach was far and away the most uncouth author in Moorehaven right then.

"Hurry, Pippa. Please!" Tru was as stiff as a board, and her fingers dug into my arm. She knew something about Gabe that I didn't.

Zach shoved Gabe in the chest, pushing him back a couple steps. *And there's my cue.* I made sure my feet thudded loudly on the front steps as I dashed over.

But before I could reach the men by the half-assembled fence, Ernie grabbed Gabe's left arm and kept him from returning the shove. "Go home, Gabe!" he hollered. "G'won, get outta here. Take the day off."

Heart hammering, I spun and pointed to Trudie. "Take him home, okay?"

Her eyes were wide as she nodded. I slowed my pace and let her hurry past me.

She took Gabe's other arm and said coaxingly, "Hey, baby. Hey, look at me, okay? You're all right. You're fine. You wanna get out of here with me? Let's go get something to eat, okay? Maybe a burger or some doughnuts? Yeah? Come on, baby. You come with me. I'll take good care of you. You know I will."

Gabe's shoulders relaxed at the sound of my sister's voice, and I realized just how tense he'd been. His head drooped a little, and as Tru led him away, he mumbled, "Sorry, Ern."

Zach stared angrily after Gabe, clearly not finished with his side of the argument.

Before Zach could regain his head of steam, I cleared my throat. "If you'd kindly return to Moorehaven, Mr. Finney, and refrain from causing any more disturbances on my property, I would be deeply grateful. I do have several other guests who are trying to write novels right now."

Zach's dark eyes cut over to me, and he seemed more frustrated than angry. "Yeah, sure, Miss Winterbourne." Without another word, he stalked across the bright grass toward the porch and disappeared inside.

I took a deep, calming breath. "I apologize on behalf of my unruly guest, Mr. Ross. I'll do what I can to keep him away from you and Gabe while you finish your work." Ernie nodded but in a vague way that worried me. "Unless you're considering quitting the job? Which I'd completely understand."

"Oh, no. That guy's harmless. Just started motormouthing about how Gabe should do his job. He'd do well to steer clear of Gabe from now on. Gabe's got a low tolerance for his kind o' stupid."

"What do you mean?"

Ernie's deep frown told me he was reluctant to share, but he spoke eventually. "You know about Gabe's record?"

"I know he has one." All sorts of heinous crimes flitted through my mind's eye, and I really, really didn't want my sister dating Gabe.

"Second-degree assault, for helping some jerk fall down when he tried to steal Maggie's shopping bags," Ernie said. "Helped him fall down four or five times, I believe. Did three years, let out early for good behavior. Hard for ex-cons to get jobs around here, you know, so I took the kid on for Maggie's sake. He's a hard worker, and he has an eye for the kind of décor that looks good in this town. I can build a good fence or mend one stronger than it was, but Gabe's the one who brings in compliments from locals and tourists alike."

"You need him for your business," I translated, "and if he goes back to jail for beating up someone who may or may not deserve it, your business will suffer."

Ernie stared at me for a long moment, his blue eyes assessing my face through deep seams in his own. "That too." He dropped his gaze and studied the fence line he was constructing. "Now, if you'll excuse me, I gotta get back to work."

"You don't want to take rest of the day off, like Gabe?" I gestured to his old-fashioned bicycle, similar to mine but in burnt orange. He was probably in pretty good shape from biking around town, but I still worried he'd get hurt if he tried to work alone.

But Ernie snorted at the suggestion. "I spent the last fifty years mending fences, Miss Pippa, and I see no reason to stop now."

Since Trudie wasn't willing to help me out, I took a deep breath and waded in. "Ernie, Hilt's pretty cut up over learning Ramòn's been dead all this time. I imagine you are too. I'm sorry for the loss of your friend. It must come as quite a shock, even after all these years. I hope you can help me with something, though, and maybe you're in the best position to do it. Can you think of anything I can pass on to my uncle that might give him something to focus on, something to do?"

Ernie shook his head and looked away. "I don't like to talk about it."

Disappointed, I nodded in temporary defeat.

"He did owe Ritchy money, though. Ramòn, I mean. Even back in the day, Ritchy was a slimy son of a gun." His voice held a hard knot as he spoke of someone he'd supposedly been good friends with.

"Did you ever owe Ritchy money?"

Ernie snorted. "Yeah. Had to sell my car to clear my debt." He nodded toward his bike. "Decided I'd never make that mistake again. 'Specially since Hilt decided I might've murdered Ramòn in it and sold it to get rid of the evidence."

"That must've been horrible. How long did he suspect you?"

"For about a day. Until he found my car, safe in Ritchy's carport and entirely blood free. Hilt apologized and bolted. I don't think he liked the idea of suspecting a friend of murder any more than I liked being the suspect. Ritchy probably still has my car somewhere—the packrat—but I never had the notion to buy it back, even when I could. I like my bicycle too much."

I shivered at the thought of suspecting close friends of murder. I'd have bolted too. "Oh. Well, your doctor's probably very proud of you for getting all those decades of exercise."

Ernie grinned. "Doc Stevens ain't one to show pride, but she does keep the glowering to a minimum during my annual checkups."

"High praise, indeed. Well, I'll leave you to it, then. Thanks for being patient with Gabe. I'll make sure Zach knows not to antagonize him." Inside again, I saw no sign of Zach, but several of my guests who'd been writing were now milling around the hall and peeping through the windows, even Jennifer. They saw me come in and converged like a cluster of torpedoes.

"What happened, Miss Winterbourne?" Gabby asked.

"Zach stormed up to his room like a petulant tween," Butch said disapprovingly. "Even slammed his door."

"I'm surprised you know what a tween is," Jennifer said from the back of the group.

"Hey, I have granddaughters. God help me," Butch replied.

Ashley added, "He woke Sarah's baby with that door slam. She had to stop writing to go soothe the poor thing. So insensitive! And I was in the middle of a critical scene with Scarlen pitting an angel and a demon against each other, and now all my mojo is gone."

"Mine too!" grumped Abby. "No more clandestine sex in the hold of the pirate ship until further notice."

Everyone paused and glanced at each other and then at Abby.

Abby replied, "How else is Lady Lisbet supposed to find out if the pirate king is smuggling her royal lover's enemies to Calais, including an assassin, unless she seduces him?"

Butch cleared his throat and tried to rise above his blushing cheeks. "With that kind of logic, you really should be published by now."

"So," Gabby prompted again, "what happened out there? Abby and I heard arguing."

"Yeah," Jennifer added. "Ogden just texted me, wondering if I know what 'all the ruckus' is about."

I raised my hands to placate the curious and slightly disgruntled group. "It was just a minor disagreement over fencing."

"I bet it was," Butch said. "Probably tryin' to tell that young man what he was doin' wrong."

I gave him a noncommittal smile, but Butch had Zach's number.

"I'm still surprised he's published anything," Butch continued.

"That man is as smooth as a porcupine's back." Ashley sounded like she was just getting warmed up.

Maybe if I let my guests vent a little steam to me, they won't vent it directly at Zach, and I can keep a little more peace around here.

"Why don't you follow me up to the Oubliette," I invited, "and I'll address any specific concerns you have. I want your stay to be as comfortable and stress-free as possible." *And there's no chance of their complaints being overheard up there.*

The group trooped after me. We wended our way through the parlor and the library then into the back corner and up the winding stairs. A golden shaft of afternoon light flared through the highest stairwell window. Chloe had made some progress with decorating now that the drywall and painting were complete, but I'd hoped for a more finished look. *Oh well. We're not here for the décor.*

The bed and chair were in the room, at least. Ashley, Abby, and Gabby piled onto the bare mattress, giggling like they were getting ready for a slumber party—or a pillow fight. Butch seemed to find their level of enthusiasm unnerving, so he stood by the open door, gesturing for me to take the single chair. Jennifer lingered in the doorway. I had a quorum of authors and trusted that any concerns Sarah or Ogden brought up later could be addressed by this group as well as by me.

"If you could only speak to him about his constant bragging." Abby wore an expression of winsome entreaty worthy of her heroine. "I work very hard for the sales I get, and poor Gabby hasn't even gotten published yet, though she tries as hard as anyone I know. And to have this country rube running his mouth about how he sells books without even trying... It's just hurtful."

"It's rude," Butch blurted. "He's got no business sense. If he did try his hand at marketing, he'd sell more than he is now. I mentioned it to him, helpful like, but he laughed at the idea. Laughed! And he's got no sense o' people, either, on account of how he laughed in my face." He folded his arms and glared from under his bushy brows.

"I wonder if he even wrote that book himself." Ashley raised a penciled eyebrow.

"Well," I said, "I'm not here to judge anyone on their writing. I'm just here to keep you fed and watered while you work."

"But we can judge him on his actual behavior," Abby said. "He had the nerve to tell me on the stairs to breakfast this morning that the only reason I write so much romance into my mysteries is because I couldn't find a man to marry me. And he can't believe I got published at all, 'on account of all the dirty stories' I write, and apparently, I should be ashamed of myself." She smirked sassily and struck a pin-up pose on the bed.

I kept my smile hidden, but Butch guffawed supportively. "Don't you listen to that goofball, Abbs. From that snippet you read to us in the library yesterday, you ain't nowhere near 'dirty story' territory."

Abby squinted one eye at him. "Yes, *thank you* for that *expert* evaluation, Butch."

The ladies tittered, and Butch blushed under his weathered tan. "Zach's a toddler."

We all turned toward Sarah, who stood in the doorway to the parlor, wearing baby Jackson in a padded sling. She stepped into the room, shifting rhythmically from foot to foot to keep her snoozing baby soothed. "Zach's acting like Penelope does whenever she knows what she's doing and wants to prove it to grownups. She wants to show them that she belongs with them, that she's smart too. She gets pretty pushy, and her way has to be the only way. Everyone else gets lectures on how they're doing it wrong. And..." She sent a sympathetic mom-look around the room at us all. "She gets pretty hurt when you yell at her for being wrong because that's the best she can do with what she knows."

It took a minute for my brain to apply Sarah's toddler explanation to what I knew of Zach, but once I did, I was surprised at how well it fit. My estimation of Sarah went up several notches. She was still a new mom, but she was already seeing the world differently. *She understands humanity on a different level than I can. And she seems more forgiving than the rest of us, which is probably a good thing.*

"So you're saying we should give him a break because he's a man-child?" Jennifer's tone was soft.

Sarah offered a patient smile. "He's a grown man, so he's responsible for everything he does. But remember, he told us this trip was a present from his brother and his sister-in-law. He's probably never been around other authors before. He's just trying to show off how he does things. He doesn't want us to treat him like a country mouse."

"Because he knows he *is* a country mouse," Ashley finished.

Svetlana jumped up next to Abby, and she petted her glossy white back. "And the mouse wishes he were the cat, right, kitty?" Svetlana purred in response, and the conversation shifted to other topics for a few minutes. The authors gradually drifted back to their writing, leaving me with my cat.

I let out a sigh. Svetlana looked at me through slitted eyes, one blue and one green, as she sprawled on the warm spot left by Abby and Gabby. "That went okay, I think. Maybe Sarah's perspective will help everyone else get by while they stay here."

Svetlana blinked slowly at me, and I nodded. If Svetlana could be patient, so could I, though I had a few concerns I really couldn't ignore much longer.

9

"HILT, I NEED TO TALK to you." It was time I found out if he had anything to do with the break-in at the archives building.

A wary look entered my uncle's blue eyes as we stood in the hallway. "Hurry up, Chloe," he called behind me. To me, he said, "We need a supply run to the hardware store. I'm teachin' her some of the ins and outs of Moorehaven's repair work."

Chloe brushed past me. "And its long and glorious tradition. Lucky me. I think he mentioned there'd be a test later. Might want to warn everyone there could be power outages and maybe explosions." She flashed a grin at me, but I was too focused on my mission to return it.

"Hilt, please, just a minute," I insisted. "I just need to ask you—"

My phone rang, and as I checked to see who was calling—Lake—Hilt took the opportunity to toss me a quick salute with a couple of fingers. "Back in a flash, Pippa."

"Seriously, wait!" But he had booked it out the front door like a man half his age with Chloe on his heels. *Is he avoiding me?* I hated feeling suspicious of him, but I couldn't help it. Staring after him in frustration, I finally answered Lake's call.

"Hey, Pippa. You got a minute?"

"For you, absolutely." I was glad to hear his voice, but I could hear tension in my own.

Lake apparently couldn't. His tone was a little intense. "You should've told me you were at the marina earlier."

Still trying to decode Hilt's behavior, I didn't follow Lake's remark. "What? When?"

"The Baker Twins?" he prompted.

That crowded, crazy, awkward morning rushed back into my mind, along with the image of Mandy flirting with him. My face went stony. "I didn't go there to see you."

"Harry says you saw me anyway and that you stormed off. You should've waited for me."

I bristled. "'Should've waited'? I'm sorry, did I miss the clause in our relationship contract where I'm supposed to serve as your personal handmaiden?" I winced at my snippiness and bit my lip to keep more angry words from spilling out.

"What? No! I mean, I just wanted to explain. That's all. I don't want you thinking... whatever you're probably thinking right now."

"I wasn't thinking anything, Lake," I lied. "But maybe I should be."

"No, you shouldn't."

Again with the "should"ing. "Then please, *do* tell me what I *should* be thinking about Mandy draping herself all over you like a heavy morning fog."

Lake sighed, a long breath that told me he was calming himself down. He always tried to keep things smooth and easy, and here I was, splashing around like a bully in the pool. "I just didn't want you to worry. It's nothing. Happens every now and again, and I just have to roll with it."

"You 'just have to roll with it'?" I blurted, aghast.

"Yeah. Mandy's not the first, and she won't be the last, I bet. It's part of the job. I'm a handsome guy. I look *great* in my captain's hat. It happens."

I sputtered, flailing. "Letting someone paw you because you're afraid they won't pay for the tour they booked if you don't—that isn't right. Not cool at all."

"It's not that bad, really. If things ever get out of hand, I can just 'accidentally' push someone overboard." I heard the good humor in his voice. "The ocean's always got my back."

I could almost see the dark cloud forming over my head. *If only I could be so casual. How nice it must be to be taller and stronger than the people who pester you.*

Lake must've heard my unspoken thought. "C'mon, Pippa, I bet there's plenty of stuff you have to do, or can't do, for your authors."

"Yes, but—" I bit back a dozen stories where I'd extricated myself from awkward author requests, some romantic, others just bizarre.

"You can't simply tell an author their writing stinks, right? Or that their whole plot is silly, or derivative, right?" His tone invited my consent.

Are you really this naïve? How many clients have assumed you'll take it as a compliment if they feel you up while you're washing their breakfast dishes? How many of them had fifty pounds and eight inches on you? How I wish I had an ocean I could conveniently tip them into! "I've had to do a lot of things at work I haven't told you about, Lake."

"Well, tell me."

I gripped the phone in frustration. I desperately needed to talk to Hilt, but here was Lake, asking me for uncomfortable details out of the blue. *Do my awkward stories justify his?* Lost in a fog of too much stress, I couldn't think straight, couldn't find an obvious an-swer. "I don't have time right now, okay? But sometime. And please, don't let me see Mandy all over you like that. You're a perfectly capa-ble pilot without her fingers sliding inside your collar."

I hung up. Then I stared at my phone. It didn't ring and kept not ringing. *Our first argument, and I ended it like a horrible shrew.*

But I wasn't going to apologize for feeling the way I felt.

I tended to a few author requests and got another couple chapters of *The Brass Artifice* read before Hilt and Chloe came back. I heard them on the porch and zipped out to catch my uncle before he could escape me again. "Chloe, go on in. Hilt will be right there."

Without a word, Chloe took the shopping bag from Hilt and headed inside. Her I'm-outta-here face told me she had plenty of experience avoiding family arguments, and a swirl of guilt hit me as I realized I'd sounded harsher than I intended to.

I stepped out into the breezy warmth, and Hilt studied me. "You okay? You look tense."

"Lake and I had a difference of opinion."

"Aw, that's too bad. I assume you're right?" He offered me a supportive grin.

I grabbed onto his camaraderie like a life ring. "I'm not sure yet, actually. Listen, I just need to ask. Did you have anything to do with the break-in at the police archives?"

Hilt went still. His blue eyes latched onto me. "Why would you ask me a thing like that?" His voice carried a thread of steel.

With a deep breath, I pushed further. "Vic said the thief took the file for Ramòn's disappearance from the 1964 drawer."

Something in my uncle's face went brittle and crumbled. Finally, he lowered his gaze. "You ain't got any epic failures that're fifty years old, Whip, so you might not know this, but I don't need that file to remember everything about Ramòn's disappearance, every move I made, every person I talked to, every lead I couldn't follow up on 'cause of the tsunami cleanup I had to do." He shuffled his feet and sighed, sinking in on himself like a parade balloon after a long day of acting balanced and rounded. "I ain't gonna try to convince you I'm handlin' this well. I probably ain't. But I got no need to go stealin' my own history."

His brave expression tried to mask the pain in his eyes, but I saw it, anyway. I put a hand on his arm in apology for my suspicion. "Then who did it?"

Hilt's tired grin was a good impression of his usual smile. "That's a real interestin' question, ain't it? I'll see if Vic will drop me a clue or two about that. 'Scuse me." Hilt pulled his phone from his pocket and headed inside.

I followed, almost entirely convinced he was innocent. *If I can't trust Uncle Hilt, I can't trust anyone.*

As the smudgy sunset morphed into a periwinkle sky with violet streaks, I got the final word from the Oubliette repair team—and their sizable bill—and whipped up a big batch of crepes for the next day's breakfast blintzes. The glorious smell of warm vanilla permeated my kitchen, drawing Svetlana to the kitchen windowsill, where she watched intently. Rex was missing out, though, since he was upstairs, letting little Penelope rub his tummy. Tyleen tapped on my kitchen window, startling me out of my rhythm of *pour, smooth, stack.* I gestured that I'd meet her at the back door, lifted the crepe in the skillet to safety, and wiped my hands on my apron.

At the back door, Tyleen wore a canny look that gave her a WWII-spy vibe. "I have new information," she murmured in a self-satisfied tone. "The Baker twins overheard a conversation in On The Rocks about treasure hidden in the marina cliff. That's why they dug there in plain sight and caused all that ruckus."

I sighed and leaned against the doorframe. "Not the brightest bulbs, but always good for entertainment. Who'd they overhear?"

"Their mother loves my pot pie recipe at the Fork and Dagger, so when I saw her in the diner today, I gave her a free plate and chatted her up. She told me it was some woman on her cell phone. Whoever the woman was talking to seemed to be giving her secretive information, and she tried not to be overheard, but she picked the worst spot to hide from eavesdroppers—right next to the Baker twins' regular booth in that back corner. Or did she sit there on purpose? Someone's pulling some strings in town—old Mrs. Baker and I agree." Tyleen's nod was sharp with confidence. "Mark my words. We'll see more shenanigans before this treasure fiasco is over and done with. And I'll bet you dollars to doughnuts that the Potts woman is tied into it somehow. The Moorehaven cats are never wrong about people."

I nodded seriously and thanked her, but as I slid the glass door closed and returned to my crepes, I couldn't help thinking that Tyleen was going Full Conspiracy Theory with the strange happenings at the marina and with my plump, middle-aged author. My cats had disliked plenty of people over the past six-plus years. *Then again, this is Seacrest. Anything can happen.*

I woke up troubled an hour before my alarm went off the next morning, which made the cats grumpy. I hadn't checked in with Tru like I'd meant to. She was my sister, of course, and I wanted her to be okay. The incident with Gabe and Zach had left a bad taste in everyone's mouths. But while I had several authors-slash-witnesses at Moorehaven, Tru had gone home alone with a guy who'd done time for assault. *I should've called. I shouldn't have left her all day with an upset guy who has violent tendencies.*

Rex did his best to ignore me and snuggle back to sleep. While Svetlana looked on disapprovingly, I threw on a pale-orange T-shirt with a large cartoon Georgia peach on it, matching seersucker shorts, and some old watermelon-themed flip-flops that were worn enough that they wouldn't survive to see the next summer. Then I flip-flopped my way around the corner of the block to Glazin' West. Through the large plate-glass window, I saw Emily arranging a muffin with sprinkly bits on the top tier of a display, turning it just so. I let myself in, jingling the door's bell, and Emily waved a surprised greeting at me. She had a couple of early customers in business attire who ate in the hurried manner of people on their way to work, and I made my way past them to the front counter.

"What are you doing up and out so early?" Emily asked in a low voice. "Is something wrong? Do you have an urgent curiosity for Glaze and Gossip?"

"No, no." I waved away her concern. "No pressing questions, just a pressing need for some breakfast muffins. I'm headed over to see Trudie."

"Ohh," Emily breathed. "The fight. I hope she's okay."

"I'm sure she is. I just want to check in. Zach can be a handful, but so can Gabe."

My friend nodded understandingly. "You want carrot-maple or peach cobbler?" She indicated different tiers on her muffin display.

"One of each, and I'll let Tru pick."

"Such a generous big sister." Emily packed two enormous muffins, each topped with glaze and crumbles, into a take-out container for me. "Let me know how it goes." She handed it over.

I nodded, though there wasn't much I could do to control the needle on the Winterbourne Gossip-O-Meter these days. Two weeks after moving to town, Tru had shacked up with Gabe. She was unapologetic in her interest in back-east politics. And that viral picture of her wearing '40s-style stars-and-stripes body paint—and nothing else—in Seacrest's Independence Day Parade had definitely caused a stir. I didn't feel like I could be nearly awesome enough to counter the growing—and darkening—local opinion of my beloved little sister.

Out in the brisk early morning, I made my way toward the nearest bridge across the Silver River. Several downtown streets crossed it, making the thirty-foot gorge look like a poorly stitched, if brightly gleaming, tear in the land. The sun was eagerly clambering to top the eastern ridge, and the sky was a bright, distant blue filled with high golden streaks of cloud. Seacrest itself remained shrouded in half shadow, an almost-town of endless possibility, not quite anchored in the world.

My heart spun out a kaleidoscope of emotions when I saw that the lights were on in Blade and Boom. I didn't like the way we'd ended our "discussion" the day before. But if I wanted a more mature relationship with Lake, I had to be more mature myself. I prodded a molar with my tongue and took a deep breath. *I can do this.*

But as my feet reached the groomed river stones that bordered the office property, the door opened ahead of me, and Lake stepped out, followed by the entire marine-salvage team. I recognized Patrice by her leggy stride and dark poof of hair and Connor by the way he trailed after her. The short, stocky fellow had to be the diver, Wade, and the tall blonde was, of course, Mandy. She hovered at Lake's elbow, but the second he saw me, Lake stopped, excused himself for a minute, and stepped over to me.

His entire face lit up. "Good morning, beautiful." He leaned down and gave me a long mochaccino kiss, and his ardent body language told me he wanted everyone—me, Mandy, the passing newspaper boy on the bike—to see how much he was into me. I threw my arms around him and reveled in that kiss, playing it up for all it was worth. And it was worth a lot.

I came up for air and placed a hand on his chest. Meeting his deep blue eyes, I tried to convey the different levels of my gratitude with one single "Thank you."

His smile lit my morning. "No, thank *you*. Long time no see. Where you headed on this fine morning?"

I needed a minute to catch my breath after Lake and his heady scent enveloped me. "Uh, going to see Trudie for a minute. Make sure she's okay."

He nodded wisely. "Oh. The fight."

Dang this small town. "You're out early again. Still treasure hunting?" I asked lightly.

"I'm just the pilot, ma'am." Lake tugged on the old white captain's hat he'd inherited from his old boss. "I leave the hard work to them."

"Well, pilot safe, then. I'll see you later, okay?" I stood on tiptoe, grabbed the front of his shirt with my free hand, and kissed him hard.

"Oh, absolutely," he said breathlessly.

"Hey, lover boy! Can we go now?" Wade called from the top of the marina stairs.

"Gotta go," he murmured in my ear before giving it an ardent nibble.

Shivers of delight arched my spine, and I gasped involuntarily.

"That's my girl." His smile was wicked and steamy, and I wanted nothing more than to tackle him right there and have my way with him. *See how Mandy likes* that *move.*

Instead, I stood smiling like a mannequin full of molten lust as he walked over to his clients, where the blonde hooked her arm possessively around his. I squinted. *Did... did she just shoot me a Look?* Half a dozen murder plots flickered through my brain like a Rolodex on crack. *And no one would ever catch me. You're lucky I'm not a murderer, lady.*

Lake and his troupe disappeared down the marina stairs, so I tucked my irritation at the blonde into a box next to the Lust Vat and walked onward.

As I crossed the river at Cedar Street and made my way back toward the sea, I saw Wallis sitting on a bench facing the river. I angled toward her and sat down on the bright-blue bench. "Such a lovely morning, isn't it?"

"I think I'm going to have to close my shop," Wallis said from behind a curtain of blond hair.

I blinked. Wallis had always been what one could charitably call pessimistic, but I'd never heard her speak about her own business in that tone before. "Is business really that bad?"

Wallis laced her fingers around one knee. Her curtain of hair shifted, but she still didn't look at me. "Who would have thought that a florist could fail to thrive in the biggest little murder town in the world? But that's the trouble, isn't it?" She finally met my gaze, and her brown eyes were full of the remote sadness of helplessness. "From day to day, we all take each other for granted. No one buys flowers of congratulation or appreciation because we believe our friends and family will still be there tomorrow. Everyone wants the happy ending. And only when it's too late, after tragedy has struck, do we understand what we have lost. We pour our regret into petals and vases, into ribbons and cards. No one wants to afford connection, but like Moore said, everyone can afford regret."

Moved, I clasped Wallis's hand. "That's so true, isn't it? We really need to reach out to each other—"

"Except for that new policeman, Vic," Wallis interrupted. "He buys flowers from me every morning like clockwork." She frowned in puzzlement. "He has a lot of regrets for a man who only moved to town a couple of months ago."

"Who are they for?"

"He never says. They're always bright and cheery bouquets. Lots of yellows and oranges. It's nice to see someone buying my favorite colors. Whoever they're for, I hope they forgive Vic."

"Or maybe he's just more enlightened than most. Maybe he's buying flowers to avoid having regrets later?" The very idea seemed to baffle Wallis into contemplative silence, so I wished her a good day and left her to her musings. I had a suspicion that Vic wasn't delivering those flowers to the person they were meant for, but I had no proof. *The gossip group couldn't look into this without Wallis finding out. And spying on a policeman is a big ask. I'll have to keep my eyes open for more clues.*

Just a couple of blocks from Lake's mid-remodel lighthouse, Gabe's Airstream trailer sat in a small empty lot behind a row of kitschy tourist shops. I stopped and watched it for a second to make sure it wasn't rocking. Then I took a deep breath, crossed the lot, and knocked on the silvery door.

"Yeah," Tru called loudly.

"It's me, Trudie. I brought breakfast."

"Oh, Pips!" A couple of thumps emanated from inside the trailer, and the door flew wide. Trudie stood at the edge of the trailer's floor, wearing a thin white T-shirt over brightly patterned pink panties. "Gabe's out getting some supplies for your fence." Her sleepy but bright smile faded as she caught me staring at the light-blue box in her hand.

Plan B. The morning-after pill.

Disappointment flooded me, and it must've showed all over my face because Trudie said, "I'm a grown woman, Pippa. I can do what I want. Did you really think I was a virgin or something?"

My lips tightened, and I felt like a judgy grandma. "No, Trudie. But I did kind of hope that, between the two of you, you and Gabe could manage a Plan A."

Her eyes narrowed. "At least I'm taking action instead of sitting back and hoping for the best. That's what you always used to do, remember? You 'just hoped' Keenan would ask you to prom—and he didn't. You 'just hoped' Dad would enroll you in the college you wanted—and he didn't. You 'just hoped'—"

"Yeah, well, then I grew up, Tru!" I said, louder than I intended. "I have a business now. I have to make decisions, or things fall apart. I hold them together, Trudie! Me! But I can't hold you together, not when you refuse to grow up."

"I don't want you to hold me together, Pippa! That's *my* job. And I'll do it my way, in my own time. I never asked you for help when I got here."

"And look where you ended up." The words shot out of my mouth before I could stop them.

Trudie's big eyes stared down at me with a deeply injured expression.

Oh, geez, Mouth. That was not *cool! Why did you go and say that? Because I'm a bad sister, that's why.* After an awkward silence, I waved my free hand back and forth in an attempt to dispel the bad vibe between us. "Here." I opened the take-out container and made a peace offering of its contents. "I got you a muffin."

She stared suspiciously at the sudden appearance of Emily's delectable creations. "Which one's for me?"

"You pick," I grumped.

"Is this one peach?" she asked tentatively.

"Peach cobbler. Yeah."

"You don't want that one? You're wearing a peach on your shirt."

"My shirt is not a legally binding document. You can have it."

Trudie hesitated another moment, clearly wanting the peach cobbler muffin. I'd always been able to read my sister's face. She was afraid of offending me by greedily grabbing it, even though I'd already offered it to her. Sisterly politics were a quagmire that required delicate steps. Then she delicately scooped it out of its holder and held it in front of her. When I didn't frown at her, she finally accepted my grudging contrition. "You, um, wanna come in?"

"No, I need to get back for breakfast. Here, just take the other one too. For Gabe." I folded the Styrofoam tabs back into their slots and handed the container to her.

She took it but held it distractedly.

"Are you okay?" I asked. "After yesterday, I mean. The fight at Moorehaven."

"What? Oh. Yeah. Everything's fine. We went to the movies, and then we sat in my studio and talked about it while I made some more sea-glass necklaces."

"You have a studio?"

She shifted her shoulders defensively, but her tone remained light. "It's one of the public picnic tables in the Green, but I kinda claim it. It's never shaded by the trees, so no one else wants to sit there, but I like having the extra light when I work with glass. And Gabe's not the monster everyone thinks he is. He made *one* mistake. You could be more forgiving."

Maybe I should. "So what are you up to today? More glasswork?"

Her face brightened, and she delicately bit her lower lip with her front teeth. "Actually, Fallon—the hotel guy, I met him on your widow walk—wants to meet up for lunch. He said he has a proposition for me."

"I bet he does." My stomach squirmed. "I warned you about him when you first got here. He likes interesting women. And *you* have a boyfriend." I nodded toward her Plan B box. "What are you thinking, Tru?"

Trudie cocked her head and studied me. "Well, I was thinking that lunch is two people sitting at the same table for a midday meal. A girl's gotta eat. That 'starving artist' thing didn't come out of nowhere, you know. And you really should do a better job of criticizing my choices. You can't insult me for being with Gabe and then insult me for having lunch with someone far higher up the social ladder."

My hypocrisy made my left eye twitch. *Oh, yes, I can,* I thought mulishly. "Look, just be careful, okay? If you need anything, you call me." I took a step back. "I mean it."

She sighed and rolled her eyes. "Yes, *Mom.*" She knew I hated it when she called me that. But I let it go. I was the older sister. And I had breakfast to make.

After a block or so, I walked into the first light of the day and squinted against its piercing rays. *I shouldn't have yelled at her. If only she weren't so stubborn and immature!* After a deep, cleansing breath, I picked up my pace. Breakfast was waiting, and I had guests and imaginations to feed.

10

"*I can't die now; I haven't seen everything yet.*"
Raymond Moore, 1981

A DELIGHTFUL VARIETY of smells greeted me when I stepped back through Moorehaven's front door: maple syrup, scrambled eggs, raspberries and strawberries, coffee, cinnamon, and whipped cream. *Is Hilt cooking up our entire breakfast selection at once?* I hurried through the dining room, tossing a quick "Good morning" to the guests around the table—Zach seemed to be behaving himself this morning—and darted into the kitchen. Chloe, Sebastian, and Hilt were all busy chopping, mixing, and frying. Sebastian apologized for his mother's absence, but I assured him that I already knew Tyleen was donating her time to decorating for the Treasure Fair.

My stomach growled demandingly. I had been experiencing mixed feelings about giving my muffin to Trudie, but now that I stood in my own kitchen, surrounded by friends and family and all my favorite recipes, the last tiny regret I held about not eating one of Emily's delicious muffins faded away.

"Smorgasbord this morning," Hilt called over the skillet he was minding. "Butch found a new love for those blintzes of yours. Likes 'em with red berries piled on top." He pointed to Sebastian's cutting board, which held an impressive collection of leafy tops next to the strawberries he was slicing.

"These go great on oatmeal too," Sebastian said. "And little Penelope is in a red-food phase, so this is about all her mom can get her to eat right now." He moved a double handful of sliced strawberries into a cute little strawberry-shaped bowl and handed it to Chloe, who added it to a platter laden with three other dishes and took it to the dining room.

As soon as Chloe stepped out, Hilt approached me and lowered his voice. "I been meanin' to say, but it's been crazy around here, with... everything and all. But Rhonda called again. Bad news."

"What do you mean? I thought everything was worked out. Is it about the Oubliette?"

He shook his head, looking more like a guilty little boy than my competent uncle. "She called a couple days ago, and I plumb forgot to tell you. The fence ain't gonna be covered. 'Act of God,' if you can believe it."

I'm no angel, but I'm pretty sure I haven't annoyed God so much that he's punishing me with a tsunami. But I had a more pressing concern. "Why do we have an insurance policy that lets them get out of covering us for acts of God? This is Seacrest, after all. Weird nonsense happens here on the regular." I sighed through my nose, unwilling to get upset over a decision that had been made two days prior. If the cost got prohibitive, I could always write to the Moorehaven Trust for a special dispensation, but I was mostly sure we could afford Hilt's fancy fence on our summer traffic. "Well, we've already hired Ernie and Gabe. How much are we going to have to pay them?"

Hilt hunched his shoulders as if bracing for my ire. "Gonna be a fair chunk, I'm afraid, with the special-order fencing and the decoratin' and such. I'm sorry, Pip. This one's on me."

I squeezed his arm. "It's okay, Hilt. I know you have a lot on your mind. And there's nothing we could've done to change the policy, anyway. But if you would, call Rhonda back and get that policy updated as soon as you can."

Hilt nodded.

When Chloe returned, she brought me coffee in a mug given to me by one of my past guests. A token of thanks as well as a portable advertisement, the mug bore the image of a hen, a tabby cat, and a big ball of orange yarn between a pair of a purple curtains, bracketed by a book title and the author's name in a quirky font. "You look a little frazzled, Boss Lady," Chloe said.

I took a couple of grateful gulps. "I'll be okay. Let me finish this cup and get something to eat." Immediately, everyone peppered me with suggestions: blintzes, egg scramble, oatmeal, cinnamon rolls. "I'll start with a cinnamon roll."

But Hilt saw me eyeing his skillet. "I'll make you a blintz or three for later too."

"I love you all so much."

"You going to the Treasure Fair tonight?" Hilt asked.

"Depends if anyone wants to stay behind. I'll be sure the authors know it's happening." At least one of them would come back from the fair with a fresh plot device, guaranteed. I devoured my cinnamon roll and the peach blintzes Hilt made for me, but I felt a little less love for Chloe when she disappeared again after breakfast, leaving all the dishes for someone else to wash. I sighed. *Maybe I should be speaking to her father instead of her. Whatever's going on with Mercer, I doubt he specifically needs the aid of a bed-and-breakfast hostess's assistant.* Rex hopped up on the counter and offered his dish-cleaning services, but I shooed him down. Svetlana stopped drinking water from her bowl long enough to sneeze at him as if to say, *Fool, that was never going to work.*

Hilt disappeared, too, and I hoped he was being sensible with his inquiries. Sebastian offered to stay until one of them came back, since that was what his mother would have done, and we chatted as he helped me straighten up various common rooms. Best of all, he stood in the hallway to listen to Zach's latest conspiracy theory so I could slip away and be productive.

When Sebastian finally escaped and found me in the library, he helped me rearrange the library table's chairs into a straight line. Then I got a text from Lori.

FYI Hilt is pestering Doc Stevens for details about Ramón's skeleton.

I texted her back. *Anything new?*

Not yet. Just looping you in.

I thanked her and put my phone back in my pocket. *Glad he's not breaking into anywhere, at least.*

Sebastian seemed content, even pleased. "Being around you is just like being around my mom. You guys get such mysterious texts all the time. I bet the spies in the thrillers you sell don't have such an efficient network as Seacrest."

In the sunroom, we organized and straightened the magazine racks and bookshelves. An hour or so later, I spotted Chloe sneaking down the main hallway as I came downstairs with Sebastian. "Now that you're back, Chloe," I said nice and loud, "can you finish off the last of the dishes?"

She jumped guiltily and spun to face me. "Yeah, absolutely. Sorry about that. I had a, uh, family emergency."

"Oh, is your dad all right?"

"He's fine. I'll get right on those dishes. Have 'em done in two shakes of a lame tail. Or however that goes." She hurried back toward the kitchen.

"She seems distracted," Sebastian said. "Is she okay?"

I frowned thoughtfully. "I think so. But she has gone missing several times lately."

Sebastian tucked his hands into his pockets. "How mysterious. Does your group investigate disappearances?"

I chuckled at the thought of the grown women from the Glaze and Gossip group stalking my teenage assistant. "As fun as that might be, I think that might spook her even more. And there's a family element to it, somehow, so I don't want to just barge in on her life. Let's give it another day or two. If she still hasn't talked to me, I'll have to be more direct."

Sebastian dipped his head with an agreeable smile, and his green eyes twinkled. "All right. I'll leave you to it." He slipped out the back door to head home. *He's the complete opposite of his mother. Not a curious bone in his body.*

Chloe stuck around for the rest of the afternoon, but Hilt only reappeared in the evening, looking somber. While his generation didn't put much stock in the touchy-feely, I'd lived in the same house as Uncle Hilt for six and a half years, and I'd never seen him this troubled and withdrawn before. With a firm grip on my sympathy, I followed him down the side hall that led to his room and stopped him outside the door.

Hoping my face brooked no resistance, I said, "You need to talk to somebody about this. It's tearing you apart. It doesn't have to be me, but you know I will make time for you whenever you need me. You saved me, remember? So I won't let you get lost in this quest to figure out who killed your good friend. It's been so long. Anything could've happened to whoever did it. Maybe it's time to let go of this, if only for one night."

Hilt blinked his bright-blue eyes at me. "Yer a sweet girl, Pippa. I've never regretted taking you on. But right now I really gotta pee—"

"Oh God. I'm sorry—"

"And get myself out to Jimmy's magnetic fishing booth over at the street fair."

Speaking of fish, my face did a great bigmouth bass impression. "What?"

His half smile was brief but genuine. "Jimmy had the same idea about distracting me. He roped me into helping him man a booth for the kiddies. Magnet on a fishing pole, little plastic fish in a wading pool. Every fish has a number; every number gets a prize!" He sounded like a carnival barker. Then he gently nudged my shoulder with his fist. "I'll be okay, doll. Long as I empty this bladder in the next minute or two."

"Of course. Sorry." I retreated out of the hallway and left him to his business. Relief settled over me like a beam of light, and I sent a bright wish of gratitude to Jimmy Craig for getting Hilt to break his obsessive behavior, even if it was just for the evening.

Sarah and her husband came down the stairs, carrying their little ones. They each wore a backpack, no doubt full of baby supplies. Penelope babbled happily about fairs and cotton candy, and her father murmured back in that encouraging tone parents used when conversing with excited toddlers.

"Off to the street fair?" I asked.

"Yes," Sarah said breathlessly as she reached the bottom of the stairs. Her sweet little boy rode in a soft carrier on her chest, wide eyes taking in everything. "We go early to things like this. That way they're not tired yet, and they're usually ready for bed when we're done."

"Look at you with your clever plan. I hope you all have a wonderful time."

"Tweasure!" Penelope cried in a surprisingly intense pirate growl. Her tiny fist pierced the air.

"We'll find some treasure, Penelope," Thad assured her.

I bustled around, tidying my hostess station area, until they left. Then I wandered into the front parlor and flopped on the red couch, grateful for a small break from my duties.

I'll never be as wise and calm and confident as Sarah. Babies and books and a marriage and everything! I'm a gawky half-grown stork, and she's a swan. And I screwed up by yelling at Tru this morning. Lake seems like he wants to be around me, but only when he sees me. Am I reading him wrong? Maybe we don't have what I think we have. Maybe

I'm not who I think I am. Maybe my whole life is a— I caught myself before I finished that thought. I'd been down that road a thousand times, and I couldn't afford a depression detour right now. Hilt needed me. Chloe needed me. My adorable authors needed me. And I needed Lake.

I sat up and lifted my chin. "I don't have time for you right now, Depression Dragon. Things to do! So get back in your cage." I rose, mentally scrambling for something to do, something to derail my oncoming funk. *Crepes! I'll make a new batch of crepes, since everyone's enjoying my blintzes so much.* The easy recipe, with its simple, repetitive motions, could keep me busy until something else came up.

As I stepped into the hall, Butch came downstairs and paused at the parlor doorway, sporting Abby on one arm and Gabby on the other. "You coming out to the street fair, Miss Winterbourne?" His tone indicated pride at escorting fine ladies out for the evening. "Moorehaven's about empty. You should take a break. You've more than earned it."

"I'll wander over later, Butch. Thanks." Though I'd decided earlier to attend the street fair if Moorehaven emptied out, I had plenty of time before evening, and the crepe recipe still called my name.

Butch and his entourage left, and I heard Chloe call me from the library. I peeked in around the corner and saw her chilling with a thriller on a sofa, her finger marking her place.

"Did you need me?" she asked.

"No, that was just Butch leaving for the street fair. You want to go?"

"No, I'm fine."

"Well, I'm just gonna make some more crepes, so you might as well head on out, anyway."

With a stubborn expression, she said, "No, I'll stay here until I finish this book."

"You can take it home with you. I do trust you to bring it back."

Her long dark curtain of hair shook once. "Couches are nicer here."

I nodded. The antique couches at Braxton House were more expensive than mine, no doubt, but her father's obsession with preserving the heritage of his ancestors probably meant that Chloe wasn't allowed to sit on them.

Poor kid.

"You can tell me anything that's bothering you. I'm worried about you and your dad. If I can help out in any way, I hope you'll let me know. I'm your friend as well as your boss, and I'm here for you."

Chloe's mouth opened as if she was about to speak. But she simply nodded. "Yeah, cool. Thanks. I, uh, I'll do that."

I nodded, disappointed but willing to be patient, and left her to her book. In the kitchen, I blended and poured and fried and stacked, wreathed in a heady cloud of vanilla, until my pile of crepes stood so high, I knew there would be leftovers even if Tyleen and Sebastian came over for breakfast. *See? I'm good at something.* I smiled, content, and felt my dragon retreat.

Feeling confident, I texted Lake. *Hey, handsome. You have a few minutes to hang out tonight?* I'd gotten distracted from asking him about the golden coins the salvage team was looking for, and our fight hadn't helped matters. *Looks like I might be free to go to the street fair. Wanna be my date?*

Lake replied, *For you, I have all the time in the world. I'll swing by in an hour. Gotta get this engine grease off. Not the best cologne.*

I sent him five heart emojis and a row of golden coins. Right around sunset, Ashley and Zach headed out singly for the evening. When I peeked into the library, Chloe had finished her book and was dusting the shelves. Touched, I left her to her work. *Her heart's in the right place.* As I waited for Lake to come over, I sat down at the tiny kitchen table and worked on meal-planning charts.

I'd only worked through two breakfasts' worth when a tap on the window made me jump. Tyleen smiled brightly, her face and glasses reflecting the warm glow from my lights. She held up a small crockpot with a steamy glass lid. I opened the sliding glass door in the dining room.

"I've just finished putting up the last of the decorations over at the Treasure Fair, but I had this baby cooking all afternoon. You're gonna love it," she trilled. She lifted the lid, and a curl of delicious steam rolled up under my nose, bringing the aroma of potatoes, cheese, and bacon.

"Then come right in." I waved her on into the kitchen.

She zoomed past me, holding the hot dish in front of her like an offering for the culinary gods, a unique priestess in a black miniskirt and grandma sweater. "You'll never guess what I just heard," she called as she walked ahead of me into the kitchen. "The Baker Twins swear up and down that they saw one of those marine-salvage people lurking in the shadows near the archives building today. You know, where that break-in happened, right across from the police station."

My spine stiffened in surprise. "Really? Which one?"

"The blond one."

Connor, who'd come to my Shelf with Patrice and bought books. *But consider the source.* "He's gotta be out looking for that treasure, though. Is the Baker Twins' eyesight better than yours, Tyleen?" I asked with an apologetic smile.

Tyleen knew she'd gotten eyewitness details wrong before because she'd been too proud to wear her glasses. But she had them on tonight. "Their eyesight, or their judgment?"

Before I could answer, someone knocked at the front door. Tyleen plunked her pot down on a counter and shed her oven mitts. "Let me get that. You look run off your feet."

Tyleen let out an admiring *ooh* as she opened the door. My eyes widened. *It has to be Lake. And he must look very good.* I leaned out the kitchen door, heart racing.

Lake's deep voice carried down the corridor, but I couldn't see him past Tyleen's bulky sweater. "Hi, Tyleen. I'm here to pick up Pippa. Hilt's going to want to know when I'll have her home, though. Is he in?"

"Oh, I'm not sure..." Tyleen began.

I hurried down the hall. "Hilt's already at the street fair," I told them. "He's helping Jimmy with a booth—" I could finally see past Tyleen when I reached the door, and I stopped midsentence.

Lake stood on the porch, holding at least two dozen deep-pink roses—my favorite. He wore black slacks and a royal-blue shirt that brought out his eyes, and he'd done something incredibly sexy with his hair. My fingers fairly ached to run through it, to make hot fists in it, to pull his lips down to mine. I'd wanted to ask him about something, but suddenly, I couldn't for the life of me remember what it was.

"I'll take those, shall I? And you two can be on your way. The food will keep." Tyleen's voice sounded faint, as if Lake and I were the only two people in the room.

I nodded mutely, eyes locked on Lake's face. He hadn't moved or said a word since he'd laid eyes on me, either.

Tyleen slid into the doorway and rescued the bouquet from Lake's unresisting arm. With his eyes gazing into mine, he didn't even seem to notice. She gave me a gentle push out the door. "Go have fun, darlings."

And she shut my own door behind me.

11

"You can't choose who you fall in love with, kid, any more than I can choose who my characters fall in love with. Love just happens. If you don't know that, you haven't been paying attention."
Raymond Moore, 1934

"WOULD YOU LIKE TO TAKE an evening stroll with me?" Lake murmured.

My hands replied, reaching for him. I left his beautiful hair alone, but I pulled him down and kissed him, hot and gentle, relishing the taste of him, his radiating warmth. "Yes. I want to stroll."

"Yes, ma'am." The breathlessness in his voice boosted my confidence.

I tucked my arm through his. "Lead on, then."

With the sea at our backs, we approached the blocks that had been cordoned off from traffic. Chatting came effortlessly, as if Lake and I had spent no time apart at all. My worries about losing him retreated into the dim cage with my dragon, and I lifted my chin a notch higher as we ambled onward. I even remembered what I wanted to ask him about.

"So what's the salvage team's take on the coins? Are there more? Do they have a good idea where to look?"

Lake studied the star-spangled sky as he gathered his thoughts. "They're narrowing it down, and they definitely think there's more treasure out there. They try to keep their discussions private, but on a thirty-foot boat, everyone can hear pretty much everything. The his-

"

torian, Patrice, figures there should be plenty of cargo from this damaged galleon she knows about. Wade, the diver, keeps poring over the seafloor charts. Connor was considering several locations—Perpetua Bay, Devil's Riding Crop, Diana's Chute, and the like—despite some tattoo map Patrice has found. He—"

"Thinks everything rocks. I know." I chuckled.

"Actually, he wasn't with them today. Not sure what's going on there, since he needs to do his job from the boat."

I remembered what Tyleen had said about Connor being spotted lurking in town. "Did he ever act strangely? I have a somewhat dubious account of him lurking near the archive building today."

"You think he could have something to do with those stolen 1964 files?" Lake's tone was doubtful.

"I don't know what to think, honestly. It could be nothing. But this treasure doesn't sound like nothing." *Until they narrow down its location, though, I won't have any new information for Hilt about Ramón's whereabouts before he died.* "Any idea how long the team is planning to look for it?"

"They've booked my boats for at least one tour every day through next week. Expeditions like this run on funds, though, so they'll eventually need to take a break to shake down their investors or whoever's financing them."

"Well, I wouldn't mind a break from this whole treasure-hunt thing, myself." I wished Mandy would go away and never come back.

Lake evidently picked up on the shift in my mood and switched gears. "I ran into Zach earlier today. He asked me if there was such a thing as a salamander fish."

At least he's not arguing. "Is there?"

Lake shook his head. "Not as far as I know, but get this. His main character..."

"Chuck."

"Yeah, Chuck. The guy needed a code phrase to tell his buddy to follow his lead while he distracted the killer in a remote mountain cabin, and Zach thought something with a fake kind of fish would be cool."

"What was the code phrase?"

Lake started to speak then started laughing and had to start over. "'You know what they say about salamander fish at low tide.'"

I chuckled. "A low tide reference in the mountains. I like it." As we passed the marina, I asked, "You're not doing moonlight tours or anything tonight?"

"Nope. Don't wanna steal money from the street fair."

"That's awfully generous of you."

Lake's smile was self-deprecating. "It was Harry's idea, actually. He thinks I'm working too hard."

"And whose idea was the bouquet?"

"Wallis's, of course. But she only suggested the number of flowers, not the color. I know what you like."

I chuckled at the mental image of the funereal Wallis encouraging Lake to be more romantic. "She got you to buy all of her pink roses, didn't she?"

"That she did. And I'd do it again. The look on your face was almost worth all the time we've been apart."

"I could've eaten you up right there," I confessed, "if Tyleen hadn't been present."

He took my hand and squeezed it. "I'll be edible all night."

Heat flooded my cheeks. I glanced around for a quiet spot to be alone with him for a moment, but we'd reached the first block of the street fair, and the crowds were growing. Lights, music, and sound effects washed over us. I gave Lake a hot look that promised delicious action later in the evening and dragged him into the fun.

Several locals had braved the tourist-laden streets to experience the treasure fair for themselves, no doubt relishing the odd sensation of seeing something that had never happened in Seacrest before. I waved to Lori and Naoma, though Naoma didn't notice me because she was taking pictures for the next edition of her paper.

Mozzie, the sandwich maker who supplied Moorehaven's guests with lunch orders at least twice a week, called me over to a broad table in front of his shop. "A free sandwich for the *signorina*, for her inestimable loyalty," the big Italian said, arms wide in welcome.

I was too hungry to refuse.

"You are on a date, yes?" His dark eyes regarded Lake. "I make you one also, Pilot Man. You're good for Seacrest. You like meatballs, yes?" Without waiting for an answer, he whipped up a Swiss meatball sub for Lake, whose eyes lit up.

"How did you remember that, Mozzie?" he asked. "I haven't had time to get this deliciously messy sandwich from you in ages. I always have to get the turkey so I don't spill sauce all over my boat. Oh my God, that looks so good."

Lake was fairly drooling, and I found myself in the odd situation of being jealous of a sandwich. I pretended to wipe some of it off his chin for him.

"Mozzie knows all the sandwiches for all the people." The sandwich-maker's smooth gray curls beamed around his head like a halo as he handed Lake his creation.

"I'll sing your praises to all my clients after this," Lake said through his first big bite.

"No." Mozzie's hair shook with denial. "You, I have heard with the 'Somewhere Beyond the Sea' from across the way in the mornings. You cannot sing. You stick to piloting."

"Ooh, ouch," I said through sudden laughter.

Lake made a mock grumpy face at Mozzie's good-natured teasing. "Fine. Just send some more menus to my office. I'm almost out."

Mozzie's smile was beatific. "This, I can do."

I took a bite of my pulled pork and nodded my delight at Mozzie before heading back into the crowd. As Lake and I left Mozzie's table, the man raised his voice and belted out a truly magical rendition of *O Sole Mio*. Lake and I glanced back at him, his eyes closed in bliss, singing after us.

"Okay, that settles it. I'm never singing outdoors again," Lake said. "That guy puts me to shame. He could sing in an opera."

I nudged him with my elbow before taking another bite. "I think he has. I know he sings in our local plays. You should hear him at Christmas. He's a one-man caroling dynamo."

Lake let out an amazed laugh, free and uninhibited, drawing a few stares. "I love this town. Every day it grows on me a little more."

"Like mold?"

"Like barnacles. It's never gonna let go of me."

We walked on into the depths of the Treasure Fair. Spanish galleons and gold coins were painted or crafted everywhere. Kids ran amok with corn dogs, miniature kites made of glow-in-the-dark sticks, and pirates painted on their cheeks. On The Rocks, the old bar, had expanded its service to a series of tables outside on their porch area, and all their umbrellas were decorated with golden lights. Food carts sported long lines, and the air was bursting with hot, cheesy, greasy deliciousness. Everything smelled amazing, even though I was actively stuffing my face.

As I was polishing off my last bite, Lake dragged me by the hand to a food cart offering cotton candy burritos and ordered us a couple of the delectable desserts. In taste and texture heaven, I inhaled a blue cotton candy wrap with almond sprinkles on raspberry-and-vanilla ice cream filling.

Trudie waved to me from a table outside one of the many art galleries down Seacrest's main drag, surrounded by artistically twisty twigs from which she'd hung her sea-glass necklaces and earrings. Lake parted the crowd like the bow of a ship and towed me behind him by the hand. He bought me a pair of green-glass earrings. Trudie wore her Professional Smile, and I was amazed how much it resembled the one I'd practiced in the mirror so much when I first moved there. Her earrings were beautiful even up close.

"You really know what you're doing, Tru. These are amazing."

"Thanks." My sister ducked her head, and for a moment, she seemed nine again, trying to conceal her childlike excitement on Christmas morning so she could be as cool and aloof as eleven-year-old me.

Several minutes later, I spotted the distinguished black wavy hair of Chloe's dad, Mercer Braxton, attorney-at-law. On impulse, I angled toward him and touched his herringbone-jacketed arm. He smiled his usual vapid-senator greeting, acting pleasant before he even recognized me.

"Ah, Pippa! So good to see you." His eyes took in Lake, hovering at my shoulder. "And it looks like you're enjoying a fine evening with your gentleman. How lovely for you!"

"Mercer." I kept my voice low. "May I ask, is Chloe doing okay at home?"

"Whatever do you mean?" He sounded like a delicate old grandmother had crawled inside his senatorial skin.

"Well, she's just been... distracted lately." I put it delicately, not wanting to accuse. "She mentioned she was helping you, and I wondered if she'd mentioned any... conflicts to you."

His brilliant smile attempted to blind any doubts I might be harboring. "I'm sure she's just fine, Pippa. It's been a busy summer for all of us."

"Of course." I smiled back, but I could tell by his tone that he would prefer it if I didn't bother him anymore right then. Perhaps it really was none of my business. Maybe he didn't like being disturbed at the Treasure Fair. But my gut had other ideas—even if I wasn't quite sure what they were yet. For Chloe's sake, I'd follow my gut, even if she wouldn't thank me for it.

Lake and I moved on and finished off our sandwiches. "She's still slipping out somewhere, huh?"

I nodded. "Even more often in the last few days."

"You'll work it out with her. I have the utmost faith in your communication skills."

"That's because I always text you back within a few minutes."

"True. But you're good with people. And Chloe looks up to you. I know you two can come to an understanding."

I sighed. "I just hope we don't end up understanding that Chloe's no longer a good fit for Moorehaven."

"Pips!"

A weight on my chest lifted at the sound of Jordan's voice. "Girl, I heard you moved to Timbuktu," I teased as she grabbed me in a big hug.

"No such luck," she shot back. "Just working nights the last couple of weeks. Hey, Lake."

"Jordan," he replied.

I shook my head in baffled amusement at his aloof but challenging stare. He and Jordan had held a not-at-all-serious discussion right in front of me shortly after Lake and I started dating, and they'd duly decided to both be equally jealous of the time I spent with the other. The entire summer had passed, and they were still at their silly game.

Jordan grabbed my arm and leaned in, capturing my entire attention. "You won't believe what happened last night."

"This sounds very Glaze and Gossipy," I commented.

Lake moved in behind me and started to rub my shoulders.

Jordan pointedly ignored him. "That treasure-hunting team that's staying at the hotel? One of them bolted in the middle of the night!"

I swatted Lake's sensuous fingers so I could concentrate. "What? Who was it? Why did they leave?" *Please say it was Mandy.*

Jordan shot a triumphant grin at Lake, who harrumphed in mock irritation. He leaned in against my back, as eager to hear the juicy details as I was.

"It was Connor Dockins, the geologist. Right after two in the morning, he called down from his room to say that he was checking out immediately. He sounded like he was angry enough to commit murder on the spot. Then he caught his rolling suitcase in the elevator doors and nearly ripped the handle off, trying to yank it free. I wished him a good night from my desk, but he didn't even look over, just stalked out into the night. If he didn't straight-up kill someone before dawn, I'll eat my sandals."

I eyed her snazzy leather sandals. They didn't appear very edible. On top of the other news I'd gotten about Connor, this latest didn't shine a positive light on him at all. "No news from the housekeeping front on what went down?" I asked. Jordan shamelessly cultivated friends among the cleaning staff to keep her fingers on the pulse of everything that happened at Seven Vistas.

"His room was a little messy, but there were no signs of a fight or anything. The other members of the team all had Do Not Disturb signs on their doors, but that's relatively common."

I made a thoughtful frown. "Don't they kind of need their geologist, though? They've only been here a few days."

Jordan shrugged. "Lake would know more about that than I would."

We both turned to Lake.

He looked pleased, and a little smug, to be able to contribute. "I was just telling Pippa because we tell each other *everything*"—Jordan stuck her tongue out at him—"that from what I've overheard, they weren't done surveying the coastline. Connor made sketches from various spots offshore and took lots of reference photos, but he was missing today. The team's got several more tours booked. No way they were done hunting for treasure spots."

Jordan and I locked eyes. "And no one else on the team checked out today?"

"Nope."

I filled Jordan in on what Tyleen had told me regarding the archive building. "This sounds like a curiosity for sure," I said, using the Glaze and Gossip term. "We should let the group know."

My fiery-haired friend smirked. "Yep."

"Then let's consider ourselves on the Case of the Missing Geologist. Even if that wasn't Connor, and he had nothing to do with the archives theft, some harmless gossip and snooping will be a great change of pace from all this mayhem and treasure fever we have in town." We nodded to each other like the conspirators we were, and Jordan squeezed my hand and melted back into the bustling crowd.

"She needs a boyfriend." Lake watched her bright-red hair move through the crowd.

"It's perfectly healthy for her to be obsessed with harmless mysteries. This is Seacrest, after all."

His smile asked forgiveness for his insensitive remark, and I gave it with a kiss on his cheek. "*Touché*. Even after six months here, I still manage to forget how murderously unique this town is. It's kinda infectious too."

Who's he getting the itch to murder? Oh. "Mallory?" I guessed.

Lake didn't quite nod, tipping his head to the side in equivocation. "I got her to agree that if I can find a suitable roommate to take the lighthouse guest room, she'll let them take it. She clearly plans to reject any suggestions I make. And when am I gonna find the time to vet roommates, anyway?"

"Don't worry. Something will work out." My false confidence rang sour in my own ears, though. Out of everyone in Seacrest, I could think of about three people I'd be happy to let Lake room with, and they all had places to live.

Lake and I had walked most of the way around the main circuit of the fair when we finally came upon Jimmy and Hilt's fishing booth. The two retired policemen were chattering reminiscently away as three children of various heights tried their best to land a plastic fish with their magnetic rods. I pulled Lake to a halt in the middle of the street.

"Look. He's so happy, like he used to be." My heart squeezed.

"He's really having a rough time with the death of his friend, huh?"

"Murder. The *murder* of his friend. And yeah. He says he didn't break into the police archives, but he keeps leaving to investigate on his own and won't let me help. I'm afraid this could send him into a spiraling depression or break his health—even his mind. I don't know what to do."

Lake hugged me close as dozens of tourists pressed past us. "We'll find a way to help. Let's just be there for him right now. Tonight's a night for fun. Let me go win you a prize from his wading pool."

"Oh, no, you don't, mister," I said. "I'm gonna win *you* a prize!"

We paid Jimmy for a pair of rods, and he set the timer, giving us one minute to find a magnetic fish in the dyed-blue water that filled the wading pool. Lake pretended to adjust all kinds of settings on his molded plastic fishing rod, rattling off a running commentary about the best way to fish under wading-pool conditions.

"Obviously, these are wet flies." He studied the wading pool. "There's going to be plenty of schooling in there too." Then he patted his pockets as if he'd forgotten something. "Would you look at that? I've gone and left my Fish Finder on my other boat." Jimmy stared at him for a few seconds before bursting into laughter, and Hilt soon followed suit.

Giggling at my boyfriend's antics, I simply dropped my magnet into the water. Almost immediately, I felt a faint click through the line, and I pulled up a bright-pink fish with painted eyelashes. "Ooh, I got one!" I hollered, waving my fish in the air. "Number fourteen. What do I win, Hilt?" I stepped around the pool and handed my catch to my great-uncle.

He consulted a chart handwritten in Jimmy's illegible scrawl and said, "Two tickets for caramel apples down at Janet's booth." He pulled a pair of bright-purple tickets from a folder on his table and handed them over.

"Any two apples, even the ones with all the toppings?"

Hilt smiled at my childlike eagerness, and I almost teared up to see him so at ease. "Any two. Says right on the ticket. Also..." He pointed to the purple paper. "One in four apples contains a gold coin inside. So watch yer teeth."

The timer dinged, and Lake gave an exaggerated sigh of despair. "I didn't catch a thing!"

I handed him a purple ticket. "I caught you a caramel apple."

He brightened. "You're so good to me. What would I do without you?"

"Get more done, most likely," Hilt quipped.

"Yes, sir, that's probably true," Lake dutifully admitted.

Hilt snorted and waved us off. "G'won, git, you two. You're makin' me all mushy."

Lake led me down a side street toward the caramel apple booth we'd passed some while ago. But as we cut alongside the river, he tugged my hand and led me behind the long purple draperies of Madame Turbinado's palmistry tent. As we slipped between the tent and one of the century-old brick walls that formed Seacrest's downtown, evocative scents of jasmine and patchouli enveloped me. The heavy velvet muffled most of the sounds from the streets.

Lake pressed me against the bricks, leaning his warmth against me, and tipped my chin up for a passionate kiss. My body responded to his touch, and we lost ourselves in each other—until a third voice, not belonging to either of us, also moaned nearby. We both whirled, a little embarrassed at being caught, but I couldn't see anyone nearby. Heart pounding, I clung to Lake's arm. Then a darker shadow resolved into a pair of legs that stuck out onto the grass from the brick wall a couple paces away. I pointed. Lake approached the slumped figure with manly confidence. I slunk along behind him, ready to get scrappy if the situation called for it.

The moan came again, followed by a cough. Alarm spiked through me. Jordan and I had just put ourselves on the trail of Connor Dockins. *Is this him? Or did he catch up to whoever he was angry with?* "Someone's hurt." I darted around Lake.

"Pippa, wait—" he began, but I was too fast.

The limp figure leaned against the brick wall next to a juniper bush. I crouched down and recognized her from her visit to the Shelf earlier. Patrice's dazed gaze landed on me, wandered away, then returned.

"Hey, Patrice, are you okay?"

She gave me a slow blink and a tentative smile.

She needs help. "Lake, can you—"

"Already on it." He pulled out his phone and dialed.

"Are you hurt, Patrice? Do you remember how you got here?"

The grad student's eyes seemed surprised every time they found me. I started gently checking her over for injuries, but I found none. She put up as much resistance as Svetlana did when I checked her fur for burrs as she lay in a sun spot—none at all.

"Thanks, Mal." Lake's final words before he hung up belatedly registered with me.

He hadn't called 911. He'd called his ex directly. My little green monster reared its ugly head deep in my chest.

"She's on her way," Lake said.

"Oh my God, Patrice!"

Lake and I both turned toward the new voice. Mandy bolted past the palmistry tent, looking distraught despite her lacy white top and flirty skirt. Tendons in her neck stood out as she rushed toward her coworker.

Lake stood and took her by the arms. "It's okay. She's okay. I've called the police, and they're on their way."

Mandy looked so worried, she seemed to be in actual pain. "I've been looking everywhere for her. She texted me over an hour ago, saying she was at the fair and didn't feel well. I came over from the hotel, and I've been searching for her ever since." She slipped Lake's grasp and strode over to Patrice and me. She got right down on her knees and took Patrice's face in her hands. "Sweetie. I'm here. I found you, and it's going to be okay."

Patrice nodded muzzily.

"Try to stay awake, okay?" I encouraged her.

Virtually ignoring my presence, Mandy rubbed Patrice's hand and began telling her a meandering story of all the things she'd seen at the fair, trying to keep her awake. "And there was this one guy dressed like a pirate. He had a real live parrot on his shoulder. A green one. It was so gorgeous. You'd have loved it."

I held Patrice's other hand until Mallory rolled up a few minutes later, *boop-boop*ing her siren to force the pedestrian crowd on the street to part. She nosed her car right up beside the purple tent, and Madame Turbinado poked her head around the side of the velvet draping and warbled, "I *knew* this was going to happen!"

If only she'd mentioned it earlier, I might believe her. I backed against the brick wall as Doc Stevens followed Mallory from the cruiser, old-fashioned medical bag in her hand.

Wearing her crisp uniform and tight brunette bun as always, Mallory took statements from everyone, including Lake and me. She maintained her ice-queen demeanor the whole way through, but from the tiny frown lines between her perfect brows, I knew she'd instantly deduced the reason Lake and I had stepped behind the tent in the first place, as if she were psychic herself. The way she kept studying me, even while she asked questions of the other witnesses, gave me the willies. *She knows she intimidates me, and she's messing with me right now because she can. I can't believe Lake put up with her for two years. Vic must have the patience of a saint.*

Mallory glanced over at Lake and me as she finished interviewing Madam Turbinado. With careful nonchalance, she went out of her way to walk past us on the way to Doc Stevens, at Patrice's side. "No takers on your guest room yet, Lake?" she murmured. "I was going to crash there tonight, until you called to report this. But now it looks like I'll be working late. Too bad, huh?" After a cool glance that became a stare, Mallory broke eye contact with me and joined the doc.

I clung to Lake's hand, feeling helpless, while he murmured calming words I didn't quite hear. *She's as bad as those demons Ashley writes about!*

Mandy stayed by Patrice's side the whole time Doc Stevens examined her. Finally, the frizzy-haired doctor stood and reported to Mallory. "I'd have to run some blood tests to be sure, but she probably has something in her system. I don't think she's been assaulted in any way. Not even a bump on the head. But either she took way too much of something on accident, or someone slipped her something."

Lake's hand tensed on my waist, but I felt my face and chest heat from sudden anger. *Who would dare attack Patrice like this? If Connor's really still in town... I thought he liked Patrice. But I barely know them.* "She'll be okay, then?" I asked.

The doc nodded. "The drug should pass from her system in a few hours. Depending on what she took, she might not remember much from this evening, though."

Mallory frowned. "She won't be able to remember who drugged her?"

Doc Stevens tipped her gray frizz apologetically. "Possibly not."

Mallory ushered Patrice and Mandy into the cruiser, and Doc Stevens rode in front as they eased off toward Seaview Hospital, leaving Lake and me alone behind the purple tent again. The romance we'd been unable to resist had been shattered by ugly violence. Lake held me tightly.

"I don't want you to be alone tonight." His voice was rough with emotion.

"I'm fine. We're not even sure what happened here. Don't worry about me. I can take care of myself."

"But what if I can't?" He turned me to face him. His expression was raw and aching. "What if that had been you, and I had no idea where you were? Let me say what I mean. *I* don't want to be alone tonight."

The stress of the last few minutes broke, and the pent-up feelings I'd been struggling with all summer rushed out. Lake was everything I wanted, and right then, he was everything I needed. I pulled him down to me by his collar and kissed him hard. "Get me out of here, Lake."

Hand in hand, we left the bright chaos of the Treasure Fair behind and walked out to the edge of the sea. He opened the door to the broken-topped lighthouse, and we slipped down into its welcoming depths.

I couldn't quite bring myself to text Hilt about my nighttime plans, but while Lake snuggled against my back, I texted the entire G&G group. They'd already heard about Patrice's attack and promised to look after Moorehaven and my guests overnight—and break the news of my location to Hilt. Then I turned off my phone and rolled back toward Lake.

Though Lake and I didn't get much sleep that night, I set an alarm on my phone so I could get back to Moorehaven nice and early. After a quick shower, I kissed a still-drowsy Lake good morning and hurried outside. But as I stepped outside under a soft-pink sky, I spotted Mallory's cruiser across the river in Moorehaven's parking lot. My stomach clenched. *Will that demon woman ever stop hounding me? Too bad Scarlen Fate can't just dispel her for me.*

I jogged down the street to the nearest bridge then back past the marina and Seven Vistas, finally rounding the corner to Moorehaven. Mallory was standing on the porch, notepad in hand, as I slowed, breathless, to climb the porch stairs. Hilt stood beside her, still in his blue-and-white striped pajamas. They both wore mortally serious expressions as they waited for me.

You have got *to be kidding me. It's my life! As long as I'm not hurting anyone, I can do whatever I want with it! Mal's not his wife anymore, and Hilt's not my dad!* I stalked up to the pair of them. "If you have a problem with my personal life, I suggest you keep it to yourself," I clipped.

Mallory took a deep breath and flipped a page back on her notebook, wearing that professional ice-queen look of hers all the while. "Ms. Winterbourne, I'm here to inform you that one of your guests was found dead this morning."

12

"*M*oorehaven is my sanctuary from the world. Only the cats boss me around in here."
Raymond Moore, 1940

MY SAFE LITTLE WORLD crashed in around me, and I stood rooted to the porch. *But—but that can't be,* my mind stuttered. *No one has* ever *died at Moorehaven, not even Aunt Felicity!* "Who... who was it?" I stammered. *Please, God, don't let it be Sarah. She's got babies.*

Mallory checked her notes. "The driver's license in his wallet identified him as one Zachary Finney."

My God, no. I glanced up at the second floor, where Zach had been staying. "Where is he? Do you have any suspects yet?"

Mallory *tsk*ed at my apparent stupidity. "Mr. Finney didn't die on these premises. His body was found in a beach-access parking lot just north of town. And though we're treating his death as suspicious, we don't have any evidence of foul play at this time."

I blinked. Had I really just assumed that Zach had been so unpopular that someone had murdered him? *Of course I did. This is Seacrest.*

Chloe's voice invaded my shock as she arrived for work behind me. "Wait, for real? Zach's dead? Like, *dead* dead?" She stood at the bottom of the porch stairs, hand frozen on the railing, heavily lined eyes wide.

"I'm afraid so, Miss Braxton," Mallory said.

Chloe took a deep breath and nodded thoughtfully. "You'll want his contact information, then. He lives with his brother and sister-in-law. We have their number inside. If you'll follow me." She brushed past Hilt and me as calmly as a nurse in an overwhelmed ER, exuding a poise I didn't think I could muster.

Mallory was pulled into her orbit as naturally as the sun rose. She followed Chloe inside, leaving me with my uncle in the cool morning air.

He met my eyes. "This is my fault." His voice was gravelly, and his eyes were beginning to water.

I set my fists on my hips. "Did you sneak out and murder him in the middle of the night? No? Then it's not your fault. Come inside, and let me get you some coffee." I guided him in through the door as if he were a lost child.

We passed Chloe and Mallory at the hostess station. Chloe was looking up Zach's information on the computer, and Mallory was scribbling in her notebook. The rest of the house echoed with the silence of a tomb. No one else was stirring yet. In the kitchen, I poured Hilt a cup of coffee and settled him at the nook table.

He held it unseeingly while Rex rubbed his head against Hilt's ankle. "You don't understand, Whip. No one's ever died here before. No one. Not Miss Felicity, not Ray, and never any of the authors who've stayed here."

I clutched his hand reassuringly. "Zach didn't die *here*, Hilt." But the technicality meant as little to me as it did to him.

Hilt seemed as if he'd aged a decade and suffered a week of sleeplessness. "He might as well have. He was staying with us. He was under our protection. I shoulda been looking out for him better."

"We still don't know what happened." *Which means I should've been paying closer attention to things. I have no idea what Zach was up to that led to his death. Did I see a clue and dismiss it? Everything's important now, and I was off dallying with a lover while he died. My God.*

"It doesn't matter what happened, Pippa! I've been so focused on tryin' to figure out what happened to Ramòn that I haven't been mentally anywhere near here. Haven't been here for you, or the guests, or anyone. I've been a useless wreck. No good to Ramòn, no good to Zach, no good to anybody."

I took both his hands in mine. "That is not true. You're a vital part of Moorehaven. You've always been here for the guests, and you've definitely been here for me. So I'm here for you too. I should've been doing more to help you find out what happened to Ramòn—"

"You been busy," he said gruffly. "This place is a madhouse right now." He finally took a sip of his coffee, and I relaxed a little.

"It is. And we need to stick together. Today is going to be the maddest of madhouses. Everyone's going to be upset. Let's work out a plan to look after everyone." *A plan that should include me never sleeping over at Lake's, ever again,* I added in silent regret. I tried to text him to explain about Zach, but I couldn't find the words. *Where's a "one of my guests died suspiciously while we were doing the horizontal mambo" emoji when you need one?* Embarrassed and angry with myself, I shoved my phone back into my pocket.

I eased Hilt into an analytical frame of mind, and I got Rex to settle into his lap. We made a list of local resources we could offer to our distressed guests. But before we'd wrapped up our impromptu planning session, Butch clomped into the kitchen, followed by Abby, Gabby, and Ashley. Sarah, who still wore a robe over her Star Wars Rebels jammies, trailed in a few seconds later. Jennifer hovered behind her, thumbs poised over her phone to text Ogden, no doubt. Their expressions were slack with disbelief and wisps of sleepiness, like kids who'd been woken and told Santa wasn't real.

"Is it true, what the girl's saying?" Butch asked in a hoarse voice. "Zach's dead?"

Chloe must've blabbed to everyone as they came downstairs after Mallory left. But they'd all have found out very soon, anyway. I stood up from the table. "Let's all move to the dining room, and I'll tell you what we know so far."

Everyone obediently shifted to the chairs around my big table, even Hilt, who took his usual spot next to my chair at the head. I summed up what little Mallory had told us. "We don't even know how he died yet."

Butch stared at the floor and rubbed a hand across the back of his neck. Ashley seemed determined to be brave and make eye contact with me. Others stared at the table. Gabby covered her eyes as if hiding from the whole situation.

"So it might be a heart attack or something?" Jennifer's voice was querulous.

"Maybe. We'll know more after they do the autopsy."

"How long will that take?" Ashley asked.

"Well, unless someone else died in Seacrest last night, Doc Stevens should be finished around lunchtime. I'll share any relevant news with you as soon as I have it. Now, I don't know if any of you are hungry, but—"

A tap at the sliding glass door behind Butch's chair drew everyone's attention. Tyleen stood on my back porch in a bright-yellow sundress and matching hair kerchief, holding a massive warming platter, its lid obscured with steam. Butch leaped up and slid open the door for her, and she sashayed in and placed her warmer in the center of the table.

"Pippa, dear, I heard from Lori," she said by way of greeting, "and I figured you might not be up for much cooking this morning. So I made a whole mess of pancakes for everyone. I hope that's okay."

My heart melted like hot butter and sweet maple syrup, and my eyes got damp with gratitude. "You're an absolute gem, Tyleen. Let me get some plates for everyone. Hilt, can you fetch the syrup caddies?"

But someone knocked at the front door before I'd taken three steps.

Hilt nudged me toward the door. "I'll get the plates."

I took steadying breaths on my way down the hall, bracing for as many different kinds of news as I could imagine—maybe Zach had been in a terrible accident, or he'd had a heart attack, or he'd actually been murdered. Or maybe he wasn't dead after all, and there'd been a terrible mix-up.

My visitor wasn't Mallory or Vic, but Emily. She stood on my porch, arms full of stacked pastry trays. "I heard from Lori and Naoma within three minutes of each other this morning. You know how I bake when I'm worried? Well, I'm worried for you and your guests. So here's a platter of tarts. And some bear claws. And a couple of all the different muffins I have—"

I couldn't help it. I broke down right there in my doorway, touched by her thoughtfulness and kindness. I clapped a hand over my mouth and sobbed.

"Oh, Pippa! I'm so sorry. I didn't mean to—" Emily looked around frantically for a place to put down her towers of delectable treats.

That snapped me back, and I swiped at my tears. "No, I'm sorry. I'm okay. Let me help you with those." I took half of her trays and backed up to let her come in. "I... Tyleen just brought breakfast, and here you are with all this amazing food, and I... it's so good to know that you're there. That you're *here*."

Emily pressed her shoulder against mine then led the way down to the dining room. "Of course we're here. We're your friends. And what are friends for, if not to stuff each other with comfort food when they need support?"

Emily and I added her baked creations to the table wherever we could find room, while everyone else loaded pancakes onto their plates and drenched them in warm, gooey toppings. Jennifer texted Ogden about the food choices, and when he replied, she passed on his preferences so I could send up a tray. I made sure everyone else had food, barely aware of the cramp in my own stomach. I brought Hilt a bowl of warm cinnamon applesauce, his pancake topping of choice. Then Chloe pressed a cinnamon walnut muffin into my hands.

"Eat. You need food too." She nodded emphatically and disappeared back into the kitchen.

I took a grateful bite, which woke up my stomach. In four giant bites, I ate the whole thing. Chloe must've been fixing me blueberry pancakes with syrup and almond slivers while I inhaled the muffin because she swung a bright-blue plate loaded with them into view as soon as I downed the last swallow. I took it in both hands with a grateful smile.

"Where did you learn to be such an amazing person?" I asked, not really expecting an answer.

Chloe offered me one of her own rare smiles. "From you. Food, mouth, now. Mozzie says food fuels the soul."

"We all need that this morning." I took a big, healthy bite of my blueberry pancake.

After a few minutes, Ogden appeared at the dining room doorway, plate in hand. He'd barely started eating his stack of pancakes, but he'd carefully combed his hair and dressed in a blue button-front shirt and jeans. With his looks and his careful study of us all, he reminded me of Andy Dufresne from *The Shawshank Redemption*. "I thought I might eat at the little table in your kitchen?" He gestured with his plate to indicate all of us. "Just for today. I didn't want you to think I was insensitive. A death is more important than my anxiety. At least, that's what I told it in the mirror just now."

"Thank you, Ogden. We all appreciate your support right now." It had cost him a lot to come downstairs and experience such an intense social environment, and I was touched by his determination to endure it with us.

Chloe and Tyleen made room at the nook table for him, and to my pleased surprise, he asked them to stay and eat with him.

"If I feel like *I'm* helping *you* guys, I can do okay," he explained.

Rex and Svetlana parked themselves by the sides of his chair, studying his every move. We all ate in relative silence, and no one wanted to leave. Conversation gradually picked up as people finished eating.

"He wasn't really that bad of a guy," Butch said. "He waddn't even that old."

"He could be my son," Gabby added with a hand at her throat. "Well, my nephew, anyway."

"I feel like I should memorialize him somehow," I said. "Maybe a plaque."

"I'm going to add him to my book," Sarah said firmly. "With a little explanation in the author's note section. He can be the character who sees where my second victim disappears to, and he'll tip his cowboy hat back on his head and point my detective in the right direction."

"He'd like that, I bet," Hilt said. His gaze drifted to the far wall after he spoke. I squeezed his hand. *He's probably wishing a fictional version of Ramòn would point him in the right direction to solve his murder too.*

The next couple of hours passed in quiet conversation, with shared stories of loss, a discussion on the difficulties of adding real people to novels, and other supportive talk. Every time the phone rang, Chloe slipped away to answer it as we all hoped for news from Lori, but she never wandered off.

Tyleen kindly cleared the table and did the dishes. When she returned from the kitchen, she said, "I remember when my first husband died. And I remember when my second husband died too—one doesn't forget things like that—but that one was a violent gambler, and he pretty much deserved what he got. No, I'm thinking about Sebastian's father, Charles. Keeled over on the golf course, middle of a bright June morning. No one saw it coming, except for the golf cart driver girl he fell on top of. Poor thing, she got a sprained elbow out of the incident. But what I want to say is"—she looked right at Hilt—"survivor's guilt is a powerful idea. Sometimes, there's really nothing more we could've done at the time. Learning more information later, like how Charles had an undiagnosed brain aneurysm and it just let loose one day, can't change what's already happened. The past is set, for good or ill, just like a Jell-O salad. Once the celery and julienne carrots are in there, there's no getting rid of them." She squeezed Hilt's hand and nodded supportively.

Hilt digested that with an expression of distaste. "I thank God every day that vegetable Jell-O salads are trapped in the seventies where they belong. But thanks, Tyleen. Some things really do belong to the past."

"Like corsets," Abby piped up cheerily. Her random comment broke the emotional tension and set us all laughing.

The phone rang again, just shy of noon, and Chloe left to answer it. A minute later, she bolted back into the dining room. "Pippa, it's Lori." Her tone told me that Doc Stevens's autopsy was finished, and that Lori had news. Bad news.

My stomach went cold, and I had to brace myself on the table as I stood up. The entire table went silent, watching with wide eyes and bated breath as I left the room. Out in the hallway, I picked up the handset. "It's murder, isn't it?"

Lori replied, "Zach Finney was definitely murdered, though Doc Stevens is sure someone tried to make it seem accidental."

"How did he die?"

"Some kind of suffocation. He'd been bumped on the head, too, but not hard enough to kill him. The injury was perimortem—right around the time of death."

"So his killer knocked him out and then suffocated him?" I asked. Zach was average height, but he was a burly guy, so knocking him out might've been the only way a smaller or weaker person could've killed him.

"That's probably how it went down, yeah. The funny thing was, Doc Stevens didn't find any fibers or anything in his throat. Something was definitely held over his face, though, because—get this—Mr. Finney had a latex allergy, and the very gloves that the killer wore to avoid leaving fingerprints left a slight rash on his skin. There are a couple of distinct finger shapes in the rash. But no—'cause I know you're gonna ask—not distinct enough to tell us details like sex, height, et cetera."

"Killing my hopes for a good clue before I can even ask, huh? I see how it is. I remember Zach told me he had a sensitivity to latex when he called to book his stay. I never imagined that detail would prove he'd been murdered."

"Crazy, isn't it? I've never seen anything like it." Lori's tone was more jaded than mine, owing to her medical-profession exposure to the weird and fatal side of humanity. "He wasn't manually suffocated, though—you know, hands over his nose and mouth. The marks are less distinct than that, and there's no rash around his nose to indicate the killer held it shut or blocked it. The doc also found some water in his trachea but not in his lungs. We're running some tests, of course, but right now, Doc actually doesn't know exactly how Mr. Finney was killed."

I digested that information with a knot in my chest. "So, an actual murder mystery."

Lori sighed. "I suppose it is. Moore would be fascinated."

"He might've been. But I bet Aunt Felicity would've been furious."

13

"I know these groovy surfer dudes, and I let them stay with me when they're passing through. What? No, I don't smell any weird smoke in here. Old houses get musty sometimes."
Raymond Moore, 1967

FOR LUNCH, I ORDERED Mozzie's sandwiches for the guests who wanted them, but we were still swimming in food donations from Tyleen and Emily. I bicycled over to his shop to pick up the sandwich order, but Mozzie refused to charge me, and he pressed so much extra food on me, along with a gallon of his famous lemonade, that my usually roomy bike basket was overbalanced on the way back to Moorehaven. I nearly spilled half a dozen bags of homemade potato chips right in front of Sebastian's pet psychic shop.

Chloe was waiting for me on the porch steps, and she came down in a hurry to help me unload all the food and drink from my bike basket. "How're we gonna eat all this food?" She hefted the lemonade jug.

"One bite at a time, as usual, I guess."

She let out a careless puff of breath. "It's nice that everyone's being so caring and all, but c'mon, no one really liked Zach. Is this guilt food?"

I paused, arms full of wrapped sub sandwiches, and recalled a conversation I'd had earlier that week. "Wallis says that regret is stronger than any other emotion. But I don't think Zach had annoyed Tyleen, Emily, or Mozzie so much as he did the authors here in Moorehaven."

Chloe's lips quirked. "So more like guilt *eating*, then."

"Maybe, but—"

"You think one of them killed him?" Her words flew casually over her shoulder as she climbed the steps with the lemonade and the chips. "He did die mysteriously, and everyone here is pretty clever with killing people."

"Hah, everyone here is too busy writing fictional murders to take the time to plan a real one." But as I followed her up the steps and down the hall to the dining room, a cold knot of doubt formed in my stomach. *Is it Connor, still lurking in town for some unknown reason? Or is it one of my guests? What if one of them had already planned out this murder in one of their books, and they just copied it into reality? Most of them didn't get along with Zach, anyway. There's their means and motive.* I felt a sudden, forceful urge to snoop through everyone's unfinished manuscripts. *But I'm not the police—*

A sudden screech of tires—more than one car's worth—sounded from out in the parking lot. Concerned that some tourist had crashed into my property yet again, I dumped the sandwiches onto the table and hurried to the porch. As soon as I opened the door, two sets of red-and-blue light bars flicked their beams over me. Mallory and Vic stepped out of their cruisers, looking incredibly badass in their sunglasses and uniforms.

I moved to the porch as if to defend the sanctity of my home and business. "What's going on, Mallory?"

She stalked up my steps, Vic in tow, both wearing equally neutral expressions. I hated that I couldn't see their eyes behind their reflective sunglasses. Vic stood behind Mallory's shoulder with one hand clasping his other wrist. He didn't lower his shades for me today.

Mallory lifted her chin, even though she was a couple inches taller than me. "Miss Winterbourne, we've had a credible report of illegal drugs inside your establishment." She produced a folded white paper. "We have a warrant to search these premises for any and all illicit drugs and related paraphernalia. Please step aside."

My spine stiffened. "Are you *kidding* me with this? One of my guests was just murdered today, and now you want to barge in and toss the place? Have a little respect, Mallory."

My reflection in her sunglasses remained perfectly steady as she stared me down. "This isn't personal, Miss Winterbourne. And it's all perfectly legal. If you'd care to examine the warrant, you'll find Judge Hannity's signature all in order."

I was getting tired of her official use of "Miss." Whenever we casually ran across each other, she'd just address me by my last name. I never thought I'd miss that. I snatched the warrant she offered, but I didn't open it. Mallory was nothing if not excruciatingly precise. Of course she'd gotten the judge's signature. "You could have waited."

Her brows lowered fractionally above her frames. "And give the perpetrators time to dispose of the evidence? I don't think so."

"There are no perpetrators!" My voice cracked with the effort of keeping my temper under any semblance of control. The urge to smack that smugly blank expression off her face was swiftly becoming irresistible, and anger pricked a hot path up my back. *I swear, this woman is a demon sent to torment me!*

Vic must've read my body language because he stepped up next to me. "No one's tossing anything, Pippa. We really did get a credible source on this one. We can't ignore it, but we're not gonna wreck your place out of spite."

My glaring gaze refused to leave Mallory's face. "Fine." The word struggled to get past my stiff lips. "But I'm billing you for any damage."

The corner of Mallory's mouth twitched into so brief a smile that I questioned whether I'd actually seen it. "Just doing my job, ma'am."

My nostrils flared so wide I probably looked like a furious horse. Vic's arm, so bulky with muscles that it stretched the cuff of his short-sleeved uniform shirt, gently guided me to the side. He and Mallory stepped inside, leaving me on my own porch.

They're invading my home, I fumed. *They won't find anything. This is such a pile of crap! And I'm not gonna stand out here while they do it.*

I darted back inside. From the dining room, I heard voices raised in confusion and irritation. "They're herbal soothers!" Tyleen hollered. "Totally legal in the state of Oregon!"

"Mrs. Pliczek," Vic said in a sturdy, calm voice, "we're not searching *your* house."

Mallory's orders boomed through the first floor. "Everyone, please return to the dining room and wait there while we conduct our search."

I stumped down the hall, ready to defend my authors, but Hilt caught my arm as he emerged from the side hall. "Best let them do their job and get it done."

I jerked to a stop, surprised and hurt by his taking Mallory's side. A moment later, it sank in that maybe he knew a little more than I did about how hard it was to investigate people he knew. "It's not true," I insisted. "No one's selling drugs out of Moorehaven."

"Then there ain't nothin' to find, is there?" Hilt's usual good humor was muted, leaving his statement sounding hopeless.

Vic appeared in the archway at the end of the hall. "If you two could move into the dining room while we conduct our search?" His tone told me he wasn't really asking.

"Sarah and her baby are still upstairs." I crossed my arms. "I trust you won't disturb her if she's feeding him."

Vic jerked to a halt and tried to hide a goofy grin. "There's a baby here?"

"Yes, Vic. Do make sure you test any powdered formula Sarah might be carrying. I'm sure it must be cocaine or something." My tone was as dry as the Sahara.

Vic considered my response with a disappointed frown and headed upstairs without a word. Hilt ushered me into the dining room, but I couldn't sit, let alone stand still. I paced back and forth in front of the library door while my guests sat and nibbled at their food. Ashley jotted some notes, as if recording our reactions for research purposes. Butch twiddled his thumbs half-heartedly. But no one seemed concerned that their secret stash was about to be found by the cops. *No one's acting guilty. This raid is such a pile of strawberry tops.*

A few minutes later, Sarah came in, carrying Jackson, who was happily gnawing on the earpiece of Vic's wraparound sunglasses. *Who knew Vic was a baby-fan?* Sarah's husband followed her in, laden with toys and a diaper bag, and his daughter came in singing about sea anemones and tides.

"Yes, Penelope," Sarah said, "the nice policeman is going to check our room for monsters first, and then we can go right back in, okay? You can keep watching your video as soon as we get back there."

Penelope nodded with the easy belief of all young children and began skipping around the table. *The necessary lies we tell those we love. I wonder who's lying to me.* My eyes darted to Mallory. *She's not lying. She's reveling in whatever truth lets her mess with me. Well, let's see if we can get some truth out of her for a change.*

Eventually, Mal and Vic finished searching every room in my beloved bed-and-breakfast and returned to the first floor. I met them at the base of the stairs. "There's no way anyone under this roof would be involved with drugs," I said, "and anyone outside Moorehaven wouldn't be a credible source. Tell me who your source is."

Mallory rested a hand on my shoulder as if to comfort me, but then she said, "Revealing the identity of a confidential source would be a serious breach of trust, Miss Winterbourne." She scooted me out of her way. She stopped in the foyer, jotting notes and conferring with Vic.

While I stewed at Mal and her heavy-handed tactics, I heard Hilt's voice reassuring our guests that everything was going to be fine.

Sarah touched my arm as she shepherded her family back toward the stairs. "I don't know about the others, but I'm gonna put a raid in my book the second my hands are free." Her eyes sparkled with excitement.

I blinked in surprise and felt a rush of gratitude. If anyone could take a step back and appreciate a real-life plot twist that inconvenienced everyone and practically accused them of a crime, it was my mystery authors. I smiled at Sarah. "Let me know if you want any details from me. I'll be happy to share."

"You're the best, Pippa. You stayed so calm during this whole thing, even with all that tension between you and the police chief. It was easy to take our cue from you. Thank you, for me and for my kids." She squeezed my arm.

Calm? Did I really look calm? If only she knew!

"Note-taking blitz in the second-floor sunroom in five," Butch hollered from the top of the staircase. "Get your drug-raid details here! Read all about it!" he added in a newsie voice pitched to carry. The other authors' voices merged into an excited babble.

Mallory pinched the bridge of her nose and sighed, while Vic gave off an air of resigned amusement as he watched the authors trooping upstairs.

Me, I needed to sit down before my legs gave out. In the dining room, I slumped into my usual chair.

Chloe silently slipped me a cup of tea.

"You get one too," I urged her.

"I haven't converted to tea just yet. I'll grab a soda and sit with you, though." She'd been quiet during the raid. *Was she just being calm again? Or is there some connection between her disappearances and this "credible report" of drugs? God, I hate this. I'm sitting here, suspecting my own assistant of drug running. The Seacrest mentality sure does have its dark side.*

While Chloe was in the kitchen, Mal stepped back into the dining room. "You should be aware," she said to Hilt, "that we confiscated anything of interest among Mr. Finney's belongings while we were here. If you could endeavor to keep your nosy authors from bursting past the crime scene tape out of perverse curiosity, that would be helpful. And if I might comment, that's quite an octopus of a laundry chute system. I'm surprised you haven't replaced it or blocked it off."

Hilt placed a hand on my shoulder. "Why fix what ain't broken? I take it you didn't find any drugs among anyone's stuff, Chief? Nothing dangling down anybody's laundry chutes?"

Mal took a minute before she tipped her head just a little to the side. "Not at present. I'll be looking into the anonymous tip. Perhaps if I had more credible information, I'd find what I was after next time."

I felt fiercely vindicated, and I couldn't resist saying, "I did tell you there were no *perpetrators* here."

"I think we should take the L on this one, boss," Vic said from the doorway behind Mal.

Mal offered him a cool glance. "It's never a loss when the truth is revealed, Vic. You have a good day, Winterbourne. Sorry for any inconvenience." She slipped out into the hall, leaving Vic behind.

I sighed and worked my jaw in annoyance. *Back to just "Winterbourne," at least. But she's still a pestiferous demon.*

Chloe slipped in then and sat beside me, clearly having waited until Mallory was gone, and popped the top on her Dr. Pepper.

Vic quirked his lips, as if debating whether to speak. Then he rubbed his nose with his thumb and said, "She found your room pretty quick, Pippa. Like she already knew where it was. But—funny thing—she stepped in to search it, and then she backed up and had me do it—I was real careful with your stuff. Don't worry. Don't think she was particularly comfy in there, if you know what I mean." His gaze flickered to Chloe, but she just smirked. She knew perfectly well what he meant. So did Hilt, but he seemed to be trying to light the wallpaper on fire with his eyes so he didn't have to think about it.

"Thanks, Vic. No idea who called in the tip? Any connection to Zach's death?"

He shifted his feet. "We don't have enough info yet. But the lab is testing evidence gathered from the scene."

"What kind of evidence?" I asked.

Vic's lips quirked again as he hesitated. "We found a footprint in some spilled soda."

Chloe made a face and slid her Dr. Pepper away.

"I'm hoping for some details that'll narrow it down soon. They're testing for drugs in Finney's bloodstream and in that water they found in his throat too." Vic glanced down the hall as if ensuring that Mallory was out of earshot. "I'll keep you in the loop. Sorry about this." He fiddled with his wraparound sunglasses, retrieved from Penelope only after bribing her with a chocolate coin. "Could be someone's targeting you, trying to throw you off balance."

I blinked at his casual suggestion. His tone suggested he'd seen such tactics before. "I didn't kill Zach. None of my authors did, either." *I hope.* "Why would they do that?"

"To keep you from thinking about who did, maybe," he offered. "You and your authors, you all think that way pretty easily. Attacking you could keep you focused on something other than Zach's murder."

I stared in surprise. "You really think so?"

He shrugged. "Could be. Seen it happen, and not just in the thrillers I read. Be careful who you're messing with this time, Pippa. The kind of folks who plan ahead like this, they can be ruthless."

I was so taken aback by the thought of a ruthless, scheming murderer roaming around Seacrest with a deadly schedule of events that I merely said, "Understood." My mind whirled as Vic showed himself out. *Have I already met this mastermind killer?* "Is someone watching us, Uncle Hilt? Are the rest of my authors in danger?"

Hilt swung a wiry arm around my shoulders. "I ain't never had anyone die on Moorehaven's premises, and there's no way I'm starting now. You stick with me, doll."

I felt reassured by his alert confidence, but his hand trembled when he squeezed mine.

14

"$\mathbf{T}$*hree men can keep a secret if two of them are dead. But if they're all dead, it'll keep a lot longer."*
Raymond Moore, 1938

THE CATS REFUSED TO come down from the Oubliette even after Mallory and Vic had left, and I knew exactly how they felt. To shake off the feeling of being invaded, I dialed Patrice's number. I knew I should be talking with Lake, but I was pretty mad at myself for my selfish desires the previous night. I wasn't ready to handle his forgiveness when I couldn't forgive myself. *And what if he doesn't forgive me? Ugh, I just can't. Not yet.*

Patrice answered on the second ring with a cheery tone that belied the trauma she'd been through the night before. "Pippa, how nice to hear from you."

"Hi, Patrice. I was just calling to check in on you. How are you feeling?"

"Honestly, I feel fine. No bumps or bruises." She sounded downright chipper.

"I gotta say, you sound really upbeat, and I like it. I'm glad what happened hasn't shaken you up too badly."

The pause that followed was long and heavy. I'd said something wrong.

"Actually, I can't remember a thing from after lunch yesterday until I woke up this morning. It is Wednesday today, right?" She laughed awkwardly. "Chief Tavish came by my room to ask me ques-

162

tions before I even finished my hospital-grade oatmeal. Pippa, I couldn't tell her a single detail." Her voice strained with confusion and frustration. "I'm not trying to be brave. It's just hard to be traumatized when you can't remember the trauma."

"Oh my God. Did someone hit you on the head after all?" I couldn't help remembering Lake's struggle with his lost memories when we'd first met.

"No, nothing like that. Doc Stevens got my test results back after breakfast. I got Xanaxed."

"Someone slipped you the anti-anxiety drug?"

"Yeah. Apparently, once you fall asleep, you can forget everything that happened while you were on the drug. I asked Doc Stevens to please tell Chief Tavish so she'd understand why I was such a flake. I hate that I can't be a useful witness in my own assault."

"I hear you. And I have every confidence that whoever attacked you will be caught. Are your other memories okay?"

"Yeah, everything else is fine. Thank God. I've just had a breakthrough with this tattoo I've been working on, and I think I finally understand what it means. If Connor hadn't left town, I'd be able to work with him on pinning down the location of the treasure."

If he left town at all. For all I know, he assaulted you himself. "Do you know why he left like that yesterday morning?"

"I really don't, and I'm pretty annoyed about it. I went down to breakfast yesterday, all excited to invite Connor to the treasure fair with me, so we could get away from our constant grind for an hour or two. A first date, I hoped. But then Wade and Mandy told me he was gone. They seemed cagey about it, but now I wonder if that was because they knew I was into him, and they found out he was some kind of creeper or something."

"And you haven't seen him since he supposedly left?"

"No." She paused. "Why? Have you?"

"There are rumors he's still around. If you see him, let Mallory know. But now, tell me about this tattoo you're working on."

I heard Patrice's hospital bed creak as she shifted position. "Okay, but I'll have to back up and explain some things first. As part of my thesis research, I was able to identify a Spanish galleon that left a good portion of its treasure along the Oregon Coast in 1691. I say that like it was easy, but it took me a full year and a trip to Spain to examine their archives. The ship was the *San Gabriel de la Costa*, and it limped into New Hispaniola two months overdue and with about half its cargo. The ship was repaired and sent back to the Philippines, but it sank in a typhoon before reaching port. No one ever returned for the rest of the Oregon cargo. There is some argument about its market value—doctored manifests and wounded pride could be factors—but the historical value of such a recovered hoard, found untouched? It's truly incalculable. The looks on their faces when I told them—Wade nearly hyperventilated, and Mandy, I think she was literally crying with joy. Pretty sure Connor couldn't quite wrap his head around my words."

"And this ship is the one you're hunting for now?" *The treasure seems way more real when a historian explains it. No wonder Tibbsy and Marco thought their burgled cannons were actually made of gold.*

"Yes. The coins found with that skeleton on the overlook—"

"His name was Ramòn. Ramòn Moreno."

"Right. Of course. The coins Mr. Moreno was carrying were dated before the wreck, and this coastal area is generally where Captain Rodriguez indicated that he stowed his cargo. As far as we're concerned, Mr. Moreno found the treasure of the *San Gabriel de la Costa*—or knew someone who did."

And he was killed for it. Hoping to stay away from dark topics, I asked, "What kind of cargo did the galleons carry?"

"The usual fare was a combination of gold, silks, Chinese ceramics, and beeswax."

"Wax? Really?"

"Yeah. They pressed it into giant cakes. About ten thousand pounds' worth spilled out of a wreck near Nehalem, a couple hours north of here. The native tribes used the wax for fuel, and the first white settlers 'mined' it off the beach and traded it."

My mind boggled at the sheer weight of what the sea had so easily reclaimed from one single ship. "Those galleons must be huge. You'd think that much cargo would be worth coming back for. Was it too far off the trade route?"

"That, and the map that Captain Rodriguez left with his superiors in New Hispaniola had no real identifying marks, no latitude or longitude."

"Like the map from *Indiana Jones and the Last Crusade.*"

Patrice's voice brightened. "Exactly! But—and here's where it gets a little creepy—the typhoon pushed the *San Gabriel de la Costa* ashore on the Philippine island of Luzon, and Captain Rodriguez's body was recovered. He had a new tattoo on his chest, which was removed and preserved at the insistence of the Spanish government. It's currently on display in a museum in Manila. And it looks a lot like the map he'd handed over in New Hispaniola."

The excitement in her voice was contagious. "Oh, no way. Map tattoo!"

"Right? But no one ever found a match to any stretch of coastline. Historians and archaeologists have been arguing for centuries about whether the map shows the shoreline of California or Washington instead. One historian I know insists this treasure is located on Maui. But I think I figured it out. Not where the treasure is—I'm no geologist—but how Captain Rodriguez disguised the treasure's location."

I could barely breathe. "How?"

"My working theory is that he mirrored the tattoo two different ways. North is south, and land is sea. He put the tattoo on his chest so when he looked down, he saw the coastline as he would if it were on a parchment in front of him—with the south side closest to his eyes. But he tattooed the rivers and landmarks onto the ocean side of the shoreline, so anyone else looking at the tattoo would see the coastline upside down and think they were seeing it right side up. The biggest hurdle with identifying the right stretch of coastline was that some of the tattoo's features simply don't exist on the Oregon Coast. It drove many historians to consider alternate locations that had the right kind of features. But I think Captain Rodriguez was smarter than everyone suspected. If you flip the map both ways, you see exactly the kind of features the Oregon Coast is famous for."

"So the captain was literally the only person who could translate the map."

"Yes! No way would he tell his mirroring secret to anyone else. He didn't trust the tattooing to anyone else, either. The preserved skin shows clear signs of being tattooed by the captain himself. But he died before he could sail back east across the Pacific, so no one ever returned to claim the treasure. And then, nine years later, that giant tsunami struck, the one the Japanese call the Orphan Tsunami because they couldn't identify the earthquake that started it."

I tipped my head in surprise, though Patrice couldn't see it. "No way. There's *another* tsunami?"

Patrice chuckled briefly. "There have always been tsunamis around the Pacific. 'A side effect of the Ring of Fire,' Connor told me. This one struck in January of 1700. It was gigantic, a wave maybe a hundred feet tall. And my guess is that it damaged or altered the coastline, obscuring the treasure's location and making the map that much harder to read."

Patrice's words rang in my head. "That makes so much sense. It would explain why not even the local tribes stumbled across it."

"That's what we were thinking too. I'm so glad I didn't figure this out yesterday afternoon. Can you imagine solving a centuries-old puzzle and then forgetting the answer?"

If only someone had solved Ramòn's murder. Or Zach's. Even if they forgot, I'd know it was possible to solve it again. "Well, I'm really glad you have this progress to cheer you up."

Patrice's tone sobered. "I'd trade it for being able to remember what I saw last night. Who did this to me and why? Did I see who killed your guest? Was I next? I came to Seacrest hoping for a big jumpstart to my career. I never expected a brush with death."

Patrice and I exchanged farewells and promises to keep each other updated on the murder case and the treasure hunt. After I hung up, I recognized the looks that flickered over my authors' faces as I passed them in the halls. They were worried about their own safety. By the set of their eyebrows and the way they wouldn't meet my eyes, I knew some had already decided to check out early.

I didn't blame them. Not one bit. *Eating this loss on top of paying for Hilt's designer fence isn't going to be fun, though. That big laundry room repair job is going to have to wait a few months.*

Abby and Gabby approached me first with anxious glances at each other. "Dear Pippa," Gabby began, "we in no way wish to offend you, but..."

"That is to say," Abby added with an apologetic smile, "considering today's events, we just feel that it would be better—"

"For *everyone*, really—"

"If we stepped aside and let things at Moorehaven calm down," Abby finished.

"Step aside?" I heard what they were saying, but that romantic-mystery-genre way of thinking had purpled up their request beyond recognition.

Abby smiled. "Surely another suitor will desire most fervently to court Moorehaven as soon as she is available and willing."

The double meaning of her statement settled on me even as I admired Abby's wording, but Gabby seemed to think I didn't follow. She stepped closer and gave me a blunt look. "We wanna check out."

My Professional Smile covered my amusement. "Of course. Follow me to the hostess station."

Jennifer tiptoed down the stairs a few minutes later, holding her rolling suitcase up as if keeping it from thumping on the staircase would be less offensive. She approached me with an apologetic expression. "I don't want to go. But my mom will literally kill me if I stay, considering what's happened. I hope you understand. I promise I'll be back, though. I've learned so much from you and all these amazing authors. And I'm definitely going to be a bestseller by the time I'm thirty."

Try as I might, I couldn't find anything in Abby, Gabby, or Jennifer that hinted they'd had anything to do with Zach's death. They'd all given alibis to Mallory, and though I knew how easy it was to fake an alibi, my gut told me none of them had done so. I expected Ogden Kemp to follow on Jennifer's heels, but he simply sent me a text letting me know he planned to stay since he was so close to finishing his rough draft. I sent in a grateful reply thanking him for his trust in me. His alibi for Zach's death was unprovable—"alone in my room"—and he did write a powerful main character with questionable morality. *Do I need to worry about Ogden? Why would he stay, though, if he were guilty?*

An hour and a half later, Sarah and her family trooped down the stairs. Her little girl hopped down each step individually, and Rex did his best to hop with her every time. He rubbed himself against her pink socks at the bottom of the stairs, and she gently scratched him between the ears. "Goob kibby," she cooed.

"He's going to miss you," I told Penelope as Sarah and Thad stepped up to my counter. "All of you."

A strange, intense look passed between Sarah and Thad, and I suddenly felt like an intruder. They said far more with a single glance than I felt I could manage in an hour alone with Lake. A small pang of jealousy stabbed my chest and effervesced into gentle admiration. My anger at myself faded a little more, and I decided I was ready to lean on my boyfriend for support.

"Actually," Sarah said, her eyes still on her husband, "I'll be staying here to finish my book. Thad's taking the kids home, though." She shifted her confident attention to me. "We just wanted to let you know, in case you wanted me to move to a smaller room."

A nursing mom letting her family leave a dangerous town without her? The thought leaped into my mind before I could stop it. *No, quit that. She's a person, a writer with a career she's dedicated to, not to mention a couple of black belts. She may be a mom, but I'm not, and I'm definitely not her mom. Geez, I've got to stop thinking these Old Fuddy-duddy thoughts.* "I can move you to the Lilac Room, if you can wait a bit so I can refresh the linens." I'd stripped the bed and opened the windows to let in the delightful sea air after Abby left, but I'd assumed I'd have a little more time before I needed to make it up again.

"Yer plum crazy, woman, staying here," Butch grumbled to Sarah. He'd come down the stairs behind everyone without catching my notice.

I let my feelings tumble out on a controlled sigh. "I suppose you'll be leaving us too, then, Butch? I'll be sorry to see you go."

"No ya won't, cuz I ain't leavin'. I just came down to try to get Sarah here to see sense."

Sarah studied the grizzled author, unperturbed. "Has it ever occurred to you that I might see a different sense than you do, Butch?"

He shook his head at her and even cracked an admiring smile. "Not yet, it h'ain't. But you keep tryin'. You may just get there with me yet."

Everyone, including me, stared at him with surprise. He raised his hands to ward off our shock. "Now, don't everyone have a coronary at once. Hilt's been whisperin' in my ear about how Pippa here is such a capable businesswoman and how all her friends are level-headed pillars of the community. Now, that does tend to imply that I'm a backward ignoramus when it comes to women and equality and suchlike. And I'm open-minded enough to admit that this may be the case. So I'll do what I always do: observe and listen and see what happens. And if you get attacked by raving murderers, I'll even let you try to fight 'em off first, before I dash in to rescue you."

And he was doing so well there, right up until the end. "That's very thoughtful of you, Butch," I said.

"You think I should defend myself with my karate or with my jeet kune do?" Sarah asked him. "All your time in Vietnam should make you an expert on these things, right?" she teased.

A strange expression passed over Butch's face. Sarah had struck a nerve she hadn't intended to hit.

I distracted her to give Butch time to compose himself. "I bet knowing martial arts is useful, even when you're not fighting off raving murderers."

"Trust me, the stronger core muscles really help out with hefting small children around. I'm going to help my family pack up, and then I'll be back in. I'm in the middle of a chapter, and Zinnia's currently hanging from a rickety gutter at the edge of a three-story building, waiting to learn her fate. She's probably exasperated with me for not getting her down yet."

I chuckled. Sarah wasn't the first author who'd told me she envisioned her characters waiting around—often impatiently—for their plots to be resolved. One author had confessed feeling actual guilt for leaving his main character swinging with his ankle tangled in ship's rigging for a week while he himself recovered from appendicitis.

The young family bumped and babbled its way out the front door to their car, and Butch leaned an elbow on my high counter. "If that woman ain't some kind of superhero—or *guano loco*—I'll eat my hat. But I guess I got you and Hilt to thank for introducing us. She's a real plotter, that one. A planner too. She made five backup plans for stuff going wrong on this trip, even though she only lives a coupla hours from here. When I saw her and her family headed for the stairs just now, I asked her if she was gonna head home, and I swear to God, she and her husband both said, "It's Plan D" at the same time."

"Plan D, out of five? Someone getting killed and her choosing to stay behind wasn't the very worst scenario?"

"My thoughts exactly. But she said Plan E was 'so unlikely it would make a great psychological suspense novel.'"

I shook my head at Sarah's mix of creativity and foresight. "Well, that is her forte."

"Listen." Butch adopted a paternal, worried expression. "I don't want you worrying over her baby while she's still here. She's planning to check out in a couple days, anyway. And she has plenty of extra milk frozen at home. Thad will know what to do with it, I'm sure."

I patted Butch's hand. The old vet's attempt to comfort me on womanly matters was endearing. "Let's let Sarah and Thad take care of things, shall we?"

Butch's shoulders slumped in exaggerated relief. "Yes, let's. I'd rather take on a pack of Charlies in the jungle any day."

So Sarah, Butch, and Ogden had elected to stay in the face of danger. I admitted to myself that I'd be glad of their company. *Unless I've been horribly wrong all this time, and one of them's a murderer.*

Chloe popped out of the kitchen. "I'll strip the latest checkout beds and get the laundry started." And she even smiled as she stomped up the stairs in her clompy black combat boots. "We'll get some new guests in here on the double. You'll see."

Who are you, and what have you done with Chloe? But I appreciated her presence as well as her willingness to dig in and work.

I slipped into my room and called Lake. He answered on the first ring. "Pippa, I've been worried. But I didn't want to interrupt the drug raid or anything. Harry heard about it from Mozzie, who—well, you know. It's Seacrest. Is everything okay? Are you okay? What's going on over there?"

The strain in his voice put an ache in my chest, and I let myself fall onto my bed. Curling up, I felt his presence, his love, surround me. Some of the tension in my shoulders eased, and I heaved a deep breath. "I kept thinking it's my fault, Lake," I blurted, feeling tears edging into my eyes. "I wasn't here because I wanted time alone with you, and then Zach died, and I yelled at Mallory, and everyone kept saying I was so calm, but criminy on a cracker, I felt like I was going to explode and take the whole building with me."

Lake spoke slowly and gently, as if he were whispering against my ear. "This isn't your fault, Pippa. Zach didn't die because you weren't there. You couldn't have known what was going to happen. That's not how things work. If anyone's to blame for you not being home last night, it's me. I needed you, and you were there for me. But the only person we can blame for Zach's death is his killer. Don't put this on yourself, sweetheart. Please, okay? I would never think you're to blame, and I'll chase down anyone who says otherwise—probably with a chainsaw or something. Although I don't actually have a chainsaw, so I guess they'll charge me with stealing one in addition to threatening people."

I giggled and sniffled at his attempt to ease my painful feelings. "Have I mentioned today how much I love you?"

"You might have mentioned it in the shower this morning, yeah."

"Well, it's been a crazy day, so let me say it again: I love you, Lake Ivens."

"And I love you, Pippa Winterbourne. Never forget that, or that chainsaw defending is available upon request." With his smooth baritone charm, Lake eased me around into a much better frame of mind, and we hung up after promises to get together more often.

An hour later, Chloe found me wielding a big can of Pledge in the library. "Ashley's gonna stay too. She got a little snippy with me when I tried to strip her bed, considering she was writing a letter on it when I just barged into her room. Please don't fire me or anything."

I set down my dusting rag. "You think she'll ask me to fire you?"

Chloe's gaze dropped to the carpet. "Probably not. But I know I haven't been... You know what? I'm gonna dust the chandeliers, especially that peacock pane one in the foyer. I have time now, and it's been so busy all summer that they're probably really dusty. Yeah." She dashed off, leaving me alone with the books and the dust.

I have got to do something about that girl. But first, I need to do something about all this dust. Then I'll see what Chloe's really up to when she disappears.

Moorehaven was as quiet as a tomb for the rest of the day, as if the mansion itself mourned for the loss of Zach Finney. My four remaining authors stayed in their rooms, writing or otherwise, and I found myself with enough unexpected free time that I finished reading *The Brass Artifice* in the first-floor sunroom. When I reached the part where Hilton Gray revealed how he'd figured out Tibbsy and Marco were also the murderers, I crowed to the cats as we all snuggled on the couch together. "Aha!" Tibbsy had been pretending to romance Ichabod Bellwether's spinster daughter Clarice, but because Tibbsy hadn't known her favorite flowers—he'd even sent her lilies, which made her sneeze—Gray had sussed out the truth. The burglars were after something else in the historian's house: information on the cannons. *Wallis knew who the killers were the moment those flowers were delivered. She brags about it every time she hears someone men-*

tion this book. I wonder who Vic's delivering all those yellow and orange flowers to. What's his motive?

"'When is a romance not a romance?'" I proclaimed, quoting Gray.

Svetlana deigned to bend a single ear in my direction, though Rex must've thought I was asking if he wanted a snack, the way his wide eyes fixed on me.

"'When it's a smokescreen.'"

My cats were less than impressed and laid their heads back down.

"Come on, guys. That's a great line." But it was no use. I'd lost my audience to cozy snoozing. *What if I'm staring at a smokescreen without realizing it? If only I was allergic to them, like Clarice is to lilies! It sure would be easier to figure out the truth.*

Taking their cue from Ogden, my guests ate supper—Mozzie's again—in their rooms. Hilt and I had the dining room to ourselves. When I asked about further developments on the archive break-in, he shook his shaggy head and grumbled that there hadn't been any. No one could prove that Connor Dockins was still in town or that he'd had anything to do with the attack on Patrice or the burglary of the missing 1964 files.

After a surprisingly heavy night's sleep—possibly aided by the knowledge that Mal hadn't tossed my bedcovers and put her demanding hands in my underwear drawer—I woke with a desire to wrestle answers from wherever they might be hiding. Hilt needed help—and supervision—learning what really happened to Ramòn all those years ago, and I needed to catch Zach's murderer. I also needed to know if anyone else at Moorehaven was being targeted. That false drug report had really thrown me, but I needed to get back on my feet.

Chloe arrived early enough to help with breakfast. With only four authors in residence, I'd informed Tyleen that she could have breakfast at her own table for once, leaving Hilt, Chloe, and me to manage for our small crew. Chloe strode back and forth from the kitchen with a purposeful expression on her face and delivered Ogden's breakfast to his room without being prompted. She even pulled her hair back into a ponytail, revealing the side of her face that was so often hidden behind a dark curtain of hair.

"You okay this morning?" I asked her as I handed her two plates of pancakes.

Svetlana, smelling an opportunity, hopped up onto an empty chair at the breakfast nook table.

Chloe met my eyes with cool determination. "This is my home too. You know, kind of. Enough, anyway. I won't let anyone mess with it. Not even you, Svetlana." She moved one plate out of reach just before Svetlana's paw darted out to snag the top flapjack. The white cat sat down on the chair and swiftly began licking her paw as if that was all she'd ever been planning to do. Chloe smirked and took the pancakes out to the dining room.

I stared after her with a lump of pride in my throat. *She does want to be here. I can probably rule her out as a drug kingpin, then.*

After breakfast, Ashley and Sarah announced that they were going to brave the crowded streets for some antiquing, a.k.a. book research, before the day got too hot. "And don't worry," Ashley said from the doorway, "we'll stick together. And we each have a brick in our bag, just in case."

Butch shifted and swayed in his chair. "You have my cell number, girls," he called after them. "Call if anything strange comes up."

"Yes, dear," Ashley trilled in a reassuring 1950s-housewife voice. The tension eased, and Uncle Hilt actually cracked a smile. The day was looking up.

Now, if only no one else gets killed.

15

"Why does gold fever exist? That's a question for your economist."
Raymond Moore, 1974

CHLOE THREW HERSELF into extra cleaning for the next couple of hours. "It's like spring cleaning, except after the summer rush," she explained when I brought her a burrito bowl for lunch. "I'm just getting the sand out of everything, giving stuff a good polish for fall. Ooh, extra cilantro? Yum!"

I hadn't instituted an official fall cleaning in Moorehaven, but after seeing what Chloe could do when she was determined, I decided I couldn't let her efforts go to waste. While I'd been inventorying the pantry, making reorder lists, and finishing up the laundry, she'd dusted the entire hallway from top to bottom, de-spiderwebbed the ceilings in both parlors, and given the library's wet bar a complete makeover. *At this rate, I won't need to track her down anywhere because she'll never leave Moorehaven again. Not the worst outcome.*

I was in the middle of dust mopping the hallway's gleaming hardwood when the front door burst open, and Jordan ushered a sobbing Trudie inside. I stared at them in shock, my mop forgotten in my hands. I hadn't seen her cry like that—heartbroken and at a total loss—since our beloved dog, Geranium, had run away because the neighbor's New Year's fireworks terrified her.

Jordan's face was tight as she said to me, "Your room. Now."

I leaned my mop handle against the wall, grabbed a tissue box from the hostess station, and led the way. I pulled open the pantry shelves that served as the secret entrance to my bedroom and let my sister and friend enter first. Then I pulled the shelves closed behind us. Jordan sat Trudie on my bed, and I handed my sister the box of tissues and sat next to her.

I put an arm around her shoulders. "What happened?"

Trudie blew her nose like a trumpet, so Jordan answered for her. "Gabe's been arrested. He and Trudie were walking on my block, and Mallory swooped in and cuffed him. Trudie didn't know what to do, so she came to my place, and I brought her here."

I took a moment to study Jordan. My friend's hair was pulled back into a messy ponytail, and dark circles hung beneath her eyes. "Didn't you just get to bed a couple hours ago?"

Jordan shook her head at me. "This is more important, Pippa. Mallory thinks that Gabe killed Zach."

Shocked, I looked at Trudie for confirmation. My sister met my eyes with her teary ones and nodded. "Vic came by early this morning. The police matched a footprint from the crime scene to Gabe's shoes. Mallory deduced that the acrylic paint and a tiny glass bead in the shoe tread could point to an artist. Somehow, she jumped right to us."

A hot spike of guilt pierced my chest. I'd been the one to put Gabe on Mal's radar. Of course she kept tabs on all his particulars.

Tru continued, "When Vic came to our trailer, he said either Gabe or I could be involved, and the footprint is too big to be mine. And Gabe already has a record. So Vic collected all of his tennis shoes, and then he asked if Gabe had an alibi for eight to ten p.m. Tuesday night. And, Pippa, I did something stupid."

A chilly worm of worry twisted in my belly. "You lied and gave him an alibi, didn't you?"

Trudie squeezed her eyes shut and dabbed at them with the sopping tissue.

I handed her a new one. "Oh, Tru. What happened?"

"I got busted by my own Facebook photos," she began. "I took selfies all night at my Treasure Fair table, and Gabe wasn't in any of them. He doesn't really like crowds. I didn't think. I just wanted him to be safe. Pippa, I don't know where he was, but I know he didn't kill anyone. Please, you have to help him. *Please.*"

Jordan looked at me expectantly, and I lifted my chin. On one hand, I had my little sister, with all her faults. On the other hand, I had my boyfriend's cop ex-wife, with her heavy-handed procedure and her pushiness about staying in Lake's guest room as soon as it was finished. That decision was a no-brainer. And I could secretly atone for my own mistake of putting Gabe on Mallory's radar in the first place. "Of course I will." I hugged Tru and reached for Jordan's hand, and she clasped mine. "We all will."

Jordan and I escorted Trudie back to her trailer. While I reassured her that I would do everything I could for Gabe, Jordan texted the Glaze and Gossip group with all the details we had so far.

"I feel so helpless right now," Tru said as she sat in the Airstream's doorway. She gave her brown curls a frustrated shake. "I need to go make some angry art, or I'll do something I shouldn't. Please, let me know if anything comes up, okay?"

"Of course I will. Don't worry. We'll get to the bottom of this."

Tru nodded, sniffed, and stepped inside to gather some art supplies.

Jordan squeezed my arm to get my attention and indicated her phone. "The texts I'm getting back from the girls are pretty concerning."

"In what way?"

Tru exited the trailer and pulled its silvery door shut behind her with one hand. Her other arm was full of clear plastic craft boxes. "I'll be in my studio on the Green, where everyone can see me, and I'll keep my phone handy. You call me with everything you learn, Pippa." Her hug was intense, and then she blew away on the breeze.

Jordan stepped close and leaned her shoulder against mine in solidarity. "Well, they were all on board with the Case of the Missing Geologist yesterday. Now, everyone's worried Gabe might have done it." She showed me her phone screen.

I sighed and nodded. "Seacrest strikes again."

Tyleen had texted that she'd never trusted men with shaved heads. Naoma reluctantly brought up Gabe's previous arrest for assault. Lori mentioned that a man who worked with his hands was more likely to have the strength to suffocate someone. Emily added that it didn't look good that Gabe had gotten his girlfriend to lie about his alibi for him. Wallis commented that a spade was usually a spade, especially after it had been used to dig a grave. And also did I want to order some condolence flowers for Trudie?

"Gabe did fight with Zach at Moorehaven," Jordan gently reminded me. "Maybe Gabe's temper got the best of him again."

"So he stalked a near-stranger to a beach parking lot and suffocated him because they argued about a fence post? Gabe got arrested for defending his grandma. He's loyal, not unhinged."

Jordan rubbed my back with one hand. "We'll check everything out, for Trudie's sake. But Wallis is right about one thing. Sometimes, a spade really is just a spade."

My shoulders slumped. I gave her a despondent hug. "Go get some more sleep. And thank you."

I had a cup of peppermint tea back at Moorehaven around eleven, and the beginnings of a plan formed in my mind. I found Chloe out on the porch. She had moved all the heavy flowerpots, swept the porch, and mopped it down. The dark-green accent paint looked as fresh as the day it had been brushed on.

"Chloe, you're amazing. This looks great!" I gave her a bright smile, which she returned. "Listen, I need your help. Well, more specifically, I need your father's help, his professional, attorney-at-law help. Do you think you can relay a message to him? I know a prospective client who needs his services right away. But there's a catch."

Chloe hesitated a moment but nodded decisively and whipped out her phone. "I am intrigued. You dictate, I'll text."

I laid out my plan, and Chloe texted its details to her father. As he replied that he was on his way to the jail, Ashley and Sarah returned from their shopping trip. I tucked a rebel strand of my summer-blond hair behind my ear and smiled winningly at them. "And what did you ladies find out and about this morning?"

Ashley lifted a clear plastic case from her pocket. "We found the treasure!"

"What?" Treasure fever tugged at the edges of my focus on Gabe. We wouldn't hear back from Mercer for a while, anyway.

She and Sarah giggled. "Well, *a* treasure, anyway," Sarah amended. "Ash found a gold coin, an actual piece of eight, at the pawnshop. The owner says he's had it for a while, nothing to do with the current craze or anything, but since everyone's raving about pieces of eight right now, Ash had to have it. And here it is! Isn't it gorgeous?"

My eyes locked on the small plastic case and its gleaming contents. I knew that Ritchy, who owned the pawnshop, wasn't known for his straight dealing. But the coin looked pretty real to me. "How much did you pay for it?"

"Oh, I couldn't say," Ashley simpered. "I didn't buy it because I thought it was real."

"It's a fake?"

She shrugged mischievously. "Let's find out." She strode inside like a woman on a mission.

Sarah and I exchanged a confused glance. "How much did she pay?" I murmured.

"I didn't get a clear look at the price tag, but it couldn't have been more than a couple hundred bucks."

"So, fake," I concluded.

"Yeah, probably. Why'd she buy a fake gold coin?"

I followed Ashley in and mimicked her words. "Let's find out."

We trailed Ashley upstairs and caught her as she came out of her room, makeup bottle and compact in hand. "Can we use the sunroom?" she asked.

"Of course. What do you have in mind?" I asked in return.

Ashley waggled the coin at me. "Ever since I read about this trick, I've wanted to try it. When I saw the coin in the pawn shop, I finally saw my chance." We settled on two of the couches, and Ashley set the coin on the coffee table. The cats came to the sunroom door, looking for company, but after sniffing the air, they decided not to put up with our shenanigans and ambled elsewhere. "I have mild anemia," Ashley said, "so this should work on me, but I brought my makeup if either of you want to try it as well. Basically, I rub the coin across my forehead, and if it's real gold, it should leave a black streak across my skin. I test my iron levels with a gold ring at home all the time so I know if I need to take a supplement. The same effect's supposed to happen if you put on foundation and powder and rub the coin on your foreheads. And don't worry. The black mark comes right off. Let's see what happens!"

Ashley opened the case and turned the coin so its uneven edge pressed against her forehead. She swiped it back and forth with more force than I thought she needed, until a mark actually did form on her forehead. A red one.

"Maybe you should stop," I suggested. "I don't think it's working, and I don't want you to hurt yourself. I'll try the makeup method if you want." *How many times have I been a guinea pig for my authors?*

Well, at least this won't be painful or embarrassing like that time I got literally roped into hopping down the Oubliette stairs with my ankles tied together so an author could time me. That bone bruise on my shin lasted two months.

Ashley offered her makeup, and I added a little to my forehead. I was already wearing makeup, but maybe it needed to be fresh for the experiment to work. The hue was a few shades darker than mine—Ashley looked like a woman who enjoyed the outdoors, or a tanning bed—but curiosity had taken hold of me, and I really wanted to know if the coin was, in fact, a fake. Having a local scamming our visitors with fake treasure was an issue I couldn't leave alone.

I took the coin and studied it for a moment. The edges were uneven, and the coin itself seemed warped. One side bore two castles and two lions rampant in opposite corners of a ribboned square. The little shield in the top left of the other side had a faint echo, as if the stamp had bounced when the coin was struck. Both sides of the coin bore random scratches, as if it had ridden in a pouch full of sharp stones or something. And if my eyes didn't deceive me, the name "Philippus" was stamped along one edge. I didn't come across people who bore my name that often, but sharing its male version with a Spanish king was pretty cool.

"I wonder if anyone called King Philip 'Pippus.'" I chuckled. *Maybe his name was stamped on the coins Ramòn was found with.* Less amused at myself now that I'd made a connection between this coin Ritchy had sold Ashley and the coins Ramòn was holding, I rubbed its edge firmly across the makeup on my forehead. *No wonder he turned white when he saw the coin Vic brought in for authentication. He knows something.* After several passes, I stopped and looked from Ashley to Sarah. "Well? Anything?"

"Just a red mark, like Ashley." Sarah took the coin and held it up to examine it. "I guess that means it's not even gold plating."

Ashley frowned, but her eyes seemed pleased. "See if you can chip off a piece of the gold."

Sarah glanced around, patted her pockets, and came up with a safety pin. She opened it and scraped at one section of the coin. I leaned forward, transfixed. Eventually, tiny gold scrapings fell to the tabletop. Ashley and I leaned over to get a closer look at what lay beneath.

"Whatever it is, it's gray." Sarah held the coin out for inspection.

I took it and tilted it in the light, while dark thoughts ran through my mind regarding Ritchy Axelrod. *Ritchy was one of Ramòn's friends, back in the day. This coin may be a fake, but it's modeled on a real coin. Maybe Ritchy really has had a genuine piece of eight for a while. Maybe he's had it for fifty years.* "I think the authorities will be very interested to learn about this fraud. Can I keep this for a while, Ashley?"

Her plump lips spread in a pleased smile. "Of course, dear. If it will help Hilton with his cold case too, so much the better."

I nodded crisply and went to find Hilt. Involving him in cracking open a fake coin scam might be a way to distract him from Ramòn's murder, or it might march him down the main street of his own investigation. Either way, I'd be right beside him.

16

"*My father died of Spanish flu, else I'd be a far different man—poorer in pocket, but no doubt richer in spirit. My other life is one of the few tales I can never bring myself to fictionalize.*"
Raymond Moore, 1952

I CARRIED RITCHY'S damning evidence in my pleated shorts pocket, but I couldn't find Hilt anywhere in Moorehaven. Worried he'd hared off on yet another wild investigative jaunt, I scoured the place for anyone who had seen him or seen which way he'd gone.

Chloe was, once again, nowhere to be found. As my irritation reached a boiling point, Butch ambled in off the side porch.

"Fence's coming along nice," he commented. "Ernie does good work. You sure you want it painted green, though?" His doubt dropped one eyebrow low over an eye.

"It'll match the house trim that way," I said. "Have you seen Hilt?"

He nodded his gray head amiably. "Just finished a consulting session with him. He said he was gonna take someone named Jimmy up on his offer of fishing."

Though I was puzzled as to why I hadn't run across Butch and Hilt in my search of Moorehaven, my worries over my uncle's state of mind evaporated like fog in strong sunlight. Hilt couldn't be in safer hands. "And what are you up to now?"

He waggled a notebook covered in scrawling blue ink. "Oh, I need to transcribe these notes before I forget everything Hilt told me."

"You're asking him about Vietnam stuff?"

"Oh, yeah, um. Just to clarify a few details." He tapped his temple. "Won't do to get those wrong. My readers will notice right off."

Butch claimed that he had served two tours in the Vietnam War. *So why is he asking Hilt for details? Butch doesn't strike me as the type to make up lies about his own service. What's going on? And does it tie in with any of the other mysteries I'm juggling, or is it just one more ball to keep in the air?* But I smiled and nodded. "They tend to do that. I won't keep you from your transcribing, then. See you for supper?"

He eyed me like he wanted to say more—confess, even, if his posture was any sort of clue—but he simply said, "You got it."

He tramped upstairs, eyes glued to his notes. I took a deep breath, squared my shoulders, and pulled out my phone, determined to deal with Chloe's absences once and for all.

She didn't pick up. She had agreed to act as my link to Gabe for as long as he remained behind bars, so I didn't want to go over her head and talk to her father if I didn't need to. But more importantly, she'd vanished from Moorehaven. Again. That was my cue. *I am Lady Lisbet, clever consort to the King of Germany, and I don't let anything get in my way. Even if maybe it should.*

Leaving Moorehaven unattended wasn't my first choice, but my remaining authors were all busy. I couldn't show the coin to Hilt yet. Chloe only lived a few blocks away. I got my bike from the rack.

Four blocks from the sea, I arrived at Braxton House, a fastidiously maintained sage-and-mauve Victorian home designated by Seacrest as a historical site and labeled, as many of the oldest homes in Seacrest were, with a large brass oval plaque beside the front door. Delicate sunburst-patterned gingerbread adorned a second-story gable above a pair of double-hung living room windows, and a semi-attached miniature turret rose from the center of the porch roof to create a delightful roofline. A minivan I didn't recognize sat parked along the curb right in front of the walk, so I walked my bike up to the porch and propped it against a nice old boxwood shrub.

I traipsed up the wide sage-green staircase to the deep porch and was about to use the shield-shaped door knocker when I heard Chloe's voice inside. She wasn't using her sweet, low, gospel-singer phone voice, but she didn't quite sound like herself, either.

"Pray follow, if you please, as we leave the salon and step into the parlor. To your left, you will see a cozy drawing room, from the longer term 'withdrawing,' to which the ladies would retire after dinner. Note the lovely detail on the arch as you pass beneath it, a decorative style typical of the early 1890s."

"Can I get a picture of you with the arch?" an older woman interrupted. "Right there by the lamp."

Chloe replied, "Of course, madam."

"Madam"? What the heck is going on in there? I peeked through the broad front window, shading my view from the bright reflection on the wavy old glass. Chloe stood in an archway about eight feet from me, dressed in a peach beaded gown and an upswept ash-blond wig studded with enormous fake topazes. She turned toward my window, leaned against the arch, and adopted a graceful pose for the woman, who raised her phone and tapped the screen a few times.

Then Chloe saw me through the window. Her whole body stiffened, and her lower lip stuttered as if she were about to speak.

"No, not like that," the bossy tourist ordered. "Lean on the arch again. Bobby, go stand next to her."

"Yes, Ma." A burly teenaged boy, all shaggy dark hair and tropical-themed summer wear, lumbered into view and shuffled to a stop next to Chloe. He hunched in embarrassment and hid his hands behind his back as his mom snapped a few pictures.

Chloe stood stiffly at his side, a cheaply made wax model of her usual animated self.

I blinked and backed away. My mind scrambled for an explanation. Then I recalled Chloe telling me that her father kept Braxton House historically accurate in as many rooms as possible because he offered tours for passing tourists. It had never occurred to me that he didn't give the tours himself.

Why didn't Chloe tell me? Several possible explanations whirled through my mind as I walked my bike down the front path again. *Embarrassment? Was she told not to? Has she secretly been kidnapped into a historically accurate cult?* I parked my bike by Braxton House's side door so the tourists wouldn't see my anachronistic 1970s bicycle with its oversized basket and be yanked out of their time-traveling experience, *Somewhere in Time*-style. I passed a few very pleasant minutes sitting on an old-fashioned bench in a tiny wind chime garden and listening to the summer breeze make its own unique music.

Eventually, the tourists drove away in their minivan. A couple of minutes later, Chloe burst out the side door of Braxton House in a white blouse and jeans, swearing repeatedly under her breath. She took three running steps in the direction of Moorehaven before she saw me and skidded to a horrified halt.

"I'm so sorry," she blurted.

I'd never seen Chloe afraid of anything, and I'd definitely never seen her wearing such horrified shame. She kept her emotions pretty muted compared to most teenagers I'd known, offering only glimpses of the depths she felt. But with her arms and legs splayed in surprise, hair wild and eyes wide, Chloe looked like she might burst into guilty tears in a heartbeat.

"Please, please don't fire me," she whispered. "I will literally do *anything* you want me to. I need to get out of this place. On a daily basis, I mean. I can't stay in there all the time. It's driving me crazy."

I realized that she'd taken my surprised silence for judgment, so I used a gentle tone. "I can't fire you, Chloe. I depend on you too much. I really do. I just want to understand what's going on. If you need me to cut back your hours so you can help your dad more, that's fine—"

"God, no!" she burst out. "I can't stand this stupid job. And it's not even a job. Dad doesn't pay me or anything."

I stood and motioned for her to walk back toward Moorehaven with me. "Then why do you do it?"

She fell into step with me and shrugged, hiding her emotions again. "I guess because I always have. Well, since Mom left. Everyone thought it was so cute when I was little, dressed in a fancy gown and wig. And I was so proud of myself that I knew all the historical stuff about our old house. It was perfect. It brought in extra money when we needed it, and it brought Dad and me closer together."

My heart tightened in sympathy. "You kept giving tours every summer?"

"Yeah. It was just a habit by then, something my dad and I would do together. Except it seemed more and more like it was just me."

"And he doesn't pay you."

"Nope."

"But…" I struggled with how to broach the subject delicately. "But you have a full-time paying job at Moorehaven. Why haven't you spoken to your father about how his tours are interrupting your paying job?" *Maybe this is why she hesitated before contacting him about helping Gabe.*

"Gah, I don't know *how*!" She made fists at her sides. "High school doesn't teach you how to tell your dad he's taking financial advantage of you. Your sister was really nice about it the other day."

Oh. This was the other thing they were talking about. "Did she have any advice for you?"

"Yeah," Chloe said. "She said I should talk to you about it."

That was pretty good advice. Tru probably didn't deserve me yelling at her over it. I took a deep breath. "Well, if you're asking, I have a suggestion."

"Yeah. I'm asking. Shoulda asked sooner. I was just... You know."

"Yeah, I know. Well, you're a working adult now. You have a job with benefits and responsibilities. So does your dad. That makes you equals, as far as jobs go. If you speak to him as an equal, knowing you both have job responsibilities and obligations, and tell him that the free service you provide is interfering with your work, he should understand. Ask him how his clients would feel if he kept leaving in the middle of meetings to volunteer here at Moorehaven."

Chloe blinked. "That's good. I'll use that, I think. Thank you. I-I just never knew how to say it, you know? Never thought about the equal work thing."

"I think everything will work out fine. But if you need me to have a word or anything at all, let me know. I got your back."

"You're the best boss ever. And I should know. I've had, like, twenty."

My smile widened at her praise. "Any word from your dad about Gabe yet?"

Chloe swore under her breath and pulled out her phone. "I have to turn it off so it doesn't ruin the, y'know, ambiance. Yes, Dad replied." She read through the texts. "Gabe claims he was out for a walk to avoid the chaos of the Treasure Fair when he came across Zach, already dead in the parking lot. He didn't see anyone." She scrolled down. "And he says he was too afraid to report the body because of his own criminal record. He thought they'd suspect him. Looks like he was right."

I gritted my teeth. "I wish that kind of thing only happened in novels. Did Gabe mention the soda he stepped in?"

Chloe texted, and I walked beside her in an agony of impatience until Mercer texted back. Chloe said, "Apparently the soda was right next to the body when Gabe squatted down to feel for a pulse. He didn't even notice it. I bet the soda was Zach's, and he dropped it when he was attacked. Dad figures the stickiness helped pull some of the forensic stuff off Gabe's shoe, and that's how Mallory found him so quickly. He says Gabe feels terrible about not telling anyone about Zach. My dad may be absentminded when it comes to fatherhood, but he's a great lawyer. If he thinks Gabe is innocent, then so do I."

"That's pretty mature of you, seeing your dad from more than one perspective." We walked the rest of the way to Moorehaven, and I texted the gossip group, hoping they could ask around and learn if anyone in town could confirm Gabe's story, or if anyone else would admit to finding Zach's body before Gabe had. I felt relieved to understand Chloe's situation, and she had a new spring in her step that showed me a weight had been lifted from her as well. And I was grateful to have an ally in the fight to prove Gabe's innocence.

Hilt looked up from the hostess station as we entered the front door. "You were lookin' for me?"

Ritchy's coin. I fumbled for it in my pocket and held it up like a police badge. "You wanna bust someone for fraud, Chief?" I asked in my best *Dragnet* voice.

Hilt's eyes widened, and then they narrowed with old suspicion. I suddenly worried I'd done exactly the wrong thing by showing him the coin.

17

"*I enjoy writing characters who can feel their cruel fate rushing toward them, but they can't get out of its way. We all fall short, and sometimes high tide catches us.*"
Raymond Moore, 1951

HILT MADE A FEW CALLS after seeing my dismayed face. He could tell I was worried about him running off and doing something stupid by himself. But after a clipped conversation with Mallory, he plunked the house phone back into its cradle and glared at the reproduction painting hanging opposite him. "Thanks, anyway," he grumbled to himself.

"No dice?" I asked gingerly.

"Not even a pip, Pip. No one's reported any other fake coins to Seacrest PD. My report has been taken, but Chief Tavish says it's not a priority, considering she's doing her level best to prove Gabe killed Zach."

"Well, Chloe, Jordan, and I are doing our level best to prove he didn't." I crossed my arms.

Chloe, texting madly to Jordan, flashed me a quick grin. "Jordan's making progress through her local contacts, but she still hasn't found anyone who can corroborate Gabe's story or anyone who's seen Connor Dockins since he checked out of Seven Vistas. If he's hiding in town, he's hiding well. Oh, and Lori says that she 'asked Patrice to come into the urgent care for a quick checkup, and she still can't remember anything from the night she was attacked. Sad-face emoji.'"

Hilt pursed his lips at her modern terminology, and the light glinted off his silver stubble. "All right, Pip, come on. You're with me." He stepped out of the hostess station and stalked toward the front door.

My tummy balled up and dropped. "Criminy on a cracker. You're gonna do something stupid. And you're gonna drag me into it too."

Hilt's skinny chest puffed up. "Am not. I'm just gonna ask a guy about a coin. And I'm bringing you as my witness."

"Or his," I muttered under my breath. I jogged to keep up with him. As I clattered down the porch, I sent a text to Chloe, who had promised to stay at Moorehaven for the rest of the day, asking her to keep an eye on things as I was being unavoidably kidnapped by my uncle.

Have fun, she texted back. *I got this.*

Hilt and I biked back up to the highway under the noonday sun. My hair was hot, and I wished I'd brought a sun hat. Or even a rain hat. Any hat would do. We pedaled along the edge of the parking lot along the eastern side until we pulled in at Ritchy's pawnshop. The Golden Ax's sign gleamed bright and new—*Ax from Axelrod, I guess?*—and the shop windows were clean and uncluttered, offering as tasteful a display as a pawn shop could. A broad awning protected windows and approaching shoppers alike from wind and rain and gave the building a whimsical, beachy appeal that matched the kite shop and the summer rental agency that flanked it. I parked my bike by Hilt's and followed him inside. The door swung against a bell, announcing our arrival.

Inside, the pawnshop's carpet soothed me with its rich, deep-blue color. A relaxing aroma, reminiscent of warm sand and incense, teased my nose. Shelves lined the walls, and display cases guarded them, lit from within with a warm glow. Jewelry and watches sat in easy view, but Ritchy seemed to have more than the usual eclectic collection for sale: a prosthetic leg carved in steampunk-pirate fashion, a stuffed badger sporting long, curly red locks and a ruby-sequined gown, and a dolphin-themed bidet attachment.

We were the only people in sight. "Ritchy! You here?" Hilt called.

A beaded curtain rustled in the distance, and a short, foxlike man emerged, pressing his palms together like a Buddhist. "Is that my favorite retired policeman? So it is! Hilton, it's been too long. You should visit more often. You know you're always welcome here."

Ritchy's voice held a smear too much grease for my taste. I suppressed a shudder, but I couldn't deny that I insta-disliked him.

"And who's this?" Ritchy continued. "This must be Pippa, your niece. I'm sure I've seen you around town here and there. How lovely to meet you properly." He dry-washed his hands and hunched his shoulders, offering me a thin-lipped, wide grin.

Is he trying *to go full Disney villain? If he breaks into song about how he's about to unleash his master plan or how he has creepy friends to help him, I'm outta here.*

Hilt saved me from a reply I was struggling to compose by tapping Ashley's coin on the edge of the glass case. "You wanna tell me about this here gold coin one of my guests purchased from you today? You wanna tell me why the gold coating just flakes right off like some cheap made-in-China nonsense? You wanna tell me why you're fleecing folks, people staying right here in town, and ruining Seacrest's reputation as a trustworthy tourist destination?"

Ritchy's eyes fixed on the fake piece of eight, and his face froze, locking his reply in his throat despite his open mouth. "Ehh, not particularly?" He shrugged helplessly and attempted a weak smile.

Hilt's face tightened, and he leaned toward Ritchy with menacing speed.

Ritchy veered out of range as if his spine were crafted from fine Italian spaghetti. "It's not like you're a cop anymore, Hilt. I mean, come on. You got no authority to ask me these questions." Ritchy's hands flicked and fluttered distractingly, a panicked pair of butter-flies.

I put a firm hand on Hilt's forearm. "Then maybe you can help us with some other questions," I said in my most reasonable tone of voice. "This coin's fake, but you must've made a mold from a real piece of eight. Where'd you get that one?"

Again with the fluttering hands. "I've had it for so long, I really can't recall. I get so many interesting items through here each year. You wouldn't believe the things I see."

Hilt gave a disbelieving grunt, and Ritchy's smarmy smile slipped.

"I mean, I guess I could check my records, but bookkeeping isn't one of my many talents, I'm sad to say. It could take a while."

Steam was very nearly shooting out of Hilt's ears. I needed to act. *I'm Agent Zinnia Lao, finest CIA operative in all of Central Asia. Nothing matters except the final result. And I need results.* "Listen, Ritchy. I'm sure you've noticed how upset my uncle is. He's taking this fraud of yours very personally. And you're right. He's not a cop anymore. He's a private citizen. If no one saw him leap over this counter and punch you in the nose a few times for being squirrely with the truth, it'd just be his word against yours. You feeling more upstanding than usual today? Didn't think so." I stretched my arms and cracked my neck. "But I'm feeling a powerful need for some fresh air, so I think I'll just step away for a bit." I smiled, heart pound-ing, and began to turn away. *Does this technique ever actually work?*

Hilt and Ritchy stared at me, wide-eyed and open-mouthed. I took five steps toward the door before Ritchy called after me. "Wait! Wait, okay, I-I think it's all coming back to me. Yeah, I remember who sold me the coin!" I turned in time to see him holding up a triumphant *eureka* finger.

I looked at Hilt for permission to let Ritchy off the hook for his pummeling, but my uncle was staring at me, eyebrows high and a little chagrined.

Then he nodded. "Spill all the beans in your pot, Ritchy."

"Okay. One day these delinquents trot in here, a little buzzed and a little loud. I get their type in here on the regular. But they show me this coin, see." His hands begged us to believe his story. "They say one of their dads gave it to them. I, well, I'm not in the habit of asking invasive questions, if you follow me. Bad for business. So I tested the coin right in front of 'em."

He gave us an apologetic shrug. "You've heard," he interrupted himself, "that I got a friend to test the coin found with Ramòn, when Vic brought it in to me. Thing is, I got spooked. Thought Vic was tryin' to bust me for the coin these kids brought in, is all. Didn't want to leave my fingerprints on it. No way was I gonna let him entrap me, no, sirree!" Ritchy waved his hands in a sharp negative gesture.

He picked up his story again. "So anyway, that coin they brought me, I totally thought it'd be a cheap fake. But blow me over—it's real! So now they kind of have me over a barrel, 'cause I gotta pay up if I want the thing. Well, lucky for me, only one of us in the room knew the current price of an ounce of gold, so I still made out okay, and they left happy." He smirked.

Hilt had taken in Ritchy's entire explanation with slitted eyes.

"And when was that?" I prompted.

Ritchy's hands wavered back and forth, and his head waffled from side to side. "Ah, um, well, let's see. It was raining, but when isn't it raining? Winds were nasty too. Musta been...winter? Yeah, this past winter."

"That's a steaming pile of shiitake mushrooms." Hilt held the coin in his fingers and shoved it at Ritchy's face. "You see that double strike up in the corner, where the mint screwed up and had to hit the coin again? You see it? That's the mark on *every single one* of the coins recovered from Ramòn's grave, Ritchy! *You* killed him for this gold. You kept it all this time." Hilt's voice went hoarse with emotion as his voice got louder. "And now that he and his coins have been found, you got stupid and tried to profit off the murder you committed fifty years ago! You killed Ramòn! I always suspected you had something to do with his disappearance, but I could never prove it. And now, because of your greedy idiocy, I got you dead to rights!"

Ritchy went as pale as sour milk. His hands stilled, clutched against his round little belly. Slowly, he shook his head and shuffled backward until he bumped against the shelf behind him. "I'd never. I'd *never*. Ramòn was my friend too. Please, Hilton. Please don't do this to me. I can't go through this again."

I darted forward, pulling the icy knot in my tummy with me, and stood against the counter with my arms out to my sides, mostly to keep Hilt from actually jumping that counter despite his seventy-five years. "Easy, boys. Hilt?"

"I was a cop. My job description included considering the worst. So eventually, I suspected everyone," Hilt said through his teeth. His eyes were riveted to Ritchy, who had begun to sweat profusely. "All I knew was, I didn't have anything to do with Ramòn's disappearance, but maybe someone else did. Ritchy here, he had a big-time crush on Maggie. And Maggie wouldn't give him the time of day because she was too busy mooning over Ernie. And Ramòn kept warning Ritchy off of his sister because she was spoken for. Maybe, one day, you got tired of getting warned off. Thought you'd have a better shot with Maggie if her brother was out of the way. You think you coulda taken Ernie on? He's got nearly a foot on you and twenty IQ points."

"No need to get nasty," Ritchy said lightly, though his tone was still nervous. "I understand how charm works. Ernie, well. He's more direct. I swear, I didn't touch Ramòn, but I'm just sayin', I coulda held my own just fine."

"I suppose it didn't occur to you to let Maggie make her own decision?" I asked tartly.

The two old men stared at me in surprise.

I *tsk*ed. "No, because that would be *weird*." I slapped the countertop. "So, Ritchy, these unruly teens you claim brought you the gold coin. You sure you can't remember their names?"

Ritchy shrugged, regaining some of his greasy charm. "I tend not to ask that kind of question very much in this line of work."

Of course not. "Can you tell me what they looked like? Ever seen them before?"

"I seen 'em here and there, I think. They might be local, might live up or down the coast a town or two. One of them shaved his head, which I thought was a poor decision for the winter weather. His stubble was dark, and he tried to let it grow on his face, too, but it was patchy. And one kid was really gangly, like he was still thirteen instead of eighteen. He wasn't quite a ginger. Sandy hair, maybe. The other two, eh." He shrugged again. "Just teenagers with ball caps. Snapbacks, I think they call 'em these days."

Snapbacks. Something tickled my memory, and then I remembered. "Thank you for your cooperation, Ritchy, but we're not done with you yet. Hilt, let's go."

"Go? I ain't even—"

"I know where to find your coin thieves." I grabbed his arm and towed him back outside the Golden Ax, desperately grateful for a lead that would help my uncle get to the bottom of his friend's murder.

18

"*S*wim *in the Pacific? Are you kidding? I wouldn't be caught alive out in those waters, any deeper than my wrinkly old kneecaps. Caught dead, now—that, I'd consider."*
Raymond Moore, 1977

UNFORTUNATELY, THE rebellious youths I was looking for weren't where I always saw them. I stopped my bike next to Lake's lighthouse and pressed my lips together in frustration.

"Oh, them boys?" Hilt asked. "Mal usually has them working early in the mornings. They'll be back here tomorrow. That'll be your best chance to ask them about that coin."

He was right, of course. There was no way Mallory would take time out from working on Zach's murder and policing the rowdy crowd of treasure-hunting tourists swarming Seacrest to look up some phone numbers or home addresses. Not for me, anyway.

I looked across the river mouth that sliced through the weathered gray basalt lifting Seacrest above the ocean. Lake's marina office was just over there, behind Seven Vistas. I could be over there in a few minutes. *Wait. Is that Lake waving at me in the parking lot?*

My tall, dark-haired boyfriend was waving with both arms. I could see his smile from where I stood. My heart thrilled, and I could have sworn I floated a few inches off the ground.

I waved back excitedly and shouted, "Lake! Hi!"

He waved back again—but strangely. He held his arms out straight in stiff positions, then moved them, then bent one elbow.

I squinted in confusion. "What's he doing? The Robot?"

Hilt stepped up beside me. "I'd say yes, but Lake's not that cool. He's giving you a message in semaphore."

"Semaphore? That thing with flags?"

Hilt nodded.

"I don't speak semaphore, though." I reached into my pocket, intending to drag Lake into the twenty-first century with these new-fangled doohickeys called smart phones.

He'd just texted me with semaphore-flag emojis.

"Well, shut the front door," I exclaimed in surprised amusement.

Hilt peered over at my phone screen, but he merely snorted at my boyfriend's antics. I dialed Lake's number, and I stared across at him as the connection rang in my ear.

Lake stopped signaling me and answered. "Hey, beautiful. Did you get my message?"

"I'm not fluent in flag. Sorry."

Lake chuckled. "My messages said, 'I love you.'"

"You are such an adorable geek. I love that you thought of me just to mess around with your emojis."

"I'll mess around with *your* emojis if you want," he said suggestively.

"I'll bring the peach, you bring the eggplant?"

Hilt, hearing only half the conversation—and not speaking emoji—made a baffled face, but Lake's laugh was pure joy. My chest filled with happiness so fast it nearly made me dizzy. If only Lake knew how much I stressed over how well we connected. My confidence boosted itself up about seven notches.

"Listen," he said impulsively, "let's get a picnic."

"Ooh, I love a picnic. When do you wanna—"

"Right now! Let's do it. Let's run away and stuff our faces and make out in the middle of nowhere, just you and me."

My to-do list fast-forwarded in front of my mind's eye. I had obligations, chores, responsibilities. *Finding proof of Gabe's innocence. Proving whether Connor is still in Seacrest. Tracking down proof of Ritchy's claim about that piece of eight. I have a lot I should be doing.*

And it seemed Lake could hear them ticking past. "No, stop thinking about all that. You and I have barely seen each other, especially the last few weeks. When I do see you, we don't really talk. And I love to talk with you. We won't get any time handed to us. We have to carve it out of our lives. And you're worth carving up my life for, Pippa. Please."

For one wild moment, I felt like Bonnie, hearing Clyde's voice, wanting to shoot everything up and go on the run forever. Then I wrenched practicality back into my mind. Okay, it was sensibility. Okay, it was impulsivity mixed with the intent to ask for forgiveness afterward. *Chloe's doing great, marshaling all the gossip ladies through Jordan. An hour or two off will reset and refresh my mind, and I'll be back better than new.* "Yes! Let's do it. I'll raid the Moorehaven kitchen and pack a lunch. Meet me there in twenty. We can take my car."

"You got it, doll." Lake borrowed Moore's favorite term of endearment and hung up.

I'd completely forgotten that Hilt was standing right beside me for the whole phone call, and I nearly fell off my bike in surprise when he said really close to my ear, "Takin' a trip?"

"J-Just a picnic with Lake. I'll be back this evening." Worries crowded into my mind now that I'd made a decision. *What if Hilt hares off and investigates without me? What if Chloe needs me to run down a lead? Wait...* "Listen, if Chloe needs *any* help with proving Gabe's innocence while I'm grabbing lunch, will you lend a hand? Please? It's Gabe, and Trudie's depending on me."

"You know I'm always there for family." My uncle smiled with gentle approval. "'Bout time you quit being so dern responsible, anyway. I'll keep an eye on Chloe for ya. And she can keep one on me. We'll be fine. Now you better start pedalin' if you wanna be ready in twenty."

"Yessir." I eagerly leaped onto my bike.

Twenty minutes later, I'd stuffed a selection of picnic food and finger foods into a basket, loaded it into my tangerine hatchback, and pulled out of the garage, ready to hit the road. I'd even found a minute to pull my hair back into a short ponytail, throw on a summery white blouse, and strap on some sandals.

Lake sauntered up and folded himself into my passenger seat, wearing jean shorts and a Fiji-themed T-shirt. He squeezed my hand and smiled excitedly. "Lead on, driver."

I shifted into drive and jammed on the gas. Half an hour later, we'd crawled through Seacrest traffic and inched along the crowded highway far enough to reach the big curve around the Mount Watch Headland. I spotted a narrow pullout on the ocean side of the highway and darted across incoming traffic to claim it, jamming on the brakes before we slammed into the safety railing.

"Are we in an action movie now?" Lake teased as he eased back from bracing himself on the dash.

"Just upping your adrenaline a little."

"Ooh, yes, please."

We bailed out of my hatchback, and Lake fetched the picnic basket from the back. I carried the blanket, which would definitely be big enough for two. We slipped over the railing and made our way down a stony step-path chipped out of the basalt. The land eased its slope into a narrow nose that stretched out into the sea, protruding down and out from the windswept headland that loomed teasingly behind us. The stretch of land before us was mostly topped with hardy, windblown grass, but toward the far end, a tangle of coniferous trees grew along the ridge, offering both windbreak and privacy.

Just us, the trees, and the sea. I'm so glad we did this!

Lake and I spread the blanket in a patch of sun past the farthest row of trees. We sat down eagerly, but I hopped right back up in a hurry. After fishing a poky branch out from under the spot where I'd sat down, I gingerly eased myself back down again and sighed with contentment.

Lake's eyes held a gleam that matched the sultry intensity of his voice, and I couldn't stop leaning against him for warmth and support. But we were trying our best to enjoy a grown-up interaction, so somehow we managed to eat our meal without tumbling romantically to the blanket. We both kept starting sentences wondering about the murders or the treasure then catching ourselves and laughing. Our eyes would meet, and we'd silently agree: no serious topics. Not now. I'd whipped up a caprese salad, some cucumber sandwiches, and some melon-and-prosciutto skewers. We devoured them with gusto—and fed them to each other—unable to deny the second layer of our hunger.

Before we opened the chocolate cake bites, Lake pulled his warm, undivided attention away from me and looked south along the coast. "You hear that?"

I nibbled on a mozzarella drop with my best sexy nibbling, assuming he'd say something about how hard his heart was racing. "Hmm?"

But he wasn't being romantic. "That's the *Mazu II*. I don't remember a tour for right now on its schedule, but maybe Harry accommodated a last-minute customer. It's got to be close for me to hear it up here. Let's go take a peek." He slipped out of my arms and stood up, ignoring my overly dramatic, lonely flop onto the blanket.

I can take the boy out of the sea, but I can't take the sea out of the boy. I sighed. "Sure." Standing, I slipped my hand through his, and we crossed the open grass toward the stubby end of the headland.

Lake gave me an uncertain glance. "It'd be weird to look up and see the boat's owner spying on you, right?"

I shrugged. "Depends what mystery genre you're living in."

He snorted with laughter. "No, really. Let's crawl up to the edge. I don't want to spook a customer."

It was my turn to snort. "But you're okay with spying? Okay, let's do this. I'm sure either Sarah or Butch will be interested in exactly what army-crawling to the edge of a cliff on a warm summer day is like."

Lake squeezed my hand. "That's my girl."

I squeezed back. "You owe me."

"I really do."

We dropped to hands and knees as we approached the cliff. Soon, I was belly-wriggling my way to the very edge. The grass retreated to cracks in the weathered stone, and I carefully avoided dragging my nice white blouse through blobs of seagull poop.

The view from the crest of the cliff was worth all that silly effort. About sixty feet below, the crystal-blue water of the Pacific foamed gently at the foot of the rock. A couple of seabirds wheeled below me, nipping insects out of the air. I could see the undulating lines of approaching waves. And Lake's new tour boat, the *Mazu II*, idled a hundred feet or so from shore. Its shadow rippled with the waves.

"I don't see anyone," I said. "Harry must be piloting it, right? Where are his guests?"

Before Lake could answer, a diver flopped onto the rail from beneath the sunroof, arms dangling above the water. Then he slipped over the edge and splashed bonelessly into the ocean. Lake and I glanced worriedly at each other. Whoever that was, he hadn't seemed fit for diving. *Drunk, maybe?*

Then another man's arms appeared below the boat's roof as he flung something the size of a breadbox after the diver. He wore a long-sleeved red flannel shirt, which Harry wouldn't be caught dead in. Then he tossed over a small coil of dark rope. I realized with horror that it was attached to the weight and the diver.

I gasped. *How many times have my authors written villains who murdered their victims this way?* "Lake, that's not Harry! Some guy's drowning that diver! He just tied him to a weight! The diver's floppy because he's unconscious."

Lake rocketed up and ran back from the edge. I was slower to follow, and my mind was frantically thumbing through its Rolodex of What To Do When I See Someone Being Drowned. Almost all the pages were blank.

Below, the boat gunned its engine and shot off up the coast. Lake ripped his shirt off and kicked his shoes on top of it. "Pippa, call 911. I'll bring the diver to the beach right down there." He pointed to the tiny strip of sand just south of where we stood, between our headland and the next.

I whipped my phone out of my pocket even as my eyes locked onto his sharply defined abs and the dark curls in his chest hair. "I'm on it, but why—"

He ran for the cliff's edge. I stood rooted to the spot, stunned, unable to process what was happening. Then my boyfriend hurled himself into thin air—empty space—off the edge of a cliff.

"Lake, what are you *doing*?" I screeched. My feet somehow got me to the rocky tip of the headland without pitching me over in his wake. I stared down in utter panic, gripping my phone like a vise.

Lake dived, arms spread wide, body perfectly arched. He fell, somersaulted twice in quick succession, and kept falling, with the warm wind seeming to buoy him up. Then he straightened out, feet together, and stomped his way into the sea with his arms at his sides. The ocean parted with a mighty tearing sound. I could have sworn Lake simply ripped the Pacific apart with the beautiful force of his will, and it recognized one of its own and let him pass unharmed.

I had never fully understood Lake's skills as a former junior Olympic diver so clearly before, but his mastery was absolutely undeniable. My shoulders sagged in relief and awe. *Jason Momoa, eat your heart out!*

He dived deep, and his outline grew dim, but I saw him swimming down for the diver. The man's mortal peril snapped me out of my gawking, and I called emergency services. After giving them all the pertinent information, I hung up and stared downward. I felt compelled to hold my breath for as long as Lake was under the surface, but I was so worried for both men that I couldn't manage it. I was drowning in the moment, in all that briny uncertainty. I gasped like a heroine wearing one of Gabby's corsets.

Finally, Lake surfaced and flung water from his dark hair. He began towing an unmoving man in a wetsuit to shore, lifeguard style. My heart unclenched. *The man I love is so amazing. An actual hero. He literally just dived off a cliff to save someone's life. I sure hope the things I do make him proud too. Otherwise, I'll just be disappointing him.*

I grabbed Lake's shirt and shoes and bolted back up the crest of the headland, abandoning the picnic. We'd passed a tiny pullout that let about three compact cars park for access to the narrow beach below, so I hopped back in my car, pulled a daring U-turn in the middle of Highway 101, and sped around the curve. I skidded into the tiny, empty parking spot and backed as close as I could to the railing to leave room for the ambulance. I thudded down a set of old wooden stairs and down the trail that followed a barely damp creek through the tiniest primeval forest I'd ever seen. Or maybe it flashed by because I was too scared to track time properly. When I reached the open sand, I saw Lake in the distance, performing CPR. I dashed over, flinging clumps of wet sand from my shoes.

"Is he alive?" I fell to my knees on the other side of the man. It took a second for me to recognize his face, slack with unconsciousness: Wade, from the marine-salvage team.

Lake, doing chest compressions, simply said, "Well, he isn't dead yet."

I took turns doing CPR with Lake for a few minutes until a trio of paramedics ran up, bearing a stretcher and bright-red bags. They took over from us, and Lake and I flopped into the warm sand, exhausted.

I reached over and squeezed his hand. "You did good, Hero."

Lake brushed away my accolade with a shake of his damp hair. "When I got down to him, he was wearing his regulator, but the tank was empty. If someone was trying to make his death seem accidental, they failed spectacularly by tying him to some cement blocks. Good thing I always carry my dive knife."

Two paramedics loaded Wade onto the stretcher while the third squeezed one of those clear bags over his nose and mouth. A hundred urgent questions flooded my brain. Who had been on the boat with Wade? Who would Wade have trusted enough to get on the boat with? Or had he been kidnapped? Once he woke up, surely the police would catch the guy who'd just tried to kill him.

"It can't be Gabe," I said with triumphant breathlessness. "Whoever did this, it can't be him. Gabe's in custody right now, so Mal has to let him go."

"You know it's not gonna be that easy." Lake's tone implied a double meaning, and I caught both sides. Just because Gabe hadn't tried to kill Wade didn't mean he hadn't killed Zach. And trying to force Mallory to release a prisoner she wasn't fully confident was innocent would be as impossible as desalinating the ocean.

North past Lake's shoulder, a dark streak of fresh smoke rose from behind the headland we'd just been picnicking on, into the midday sky, marring its perfect blue. "Uh, Lake?" I pointed.

We both stood again, staring at the ominous black smoke. "Is that my boat?" he breathed.

Somewhere in the distance, the *Mazu II* exploded. The faint boom rolled across the sea. Slowly, Lake sank to his knees in the damp sand, as if the explosion had struck him hard enough to topple him.

In a way, it had.

19

"I never eavesdrop. I just happen to overhear a whole lot of interest-ing conversations."
Raymond Moore, 1937

"I'M SO GLAD YOU'RE both okay." Jordan squeezed my arm and picked a piece off the strawberry delight muffin I'd smuggled in-to the coffee bar from Emily's shop. I'd barely touched mine or my dirty chai, even though the Coffee Breezes barista added exactly the right amount of bitter coffee to the sweet and spicy chai. "I can't be-lieve Lake lost *another* boat named Mazu," she continued musingly. "I think that name is cursed now. He should pick something else for his next boat."

After my picnic with Lake was interrupted by his dramatic water rescue and the explosion of his boat, I'd left Lake to deal with the wreck—at his insistence—and returned to town to seek solace with Jordan at the coffee shop inside Seven Vistas. I couldn't embrace her attempt to cheer me up, though. "If Lake had been on the *Mazu II*..." My gaze vacantly aimed over Jordan's shoulder, where I could see the glistening Pacific through Coffee Breezes' floor-to-ceiling windows. *Would he have been overpowered and killed?* My mind shied away from Lake's last brush with death aboard another *Mazu. He's a strong swimmer, strong everything. Maybe he'd have caught the person who tried to kill Wade.*

"But he wasn't, and that's why he was able to save Wade's life," Jordan said firmly. "Was Harry able to say whether the guy who took the boat from the marina looked like Connor?"

I shook my head. Lake's new pilot was nearly beside himself with frustration and embarrassment. While Lake was busy talking to law enforcement about the incident and checking on Wade in the hospital, Harry had taken to texting me so I could update Lake later. "Harry says no one was scheduled to take the *Mazu II* out. He talked to everyone who was anywhere near the marina, and the best info he got was that a couple of guys walked onto the boat like they belonged there. He doesn't know how they got a key. All of Blade and Boom's keys are accounted for."

"That sounds like Wade walked on with his would-be killer. But honestly, it could be anyone, with any sort of motive." Jordan made a sour frown. "And now I've fallen victim to the Curse of Seacrest—suspecting everyone. Again."

"Welcome to my world." I squeezed her hand. "We all succumb to unnecessary suspicion eventually. Me, I kind of have to live there."

Our phones blooped text alerts at the same time, and we scooped them up. The text was from Lori, and my heart lodged in my throat. But Jordan read the text out loud. "Wade still unconscious. Will update as info comes in."

"If he wakes up soon, he can tell us what really happened." Another text came in, this time from Lake. "Lake's left the hospital. Says he's going to be in his office, filling out insurance forms. He didn't even attach any emojis. He must be exhausted."

Jordan's voice dropped to a whisper. "I think it was Connor, that he's really still in town, attacking his former team. Who else could it be?"

I shrugged helplessly. "It's the best guess I've heard so far, but I still don't know what his motive could be. I should check in on

Patrice and see how she's doing. Maybe she can shed some light for me."

Jordan pursed her lips in a thoughtful moue. "What if... and I'm just guessing here... what if Patrice drugged herself to throw off suspicion? We know for sure she's still around."

I gave her idea an admiring nod. "Seacrest Curse or not, that's clever. No one suspects the victims, do they? Like Ogden's Deadly Damsel. She tricks one character into attacking her, and then she manipulates a couple of other characters into actions they believe will avenge or defend her. She acts like the helpless victim, but she's the mastermind all along. Maybe Patrice is doing something similar—forcing someone to act on her behalf until she's the only member of the team left, and she can claim the treasure for herself."

Jordan rested her hand over mine for a second. "Let me check in on her. She's here in the hotel, so I can just pop up to her room or catch her if she heads out."

I tilted my head and gave her a cynically raised eyebrow. "Yeah, great idea. Waltz in all by yourself to confront a potential murderer. That's never gone wrong, ever. Do you even *read* mysteries?"

Jordan only chuckled. "I do, and you know it. I was going to make it clear that I only wanted information on Connor."

"Ah," I proclaimed sagely, "the old Alternate Suspect Distraction Gambit."

"It's not really called that, is it?"

Jordan's tone indicated that my impromptu trope title wasn't quite up to snuff, so I caved and giggled, shaking my head.

"Yeah, don't give up your day job. Anyway, if it'll make you feel better, I'll take someone with me. One of the Gossips."

"At *least* one."

A lanky figure caught my eye out in the broad hotel hallway. Mandy shambled toward the lobby, covered head to toe in dirt. A harness and utility belt bore spelunking tools that appeared as encrusted with dirt as the rest of her. Her blond ponytail was dark with sweat and grime, and she held her left wrist against her chest as if she'd injured it. My suspicious side teamed up with my jealous side, and I gave Jordan a silent nod that said, *I'm going to follow that woman*. Jordan subtly nodded in return, and following Girl Code, pretended to study her phone so I could slip away without drawing any attention from other customers in the small coffee shop.

I'd barely stepped onto the thick carpet of the hallway when I saw Lake loitering by the potted palm tree at the corner of the lobby ahead. *But he said he'd be filling out forms in his office,* I thought, trying not to be suspiciously stalker-esque. From his perspective, I was still hidden behind the palm leaves, so he didn't see me.

He saw Mandy, though. "What happened to you?" he blurted, heading for her.

I veered into a side hallway that led to an ice machine and pressed myself against the wall. "Lake, hey," Mandy said. "I think I'm onto something with the location of the treasure. But I started a little rock fall and hurt my arm. Gotta take a minute to patch myself up before I head back out."

"You heard about Wade?"

"Yeah, Patrice sent me a text. I'm so relieved he's safe in a hospital. Wade's a great guy."

"You sure you want to keep chasing this treasure right now? Someone clearly has it out for your team."

"But I'm so close now! I can almost smell the gold." Excitement radiated from her voice. "I'm sure I'm on the right track."

"That's great!" Lake's voice sounded just as excited, and my mood soured further. "You need some help upstairs?"

She doesn't need any help, I thought firmly at Lake, doing my best impression of the Jedi mind trick.

"I don't need any help, but thank you, really."

Holy handbags! It worked!

Mandy continued, "Listen... Lake, can I trust you?"

No, you can't trust him, I thought, trying my luck again.

"Of course. Anything."

Cripes, I should've saved my Jedi powers for this one instead.

Mandy took a couple of seconds before she spoke, so I dropped to my knees and peered around the corner with one eye. Mandy had pulled Lake right up against the wall behind a closer palm tree, farther from the ears in the lobby but only a dozen feet away from me. When she spoke, her voice was barely above a whisper. "I'm afraid. I'm sure it's Connor out there, hunting everyone down out of some sick, twisted sense of revenge."

"Revenge for what?" Lake asked.

But Mandy kept talking over him. "See, you were there when Patrice got found in that alley. And you actually rescued Wade. You're literally the only person who can't possibly be trying to kill people all over town."

"Well, Pippa was with me both times, actually. She can't be the killer, either." My heart warmed at Lake's matter-of-fact defense of me to the woman who was doing her darnedest to sway him.

"I trust *you*, Lake." Mandy met his eyes directly and rested a hand on his upper arm. "Come with me tomorrow while I find the treasure, once and for all. I would've taken Wade, but... I really need someone to watch my back. It would make me feel so much safer to know you're there with me."

Lake hesitated, and though I couldn't see his face past the palm tree, I could picture his perplexed expression. I rolled my eyes and slipped back around the corner. *Do men actually fall for that crap?*

Lake's voice sounded hesitant, but it held way more interest than I was comfortable with. "Well, I am down one tour boat. I guess I do have a little free time on my hands until I can wrangle a replacement. Text me the details, and I'll be ready."

A soft smack reached my ears. She'd kissed him! *Oh, no, you did not just get lippy-skippy with my boyfriend, you—* I shot up to my feet and rounded the corner in time to see her shuffling tiredly for the elevators, with Lake watching her go, one hand rubbing his cheek as if to subtly erase her touch. *Oh, a cheek kiss? Well... still! Not cool!* The elevators opened, and Mandy waited for a group of well-to-do people to exit before she slipped inside, out of view. Lake strode toward the elevator she chose, and I stalked out after him, raring to claim my man from her dirt-encrusted clutches. But Lake didn't wave to Mandy. He flagged down the family that had left the elevator.

"Mr. Masaki. I was hoping to catch you," Lake said.

I ground to a halt in the hallway.

"I'm afraid there's been an unfortunate accident with the tour boat I was supposed to use for our sunset tour this evening. I wanted to let you know in person that I'm scrambling for a replacement boat, but I might not find one in time."

Mortified, I whirled around and quick-timed it back to Coffee Breezes. Lake hadn't lied about his whereabouts and sneaked over to Seven Vistas to find Mandy. He'd obviously stopped by on his way to his office to smooth over the loss of his boat with one of his richest clients. *I'm such an idiot!*

I slipped back into my chair at Jordan's table. "Well, that went poorly," I grumbled, comforted only by the fact that Lake had wiped her kiss off without even knowing I was there.

"I know, I stuck my phone into the hallway and got it all on video." She waggled her phone at me.

My eyes widened.

"Even got your head peeking around the corner to spy on them. Adorable stuff, really."

"Since when is it okay to spy on a spy like that?" I asked, nonplussed.

"Don't worry. I've got your back. Girl Code, remember? I only recorded them for proof of their conversation, in case we need it."

"What would we need that for?"

"Justification for you murdering her, of course. I'll be your star witness. She had it coming."

Jordan's wicked smile managed to cheer me up. "You're the best. I guess I should let you get back to work. I gotta get back to Moorehaven, anyway."

"Call me if anything comes up." Her tone told me she wasn't referring to the local attacks. "And in case it becomes relevant, I have a new shovel, and we can steal a body bag from Lori's office." She dropped her coffee cup in the trash and walked with me back toward the lobby.

I nudged her shoulder with mine. "I do not deserve you."

Jordan studied Lake and the Masaki family. "It's *him* who doesn't deserve *you*." She nodded toward Lake. "I bet we can get two body bags, easy."

"No, no," I said, warding off her murderous friendliness, "there's still hope for him."

I caught Lake's eye as he stepped away from Mr. Masaki, and his whole face brightened.

"Lots and lots of hope," I told Jordan.

I wrapped my arms around Lake in the middle of the lush Seven Vistas lobby and kissed him to within an inch of his life. Then I strutted out, leaving Lake breathless and dizzy and Jordan laughing so hard behind her concierge desk that she could hardly breathe, either.

20

"*K*id, *you got heart, but if you model your writing career on my life, it's your liver I'll be concerned about.*"
Raymond Moore, 1972

"I UNDERSTAND IF YOU can't. I know the charter." Chloe's slim fingers clutched the handle of her black-and-red fleur-de-lis-patterned rolling suitcase as she stood on Moorehaven's welcome mat. Her expression was a combination of sadness and determination, and she refused to come in off the porch until she had her answer. The cats had already made up their minds, though. They both twined around her feet and rubbed their cheeks against her suitcase.

Hilt and I exchanged shocked glances. Then Hilt reached out with a weathered arm, grasped Chloe by the elbow, and bodily hauled her inside Moorehaven. "Ain't no question, doll. You're staying here. You're family."

Chloe's eyes were unusually wide and vulnerable, and she glanced uncertainly from Hilt to me. "Are you sure?"

Moorehaven belonged to me, not to Hilt. As much as Hilt might want to shelter Chloe, it did go against the charter I was obligated to follow in order to continue my ownership of Moorehaven. It took me less than a second to make my decision. "Of course I'm sure. I won't tell if you won't. We do happen to have a few empty rooms at the moment. Which one do you want?"

Chloe dropped her eyes to her gaudy suitcase. "I'll stay in the Oubliette, if that's okay. If I come and go by those back stairs, no one

"

else will even know I'm staying here." She glanced down the main hallway and into the parlor, planning her route to the back corner of the mansion. I was fully confident that, if any of my authors had been around to pick up on her situation, they'd have been all for letting her stay too.

Hilt sensed her discomfort, so he picked up her suitcase and telescoped its handle shut. "Rule number one about breaking the rules: act like you're supposed to be doing it. I work here, for criminy's sake. I'm supposed to carry people's luggage around." Without another word, he sauntered through the parlor.

I put an arm around Chloe's shoulder as she followed Hilt into the library. "Your father didn't make you move out, did he?"

She shook her head. "I left. But don't get mad. I did what you told me first. I told him it wasn't fair to ask me to work for free, especially when I already had a full-time paying job that he was trying to drag me away from. I asked him if we could make the schedule outside of my work hours here, I even told him I'd be more available once the summer season's over, and I also asked him straight up to pay me for my work. I *am* a skilled tour guide. I deserve compensation."

"Good for you! Did he get angry with you?"

We reached the winding stairs up to the Oubliette, and Chloe paused while the cats trotted up and out of sight. She stared up the steps and sighed. She probably couldn't see her future much further than the curve of the stairwell, and I knew how daunting that feeling could be. Before I'd come to Moorehaven, I couldn't see around the next corner either.

"Actually," Chloe said, "he kind of stared at me and waited for the punch line. He honestly thought I was joking." She started up the steps, and I followed. "All at once, it hit me that he still saw me as that little seven-year-old kid. I knew I'd have to do something drastic to change his mind. So I said I was moving out, and if he changed his mind, he could reach me through you. I hope that was okay."

"Of course it is. How'd he take that news?"

"Basically more baffled staring. Dad doesn't handle change well."

We reached the upper landing. Hilt, as spry as ever, was already setting Chloe's suitcase on a chair. Rex and Svetlana had already claimed the very center of the unmade bed for themselves.

"I'll go fetch some linens for you. The mulberry sheets are freshly laundered. I know you like that color."

My heart warmed at his attention to detail. Tiny personal touches like that were what made Hilt such a good host. A small, grateful smile flashed across Chloe's lips.

After Hilt descended around the first curve, she said, "I promise I won't stay here any longer than I have to. I don't want you to get in trouble over me. I love this place. First thing tomorrow, I'll start looking for a place of my own. I mean, I have my own money. I can pay rent and everything."

I grinned. "See? Totally an adult."

We got Chloe settled in for the evening, and then Hilt and I made the rounds, making sure windows and doors were secure, and that all our authors were present and accounted for. They fussed a bit over the attention, but I could tell they appreciated our concern.

"It ain't against the charter if it's an emergency, Pippa," Hilt said as he wiggled the lock on the rear sliding door, our last check for the night.

"You're preaching to the choir," I replied. "I'll build a secret room with my own two hands and hide her in it if I have to. I'm glad you're as on board with this as I am."

Hilt's hands fell to his sides, and he stared at the door latch for a few seconds before meeting my eyes. "She reminds me of you a little, is all." Taken aback, I could only smile.

Hilt's offer to take me on as paid staff seven years prior to the next Christmas had changed my life and might even have saved it. I had always been amazed by and grateful for his generosity, but I'd never stopped to think how he might have felt about *me*. What he'd said about Chloe gave me a big clue, though: he cared enough about her—about me—to break the rules.

My parents hadn't been the most understanding when it came to the depression I suffered right after my senior year in college. Hilt hadn't simply wanted another pair of hands around Moorehaven. He had breached family taboos and broken unwritten rules in order to reach through my tangled family ties and pull me to safety. That hadn't been the only assistance I'd needed, but without Hilt's magnanimous gesture, I didn't want to think about where I might have ended up. He'd broken rules for me, and now we were breaking rules together for Chloe.

Finally, a smile broke out across my face. "Uncle Hilt, you're just an old romantic hero, aren't you? Bucking the system and saving damsels. Moore rubbed off on you *hard*."

He ducked his chin like a shy schoolboy, and all at once I was certain he'd been telling the truth about the 1964 drawer. He couldn't possibly be a thief. "It really wasn't you who broke into the police archives."

Hilt shook his head. "Honest to God, Pippa."

I lowered my eyelids, thinking hard. "Well, somebody did. The question is, were they trying to frame you, or were they looking for something in the old records?"

"That right there is a great question to ponder some more tomorrow. Sleep well. See you in the morning." Hilt ambled past me in the direction of his front-turret bedroom.

A faint latching noise woke me in the middle of the night. I sat up and listened with my eyes closed in the darkness, shifting the warm, sleepy bodies of my cats enough to make them meow grumpily. I didn't hear it again, but something compelled me to get out of bed and check on things. I shuffled into my bunny slippers and slipped out into the pantry, and to my surprise, Rex and Svetlana accompanied me. That more than anything told me something was going on—nothing could get my cats out of bed before they smelled breakfast.

I peeked through the rooms on the first floor, but no one was about. By the time I reached the library, I realized I had lost Svetlana somewhere. Following my own animal instinct, I retraced my steps until I found her by the front door, staring intently. She sniffed the air, and I got a hunch.

I grabbed a spare umbrella from a communal collection in the corner, brandishing it as I opened the door, and both cats trailed me onto the porch. The street was blessedly empty and quiet, the night velvety and cool. In the amber glow of the old-fashioned lamps that lined the boardwalk across the street, two men sat on a bench facing the sea. Tails high, Rex and Svetlana trotted right out across the street toward them. After a jaw-cracking yawn, I followed them.

At the Moorehaven curb, I recognized Ogden on the left side of the bench. To my surprise, he was speaking with none other than Harry Shamsi. I'd been assuming that, with Ogden's anxiety, he had never met anyone outside Moorehaven. *Silly me. That man can text up a storm.* I hung back, not wanting to interrupt what seemed to be a deep nighttime conversation. But despite the crash of the waves below, I couldn't help overhearing as the breeze brought their words to my ears.

Ogden was saying, "And I started wondering about all of those lateral-thinking puzzles. You know, the ones that start off, 'A man lies dead in a room with no windows' or something?" Harry nodded, and Ogden continued, "A bunch of those have a melted block of ice involved somehow. It's a classic time-delay tool. And they found that mysterious water in Zach's throat. It seemed like a logical assumption to me."

Harry's dark hair bobbed in agreement. "Makes perfect sense to me. So how does the killer move around during a treasure fair with a block of ice?"

Ogden waved one hand, dismissing the idea. "It doesn't have to be a big block. In fact, it doesn't have to be a single piece at all. Think about it: it's hot, and people get thirsty. Half the town was walking around holding potential murder weapons. I mean, I stayed in my room because my anxiety didn't want to go to the fair, the party pooper. But Jennifer texted me pictures."

"Ahh," Harry said. "You're talking about ice cubes in soda. I heard there was nothing in his throat but water, though. No soda."

Ogden pondered that for a minute. I stood rapt several feet behind their bench, thrilled as I listened to them work through the conundrum of how exactly Zach had been killed.

Finally, Ogden said simply, "Not everybody likes soda. A hot night, an absolutely massive crowd, would the vendors be surprised if someone simply asked for a cup of ice? Would they even remember who asked?"

My brain burned hot as I realized I had all the pieces I needed to figure out how Zach died. Ice cubes weren't quite the right answer—surely they'd be too big, allowing air between them, letting Zach continue to breathe even while unconscious. I'd seen something. What had I seen? I racked my brain, and then I had it. "Have you guys ever tried the cotton candy burritos they sell here on the boardwalk?" I blurted.

Ogden yelped, stumbled up from his seat, and vanished over the edge of the cliff. Harry and I lurched forward in shock, only to hear Ogden wheezing with laughter from just out of sight. He stood up on a small ledge, resting his forearms on the grassy edge of the cliff.

"Relax, guys. If anyone's going to freak out here, it's going to be me, and as you see, I'm fine. The looks on your faces! Didn't you see the cats, Pippa?" He pointed to Rex and Svetlana, who had curled up under his spot on the bench, listening to his easy baritone voice. "They gave you away a few minutes ago. They'd never be out at night without you. And I knew about this little safety ledge here because I can see it from the second-floor bay window." He pointed to his usual Moorehaven vantage point behind me. "I told myself that if you said anything other than to call the cats back, I'd pretend to panic off the cliff. I realize now that my idea may have alarmed you without cause, and I apologize. But it was really funny in my head."

Harry, still unaccustomed to author antics, gave me a wide-eyed look of disbelief, but I had to shake my head and chuckle. "You did freak me out there for a second, Ogden, but I really should have figured out that you knew I was here because of the cats. I admire the way you own your anxiety, instead of letting it own you."

Ogden clambered back on top of the cliff and gave me a short bow.

Harry tapped a finger toward me and said, "What were you saying about those cotton candy burritos?"

I pointed at him. "I had one. They're delicious. And do you know what was being sold right next to them at the Treasure Fair Tuesday night?"

The two men exchanged glances, shrugged, and shook their heads.

"Snow cones. Shaved ice."

"Eureka!" Ogden clapped his hands over his mouth and hunched, chagrined. "Oops, I kind of forgot that it's two in the morning. My bad."

"Shaved ice would definitely be a good way to suffocate someone." Harry warmed to his icy subject. "All you'd have to do is pack it down nice and tight. You could even leave them there, unconscious, and go make yourself an alibi if time was tight."

I nodded. "The shaved ice would melt faster than cubes, leaving us with the proverbial puddle of water and, without any flavored syrup to point us in the right direction, no idea what actually happened. Guys, I think we just used lateral thinking to figure out how Zach died. The murder weapon was plain shaved ice."

"Now we just need to figure out whodunit." Ogden nibbled on a nail.

I yawned again. "Let's save that for the morning, please. We'll all think more clearly after a good night's sleep and an awesome breakfast. But if you want to," I suggested impishly, "you can text our breakthrough to Chief Tavish right now, Ogden."

He nodded slowly, warming to the idea. "Time and tides, and all that. What's her number?"

I recited it from memory, and as we said good night to Harry and left the seaside bench behind, I couldn't help gleefully imagining Mallory's indignant squawk as she was awakened by Ogden's helpful text.

At the foot of the stairs, Ogden murmured, "Good night, Pippa. Thank you for letting me help. It means a lot."

Touched, I squeezed his hand and replied, "You got us started. I'm the one who just helped out. I'll see you in the morning with your breakfast tray."

That night, I slept like the dead. Refreshed and rejuvenated from our breakthrough in the wee hours, I got up so fast that Svetlana and Rex meowed irritably at me for disturbing their slumber.

Chloe showed up to help with breakfast, looking like she'd also had the best night's sleep in a long time. My authors were worn out, though—and Ogden wasn't even awake yet—so I didn't create a pop quiz.

Once Sarah, Butch, and Ashley had eaten at least a few blintzes at breakfast and polished off two pots of coffee, I said, "So we think we've figured out how Zach was killed, if not by whom." I filled them in on the shaved-ice theory to murmurs that held an indecent amount of interest but no malice. Everyone seemed surprised—or impressed—and my gut told me none of them had been responsible for Zach's murder. I continued, "And I also think we're close to solving Ramòn's murder. It's about time, isn't it, Hilt? And we'll do it together."

Everyone stopped eating and stared. I glanced at Hilt. The wrinkles around his eyes pulled tight in a pained but intense expression.

"Hilt and I will be heading to the lighthouse after breakfast to tackle the next step," I explained.

Ashley leaned forward, putting her elbow in a bit of leftover whipped cream on her plate. "You have to let me come with you."

Sarah glanced between Ashley and me. "Hey, I want to come too. Don't you leave without me."

Everyone turned to Butch. He leaned back in his chair and sighed. "All right, all right. I'll come along and keep everyone safe." I saw the smile hiding at the corner of his mouth. Perhaps having a couple of formidable older gentlemen with us wouldn't be a bad thing. Teenagers weren't always predictable, as Chloe had demonstrated.

Soon, we had a whole troupe formed and ready to depart. Svetlana curled around everyone's ankles except Ashley's, begging us not to leave. The next clue called to me, though, and I had to listen. Hilt needed to know what happened to his friend.

I texted Lake. *You still at home?*

Nope. Getting ready for a tour. What's up?

Can I pop over there to ask the repair kids a question?

Yes, but what are you really doing?

Thanks! I followed up with lots of hearts and big cheesy smile emojis and stuffed my phone back in my pocket. *I have my posse. Nothing will go wrong in Lake's place.*

My uncle and I led the way down the street and across the bridge to the other side of town. As we stepped off the bridge's sidewalk, a pair of familiar folks caught my eye a block ahead. Ernie Ross and Maggie Skinner were holding hands like a pair of young lovers and strolling among several groups of coffee-buzzed tourists who were talking too loudly and taking pictures of perfectly ordinary business signs and fire hydrants.

My heart melted. Maybe time could heal all wounds, after all.

We turned toward the lighthouse. The wind picked up, gusting crisp and cool against my face. I felt close to the final truth about what happened to Ramòn Moreno, and my own troubles seemed to blow away behind me on the breeze. We reached the lighthouse, and sure enough, four bikes rested against the whitewashed curve of the broken-topped building.

"What's this place?" Sarah asked.

"It's the old lighthouse," Hilt said in his best Captain Obvious voice. "Built during Prohibition, but it didn't outlast the era by much. Now Pippa's gentleman friend lives in the basement. The police chief assigns local delinquents to repair work instead of fines or jail time." He pointed to the bikes.

"And we're here to ask about one particular crime of theirs." I led the way down the tightly curving metal staircase into a small open area that took up a third of the circular floor space, judging by the curve of the wall. A closed door led to the guest room—the room where Mal kept threatening to "crash for the night." Four teenagers, working in different spots around the space, looked up from their half-hearted tasks in alarm.

My attention riveted on the guest room, and an answer to two problems at once blossomed in my head. Chloe needed a place to stay, and Lake wanted to keep Mallory from horning in on the guest room she technically owned. How could Mallory refuse the room to the daughter of a town councilman? For one bright, shining moment, I forgot where I was and smiled.

Then the beefiest of the teenagers put down his paint roller and faced us. "Can I help you?"

Before I could speak, a skinny kid with shaggy dark hair, a dark smattering of freckles, and a bucket of spackle said, "Dude, Cody, should they even be down here? I mean, the chief said—"

"My boyfriend lives here," I said. "But I need to talk to *you* right now."

"Whoa, we didn't steal anything," a guy in a blue plaid shirt said from the back of the small room. He innocently held his paint roller up. "Mr. Ivens locks his door downstairs, like, every single morning. We just do the repairs. If you lost, like, some panties or something, you'll have to talk to him, okay?"

Sarah snorted with laughter, while Butch and Hilt turned pink. Ashley just shook her head and smiled.

Cody mumbled, "Dude, Lonnie. Geez."

I put my hands on my hips and wrenched the conversation back on track. "I need to know whose house you burgled when you stole all those vinyl records last winter."

All four boys' eyes widened, and they stiffened as if they'd been overinflated. They glanced warily among themselves. Then Cody, the implicit leader, said, "If we *did* do that, what business is it of yours?"

A low growl emanated from behind me, and for a split second, I thought Hilt was losing his temper. But Butch pressed forward past me and barked, "The lady asked you for a simple piece of information, youngster! Are you telling me you're incapable of respecting your elders, or are you so dense that you can't remember back that far?"

The boys stiffened again with alarm at Butch's impression of a drill sergeant. "No," Cody admitted.

"No, what?" Butch snapped back.

"Uh, no, sir?" Cody replied, squirming a little.

Butch sucked in a forceful breath through his nose, and Cody flinched. I stifled a giggle. I was pretty sure that Butch had only been asking Cody to pick one of his two options.

"This is the part where you answer the lady, son," Butch said in a gentler tone.

Cody blinked and started to turn his head toward his compatriots then thought better of it. "Uh, what was the question again? Uh, ma'am?"

"Whose house did you burgle those vinyl records from? It's the same house where you found that gold coin." Behind me, my authors murmured interestedly at my latest clue.

"Oh, dude." Lonnie pointed his paint roller toward Cody. "That coin, dude. Remember? We found it in the junk drawer."

"I can't believe the pawn shop guy bought it," Cody said smugly.

I was losing them again. "It's a genuine golden coin. A piece of eight. And, you know, just coincidentally, it came from a *murder scene*."

"Holy sh—uh, holy cow! Really? No, we had nothing to do with that." Cody held his hands up and took a step back from Butch, who glowered at them from beneath his bushy eyebrows.

"Unless you boys have mastered time travel, we know you got nothin' to do with that murder," Hilt said. "But you can help us figure out who did. Whose house did you steal the coin from? Please."

Hilt's "please" seemed to strike home with Cody. He scratched his nose and slumped his shoulders. "That fence guy. Those vinyls were his. And the coin. I swear, we didn't even know it was there. We found it by accident. Look, we're paying for other stuff we did by fixing this place up. You don't need to tell the chief about that too, do you?"

I looked over when Hilt didn't reply. His face had gone an unnerving shade of white. Belatedly, I realized what Cody's words meant. *That fence guy.*

"Let's go, Hilt. Let's finish this." I pressed on my uncle's shoulder until he began climbing the staircase like a tottering robot.

"Wait, which fence guy?" Ashley asked. "The one with the criminal record?"

I was too busy keeping Hilt moving to answer her. I had to get him outside. A breath of fresh air would help.

Behind me, Sarah and Ashley followed us, but Butch wasn't quite ready to leave. "You boys get back to work. I want this place finished and done with, pronto! Don't make me come back down here."

The boys straightened up one last time and replied in unison, "Sir, yes, *sir!*"

I nudged Hilt upward toward the lighthouse's outer door, murmuring soothing words from behind him all the way up the stairs. Hilt burst outside onto the old concrete pad and heaved like he'd come up for air after being underwater too long. A tsunami of guilt and loss had held him under for fifty years, and that first breath of air had to be painful. He clapped a hand to his forehead and leaned against the bright outer wall of the lighthouse.

Sarah touched my arm. "We should call the police. Your uncle's in no fit state to go confronting anyone right now."

I nodded and reached for my phone. "I just saw—"

"Hilt, wait!" Ashley cried.

I spun to see my uncle legging it up the street along the river, already a dozen yards ahead.

Butch stepped out of the lighthouse. "Dang fool, what's he gonna do?"

"That's what I'm worried about!" My legs rocketed into motion as I gave chase. "Ramòn was one of his best friends!"

"C'mon, then, let's go!" Butch hollered, wrangling the others into a posse.

With my heart in my throat, I led my authors after Hilt. He hadn't gotten his man fifty years ago. He'd do whatever it took to get him now. But I couldn't let him break the law. As a former police officer, he'd never forgive himself.

"Uncle Hilt, no!"

21

WITH MY AUTHORS POUNDING the pavement behind me, I dashed up the street after Hilt. With trembling fingers, I dialed Mallory's number.

She answered after the second ring. "Winterbourne. What do you want?"

"Mallory, please help me. Hilt's learned who killed Ramòn Moreno, and he's running him down."

"Justice is a good thing, Winterbourne." Her tone was infuriatingly casual.

"No, Mallory, I mean he's literally chasing after him down the street! If you thought your best friend went missing, but they were actually murdered, and fifty years later you figured out who got away with their murder, what would you do to them?"

My heart pounded in my ears, and my lungs wheezed, as I waited for Mallory's reply. "What's his twenty?" she asked coolly.

Hilt was nowhere to be seen. *Crap, I've lost him!* "He was on North River Street a second ago. He must've turned onto Cedar." I stopped at the end of the Cedar Street bridge to catch my breath. "Probably going south. We passed Ernie and Maggie earlier. We all saw them. They were heading south. Hilt's gonna be looking for Ernie."

Over the phone, I heard Mallory's cruiser siren come to life. "I'm on my way. If you find him first, do what you can, Winterbourne, but don't be stupid." She hung up.

I stood panting at the corner and stared down the streets that met at the intersection. I couldn't see Hilt at all. My authors puffed up behind me. "Did anyone see which way he went?"

A running figure caught my eye down the bridge. For a split second, I thought it was Hilt, and that he'd changed his mind. But the man's gait was fluid and graceful, and I knew that dark hair and French-artist profile intimately.

"Lake?"

"I was at the marina when I saw Hilt take off and all of you chasing him." He eased to a stop, breathing normally despite his sprint. "What's going on?"

"Ernie killed Ramòn," I gasped. "And Hilt knows it."

"My God," Lake murmured.

"We passed Ernie and Maggie on our way to the lighthouse," Sarah said. "Hilt saw them too. He knows Ernie's close by."

"Didja see 'im?" Butch's voice was thick with breathlessness and worry.

"No, but I saw Ernie and Maggie head that way." Lake pointed inland along South River Street.

"If we can get to Ernie before Hilt does—" I began.

"We can keep Hilt from doing something he'd regret," Ashley finished.

We all broke into a run again. Powered by adrenaline, my lungs seemed to awaken from a long, deep sleep, eager to huff and puff for as long as it took. Lake kept his pace slow to run alongside me with my shorter legs, but I pushed him forward.

"No, go faster. Time, essence, et cetera."

Lake nodded and dashed ahead, crossing the bridge and hanging a left. Sarah paced herself beside me, and Ashley and Butch brought up the rear, scanning in all directions to compensate for their slower pace. A rush of gratitude filled my heart. For all I knew, Hilt was behind us somewhere. I couldn't do everything at once. But these amazing people, whom I saw infrequently or had met for the first time, were all willing to do whatever it took to save two people from a terrible mistake.

They may write about murder and mayhem, but deep down, people are precious to them. I'd cry, but I'm too busy gasping for air!

For two blocks, I kept the white soles of Lake's boat shoes in sight. Then he paused at a corner, glanced around, and ran left past a corner pharmacy, back toward the river. Worry mixed with certainty. *He's found Hilt.*

I sped up, and Sarah easily kept pace with me. "How do you do all this?" I puffed. "Mom, author, sprinter, goddess of all things?"

Sarah laughed. "Most days I feel like I'm barely keeping my head above water. Really, I'm just doing the best I can, day to day."

Coming from Sarah, that advice seemed like the simplest and easiest idea ever. And then it hit me: *that's what I'm already doing.*

"Pippa!" Lake's voice echoed off the buildings. Strolling tourists for blocks around paused to glance around. I picked up a strong note of *You'd better get over here* in his voice and hurried toward him with Sarah on my heels.

"That guy's got a set of lungs to rival Jackson's," she commented.

"It's all the cliff diving he's been doing," I replied.

We reached the corner and jinked to the left. On the far side of the bridge, Maggie stood, hands on her cheeks in shock, as Hilt held Ernie against the railing. Ernie's light jacket bunched in Hilt's liver-spotted fists. Thirty feet below, the Silver River swirled, just past high tide. *If Ernie falls, the sea will suck him right out and drown him.*

Lake stood in the middle of the street, keeping his distance from Hilt. Mallory's siren got louder as she turned the last corner before the bridge. She parked across both lanes, blocking access to the bridge, and strode toward us. And out of nowhere, Naoma trotted onto the bridge in her wake, notepad and pen in hand, apricot suit and matching pumps bright in the morning sun.

Mallory stopped a short distance from Hilt and Ernie. Neither of them acknowledged her. "Everyone, stay calm."

Naoma rushed up to us, and we met up with Lake and Sarah on the painted yellow line down the middle of the road. She clasped my wrist. "Pippa, what's going on?"

Tense, I barely glanced over. "We believe Ernie's responsible for Ramòn's death back in 1964."

"It was an accident!" Ernie howled.

Butch and Ashley finally arrived, and everyone stood rapt. I'd been determined to help my uncle find closure regarding the death of his friend, but with fifty years of pain, anger, and guilt pumping through his veins, Hilt suddenly seemed like a younger, more dangerous man, one I didn't know. I hesitated, clasping Lake's hand, and his grip anchored me to his side. Hilt and Mallory exchanged a tight, wordless look, and Mallory nodded, giving him permission to lead.

"Then why didn't you come to me?" Hilt's voice held a rough frustration as he addressed Ernie. "I would've understood!"

"No. It got... complicated." Ernie pulled away from Hilt. His sorrowful gaze landed on Maggie, who stared at him with wide, uncertain eyes. Her fingers trembled against her lips.

"Tell me what happened," Hilt growled.

"I owed Ritchy a lot of money. Ramòn and I both did, but I owed more. I didn't know what I was gonna do. He had some pretty violent friends back then, and you remember what his ego was like. But one night, Ramòn told me to meet him out in the middle of nowhere. He had something to show me. A secret. And he had this handful of old Spanish coins. It was like God had smiled down on me, you see? My good friend had all the answers I needed." Ernie's smile was bright and bitter, full of self-loathing. "But when I asked him for one of them, he turned me down. Said they belonged in a museum, but I didn't trust him. Thought he was hogging them for himself. I'd never felt so betrayed in my life. So..." He glanced at Maggie again.

Her face was pale stone.

"So I hit him. I was desperate. I needed that coin! I swear I didn't mean to do anything else to him. But he stumbled backward over a drop-off. And he landed with his head on a rock. He was... He was gone by the time I got down to him."

Everyone stood frozen, like statues in the humid wind. Ernie stared at the road. Maggie wrapped one hand over her mouth. Hilt's torso sagged to one side, as if he'd been shot, and his face radiated pain. Mallory watched with wide eyes, as off-balance as I'd ever seen her. The rest of us were rooted in place, captured by the unfolding drama. I squeezed Lake's hand until mine went white.

"But why did you leave him out there?" Maggie's question was a bare whisper, but it carried over the river's rush.

"I panicked. I was scared. I knew I'd done wrong. But... those coins were still in his pocket. I blamed him for his own death right then. That wasn't fair, I know. But if he'd only given me one coin..." Ernie's face was wreathed with entreaty, begging us to understand.

I glanced around again and saw only shock and sadness.

Ernie continued, "So I took one. And I buried him there on the headland. And then the tsunami came. The sea rose, and I thought God was punishing me. It nearly ate the North Fork Bridge out from under me as I drove back to town. I never shook so hard in my life. I thought God had seen what I'd done and that it was Cain and Abel all over again to Him. I stayed awake all night, shaking. But in the morning, everyone was talking about the tsunami. And everyone—even you, Hilt—everyone thought Ramòn had been taken by the sea. Maybe God wasn't punishing me after all. Maybe He understood. But I knew—I knew if I spent that coin on anything, ever,

God would bring His wrath back down on me. So I tucked it in a drawer and left it there. Sold my car to Ritchy as a down payment on my debt and never bought another one."

"The flowers, the candles at the church on the anniversary of his death," I said. "You didn't do that out of sorrow. You did it out of guilt."

Ernie nodded. "When those kids stole my records and found the coin in my junk drawer, I couldn't bring myself to report the theft. It felt like God was finally taking back what wasn't mine. I knew I never should've grabbed it." His eyes sought out Maggie's. "It was always Ramòn's."

Mallory unsnapped the cover on her handcuffs, but she hesitated as Maggie stepped away from the rail and stood tall. Maggie stepped forward, one step at a time, testing her new courage, until she stood face-to-face, nose to nose, with Ernie. Hilt stepped back and gave them their own bubble of space. I could almost see the tension and emotion whizzing around them like electrons surrounding an atomic nucleus. Their pairing contained so much energy, it had the potential to destroy both their worlds.

Maggie's voice was quiet, but it shook with power. "You killed my brother. *You.* All this time, *it was you.* My life fell apart when Ramòn died, and nothing I tried could put it back together. I lost him. I lost you. I lost my confidence in myself... But *I* wasn't what was wrong with my life, Ernie. It was *you.* It was you all along."

Lake squeezed my hand tightly as I squeezed his, as tightly as I needed him to.

"I can only say how terribly sorry I am." Ernie spread his hands in supplication.

But Maggie shook her head. Her eyes burned with the low embers of a decades-old fire. Where once there had been passion, love, and anguish, her face bore only disappointment and too many years of distance. "I was wrong. You didn't deserve better than me. You never deserved me at all. You lost me fifty years ago. You lost me the day you killed my brother." She turned away and walked down the bridge, alone.

Ernie watched her walk away from him. His shoulders slumped, and he seemed to age ten years right in front of my eyes. He held out his wrists to Hilt. "You can arrest me now."

Mallory wordlessly slipped her handcuffs from their case and handed them to Hilt. As my uncle arrested one of his oldest friends, I pressed a hand over my mouth. Too many conflicting emotions wrestled inside me. Hilt had his closure, but none of us would have wanted this outcome. But maybe Maggie could finally be free. And with her freedom, Gabe, who'd grown up with a grandmother who felt out of control of her own life, might find a stronger emotional footing in a world that felt a little more fair. Getting him freed from a charge of murder would go a long way toward that goal, too, and I was determined to make that happen, for Trudie's sake. Lake pulled me close, and I hugged him tight.

I nestled in Lake's arms for a blissful few seconds. We had laid a fifty-year-old mystery to rest. But I still had one more mystery to solve. Someone had killed one of my authors, and I was not going to let them get away with it.

22

"Ain't no shame in being wrong. I'm usually wrong about eight different things before breakfast. The trick is to find new ways to be wrong until you finally get it right. Being wrong that much takes dedication."

Raymond Moore, 1970

LAKE HELD MY HAND ALL the way back to Moorehaven, and I held Hilt's with my other hand. He didn't seem to notice or mind that he was one degree of separation from holding hands with Lake. And there was no way I was letting him feel even the slightest bit alone right then.

Behind us, I heard Sarah muttering for a pen. "I can't believe I forgot one. I bet it fell out when I was running."

"You got an idea, don'tcha?" Butch asked matter-of-factly.

I glanced back and saw him handing her a Moorehaven pen.

Sarah took it. "You little thief. You make me want to write you in as a cheeky little street rat who pickpockets the villain and ends up saving the day, even though I don't usually write such cute characters."

"Aww, Sarah. That's the nicest thing anyone's ever said to me." He raised his voice a little for our benefit. "She thinks I'm cute!"

My heart warmed at their attempt to distract us and lighten the mood. Authors always seemed to know how and when to lift my spirits.

A layer of high, thin clouds eased in from the northwest, and by the time we reached Moorehaven, our shadows had dimmed and the air had cooled off by a breath. Ashley and Sarah filed past me as I paused on the porch with Hilt, their voices low and eager with a fresh batch of plot details. Lake ushered Butch in after them and gave me a worried glance. I shook my head. I could handle Hilt by myself.

My uncle stood, lost, on the broad green porch. Behind him, Ernie's crisp green fence stood sturdy and tall. All traces of the tsunami's damage had been repaired, and I couldn't even tell where the old fence met the new. Ernie had finally mended his last fence.

"You want to talk about it?" I asked my uncle.

Hilt paused for a long moment before shaking his head.

"Well, promise me you'll go see Jimmy later today. I don't want you hanging out alone with this and getting lost in it. You did what you could do, when you could do it. No one could ask for more. No one."

Hilt nodded, but I could tell it was to appease me. "I will go see Jimmy, though," he assured me in a quiet voice. "Can't have him thinkin' I still have an unsolved case out there. Got my rep-yoo-tation to protect."

He offered me a clever smile, and I smiled back, finally believing that he'd be okay. Eventually.

"And I'm gonna take a leaf from your book, Pip. I'm not sure Maggie'll ever speak to me again, but I'm gonna tell her she can come talk to me if she ever wants to. She's done her waiting for me, and she shouldn't need to wait on me anymore. But I'll wait for her, the rest of my life, if I have to. I deserve that, I expect."

Hilt ambled to his room, and I let him go, awed at his capacity for wisdom even in the midst of his conflicting feelings. I hoped Maggie would come talk to him someday, for both their sakes.

Lake called my name from the big parlor, and I stepped in to see him sitting on the red couch. All my authors were in the room too.

Ogden leaned against the doorway to the sunroom, arms crossed. "Did you guys really go out and solve a fifty-year-old crime? Did I really just miss that?"

I shrugged apologetically. "I'm afraid so."

Ogden threw his hands in the air. "Okay, well, if you go out to solve another murder, you have to promise to take me with you, no matter what I say. I mean it. Drag me kicking and screaming if you have to."

Ashley tipped her head and considered him. "Well, that's awfully brave of you."

Lake said, "These guys want to go over the details of Zach's murder with you again, Pippa, so maybe Ogden will get his chance, after all. I need to head out, though. Got a treasure trove to locate. Mandy thinks she knows where it is."

I gave my jealousy a smack as it tried to rear its ugly green head. "Okay, hon. But before you go, can I offer you a solution to your guest-room problem?"

Lake froze with intense interest in the middle of standing up off my red couch. "You have my undivided attention right now. Like, you don't even know how undivided."

My skin warmed under his eager focus.

He continued, "You're hot, smart, clever, and now you tell me you can banish the most frustrating problem I've had all summer long, just as I'm helpless before my fate? Have I mentioned today how much I love you?"

Butch stared in bewilderment at Lake's unprompted profession of love. Ogden folded his hands and held his breath, rapt.

Sarah pressed a couple of fingers against her lips. "Aww, so romantic!"

"Chloe," I called down the hallway.

She trotted into the parlor a minute later, wiping her hands on a green-and-white kitchen towel. "Yeah, what's up?"

I held out my hand and indicated Chloe. "Lakyn Ivens, meet Chloe Braxton. Chloe, this is Lakyn, your new housemate. Lake, Chloe needs a change of address, and she will be living in your guest room."

"What?" Lake said through a giant grin.

"No *way*!" Chloe shrieked. She clapped her hands to her mouth and literally hopped up and down. "Omigod, are you serious? Seriously, Pippa, are you serious?"

I looked at Lake with love and pride. "I don't know. Am I serious, Lake?"

Lake stood tall and took a deep breath. His eyes considered me and then Chloe. He bobbed his head as if doing mental calculations. "The last time I lived in the same house with a teenage girl was the year before I medaled at the Junior Olympics. There were hair products everywhere."

Chloe calmed down and caught a swath of her long, dark hair on her palm. "You think this kind of stunning beauty just happens naturally?"

Lake blinked. "Um, maybe? Not? No, definitely not. Besides, the guest room has its own bathroom, now that I think of it. Sorry. Flashback moment."

Chloe smirked. "I'll do my best not to light my hairspray on fire around you."

"Deal. Wait, what do you mean, 'around me'?"

Chloe cackled. "Nope, too late, you said 'deal.' When can I move my stuff in?"

Lake clapped his hands on the sides of his head. "Geez, it's my little sister all over again." But his smile was a mile wide.

"Ha! You wish," Chloe shot back. "How do you feel about thrash metal?" Before Lake could get an answer past his gaping-fish expression, she continued, "Never mind. We'll find out soon enough."

Lake laughed and spread his arms wide. "You know what? I don't even mind. I'll take Chloe any day over the ills I know not of." He drew Chloe and me into a giant hug and squeezed us enthusiastically.

"Like, whoa, did you just quote Shakespeare?" Chloe asked.

My already high estimation of my clever assistant ratcheted up another notch. "Verily, he didst." The knot I'd been carrying in my chest for days finally loosened.

"I'll get you an extra key as soon as I have one made," Lake told Chloe. "I really do have to go. But oh my God, Pippa, this is awesome. Seriously. I owe you everything for this one." He gave me a big, loud, wet kiss goodbye and left for his treasure hunt with Mandy.

I stared after him, feeling thrilled and relieved and definitely in love. I hadn't realized how much pressure he'd been feeling from Mal's advances until I lifted them for him. I'd do pretty much anything to protect him and make him feel safe. And that included catching the killer who kept striking. No way was I going to let some homicidal maniac wander the streets of Seacrest and keep endangering my friends, guests, and community.

I took Lake's place on the couch and invited Chloe to join us. She sat in an empty wingback beside Butch's chair.

"Okay, guys. My sister's boyfriend is still in custody for a crime he didn't commit. Let's do this. Who killed Zach? Is it Connor? Is it someone who's been flying under our radar?"

My authors' faces went blank as they all retreated into their mental plotting zones to concoct possible explanations. Chloe opened her mouth to speak but closed it as if she'd been about to speak out of turn.

"No, go ahead, Chloe," I said.

"Well, I was wondering, can we actually rule anyone out? It doesn't seem like we really have a lot of evidence to narrow down the suspect pool."

"'Suspect pool.' You're training her well, Miss Pippa," Butch said.

"And Chloe's right too," Ashley said. "What evidence do we have? We should review."

"The shaved ice." Ogden's look was keen.

"The latex gloves." Sarah raised her chin and put on a mysterious expression.

"The rash." Butch pointed toward his mouth, the same place where Zach's latex-allergy rash had shown up.

"Looks like we're all reading from the same page," I summed. "Zach was deliberately smothered with shaved ice. The killer wanted it to seem like a bizarre accident, but he didn't know Zach well enough to know about his latex allergy. That seems to rule out all of us, which is a good thing. The gloves the killer wore to hide his fingerprints exposed his crime because Zach's face got a rash where the killer had touched him while pressing the shaved ice in his throat."

Chloe shivered. "Not sure I'll ever be able to look at a snow cone the same way again."

"Welcome to the mystery-author mindset," Sarah said.

"And how about the timing?" Ashley said. "Why Patrice and Zach in the same night? We haven't found a connection between them. Did they meet here, maybe? Bump into each other in the Shelf? Or are they unrelated attacks, as unlikely as that sounds?"

"The Glaze and Gossip team asked all over town about Zach's timeline for the night he was killed," Chloe offered. "He was never reported with Patrice."

I closed my eyes and racked my memory. "I can only remember Patrice being here once before Zach was killed. I'm not a hundred percent positive, but I can't recall that Zach was downstairs right then. But they could've met anywhere, really."

"So that's a maybe," Butch said. "What else we got?"

"There's Wade, the diver Lake saved," Ogden said.

"Lori says he's still in a coma," I added. "We still don't know what he saw."

"What is it with water names for guys who like the water?" Sarah asked.

Chloe offered a half smile. "I think they're Pokémon. Harry's full name is probably Squirtle. Mark my words."

"Wade maybe shoulda stuck to wading," Butch said. I felt the air fairly thicken with morbid puns.

"He's not dead yet," Ashley said. "Better shallow water than a shallow grave."

Sarah grinned wickedly. "They'd need underwater chalk for his outline."

"Plenty of fishes to swim with in that sea," Butch added.

"Too soon?" Chloe asked.

I shook my head. "Not in this town. And Zach would want us to do whatever it took to get our mental juices flowing. For instance, the killer has to know how to operate a boat. He took the *Mazu II* out to kill Wade, and then he drove it onto a beach and blew it up."

"That doesn't really narrow it down," Chloe said. "This is a coastal town. I'm a nineteen-year-old college dropout, and I can pilot a boat."

"We have to have something to go on," Ashley insisted. "There has to be something definite somewhere."

A hopeless darkness settled in my gut. *What if we can't figure this out? What if someone else dies? What if the killer gets away with everything? I'll have failed Moorehaven and Moore himself. I can't let that happen. I just can't!*

"No, we'll figure it out," Chloe said. "Or at least, *you* will." I realized she was looking directly at me. "You just solved a fifty-year-old murder, Pippa. Not even Hilt could solve that one without you."

The others nodded in unison, and my confidence rose. "You're right. I did solve that murder." I shook my head, introspective. "It's so fresh in my head, I'm having a hard time believing that Ramòn's killer managed to hide in plain sight for fifty years."

Of course, no one knew Ramòn was murdered until recently. If they'd found his body right away, Hilt would've been all over that case. And Ernie's guilt kept him anchored here in Seacrest, unable to move on, unwilling to confess. He tried to cover his guilt with layers of secret penitence—the flowers, never buying another car, staying away from Maggie. But like a pearl growing around a gritty secret, his guilt only got heavier with time. He knew what he'd done, and it affected everything else he ever did. Right down to mending fences—every fence but the one he could never mend.

"He was hiding in plain sight," I murmured again. My head popped up.

All of my authors stared at me, electrified. "He's hiding in plain sight!" we all exclaimed.

"Whoa, guys, not cool," Chloe said grumpily. "You left me out of the Author Brainwave."

"Zach's killer never left town." Butch leaned forward in his chair, and his knuckles went white from gripping the armrest. "He only wanted us to think he did."

Ashley sat forward. "Two of the treasure team members have been attacked. We've been looking for a connection between them and Zach. But what if they were the actual targets all along, and Zach got in the way with his conspiracy theories?"

"You think he got one theory right at exactly the wrong time," I said.

She nodded her perfectly coiffed blond hair. "Could be he was spinning a theory at the fair that night, and the killer overheard him and knew he had to take Zach out before he told the wrong person."

"Doesn't your friend Jordan work at Seven Vistas?" Ogden asked.

When I nodded, Sarah added, "She'll have our killer's contact information. A phone number. The police might be able to triangulate his position and locate him before he can attack anyone else."

"Well, look who's all high-tech," Butch said with a smile.

I grabbed my phone and called Jordan. Chloe and my authors hung on my half of the conversation. "Jordan, I need a favor. I think we're close to catching Zach's killer."

"You got it. What do you need?"

"Connor Dockins's phone number. Wait, hold on. Did I just wake you up? Aren't you still working nights?"

"I am working nights, but I am currently sipping a lovely cup of coffee at Glazin' West. And I'm really sorry to do this to you, Pippa, but I can't give out guests' contact info. I can't use it to check on him for you, either. Too many stalkers in the world." My heart sank, but my best friend came through with an alternate plan. "Just because I can't get you that information, doesn't mean you can't find it another way. Patrice is still checked in."

"You visited her, right?"

"I went to see her earlier, yes. I took Wallis along."

"Wallis? Why Wallis?"

I could hear her grin as she replied, "I figured a get-well-soon bouquet from the shop owner was a solid way in, and I, as a veteran concierge, was simply escorting her in and checking that my guest was comfortable."

"What did you learn?"

"I let Wallis distract her while I searched her toiletries bag in the bathroom. I checked everywhere—even the usual hotel room hiding spots. Patrice doesn't have a prescription for Xanax."

"So you're pretty sure someone else drugged her."

"I think so, yes. She seems like a good kid who got caught up in way more trouble than she ever wanted. She's worried about Connor, upset that she can't remember what happened to her at the fair, and stressed that this salvage-team job is going to hurt her standing in her graduate program instead of helping it. I'm pretty good at reading people's faces. I don't think she's hiding anything. Give her a call."

"I will. Thanks, Bestie."

I'd been hoping not to disturb Patrice, but it seemed like she was my best option now. "You are a cherry-flavored lifesaver. I'll talk to you later."

I called Patrice and kept my request simple, hoping not to upset her, but she was well aware of the rumors flying around town.

"It's not true, what they're saying about Connor," she protested. "I know he's a good guy. He'd never hurt anyone. I still can't explain why he left town, but I believe he's really gone. If he were here, wouldn't he have tried to contact me? We had a thing going. Well, starting. Trying to start."

"That's a fair point. I'm sure everything will get resolved soon." A doubt settled in. Patrice knew him better than I did, and she was certain he was innocent. *Only one way to find out.* After I hung up, I said, "We're on our way, guys. I got Connor's number."

Chloe shifted in her chair and carelessly slung a leg over the antique armrest. "Um, that's cool and all, but does Seacrest actually have cell phone triangulation? Is that a thing we can even do? Because that sounds a little New York City to me."

Butch *hmm*ed. "Sounds like a comment Zach would've made. And maybe he'd be right."

I took a deep breath. "Our killer could be on the other end of that phone number. And Chloe's right. This isn't New York. But whether the police can ping his cellphone from Seacrest or not, we should hand the number over."

Sarah ripped the top page off her notepad and handed it to me. I took a deep breath and dialed Vic's number. Being from the city, he'd have a good idea what Seacrest PD could do and what it couldn't—or wouldn't. After all, there wasn't a warrant out for

Connor's arrest. I left Connor's number with him, and he said he'd check on it right away. I hung up, feeling only halfway vindicated. "It doesn't feel finished yet."

Ashley waved her notepad at me. "Dial him yourself. If he answers, put him on speaker."

Sarah leaned forward. "We can listen for background noises. It's not much, but maybe we'll get lucky."

My fingers hovered over my screen. "What should I tell him I'm calling about?"

Chloe sat up straight and put her foot back on the floor. "He came in here with Patrice that day. He bought a book. Tell him his card was declined."

"And keep him talking," Ogden added. For a guy who didn't say much, Ogden knew how to make his words count.

I slowly let out my breath and remembered Jennifer, inexperienced but determined. *I am Demetria Graves, brash young heroine who takes every dare, no matter how dangerous, and somehow manages to stumble into the right choices. Please, let this be one of them.* I dialed Connor's number. My spine was stiff with awareness that I was about to speak to someone who had probably killed one person and tried to off two more.

"Hello, who's this?" Connor answered. A gust of wind dragged static over the line.

I turned on the speakerphone. "Connor, it's Pippa Winterbourne from Moorehaven. How are you?"

"Miss Winterbourne? Why are you calling?" His voice sounded calm but confused.

"There was a little problem with your card."

"That's weird. It cleared just fine when I gassed up outside Bend."

"You're in Bend now?" I blurted. *That's halfway across the state!*

My authors all leaned forward intently.

"No, I'm over in the Wallowa area. My grandpa has an old hunting cabin up here near the national forest. Since I walked away from the salvage team, I figured I'd treat myself to something relaxing for the rest of the time I was supposed to be working with them. So I'm up here, in the middle of nowhere, hiking around in a bright-orange vest so I don't get shot."

"Would you send me a picture of yourself?" I asked in what I hoped sounded like a casual tone.

"Uh, sure. Any reason?"

"All we see are ocean waves out here. Give a girl a new vista?"

"Hah, sure. One second."

After a pause, I received a photo. I studied it and showed it to the others. Connor stood low on a hill covered in dead golden grasses that bowed, gleaming, in the sun. A smattering of pine trees sprinkled the pale hill behind him. He wore a dark-purple shirt with its sleeves rolled up and an orange vest. He grinned like a man happy with his place in the world. A weathered cabin with peeling cornflower paint nestled in the corner of his picture, complete with a rusty stovepipe and a tiny covered porch bearing a magenta welcome mat.

This man couldn't have killed anyone in town. He's way over on the other side of the state. Or could he? Timing is everything. It's still possible he killed Zach the night of the fair and drove across the state overnight. "Looks great, Connor. Listen, this is gonna sound weird, but do you still have your gas receipt from Bend?"

"Uh, why?"

"I need a picture of that too."

"Look, Miss Winterbourne, what's going on?"

I took a deep breath. "Crime, Connor. Crime is going on, here in Seacrest. We have a killer on the loose, and until very recently"—*like two minutes ago*—"certain people were convinced it was you. But if you can prove to me that you weren't here in town after the morning you allegedly left Seven Vistas, we can try to find the real killer before he kills again."

"Again? Who's been killed? What the heck is going on over there? Is Patrice okay?" Connor's voice went sharp with worry.

"She's okay," I reassured him. I needed to see that receipt, and I didn't want to delay him with the details of what Patrice had been through to reach "okay."

"Okay, good. Let me go find it for you." I heard the creak of a rickety door. Then Connor put his phone on speaker, and I could hear him digging through what sounded like a backpack or something. "Argh, where is it? Maybe it's in my car still. No—got it!" He crowed with success, and soon I got another picture from him. I zoomed in on the date printed on the receipt.

"That's dated two days ago," Sarah said.

"He did leave town after all," Chloe said.

Butch coughed into his fist and said, "I think that about sinks our theory. Connor didn't do it."

"Whoa, who are all you guys?" Connor blurted. "The B&B authors? Are you gonna tell the police I'm innocent? Because I am."

Yeah, about that. "You may get a call from a Seacrest policeman named Vic Nuncio. But I'll forward these pictures to him and tell him we need to keep looking for the real killer."

"No offense, but that sounds like the least you could do. I honestly had no idea what was happening back there. I kinda wanted to keep in touch with Patrice, but I was still so peeved at Mandy that I figured I'd wait until these hills had chilled me out a little more before I called her. I guess I shouldn't have waited."

Ogden and Butch shared a wary look, which they turned on me.

I caught their vibe. "Can you tell me your side of what happened when you left Seven Vistas at two in the morning?"

Anger tinged Connor's voice. "You bet I can. Mandy called me to her room after midnight. We'd all been up late, coordinating our plans for the next day's search up the coast. And like a moron, I went over. She started flirting with me while she pretended to talk about correlating Patrice's tattoo analysis with the Spanish captain's charts. Then she popped into the bathroom. I was getting pretty uncomfortable because it seemed like she was gonna put on something slinky, and she's, like, at *least* ten years older than I am. Like, no offense, but that's not my thing."

What does he mean, "No offense"? I wondered, taking some offense, anyway. *How old does he think I am?*

"So I was just gonna say I was really tired and slip out to my own room," Connor continued, "when I saw a black leather folder sticking out from her briefcase. I thought it might be extra info she was hiding—she's a cagey one—but it was bankruptcy stuff, documents showing she'd sold her half of the company to Wade, and some kind of threatening letter from a Chicago museum. Reneging on a contract or something."

"Wow, that's crazy."

"I know, right? But she walked in right then, wearing some thin nightgown thing, as I was scanning through the papers, and she started yelling at the top of her lungs. And screaming, like she was being hurt. I started freaking out, thinking maybe she was having a seizure or something, so I tried to help her, but she got all violent and shoved me away. She ran for the door and yanked it open. Wade was just on the other side of it with his hand raised to pound on the door. She said I attacked her. Wade straight up took her side, and I, well... I admit I lost my temper with both of them. I rage quit right there, grabbed my stuff, and left. I drove the rest of the night, filled up in Bend, and reached the cabin by lunchtime. I've been here ever since. And there you have it: my side of the story."

Connor's words and their implications began to swirl and coalesce in my mind. Something big, something huge, was coming together, and I needed to understand it as soon as possible. A killer was still on the loose. "Thanks, Connor. When Vic calls, tell him exactly what you told me. I hope you find the relaxation you're looking for. And I'll tell Patrice you want to keep in touch."

"Thanks. I appreciate it."

I hung up and stared at the others. The things Connor had said felt so big, so important, that my body seemed to fade away. Something he'd said triggered a buried memory, something that had seemed perfectly innocent at the time. *What is it, Brain? Give up the clue!*

I visualized Connor's story. *It happened so quickly, Connor thought it was real. And Wade saw exactly what he was meant to see. At the Treasure Fair, Lake and I only saw what we were supposed to. We told Doc and Mallory, and they believed us. And on and on it goes.*

It's lies all the way down.

"Pippa, your face." Sarah clasped my hand. "You know who did it."

I did. "The attack on Patrice wasn't what it appeared to be. It's time to call Mallory and tell her she needs to let Gabe go." And then things got worse. "Oh my God! Lake is with the killer!"

23

"*S*ometimes being a hero makes you someone else's villain."
Raymond Moore, 1944

LAKE'S PHONE WENT STRAIGHT to voicemail. Five times. I dialed Blade and Boom with shaking fingers. Harry's cheery reply didn't dent the ice block weighing down my gut.

"Harry, help me. I need to know exactly where Lake went. He's in danger!"

"What? What's going on? Am I getting sucked into some elaborate danger-plot date, Pippa?" Harry's tone was still light and amused.

"I swear on the Eight-fold Way, Harry, I'm dead serious."

"That's... that's not something Buddhists swear on, actually, but... You're serious? Lake's in actual danger? How do you know if you don't know where he is?"

I almost tore out my hair. "Harry, Lake is being lured away by a murderer who's tried to kill three people and succeeded once already. *Where is he?*"

Harry muttered in Sri Lankan, and by the shock in his voice, I could guess what he was saying. "He was sworn to secrecy. But when Lake hired me, he told me never to go anywhere alone, because the buddy system is Lake's Eight-fold Way, if you will. So he wrote down where he was going just in case. Let me get the note."

I waited in an agony of impatience for what felt like three and a half eons before Harry spoke again.

251

"He wrote, 'Diana's Chute. Shh.'"

"I didn't say anything."

"No, he literally wrote 'Shh' because it's supposed to be—"

"A secret. Gotcha. Thanks, Harry." I hung up and bolted for the door.

Everyone sat up, alarmed.

"Wait, where are you going?" Chloe blurted.

"I know where they are!" I grabbed a light windbreaker off the coat rack.

"Hey now," Butch called, still inside the parlor. "You can't dash off alone like that."

I leaned back into the doorway to stare him down and found all the women glaring at him too.

He raised his hands defensively. "I mean, we should come too, all of us. For support."

"What's all this commotion?" Uncle Hilt stood in the side hallway a dozen feet away from me, wearing a puzzled expression.

Chloe swung around the doorway, wearing a fierce grin. "It's a rescue mission!"

Ashley power-walked out into the hallway and pulled open the front door. "Call the police, Hilton. We're going to need backup."

"Which car are we taking?" Sarah stood, already patting her pockets for note-taking equipment.

Hilt groaned, but a wry smile lurked in the corner of his mouth. He fished in his pocket. "You're taking Sadie."

Chloe brightened. "The Rescuemobile."

I snatched Sadie's keys from Hilt's hand. "That is not a classy-enough nickname, and I'm telling her you called her that."

Chloe stretched out a hand. "No, no, no need for that. I take it back. Wait." She looked around, confused. "Did I just take back an insult to a car because I was worried she wouldn't like me?"

Hilt pursed his lips as if hiding a smile. "Seems you did. Now, who needs rescue, and where are they?" He reached for the landline's handset on the hostess station.

"Lake's spelunking with a murderer at Diana's Chute. Send literally everyone!" I dashed through the door Ashley held open. Hilt reached for his phone, and everyone else followed me.

Inside the garage's side door, I pressed the big orange button on the wall, and the old wooden door rose until it stuck out like a stiff awning, revealing two cars. Next to my cute tangerine hatchback gleamed Sadie, Uncle Hilt's 1965 Rolls Royce Phantom V, the sexiest vehicle I'd ever laid eyes on. Her glossy paint job sparkled at me, well aware I'd never look that fine in black, and her chrome trim gleamed saucily even in the cloudy light. "Hello, girl," I greeted her in a rush.

"I love these suicide doors," Ashley said. "I'm sitting in the back! Wow, is this inlay made of curly maple?"

"Yes, it is." I pulled open the driver door. *But curly maple inlays won't make Lake any safer.*

Everyone piled in. Butch sat shotgun next to me. "In case it helps to get there one seat earlier," he explained.

"Did anyone bring any weapons?" Chloe asked. "I've got a pocket knife."

"I've got my Navy training." Butch flexed his wiry arm. "And Sarah *is* a weapon with those two black belts of hers."

"You always know just what to say to a girl." Sarah patted his shoulder.

"I'll use a rock if I have to." I pulled my door shut.

With four people in back, Chloe ended up halfway on Ogden's lap. "Sorry," she began. "I know this must make your anxiety worse."

I caught Ogden in the rearview mirror, wearing a strange smile despite his tense posture. "It's doing its best to tell me our quest will end in doom and blood, but for once, that could actually happen—no offense, Pippa."

"No, I agree with it." My Depression Dragon was mumbling behind the bars of its cage, telling me my endeavor was a useless waste of energy, that Lake would end up dead—in the surf, sprawled on the rocks, stabbed, shot, strangled... I mentally pointed a remote at it and hit Mute.

Ogden continued, "My anxiety makes me live in crisis mode. It's really weird to see everyone around me in the same frame of mind. Not what I'd call relaxing, but... I do this every day, so I'll be okay. We all will. Let's do this."

I turned the key, and Sadie roared to life, eager for adventure. We peeled out of the parking lot and veered past Sebastian's pet psychic shop. With my heart spasming in my throat, I laid on the horn and blew through all the stop signs, scattering tourists. Butch, Sarah, and Ogden rolled down their windows and waved their arms, yelling warnings to get out of the way. We managed to scare most of the tourists back to the sidewalks, and I avoided the slow and oblivious ones with some quick twists of the steering wheel.

We made it to the coastal highway unscathed, so I spun the wheel to the left and burned rubber. Across the highway, Ritchy stood in his parking lot, examining a stuffed sheep holding a steering wheel, but he and his customer stared, open-mouthed, at Sadie's raw animal magnetism. I gunned the engine and left them behind in a cloud of rubbery blue smoke.

"We do wanna live long enough to find your boyfriend, right?" Butch gasped from the passenger seat.

"Oh, we're gonna live long enough," I promised. "Diana's Chute is only a dozen miles up the coast. We'll be there in no time flat." My eyes were glued to the road, and blood hammered at my temples. *I'll save you. I'll save you. I'll save you.* As soon as I hit a straightaway, I swerved around a lumbering motor home from British Columbia. Then I had to edge my way around a train of long-haul cyclists whose wheels each bore tightly packed, brightly colored bags. Sadie's horn barked at cars, trucks, and cyclists alike.

"I think I should tell you the whole truth," Butch began, "in case this doesn't end well for one of us. I can tell you suspect something, and it's only fair I set the record straight, since I'm acting under your roof."

I wasn't sure where Butch was going with his confession, but I was too focused on driving to question him. I gave him a curt nod to continue.

"I'm not a draft dodger. I served my country. But I took a bad crack to the skull the last month of my tour. When I woke up, I was stateside, and I couldn't remember most of the past five years. I wanted to honor my fellow servicemen. And women," he added, glancing over his shoulder at Sarah, who studied him intently. "But I couldn't write about what I didn't remember. So I use Hilt's stories."

"What?" we all chorused.

"Yeah, he kind of insisted. He's like me—not one to brag—but he's proud of his service. Turning his escapades into fiction helps us both. So Captain McReynolds's wartime adventures are loosely based on the real-life adventures of Hilton MacKellar. That's the real reason I come here so regularly. I... I just wanted you to know. I'm not ashamed of my service—only ashamed that I can't remember it."

"Whoa, man," Ogden said. "I think you're my new hero."

"No, son, I think you got that backward," Butch said kindly.

Sarah squeezed his shoulder. "You're a braver man than I am, Butch."

Butch barked a laugh. "That's 'cause you ain't a man, Sarah. And I ain't strong enough to be a woman."

The extra tension broke, and I let out a chuckling breath.

Sarah cackled like a villain. "Oh, now I *know* I'm putting you in my book, Butch Thorsen."

"Lord help me," Butch murmured.

My knuckles had gone white on the steering wheel when we cut across incoming traffic and skidded to a Tokyo-drift-style halt in the turnout above Diana's Chute, narrowly missing a California tourist who barely glanced over. My chest hurt from tension and from bracing myself against my frantic driving, but I had no time to catch my breath. I grabbed the door handle and bailed out of the car.

My authors tumbled out after me, also short of breath and a little wobbly.

"Let's you and me make a pact," Butch said, "never to tell Hilt how you got us here so fast."

I strode for the low wall that edged the turnout, ignoring the stunning view of the Pacific and nearby headlands. "He's not going to get you in trouble for not stopping me, Butch."

"Couldn't have stopped you if I tried." He trailed after me with a wiry speed walk. "I just don't want him knowing where I got it from when it turns up in my next book."

I managed a quick grin. "Deal. Wait, is there no trail down?" I leaned over the low wall and rested my hands on its warm surface. The rough, dark-gray rock was solid and comforting, but it kept me from reaching Lake. Past its gentle curve, a nearly sheer drop-off fell a hundred feet to the narrow strip of crumbly rock that edged a turbulent finger of the sea: Diana's Chute. I saw no sign of Lake, Mandy, or anyone else below. "How do we get down there? Lake needs me!"

Ashley puffed up beside me. "Where exactly?"

I scanned the area. A hundred feet north of our turnout, the highway crossed a 1920s Art Deco-style bridge in front of a shadowy crevice that drew a line all the way down the sheer basalt cliff. Deep in that crevice, a waterfall had eaten away at the volcanic rock for centuries—maybe millennia. Its constant rush had cut through several hundred feet of solid stone and formed a cave where the sea rushed in to meet it, sandwiched between two high cliffs that still resisted the wearing of the ocean. Below the highway's bridge, tiny Diana Creek trickled out of an old rock fall and into a narrow slice in the coastline. Connor's theory was probably spot on: the tsunami of 1700 had shaken the land so hard it altered the water's flow, exposing the treasure or a path to it. The cave behind those tumbled rocks was dry or nearly so, and Ramòn had been able to squeeze his way in.

But that rock fall must've formed when the tsunami struck three centuries ago, or the treasure would've been found long before now—a different kind of protective barrier. Giant tumbled boulders littered the narrow beach on both sides of the slit. Any treasure that had been hidden down there would be nearly impossible to reach. But Ramòn had found a way in. And Mandy must have too.

But there was no trail down to the rock fall. I couldn't reach them. "How do I get down?" I yelped.

Ogden took me by the shoulders. "How did *they* get down?"

I met his eyes. "How *did* they get down?"

"Guys, over there!" Chloe pointed to the bridge. I hadn't spotted them before, but now I could make out two neon-hued ropes dangling off the bridge's railing. Lake and Mandy had rappelled straight down and vanished into the rock fall.

My stomach lurched at the thought of trying to go down one of those ropes without any safety harness. I was nearly desperate enough to try it, but Butch spotted the glint in my eyes.

"Don't you dare, missy. That ain't the way."

He was right, and I knew it. But I was running out of time to save Lake. Hilt's reinforcements might not arrive in time to reach him, and I had zero interest in waiting patiently for their arrival. Seeing Ogden's personal bravery as he faced more fear than any of the rest of us inspired me. *I am Ogden Kemp, solving crime despite my anxiety. I can't hide from this. I have to throw myself into this scary situation and hope for the best.* In desperation, I started jogging around the curve of the rock wall, eyes locked on the rough, shrubby slope that tumbled down to the rocky beach below.

An odd vehicle with oversized tires caught my eye on the seemingly inaccessible beach, and I stopped. As I leaned on the wall, I was shocked to recognize a familiar mass of curly brown hair blowing in the wind.

Trudie. My little sister was squatting beside a tire on that very expensive-looking rock crawler with Fallon Vanderveer, who was watching her with an admiring expression. *Fallon's "proposition" to Trudie was to go rock crawling?*

Inspiration struck hard, and I gasped as it sent sharp tingles up my spine. "Chloe, get me one of those ropes from the bridge!" I hollered.

She nodded with a fierce grin before running for the highway.

Ashley approached me and peeled off her fingerless compression gloves. "They're all I've got, but they might protect your hands a little."

"But these are your writing gloves," I protested.

"And that's Lake's life. Take them, you badass."

I pulled the stretchy brown gloves on and felt them gently hug my hands and forearms. Then I whipped out my phone and dialed Tru's number.

"Kinda busy right now," Tru said by way of answering.

"Look up. I'm coming down."

"What?" Below, I saw her spin around, glancing in several directions before she spotted me. She gave me a tentative wave. "Whaddaya mean, you're coming down?"

"Lake's in danger, and you and Fallon are going to help me save him, catch the real killer, and prove Gabe's innocent."

"Omigod, yes!" Tru roared. She slapped Fallon on the arm and pointed up at me in excitement. "You're not gonna believe this! My sister's coming to save my boyfriend! And hers. Hers first, actually. Then mine. I did mention I had a boyfriend, right? 'Cause I'm very taken."

"You might've mentioned it a few times." Fallon's amused voice carried faintly over the phone.

Chloe appeared beside me with a bright-orange length of rope.

Butch picked up the trailing end and made quick work of wrapping the rope in a coil from his palm to his elbow. "You've done this sort of thing before?"

I nodded. My adrenaline convinced me I was some kind of rappelling expert, even though I'd only taken one quarter of rock climbing in college, about eight years prior. *It'll be fine,* my mind whispered reassuringly. *Totally fiiine.*

Butch nodded back at me and hurled the looped rope out over the slope while Chloe held the other end. Then he, Sarah, Ogden, and Ashley took hold of it too, anchoring my lifeline.

"Then I guess we've reached the part where I let you go in first and try to take out the raving murderer," Butch said. "Holler real loud if you need backup. We'll be watching from the wall." His voice was rough with concern, but his eyes were bright with confidence.

My laugh was breathless with nerves. "Thanks, Butch."

"Good luck," Chloe called.

"You can do this." Ogden's face radiated assurance.

"Be careful!" Sarah added in her mom voice.

I nodded and arranged the rope around my thigh. I grasped it above and below that point then eased myself over the low rock wall. My mouth went dry, and my hands got damp, but I didn't dare stop. I met everyone's eyes. "Thank you. Also, if you drop me, there won't be any fresh blintzes for breakfast tomorrow."

Butch, in front, braced his leg on the rock wall. "You heard her, folks. We need those blintzes, Miss Pippa."

"Butter peach, please," Ashley requested.

"You got it." I shifted my grip and began my descent. *It's just a hundred feet or so. I can totally go a hundred feet down. That's like Moorehaven's third floor to basement level three times. No biggie.* After a few tentative steps, I couldn't help speeding up. *Lake's life depends on me getting down alive but quickly.* Soon I was leaping out from the rocky slope and letting the rope slide through my hands. Ashley's gloves didn't offer much protection from the heat of the rope's friction, though, and I felt my palms begin to burn.

I tripped over a couple of shrubby trees that I totally failed to see coming up behind me, but I managed to reach the bottom of the cliff without falling to my death. Fallon and Trudie steadied me as I stumbled on the flatter ground amid a field of small rocks, many of which I'd dislodged from the cliff.

"You're one crazy lady," Fallon said in an admiring tone. "What's this all about?"

I staggered toward the rock crawler with one arm around Trudie's shoulders, wincing at the pain in my hands. "I need you to drive me around the corner of this coastline. Lake's gone into a cave with a killer, and I need to save him."

"Oh! Oh, uh..."

Tru's grip on my arm tightened. "*I'm* the rock crawler driver. I'll get you to Lake." We reached the vehicle, and Tru shoved me into the passenger seat. She belted me in with a strap system fit for a wriggly toddler in a fighter jet.

I thought I'd heard her wrong. "But you don't own a rock crawler."

"The crawler is Fallon's," she said, with one final snap of the harness. "But he can't drive the thing. Never even taken it out before."

"I've been all excited for my first time out." He fondly patted the vehicle's side.

Tru darted around to the driver's door and climbed in. "When he heard I had experience driving them in competitions, he invited me out today to show him the ropes. And then you called." She hollered at Fallon, "Hey, flyboy, we're gonna go save our men. You coming or what?"

The hotel owner jolted out of his daze at Tru's question, though, and loaded himself awkwardly into the back seat. "Gah, how do you buckle this thing?"

"When did you get into professional rock crawling, exactly?" My voice came out breathy with tension.

Trudie barked a laugh. "Long story! It all started with an art-loving landlord with ties to the Argentinian mob, some dumpster diving for a lost engagement ring—not mine—and a four a.m. bet on owls."

"So, Chicago?"

"No, no. Reno!"

Baffled, I asked, "When did you live in Reno?"

But the time for small talk was over. "Hold on to your butts!" Tru threw the crawler into gear.

My fist clenched around the Oh Crap handle above my window as I realized how little I'd cared to learn about my sister's adult life and how much I'd clearly missed out on. But I'd clearly overestimated the rock crawler's speed.

Trudie eased over the first few rocks at the equivalent of a fast walk, and then we slowed to negotiate a deep gap between two higher boulders.

Fallon leaned forward from the back seat, elbows dangling over the front of our seats like an eager teenager. "This is so cool!"

"Can we go faster?" I begged.

"Not without turtling." Tru's tone was exquisitely professional. "And no, you shouldn't get out and walk. If you twist an ankle trying to run across the tops of these boulders, Pips, you're never going to reach Lake in time. Sit there, and let me help. Let me help both of you."

Fallon blurted, "Me? I don't need help—oh. You meant her and Lake. Of course you did. Sorry."

My little sister stepped on the gas and spun the steering wheel to the right.

"I thought you said we had to drive slowly!" I blurted.

With her eyes still on the viewpoint above us, Trudie replied, "Remember those bouldering competitions I said I entered? Did I mention I won the last three?"

The rock crawler scrambled over a huddle of boulders, and we bounced our way down the far side. I clung to my Oh Crap handle with both hands and did my best to keep my yelps of fright to myself so as not to distract her.

Trudie drove like a wildcat, scrambling over the boulders as if the tires had grown gecko fingers. I was soon convinced that not only was their rubber sentient, but it had adopted my rescue quest. I was also convinced I would be pretty bruised the next morning, no matter what happened between now and then.

We rounded the corner of the slot in the headland, and the crawler's raised cab afforded me an excellent view of the narrow, violent channel of water that was Diana's Chute. A strip of nearly impassable rocky shore ran from where we sat to the cave below the highway bridge a few hundred feet ahead. Only thirty or forty feet to our left, a mirror image of the rough shoreline formed the other side of the dangerous waterway. In between, the sea foamed and swirled, elbowing its way in past giant boulders toward the cave but never quite reaching it. Ahead, I saw the rock fall that obscured the cave's entrance, and I knew Lake was beyond it, in grave danger.

Trudie tore up the sand exposed by the low tide as she peeled around a half-submerged rock the size of a delivery van and nearly climbed the side of the cliff as she edged us around a shattered chunk of basalt that had fallen from the cliff. Despite the narrowness of the path before us, the going did get easier. The waiting didn't, though. I could barely breathe through the tension in my chest by the time

Trudie tackled the short rise to the tumble of rocks at the base of the lost waterfall. I didn't see any sign of Lake, dead or alive.

My legs spasmed with adrenaline as I climbed out of the crawler, and I almost fell on my face. "Do you have a flashlight? A big, heavy one?" Light was good. A weapon was better.

Fallon handed me a rectangular emergency light, made of plastic and barely bigger than my hand. It would have to do. "We should come with you," he said with a gleam in his eyes.

Fallon was nearly as tall as Lake, but he had quite a bit more padding on him. I had no guarantee he'd be able to fit through a hole that Lake might have had trouble with. *And even if he can fit, there is no way I'm getting the richest man in town killed.* I shook my head. "Trudie, keep him here, okay? Please. And thank you."

Trudie threw her arms around me for a quick, strong hug. "Be careful." As she echoed Sarah's concern, her face was tense with worry. I'd never seen my own mother in Trudie's face before, but right then, I could almost feel her presence.

With the rolling splashes of an incoming tide behind me, I studied the rock fall. The tumbled stones were old and weathered on all sides and rose a good forty feet—higher than I could probably climb. No one had found a way in since 1700, until Ramòn. The 1964 tsunami probably hadn't damaged Ramòn's way in, since Mandy and Lake had disappeared inside the cave. I squinted, envisioning what I might have to do to rescue Lake, and I felt every one of my authors' protagonists hovering at my back, strong, confident, determined. Just like me.

Give me back my boyfriend.

With the emergency flashlight in one hand, I started climbing onto the tumbled rocks, looking for any trace of a crevice. The faint howl of sirens reached my ears from the highway up above. It faded again as the vehicles disappeared into one of the folds of the headlands. *Backup is on its way. Good to know.*

I scrambled all the way across the spilled apron of fallen basalt, looking for the opening but afraid to turn on the flashlight in case it gave me away. When I turned back for a second pass, I realized Trudie and Fallon had been shadowing me, helping me search for gaps and openings. Trudie pointed to the rocks I'd just covered and shook her head. Then she gestured upward with one hand. I nodded and scrambled higher up on the rocks.

To my great relief, once I was several feet higher, I spotted a narrow crevice, maybe ten inches wide, black against the weathered gray stone. I scooted over to it and stuck my ear out over its empty space. But I couldn't hear Lake's voice. I couldn't hear anything at all. Then the sound of grinding stone resonated from deep inside the cave.

Sirens reached my ears again, and the faint but distinctive *whop whop* of an approaching helicopter echoed down from somewhere past the crest of the cliff. I glanced up its sheer face, past the bridge that arched a hundred feet overhead. The intimidating solidity of the stone I was about to crawl under made my mouth dry. I'd taken a big risk climbing down like I had. Emergency services would be more methodical. Slower. *Please don't collapse on me. Please don't collapse on me.*

With the sound of my heart pounding in my ears, I gingerly lowered myself into the narrow slot in the rock, feeling for footholds with my rope-burned hands. My double-Ds didn't enjoy the tight fit. My eyes didn't adjust fast enough, and I scraped my shoulder and smacked my knee on the rock on my way down. At the uneven bottom, I crouched in the dimness like a frightened rabbit, waiting. But no one reached out of the cave to strike me. The rocky scraping came again, as if someone was dragging something, and I could tell it was quite a ways under the cliff. The way it kept repeating, I was sure no one knew I was here.

I eased forward into the cave on my hands and knees, feeling my way past the rough edges of the three-hundred-year-old boulders. *I must be, what, the fourth person to touch the underside of these rocks? Now that's pretty cool.* My eyes began to adjust, and I saw the faintest glimmer of light through a gap above my head. I scrambled up, eased my way forward again through a narrow section, and found myself in a more open space.

I covered the flashlight bulb with my fingers and turned it on, making light stripes. As I played them across the rocks around me, what I saw made me gasp quietly in amazement. I had reached the waterfall cave. The stone was smooth and weathered, as if it had been exposed to millennia of beating waves, punishing winter storms, and the full force of the Diana Falls stream. The barest trickle of water reached my ears now that I had moved away from the booming surf. The waterfall had probably dried up at the back of the cave, at least for the summer. The roof was low, and the passage curved up and to the left for at least fifty feet. That was my way in.

I took a deep breath and removed my fingers from the light. The whole cave entrance lit up, revealing varied gray striations in the ancient stone and a network of ancient cracks.

"No! No, I don't understand!"

At Mandy's exclamation, I froze and nearly had a heart attack, and then another as something wooden crashed and splintered. More crashes followed, and I gave up on stealth and bolted up and around the curve of the waterfall's ancient bed.

Mandy was making so much noise that she didn't hear me approach from behind. I got to the top of the rise, where the smooth stone floor ran just a couple of feet from the roof, and hid my flashlight beam against my thigh. Lake and Mandy knelt in the light of their lanterns, fifteen feet across the cave, atop a smooth-edged boulder the size of my small parlor. *He's alive! I'm not too late.* Between us lay a low, rounded bowl of stone that had once been a deep pool. Now it held a smear of brackish water and algae that smelled like the underside of a dock. Three or so splintered wooden boxes had crashed to the edge of the water and spilled their treasure. Glints of blue-and-white ceramic shards and the tattered remains of silk cloth caught my eye, and my heart raced. *Treasure!*

A deep stone shelf had been roughly carved into the wall right below the uneven ceiling, next to some oddly carved stones. Mandy picked up another small chest and hurled it behind her in apparent frustration. *What the heck is she doing? She's breaking priceless artifacts!*

Lake was *my* priceless artifact, though. I'd come to rescue him. Yet there was no way I could reach him without getting wet and attracting Mandy's attention. If only Lake would turn around!

"Mandy, what's going on? What's the problem?" Lake asked over her impatient yells and grunts. "You found the treasure. Here it is. You're going to be famous."

Mandy shoved a small box against Lake's chest, and he reflexively clasped it. "She said its worth was 'incalculable.' But look at this trash! A couple of chests full of broken ceramics, some ruined silk, about two dozen gold coins—" She indicated the box she'd handed Lake and threw her arms in the air helplessly. "And the rest is that godforsaken *wax*!"

Wax? I followed the frustrated gesture Mandy made and saw what I had originally assumed to be stones. They were stacked too evenly, and their color was too light, though. *Oh! Wax cakes. Like the settlers "mined" off the beach in Nehalem.* Captain Rodriguez could have lightened his cargo however he chose, but it seemed that ninety-pound wax cakes had been his favorite item to offload. From where I crouched, half hidden behind a lump of rock, I could count a few dozen of them fading back into the shadows of the deep stone shelf the captain's men must've carved. The so-called treasure chests, however, numbered less than ten, and Mandy was swiftly destroying them, while Lake wisely stayed out of her way.

My arms prickled with goose bumps. *Oh my God. Mandy just melted down her cannons and realized they were only bronze.*

"This is worthless! A giant pile of crap!" Mandy yanked the tiny box from Lake's hands and hurled it across the stagnant pool—and right at me.

I ducked reflexively, and a handful of coins caromed off the rocks around me with bright golden pings.

"There's no way this'll be enough. Not nearly enough. Don't you understand? They'll *kill* me!"

As Mandy continued her rant, I snatched up a piece of eight that had come to rest against my shoe. Without thinking, I rubbed its edge across my forehead. I turned the emergency flashlight off and tried to make out my reflection in its signal mirror. *Is that a black streak? Or just dirt?*

Mandy paused, and I peeked over the edge of the rock. Lake was staring right at me. *He must've seen me dodge those coins.* But Mandy was turning to see what had caught Lake's attention. She'd spot me in a heartbeat, and my heart was pounding pretty fast. I had a split second to keep her from taking control of the whole situation.

I never thought I'd do this, but I need to be Scarlen Fate. I need to get Lake out of here safely. And I'll do absolutely anything to make that happen. Lake is mine. And Mandy's mine too. I own this room.

I flung myself into a dramatic standing pose, legs apart, head thrown back, right hand pointing accusingly. "Did you honestly think you'd get away with any part of this idiotic plan, you bumbling ignoramus?" I belted out in my best insulting voice.

"What the...?" Mandy's face was a question mark of bafflement.

"What the...?" Lake echoed, equally confused.

I refilled my lungs with the damp cave air. It tasted of algae and stone. "You're pretty bad at crime, aren't you, darling? You really should leave it to the professionals." *Did I just call myself a career criminal? As if that's a good thing?* "You left a trail about four miles wide, and you barely managed to kill anyone at all. *Tsk.*" *Sorry, Zach.*

Lake hadn't known. His eyes widened to the size of fishermen's floats, but he stayed put.

"You think I enjoyed what I had to do?" Mandy shot back. She spun on her knees atop the huge boulder and leaned forward with her hands on either side of her lantern. The tendons on the backs of her hands cast tense shadows in its light. "You don't know anything, you crazy woman. I owe money to some very powerful people in Chicago. *Very* powerful. They'll kill me if I don't pay them back. Don't you see? This treasure was my only way out. It was a godsend, a sign from the universe!"

Lake, helpful guy that he was, tried to distract Mandy from me. "This treasure trove won't be enough? How much do you owe?"

Great, the desperate murderer is staring right at my boyfriend, whom I've come to rescue.

"The price of a state-of-the-art salvage vessel and all its brand-new equipment, which sank in a freak storm on Lake Michigan this spring. I told them my plan was foolproof. There was no way I'd fail to locate and bring up the wreck of the *Nathaniel Browne*. And then, what do you know, I failed." She tightened her jaw and looked away.

"The *Nathaniel Browne*?" Tru had mentioned that name during the tsunami party—a ship lost in a freak storm on Lake Michigan in 1913. It hadn't been found yet. "That was you?"

Mandy flung her hands up in frustration. "Yes, great. Even here in the middle of Hicktasticville, you've heard of my failure." She leaned across the rock again, her body language intense. "That disaster ruined my career before it ever got off the ground. I had to sell my half of my own company to Wade just to keep my investors from fitting me with a nice pair of cement shoes on the spot. I had to sell everything I had and borrow from everyone I knew. And it wasn't enough. I jumped at the chance to find this treasure. I felt it calling to me, you know? I was meant to find this trove."

"And now you have." I kept her focus on me. "Congratulations and all that. But why did you have to kill one of my authors? He had nothing to do with your treasure hunt!"

Mandy smirked dismissively. "That hick? He was an idiot, completely full of himself. You're not telling me you actually miss him."

"He was a person, and you killed him. Tell me why!" I demanded, feeling Scarlen return.

Mandy shook her head in a rueful manner. "He guessed. He came up to me at the bar and started spinning this crazy conspiracy theory."

My jaw tensed. *Zach, you didn't.*

"And he got enough right that I couldn't let him walk away—even if he thought it was Wade's plan because I was 'just a woman.' Couldn't have it ending up in one of his books for everyone to see."

"He wrote cowboy mysteries," I said faintly. "Ranches and back roads. He'd never have used your plan."

Mandy blinked, and her brows drew together. "Well, I didn't know that then, did I? I told him to meet me later, and I'd tell him what I suspected. That gave me time to set up an alibi, except it nearly went wrong when you two stumbled in like a pair of horny saviors."

"What alibi?" Lake asked.

"Patrice," I supplied.

Mandy gave me a nod of grudging respect. "I drugged her at On The Rocks—just a little too much Xanax powdered in her martini—and left her in the alley. Then I sent myself a text from her phone. I could be 'out looking for her' for as long as I needed. In the midst of a town festival, no one would notice either of us. But you lovebirds stumbled onto her before I got back from dealing with Zach."

"And you tried to kill Wade," I said, keeping her talking. *If we can't take her down ourselves, reinforcements will be here soon enough.* "That was you on the boat with him. Everyone—including Lake and me—thought you were a man. But you're six feet tall. Put on a flannel shirt and a ball cap, and it's an easy mistake to make from a few hundred feet away. What did Wade ever do to you?"

"Bayside Buccaneers is *mine,*" she said with a possessive growl. "Wade bought me out so the business could stay afloat. But I founded the company. He had no right to order me around in the company I created. He said he wouldn't sell it back to me even if we found the treasure. He'd gotten power hungry, and he had to go."

"Murder is not the way to get what you want," I said. "And neither is deceit. Lake might've fallen for your lovey-dovey act"—Lake's eyebrows dropped in confusion—"but I saw right through you," I lied. "You tried way too hard to convince everyone you were falling for the handsome local boat pilot. You'd planned to get rid of Wade from the start, but you also needed to secure a backup partner, a trusting guy you could seduce into helping you, whom you could easily betray as soon as you got the treasure. And there was my boyfriend, just trying to be a good friend. You didn't need to lay the romance on so thick to get him to help you. But you don't know him at all. You might as well have sent him a bouquet of lilies, Tibbsy."

"What?" Mandy's nose wrinkled in confusion.

But Lake's eyes widened. He'd gotten the *Brass Artifice* reference.

"When is a romance not a romance?" I quoted.

Lake finished Gray's quote in a low, cold voice, his eyes pinning Mandy to the boulder top. "When it's a smokescreen."

I let out a dramatically long-suffering sigh. "Don't you read mystery novels, Mandy? The killer always gets caught in the end."

Mandy whipped a diving knife from its sheath on her leg. Beside her on the boulder, Lake leaned back, unable to scramble out of reach. "Not always," she said. "Three people can keep a secret if two of them are dead. And I need to have a quick word with a certain young grad student who lied to me about how much this treasure is worth."

Oh, no, you do not *get to quote Moore at me, you murderer. And I'm not letting you get anywhere near Patrice, ever again.* "Did you really think I came in here by myself, that there aren't dozens of police officers waiting outside to arrest you? Don't do anything stupid, Mandy. There's no way out for you."

Mandy paused, twiddling her blade. She looked deeper into the cave and smiled. "It's like you've forgotten my job title. I'm a spelunker. All I have to do is kill the both of you, make my way to the back of the cave, and climb up the old waterfall shaft. No one from outside will even see me because the waterfall has cut so deep into the cliff face. And once I'm at the top, I can hike out of here and take care of Patrice, and no one will ever hear from me again. Or her. Or either of you."

No, no, no! This is not the plan! Scarlen reared up in my mind again, and I frantically scanned the area for something—anything—to wrest control back from the deranged killer before she hurt Lake. Or before he hurt himself trying to take her down. By the way he was trying to hold his head so still, I knew he was actually looking for something out of the corner of his eye. *Probably a rock to smack her in the head with.* Ernie's accidental murder of Ramòn, who'd died from hitting his head on a rock just outside this cave, flooded my mind. I couldn't let Lake kill someone, not like that, not here.

Freshly disturbed dirt caught my eye. One of the boulders next to me had been moved from its spot. The tool marks dug into the damp earth, and I searched for their maker.

A crowbar rested in the shadows a few feet away. I lunged for it, clutched it with sore hands peeking through Ashley's torn compression gloves, and brandished it over my head.

Mandy laughed condescendingly. "What are you gonna do with that? Throw it at me? You run a bed-and-breakfast. Maybe if you had a killer stack of sharpened pancakes or something, you'd be a threat. But you don't, and you're not." She moved the blade toward Lake while holding eye contact with me. Her smile was cold, triumphant.

Lake raised his arms defensively, but he sat at the edge of the high boulder, with nowhere to run.

My blood thrummed at my temples. "I. Own. This. Room." I brought the crowbar down hard, and it rang against a chunk of columnar basalt that had fallen from the cave ceiling. The rock's long, thick crystals sang a low, alarming note.

Mandy barked a derisive laugh. "You most certainly d—"

I leaped onto the rock and slammed the crowbar against the wall repeatedly, right near the ceiling. Dust streams trickled down from half a dozen cracks in the rock above us and spun in the lantern light.

"Whoa, Pippa, what are you doing?" Lake yelped.

I jammed the straight end of the crowbar into the nearest crack over my head and leaned on it. More dust drifted down. I gave Mandy a wicked, hard smile. "*My* room. I decide its fate. I decide *all* our fates." I shifted my weight and pulled hard on the crowbar, and a crystalline chunk of stone the size of my forearm crashed to the dirt. My heart rate skyrocketed on a fuel boost of pure adrenaline. *Criminy on a cracker! Please don't actually collapse! Nice cave, good cave.*

"Stop, stop! You'll trap us in here, if you don't kill us all first!" Mandy scrambled off the boulder, trampled on the scattered treasure fragments, and slogged through the mucky water that separated us, knife blade flaring in the lantern light.

"Now you're catching on!" I hollered, terrified by my own actions. But I couldn't stop now.

Lake stared at me like I'd gone mad.

I leaned on the crowbar again, and a deep grinding noise emanated from the ceiling above our heads. I remembered the story Lake had told me about Zach asking him for a cool code phrase for his book. "You know what they say about salamander fish at low tide!"

Lake's head snapped up, as he grasped my message—the same one Zach had meant for his character to use: *Attack while I distract.* Mandy only made it halfway through the water before he tackled her with a mighty splash. She fell into the algae mouth-first, and her blond hair disappeared below the surface under Lake's weight. A few seconds later, her head emerged. She sputtered and coughed like a flooded engine, and her brownish-green hair plastered itself to her face. While Lake grabbed fistfuls of the back of her shirt, she swiped muck out of her eyes with both hands, having dropped her knife somewhere in the dirty water. I yanked the crowbar from the ceiling crack and hopped off my makeshift soapbox, and the cave generously stopped dropping chunks of stone at me. *Good cave.* I patted its ceiling.

Lake hauled her out of the water and onto the muddy slope on my side of the puddle despite her growling and writhing, using her collar and belt as handles, then he pinned her hands behind her back. I yanked the lanyard from my emergency flashlight and tossed it to him, and he did some kind of ropey magic and tied her hands as quick as a wink. With some rough encouragement, Lake got her up to the top of the little path, where I gave him a breathless kiss. Only then did I notice the blood on his arm.

"You're hurt!" I cried.

Lake studied his bicep. "Huh, how about that? Her knife must've caught me."

"That water is nasty. You don't want to get an infection." Remembering Captain McReynolds' jungle tactics, I unlaced Mandy's boots and took them off, along with her thick woolen socks. "You don't want a boot to the head in here, either."

Mandy scoffed, though her eyes blazed hot with fury. "Whatever. You'll never understand what's really important."

My jaw muscles bunched. Lake tightened his grip on her collar.

I held up one of her wet socks. "What's important is remembering who we are. That we're all the same. That we're all worth saving. That mercy is always a choice. Like this." I wrung her sock out, then I stuffed it in her mouth and tied it there with the other sock.

Her eyes burned fire at me, but I just patted her cheek. "I could've left it wet. See? Mercy. You're welcome."

"Dude, Pippa," Lake said, but I heard laughter behind his words.

I met his sea-bright eyes. The tension in my shoulders finally eased. He was safe. "Let's get out of here, Lake."

"Yes, ma'am."

He got Mandy on her feet and pointed her toward the cave entrance. I scooped up a few shiny pieces of eight and my trusty new crowbar and followed them.

Luckily, all of Hilt's cavalries had arrived outside, so extra hands were ready to assist us in our exit from the cave. EMTs ushered Lake to the side to treat the slice on his arm, and Sheriff Kettleman clapped handcuffs on Mandy's wrists. He chuckled at the flashlight lanyard and left it in place as he escorted Mandy away. She strode stiffly in front of him. Her ramrod spine seemed unwilling to admit guilt, but her slumped shoulders were unwilling to fight for the treasure any longer. If it couldn't save her, nothing would.

Triumphant, I stood astride the cave's vertical shaft, one hand on my hip, the other resting my crowbar across one shoulder. The sun shone down through a break in the high clouds, gilding my victory. The late-summer breeze smelled of salt and fir trees. And freedom. And success.

"You can come down now, Winterbourne," Acting Police Chief Mallory Tavish called up from the base of the rock fall, twenty feet in front of me. "We get it. You were awesome." Her words of praise were blunted by her unimpressed tone.

"Darn right I was—whoa!" I wobbled and narrowly avoided tumbling head over heels and breaking a limb or two. With one last burst of adrenaline, I righted myself and promptly plopped on my bottom before sliding ingloriously off my Boulder of Triumph. I picked my way through the rocks until I stood before Mallory.

We eyed each other for a long time. Her brown eyes studied mine so closely I felt like I'd been X-rayed. Finally, she said, "Looks like it's your turn to be the badass hero." She paused and pursed her lips as if the next sentence didn't want to come out yet. But she said it, anyway. "Thank you for saving Lakyn."

I lifted my chin. "I didn't do it for you."

She finally lowered her eyes. "I know."

"The treasure's in there, Mallory. The other members of the salvage team should be notified—Connor and Patrice, and Wade, once he wakes up. And..." I held out my hand, showing her the gold coins I'd picked up. "These belong in a museum."

Mallory's eyes widened, and she shared her gaze between the coins and me. "Okay, Indiana Jones."

"It's what Ramòn wanted."

Mallory nodded and solemnly took them. She held one up and let it gleam in the sunlight. She sighed with a frown and a shake of her head.

I knew exactly how she felt. *All this grief and heartache because of greed and desperation.*

Trudie pelted past Mal with an excited, girly squeal and slammed into me with a giant bear hug, which nearly knocked me off balance. "You did it! You're not dead! You saved him! You're amazing! You're the best sister ever on the whole planet, oh my God!" Out of breath, she squeezed me so tightly I saw spots. Then she pulled back and smiled at me. "Hey, what's that on your forehead?"

"I rubbed a gold coin there to see if it was real." I grinned. "I guess I have treasure on my mind."

Her groan at my pun rose to a growl. "Really? You think now is an acceptable moment for a pun? Did you hit your head in there?"

I could only laugh at her mock outrage.

She grinned and relented. "But I'll forgive you this time because you're okay. You did it." The pride and sisterly love in her eyes fairly glowed, and it touched me so deeply that I felt our bond strengthen all the way back to our childhood.

I squeezed her back and held her for a long time, not speaking. Over Tru's shoulder, Mal gave me a final nod and walked away. I grabbed my little sister and looked her in the eyes. "I couldn't have gotten here in time if it weren't for you. You helped me save the man I love."

"Darn right, I did," she said, echoing my earlier brag. "Besides, it was the only way to save the man *I* love. With Mandy in custody, they'll have to let Gabe go."

"That's right. But c'mon. You have to tell me," I begged. "What's the skinny on the Reno rock-crawling story?"

Trudie gave me a mysterious smile that made her seem older and wiser. "A girl's gotta have *some* secrets."

I blinked. Tru was her own person. She always had been. "Fair enough."

"Pippa!" Lake called. I approached my mansel-in-distress, and Tru trailed after me. "They say I have to go get this cut cleaned and stitched, and they're threatening me with like eight different antibiotics because of what might be living in that puddle. So I guess I'll have to catch up with you later."

"You heal up soon." I kissed him firmly. "And no mutating into Aquaman or anything."

He lifted his chin. "We both know I'm already Aquaman."

I kissed him again. "Yes, we do. So if I saved Aquaman's life, how awesome does that make me?"

His sea-blue eyes shone. "The awesomest."

I squeezed his hand as the EMTs led him away. "See you soon."

I put my arm around Tru's shoulder, and together, we followed Lake and his escorts through the cluster of emergency personnel, rescue crews, and law enforcement officers. Butch, Chloe, Ogden, Ashley, and Sarah cheered and waved from the viewpoint wall a hundred feet up the cliff, and I offered them a jaunty salute in return. A Coast Guard boat idled in the water, and a chopper hovered alertly overhead.

I smiled at all the chaos, content with my place in the world, and gave my sister's shoulders a squeeze. "You hungry?"

24

"*Women are like onions—the closer you get to one, the more likely you are to cry.*"
Raymond Moore, 1936

TRUDIE CALLED A COUPLE of hours later to let me know—complete with squeals and exclamations of delight—that Gabe had indeed been released from jail. "And no offense, but we won't be coming over to thank you in person today. It's gonna be a night in for us. I'll see you tomorrow, okay? And thank you. You're the best big sister in the world."

While my authors eagerly worked on notes and novels in their rooms, I pulled down the crime scene tape that had X-ed over Zach's door. *Case closed. We got her, Zach.*

Lake called a bit later, to let me know the hospital was holding him overnight to make sure he didn't get some Aquaman-level infection. With the cats trailing my steps as if lonely for human company, I wandered Moorehaven's halls and talked with Lake for hours, making plans for the rest of the year—from picking a weekly evening for our date nights to attending local events. That quiet time with him refreshed me like a soft rain on thirsty soil. I snuggled my cats close and dreamed of Lake all night.

Cool clouds had eased in, and on Saturday morning, I woke to a silvery sky of puffy cotton balls that let the sun gleam down between nearly invisible cracks. The air was cool and delightfully crisp. Though it smelled of fresh salt, I imagined I could pick out the faint aromas of apples, cinnamon, and pumpkin. The frenetic heat-shimmer of summer was dying, and I was happy to dance on its grave.

Word had gotten around town about the Spanish treasure being located, and the bloat of gold-crazy tourists was beginning to trickle away. Seacrest was exhaling summer, and that meant I could breathe a sigh of relief too.

Chloe showed up bright and early to help with breakfast, and Tyleen even popped by to drop off some homemade Polish sausages, which got Rex in particular very excited. I convinced her to stay and eat with us as a thank-you for all her help over the past crazy week.

"You're too kind, Pippa." She sat on the chair Hilt pulled out for her. But even after everything I'd been through with my authors—and everyone in Glaze and Gossip knew the whole story now—my neighbor still shot Ashley a calculating glance. *She's made up her mind, and now she can't change it. But her heart's in the right place. She's only looking out for me, after all.*

Ogden opted to eat in his room again, so I added an extra blintz to his plate before I took it up. Svetlana generously offered to keep him company by perching on his keyboard.

In the dining room, over a breakfast that managed to be both celebratory and sober, Ashley said, "I've packed up, and I'll be heading out when I'm done here. Keep those compression gloves of mine, if you like. They're a souvenir of a pretty exciting adventure, aren't they? I have to say, this has been the most fun I've had in a very long time. You have no idea what that means to me. I won't be forgetting you anytime soon."

Butch preened. "I'll make sure you leave with my number, then, sweetheart."

Sarah cleared her throat. "She meant Pippa."

I polished off the last bite of my eggs and bowed over my fork. "I'm glad I could oblige. Nothing says memorable visit to the Oregon Coast like solving a murder with a few intrepid mystery writers."

Sarah offered Butch a bright smile and held it for a few seconds, letting it soften into gentle regard. "I'm leaving too. I wanted to stay on to help out, and now I've done that. Time to resume my duties as a milk factory."

Butch took a deep breath and tried out a comment despite his uncertain expression. "If anyone can multitask, it's you."

Sarah patted his arm with an *Oh, you* look.

I recalled how full my freezer was getting. "He's right. You never really stopped. I can get you some extra ice to keep everything frozen."

"I appreciate that. Thanks."

After we finished up, Chloe and Tyleen tackled the dishes while I printed out receipts for my departing guests. Since Chloe had taken her suitcase—and a box of odds and ends—over to the lighthouse the previous night, the Oubliette was officially empty and ready for guests again. Hilt ran a final check on its readiness. I was definitely ready to mark it as available again on my website.

"Knock, knock!" Tru called as she sashayed in, wearing a bright summer dress printed with giant pink roses. Gabe trailed after her, hands tucked in his pockets, grin a mile wide. "Pips, there you are. We're off on an adventure, and I wanted to tell you."

"Tell me what?"

"We're house hunting today!" Tru rushed up to the counter and spread a big stack of printed MLS listings across it, disheveling my carefully organized tourism pamphlets. "Look, this one is huge—and so cheap! Think of all the rooms it must have. I could have a craft room all my own, and Gabe could have a man-cave, and they wouldn't have to be opposite ends of the same tiny table anymore!"

I frowned at the picture on the page. "That's the house everyone says is haunted."

Tru pouted. "Well, how about this cute cottage by the sea?"

I read the details upside down. "Six hundred square feet? Where's the craft room in that one?"

"Or," Tru said, cheerfully determined to share her favorites with me, "this one on a cliff. 'Great views!' Look, they have pictures!"

I turned the page right side up. "Those do look nice." I read the address. "This is on Halfway Hill, though. They had all those landslides last winter. Why do you think it's selling for so cheap?"

Tru narrowed her eyes. "You are no fun at all."

I leaned my elbows on the counter and met her eyes squarely. "Listen, I'm excited you guys are hoping to stay in the area, but this is part of my big-sister job description: keeping you safe and disgruntled since 19—"

"Yeah, yeah, okay," she interrupted. "Gabe said you'd say all those things." She shuffled the top three papers to the bottom of the hefty pile.

Gabe stepped up, wrapped an arm around her shoulders, and kissed her temple. "I'm gonna interrupt long enough to tell your sister thank you for getting me out of jail." The deep peace I saw in his warm brown eyes told me all I needed to know about why Tru had fallen in love with him. "Thank you, Pippa. You saved me from a dark fate. I owe you. You ever need a big favor, you ask me first, okay?"

That low ribbon in his tone told me he meant every word. I did him the honor of taking his offer seriously. "You got it, Gabe. Do you have a favorite house in the stack?"

He shrugged one muscled shoulder. "Not really. I've offered to build an expansion or two onto any house we get. Now that I've taken over Ernie's fencing business, I'll definitely be working on my carpentry more."

I chuckled. "Well, good hunting. I'm sure you'll find something that suits you both. You're a good fit."

Tru gave me a dewy look. "You think so?"

Ah, the power of the older sister. "Well, early returns are promising."

Tru straightened her listings with unnecessary precision, but a smile played at the corner of her mouth. "Well, we're off. I'll send you a housewarming invitation when we pick the best one."

"I look forward to it. And, Tru." She turned back. "Thank you again." She smiled and gave me a jaunty salute.

Ashley had her rental car company pick her up right afterward. Ogden checked out shyly a few minutes later, but the way he lingered, fiddling with his receipt, told me he wished he could express the big emotions he was experiencing.

"I know, right?" I told him. "I'll pay close attention to your next book in case you tuck any recognizable details in there, okay? And I look forward to your next visit."

He nodded and managed to meet my eyes for a brief, smiling moment. "Thanks. I'll see you."

And with that, the only real person I'd ever used to inspire myself walked out into the salty air and blew onward to the next adventure in his life.

Within an hour, Sarah's husband, Thad, showed up to take her home, and Butch picked up his receipt at the same time she did.

"You know," Butch said as he held the front door open for Sarah, "I'm glad I met you. You did good things for my thinking."

Sarah stood on tiptoe and kissed the older man's leathery cheek. "Same here, Butch. See you in the bookshelves." She slipped out onto the porch, pulling her suitcase behind her and carrying a couple of shoulder bags.

Butch gave me a friendly nod of farewell, but his smile melted into concern, and he whipped his head around after Sarah. "Wait, does that mean you're really putting me in your book? Sarah? Are you killing me off, woman? Sarah!"

Her voice trilled back through the closing door as Butch chased after her. "Spoilers!"

I chuckled. Opposites combined to make a dynamic team, but sometimes, they still tried to murder each other. Fictionally speaking.

Right before lunch, Chloe and I sat at the nook table and went over the list of incoming guests. "It's weird not to have a lunch order today," she said.

"We can still get some sandwiches from Mozzie's if you want."

"Oh, I definitely want." She pulled out her phone to place our usual orders.

A knock came at the front door while Chloe was ordering extra chips. I found Wallis standing on my porch. "Hey, Wallis, what's up?"

The funereal florist clasped her hands together and looked her usual mournful self. "I was hoping to speak to Chloe." Her voice was positively bereaved. "Is she here?"

"Hey, Wallis," Chloe said, appearing at my side. "What's wrong?"

"Oh, nothing at all," she said, as if consoling Chloe for the loss of a favorite aunt. "I was merely hoping for a couple of tips."

Chloe and I exchanged a surprised glance. "Tips for what?" I asked.

Wallis looked around uncomfortably, and I realized I hadn't invited her in.

"Come into the small parlor. I'll get some coffee."

In a few minutes, we all sat in the small parlor's green wingback chairs with cups of coffee— and tea for Wallis.

She took a sip. "You already know, Pippa, that my flower business might not be long for this world. Even though that fisherman thought it was funny to receive a Congratulations bouquet for losing two toes, word's gotten around that I'm losing my touch. And no one wants to die in the summer. Not even me."

Chloe gave me an exasperated glance from behind the black curtain of her hair. If the Goth girl from the fictional-murder capital of the world was getting fed up with Wallis's deathly references, I would have to tread carefully.

"Also no graduations, and the wedding rush is over for the year," Chloe added with a salty tone.

"Too true," Wallis lamented. "So I've branched out. I managed to find a small part-time job that pays very well. Too well, I rather think, but I couldn't guess why. And I thought I'd ask for some advice." Her forlorn gaze settled on Chloe.

"From me?" Chloe's surprise shook her hair from her other eye. "Why?"

"Because the job used to be yours. I'm your father's new tour guide. He's springing for a new costume and everything. I'm so tall, you and I wouldn't fit in the same coffin, let alone the same dress."

Chloe sat silently, staring at Wallis. I worried she was furious that her father had stepped up with good pay in order to lure Chloe back to a job she didn't want. Or maybe she felt rejected, since her father had found a replacement he *was* willing to pay so soon after she moved out.

"Chloe? You okay?" I didn't quite reach out to squeeze her hand, but my fingers twitched toward her.

"How much is he paying you?" Chloe's voice was nearly a whisper.

"Fifty dollars per tour. But I have a couple of weeks to learn all the information because he said something about restoring the attic to its original, creepy state."

"That won't take much." Chloe's voice was soft.

"And he made sure I knew that the mummified rat in the windowsill up there is named Cerberus."

Chloe gasped and smiled. "He's keeping Cerberus? Oh my God. That's, wow. That's amazing. This is a big step for him. I'm sure you'll be great, Wallis."

I stared at her, stunned. "You're okay with this?"

My assistant offered me a wry smile. "He's not 'restoring' the attic to a creepy state. I kept it creepy the whole time I lived there. He hardly has to change much at all. The two weeks are his period of mourning."

"Mourning?" Wallis perked up.

"He's mourning me," Chloe said. "I moved out when he wouldn't pay me or give me a schedule. He's not ready for the tour guide to be anyone else quite yet. He just needs time to adjust, is all."

"*Ohh*," Wallis breathed. Her hand delicately fluttered to rest on her heart. "I completely understand, dear. I'll be very understanding when I deal with your father."

Chloe hid a smirk, but I still caught a glimpse of it. "I'd appreciate that," she told Wallis. "Now that I think about it, I'm not sure my dad could've picked a better person in all of Seacrest to be the new tour guide for our historic home and the guardian of all my family's stories."

"Really?" Wallis leaned forward on her comfy chair. "Why is that?"

Chloe waited a beat to make sure she had our undivided attention. "Because, Wallis, everyone you'll be talking about is dead."

Wallis's hands rose until her fingers hovered just shy of her lips, which she pressed together to hold in her emotion. "That is the sweetest thing anyone's ever said to me."

Wallis stayed and chatted for a few more minutes before she excused herself to go try on her new costume, but as she opened the door to leave, someone knocked. She pulled the door open out of reflex, and we all stared at Vic, who held a bouquet of pale-orange daisies in his hands. His shaved head bore a tan line where he usually wore his wraparound sunglasses.

He smiled shyly at Wallis. "I saw you step in here, so I popped home to get the bouquet I bought from you this morning." He offered them to her, and she took them slowly, as if she'd never received a bouquet of her own in her life. "Congratulations on the new job. I hope this doesn't mean I can't see you in the mornings, though. I've kinda gotten used to it. To you, I mean." His cue-ball head tipped, and he offered her a soft smile.

Wallis seemed entirely unprepared for Vic's declaration of affection, so I stepped in to rescue her. "I guess this means he doesn't have any regrets after all, Wallis. It would be a shame if he started to get some, wouldn't it?"

Wallis blinked at me, and the frown between her brows seemed to ask, *Are you telling me what I think you're telling me?*

Sometimes, a romance really is just a romance. I shooed her onto my porch with Vic. "Go on, you two. It's a lovely day."

Wallis gave me the most dazzling smile I'd ever seen, and I nearly fainted from the shock of it. "Yes, yes, it is a lovely day, Pippa. Now, Vic, dear, would you be so kind as to escort me back to my shop?"

His hazel eyes twinkled. "Yes, ma'am."

The unlikely pair sashayed off the porch, leaving Chloe and me giggling. I whipped out my phone and began to text Jordan and the other members of Glaze and Gossip. *You'll* never guess *what just happened right on my porch!* I filled them in on the surprising romantic twist as Chloe and I pottered around in a virtually empty Moorehaven.

"Oh," Chloe said as we rose to put the coffee cups in the sink, "I found an envelope for you in Ashley's room. I tucked it in the top drawer at the hostess station and forgot about it."

"Thanks. I'll grab it." After Chloe took my cup for me, I found the envelope and slit it open. A cream page covered with smooth blue cursive slid out into my palm, surrounding something firm but bendable.

When I unfolded the note, a bundle of cash revealed itself, bound by a paper marked *$10,000*. I stared in utter bafflement for a few seconds before I remembered I was still holding Ashley's note.

Dearest Pippa, Ashley wrote, *it has been a true pleasure to get to know you these past few days. You've impressed me, and that's hard to do. I'd only intended Moorehaven to serve as a hunting hide while I observed Chief Tavish at work. And then I met you. You jumped at the chance to investigate the marina when I called in disguise—a true sleuth at heart! I almost never change my mind once I set a plan in motion, but you, my dear, are a rare treasure, able to encourage, inspire, and investigate, all in one. I even got excited about the book I started writing so I could stay at Moorehaven, and that was unexpected indeed.*

Chloe came back from the kitchen as I finished reading it. "What does she say?"

Eyes still on the note, I waved the bundle of cash in reply. Chloe gasped.

Do pass on my apologies to Chief Tavish and your uncle, I read on silently, *for the necessary deception regarding the break-in to the police archives room. I needed to be as certain as possible that you were on the right track in solving Ramòn's murder. And you were.*

I know you've had a rough time of it lately, so please accept this small token of my appreciation. Please note that accepting this favor will endear you to me in such a way that I may call on you at some future point for assistance. You're one of the family now, and should we meet again, I shall rely on you most intently. Warmly, Ashlen Potachev

Chloe's eyes were still on the greenbacks I held. She nonchalantly offered, "You want me to take care of that for you? I can blow it all in downtown Portland, easy. I can even do Amazon in a pinch, although now that I have my own place—sort of—I should probably start saving for, like, utilities or something. You could donate to my light and heat fund."

My head spun. With desperate urgency, I struggled to think back over the past few days, to everything that had happened. *She even signed this with her pen name. Did anything mean what I thought it did? I might owe Tyleen an apology for thinking she was just being paranoid about Ashley.*

"Pippa! What does she say?" Chloe repeated, nudging my arm.

"She seems to be buying me with this 'gift' of money for Moorehaven's repairs. But if I spend it," I continued, "I'm agreeing to accept her favor, and I'll owe her one in return, which I must repay whenever she calls on me."

"What the actual heck?" Chloe blurted. "Is she, like, the daughter of a Russian mobster or something?"

"I... I have no idea who she really is." I thought back to everything she'd said about her novel. It sounded completely legitimate. "She planned and wrote at least part of a book, just to come here and stay. But I don't think she ever intended to finish it. She says she came to watch Mallory, but she ended up choosing me instead." I shivered. *And I used her character as inspiration when Lake needed help. Eew.*

"So what did she really want here?"

A stiff bit of mystery-sleuth spirit returned to me. "That, my dear Chloe, is the right question."

25

"An enemy is just an ally you haven't persuaded yet."
Raymond Moore, 1942

"THE HOSPITAL HAS FINALLY let me go," Lake said over the phone. "Seventeen stitches. I'd love to see you right away, but I seriously need to drive home and get a shower first."

"I don't mind," I replied. Chloe and Hilt were playing backgammon in the library. Neither of them had been able to offer any light on Ashley's mysterious letter. Moorehaven's near-emptiness was messing with my head. I needed to have someone to take care of, and I had no guests. "Let me come pick you up."

"No, seriously. I have the nastiest slime in my hair. And you know how I love algae, so trust me, if *I* don't want to smell this stuff, *you* don't want to smell this stuff. I'll come by as soon as I'm clean. Promise."

"I'm holding you to that."

"Anything else you want to hold me to?" The smile in his voice warmed me from head to toe.

"You'll have to show up and find out. See you soon."

Restless, I roamed the halls like a wandering spirit. The Oubliette was finally complete and ready for guests. My halls were vacuumed. The laundry had been sent down the chutes, washed, dried, and folded. My kitchen was spotless. Hilt had already fixed a leaky sink in the Cobalt Suite, and Chloe spent the afternoon weeding around the flowers in the back garden and making a list of flower bulbs to buy. She'd already dusted the peacock-pane chandelier, along with every Tiffany lamp in Moorehaven. The cats lay in the sunroom and snoozed on separate couches, also having completed their short and simple to-do lists for the day.

My B&B didn't need me. It was simply waiting to be useful. I felt exactly the same way. With a sigh, I stepped out onto my front porch and grabbed the broom from its place behind a big pot. Chloe had even cleaned the porch, I remembered. But I could at least appear useful by pretending to sweep. *Maybe some mindless sweeping will help me remember something useful about Ashley.*

I meandered toward the south end of the shaded porch. My fence had been repaired, painted, and decorated with brightly colored fishing nets that captured wooden books and shells. Gabe had done a fabulous job painting the books' covers like some of the best-sellers that had been written at Moorehaven. The nets were also strewn with the occasional glass fishing float. The whole fence ensemble looked amazing, but seeing Ernie's handiwork brought a pang of sadness to my chest. I hoped Hilt would get used to seeing it out his window every day. Then I reminded myself: Gabe had worked on the fence too. And he and Tru were settling in to stay—or trying to.

A car pulled into my empty parking lot. My spirits sank a little at the sight of Mallory's cruiser. She stepped out alone, wearing her reflective sunglasses and a blank, professional expression. "Winterbourne. A word."

You could at least pretend to make it a question. "Come on in." *This isn't going to be pretty.*

I set my broom back and led the way into the big parlor. She took one of the chairs, and I sat with my back to the window, hogging the red couch so she couldn't crowd me. I waited for her to speak first. Time dragged out. I put on my best Hostess Smile and folded my fingers around one knee.

Finally, Mal took off her sunglasses and tucked them into her uniform pocket with a sigh. "Look, this isn't going to be pretty," she said, echoing my earlier thought.

I braced myself for her oncoming possessive tirade.

"But I need to apologize to you, and I figured I should do it in person."

"Wha-a-at?" In disbelief, I dragged out the word.

"The drug raid shouldn't have happened. I should never have gotten that court order. The opportunity to throw you off your game was too good to pass up. I had my suspicions that the letter accusing you was a false lead, but I ignored them, and I convinced Vic to ignore them too. And my timing was really rotten." She leaned forward and put her elbows on her knees. "I'm sorry. I was wrong. I'm a better cop than that. But I'm not sure I'm a good-enough person to do this job the way it should be done."

In shock, I blinked at her several times, fumbling for a response. Anger, sympathy, and admiration swirled in my head. *Well, I can't believe I'm thinking this, but if she can step up, then so can I.* "Thank you. That must've been hard for you to say—"

"*God*, you have *no* idea."

I bit my lip hard to keep from saying something really snarky, even though my hands literally twitched with eagerness. "And so," I continued with deliberate calm, "I appreciate you coming in person."

Mal sat back, her earnest confession over. "And since I'm here, I also wanted to say how foolish you were to climb into that cave by yourself. I'm surprised you didn't drag a handful of your novel-writing companions in after you, but I suppose I can credit you for having a smidgen of common sense."

I crossed my arms. She didn't sound like she was done, though, so I pressed my lips shut and waited.

Seemingly disappointed at not getting a rise out of me, Mal sighed and added, "But you managed to save Lakyn anyway, so...

Thank you. If anything had happened to him..." Her jaw bunched as she clenched her teeth.

"There's no way I was going to let that crazy woman kill him," I said coolly. "Not after having to watch her flirt with him left and right."

"What?" Mal's eyes widened. "That little..."

I raised an eyebrow in wry agreement. "One of us would've saved him. This time, it was me."

Mal raised her chin and studied me with a surprisingly open expression. "He does need a lot of looking after."

Basking in the sudden lack of possessive jealousy, I had a thought. "Speaking of men who need looking after, what's going on with Ritchy Axelrod? You've charged him for selling those fake coins, right?"

Mallory's lips flattened into a line. "Sadly, no. Turns out the little paper insert in his fake coin cases had the tiniest of print that read 'genuine reproduction.' We can't bust him for selling fake coins he labels as fake."

"Slippery little hagfish."

But Mallory wore a small smile. "He'll slip up someday, and he'll have made his last slick move."

Speaking of slick moves... "Wait, you said a letter told you about the drugs. What kind of letter? Can I see it?"

Mallory gave me a disappointed look. "I don't walk around with evidence in my pockets, Winterbourne." She frowned thoughtfully. "But I do happen to have a picture on my phone. My backup evidence policy. Why do you want to see it?"

"It could help me solve one more mystery."

Mal rolled her eyes, but she pulled out the phone and flicked through until she found the picture. She handed the phone to me, and my stomach dropped at the sight: bright-blue cursive on cream paper. "Oh my God."

"What is it?"

I pulled Ashley's farewell letter from my pocket and handed it over. "Ashley Potts left this for me when she checked out. The paper, the ink, even the handwriting's a match."

Mal snatched the envelope and fished out Ashley's note. After scanning it, her slim brows drew together. "I can't believe I didn't put this together before now. And... Oh my God..."

"What are you talking about?"

My urgent question wiped the alarm off her face and directed her attention back to me. "The letter that accused you of selling drugs here in Moorehaven was dropped off anonymously. But this handwriting, this card stock—all of it—matches. And not only the drug letter, but a letter I received at my home address a couple of weeks ago."

I sat bolt upright. "Ashley wrote to you? Before she even came to Seacrest? What did she say?"

Mallory closed her eyes and frowned. "Nothing special. That's why I didn't connect it with the drug accusation. It just said something about looking forward to seeing me in action. And she didn't sign it with either of her names."

I pointed at the note Mallory still held. "She said she came to watch you. So why does she tell *me* I'll owe her a favor and not you?"

Mallory's smile was sad and wry. "Because *you* solved the murders, not me. You rescued Lake, not me. Congratulations, Pippa. You've drawn the attention of a very dangerous person."

I went cold, and tingles shot up my spine. *I really do owe Tyleen an apology, and I'm going to take her intuition more seriously from now on. Even the cats seemed to know something was up with Ashley.* "But wait. Even if she did poke us so we'd jump, she couldn't have controlled everything that happened in the last week. I mean, she couldn't have known Ramòn's body would be found while she was staying here. That's what started everything. He had gold coins in his pocket, and that drew in Mandy and her team, and her desperate need to pay off her debts got Zach killed and half her team attacked. Ashley couldn't possibly have choreographed all of that." My voice dropped to a whisper. "Could she?"

Mallory stared back at me, as disconcerted as I'd ever seen her. "The money for the construction of the overlook that was supposed to be built where Ramòn was buried? It was donated anonymously." She folded her hands slowly and studied them for a second. "I could try to trace it back for you. But in my experience—and I have a lot in this area—poking powerful people is a *bad idea*. And Ms. Potachev actually seems to like you."

The wary stillness around Mallory's eyes set off a red flag. I narrowed my eyes at her. "You know who she is."

Mallory defended her knowledge with a blank look.

"Potachev is her real name, isn't it? Potts was the pen name, to fool us."

Mallory sighed. "You're mostly right. See, I follow wealthy people like some people follow baseball. I admit, I didn't recognize her in her ordinary, middle-aged-woman getup. Even in this town, running across a billionaire in disguise isn't something one expects to happen. But I do recognize Potachev as the birth name of one of the most powerful and dangerous women in the country: Ashlen Potenta, the Bombshell Billionaire."

I had to raise an eyebrow at the nickname. "Really?"

She shrugged. "One of the nicknames the media gave her thirty years ago. The Marilyn of Money was another. She built an empire through cutthroat business practices and character assassination. And then, two years ago, she sold it and walked away. No one's really heard of her since. They say she never lost out on a deal, whether financial or personal. She's perfectly ruthless. And now, Pippa Winterbourne, she knows your name." She pursed her lips in concentration. "You did not, repeat, *not*, hear this from me, but... Take the money and forget you ever laid eyes on Ashlen Potenta. If you're lucky, you'll never hear from her again."

"Wouldn't it be better to just walk away?"

Mallory shook her head decisively. "That's not what she wants. You can't make her forget your name. Your best option is to play along for now. It'll give you more options in the future. Pray you never need them."

I wasn't sure which unnerved me more—that some kind of mastermind had noticed my miniscule little existence in a tiny town on the left edge of the continent, or that Mallory, Queen of Cool Professionalism, was beginning to sweat at the temples at the very thought of Ashley Potts—or Ashlen Potenta. "Okay. If you say so. I'll trust you."

That shook her out of her worry, and she studied me. "A first for everything." She shifted in her chair, shaking off her tense mood. "Listen, um... Boundaries aren't really my thing, as you might have noticed. I grew up in a wealthy family. All I had to do was ask hard enough for anything, and I got it. Cars, trips, vacations in Bali, even police academy and a posh post guarding Sacramento's wealthiest neighborhood."

I squinted. "Did you just say 'posh' un-ironically?"

Mal squinted back. "I spent a year abroad, mostly in England. One picks things up."

"Is that why you keep calling me by my last name?"

Her lips quirked. "Partly. Lake, though, he said no to me. A lot. I couldn't control him, couldn't keep him where—who—I wanted him to be."

My heart warmed as I envisioned Lake and his indomitable spirit. "Water doesn't compress."

Mallory's expression suddenly broke. Her mouth shifted from a firm line to a soft, trembling rose petal. "Oh God. You understand him perfectly. In all our time together, I could never manage to figure him out."

I flushed with a mix of pride and confusion. Not so long ago, I'd been jealous of how well Lake and Mal knew each other. I wasn't the only woman in his orbit to suffer from doubts.

She continued, "I'll never be that person for him. I'm just too—too *me*. I can't be a normal person. I can't be a normal... friend." She met my eyes, and I read her vulnerability.

How easy it would be for me to crush her. But I'm not Ashlen. I don't manipulate people from behind my smile. I shrugged breezily. "Hey. Normal is overrated. I have authors who say it's a total illusion. And with you, Chief Tavish, I will take whatever I can get."

Mallory blinked and looked down, a tentative smile playing over her lips.

"And right now, I'll take some blintzes and coffee. You want to join me?"

"It's going to take a pretty amazing blintz to impress this palate, Winterbourne. I did say I grew up wealthy."

I leaned forward and offered her a confident smile before I stood. "Then follow me, Tavish, and prepare to be impressed."

I let Mallory choose her blintz topping—cherries and peaches—while I opted for spiced apple, a harbinger of the changing seasons. *And changing attitudes.* We carried our plates and coffee back to the parlor and ate in companionable silence until Mallory finished.

She patted her lips with her napkin. "All right, Winterbourne, I'll confess. That was a decent blintz."

I nearly choked on my coffee, and my ire rose up in defense of Raymond Moore's blintz recipe. "Decent? *Decent?*"

She held up a peremptory hand. "Do you know how many Michelin-star chefs have failed to achieve 'decent' according to this refined palate?" She gestured to her mouth.

Despite how weird it felt to bond with Mallory, my chest swelled at her compliment. I gave her a cheeky grin. "Is it more than six?"

Mallory ducked her head, but I still caught her quiet chuckle. "Winterbourne, I swear to God."

"Thank you for coming today, Mallory. I'm not sure I'd have had the courage."

Mallory recovered her poise. "Probably not," she said lightly. "Clever of you, by the way, to send Chloe to the lighthouse. You knew I couldn't object to her on any level."

A warm feeling flooded me at Mallory's praise. "Well," I began, "the whole situation just kind of fell in my lap."

But Mallory was already shaking her tight bun. "No, no. Never do that."

"Never do what?"

"Never excuse your own success. It ruins the air of mystery." She gestured around herself, as if indicating an invisible cloud, and I suddenly understood Mallory Tavish on a whole new level. "Now, I need to be on my way. I've made him wait long enough." Her eyes weren't on me any longer. They lingered on the elaborate stained-glass window over my shoulder.

I whirled around and spotted Lake through a clear pane of glass. He looked half terrified at the sight of Mallory and me together. *Maybe he thinks we might snatch up our forks and duel to the death at any moment.* I glanced back at Mallory, and we both chuckled.

She set down her coffee cup, and I followed her to the door. Its stained-glass window was afire with reds and yellows in the light of the late-evening sun. Mallory glowed like an avenging angel, and her tightly tucked bun flared with a golden halo. *Not a demon, after all.*

She opened the door and let in a crisp evening breeze. "Good evening, Miss Winterbourne." Then she slipped out into the sunset. Her voice drifted back: "See you around, Lakyn."

"Mallory." Lake caught the front door with one foot before it shut. He stared at me in wary confusion. In one hand, he held a dozen fuchsia roses, and in the other, caramel-dipped apple doughnut bites from Emily's pastry shop. *My hero!*

"Do I want to know...?"

I kissed him warmly. "Probably not. But everything's fine. Come on in."

He smiled hopefully. "I'd hate to get arrested on your porch for public indecency."

I took the flowers from him. "Actually, I'd really love to just talk. Even though we've been dating all summer long, I still don't feel like I know you nearly as well as I want to."

A small furrow of concern formed between Lake's brows. "You want to slow down."

My smile was as bright as the sunset as I took his hand and led him deeper into Moorehaven, deeper into my life. "Not slow down. I want to branch out." I threw my arms wide, embracing the hallway and the future alike.

"Branching sounds cool." Lake followed my lead. "I like branches. Rivers have branches. Marine-animal nomenclature has branches. Underwater sea currents have branches. Branches are good."

"You are such a water nerd," I teased. "I love that about you."

He pulled me to a stop in the hallway and kissed me until I was breathless and dizzy. "And I love that you own a B&B for mystery authors. You have so many amazing skills. It blows my mind."

I leaned against him and reveled in his presence—in my life, in my hallway. "Really?"

"Really, really. And speaking of amazing..." Lake gazed wistfully over my shoulder, to where my empty plate sat on the parlor table. "Do you have any more of those blintzes?"

I entwined my fingers with his and pulled him toward the kitchen. "Oh, Lake. You ain't seen nothin' yet!"

Moorehaven's Mouthwatering Blintzes

Ingredients:

Crepes:

2 eggs

2 Tbsp unsalted butter, melted

2 cups milk

1 tsp vanilla

1 Tbsp sugar

½ tsp salt

1 ½ cups all-purpose flour

Filling:

¾ cup cream cheese, softened

¾ cup small-curd cottage cheese

½ cup honey vanilla Greek yogurt

¼ cup sugar

1 tsp vanilla

Berry Sauce:

½ cup fresh marionberries or blackberries

½ cup fresh blueberries

½ cup fresh strawberries, quartered

½ cup fresh raspberries

½ cup sugar

Grapeseed oil for frying

Powdered sugar for sprinkling

Directions:

Make all ingredients at least a couple of hours beforehand to allow them to rest. The batter in particular benefits from resting a couple of hours or overnight. The crepes can also be made ahead of time, after the batter rests, and refrigerated.

To prepare crepes:

Add the ingredients to a blender in the order they are listed. Cover and blend until batter is smooth. Let batter rest at least two hours.

To prepare berry sauce:

In a medium saucepan, combine marionberries, blueberries, strawberries, and sugar. Boil over medium-high heat, stirring constantly. Cook until berries soften, about 2 minutes. Remove from heat and puree using an immersion blender, or use a blender and pour mixture through a fine strainer to remove all seeds. If desired, set aside ¼ cup of sauce to add to filling, the way Penelope likes it. Fold in raspberries. Cover and refrigerate.

To prepare filling:

Combine ingredients in blender until smooth. Cover and let rest in refrigerator, up to a day ahead of time.

To make blintzes:

Heat an 8-inch skillet or crepe griddle over medium-high heat. Coat lightly with a small amount of grapeseed oil, which tolerates high heat well. Pour ¼ cup of batter into skillet or onto griddle and immediately rotate pan or smooth batter across griddle to coat hot surface in a thin layer. Cook approximately 1 minute or until surface loses its sheen. Do not flip to cook other side. Stack to cool, or use immediately.

To fill each blintz, flip crepe over so the browned side is up. Add ~3 Tbsp of filling to the lower middle. Fold the lower edge up, then the top down over it, then fold in the two sides. The un-browned side should be outward and ready for frying. Place blintz in medium-high skillet or on griddle, folded side down, for about 1 minute, then flip to cook the top.

Transfer to plate and spoon berry sauce on top. Sprinkle with powdered sugar.

Tips:

Thawed frozen fruit may be substituted for fresh.

For a crisp raw-fruit topping for whole or chopped fruit, mix fruit with honey or sugar in a bowl and simply spoon atop your blintz. Moore thought it was most excellent on warm summer mornings.

Any fruit may be substituted for the berries, really. Blintz toppings are virtually limitless.

Want to add cinnamon? Nutmeg? Peppermint? Coconut? Sugar sprinkles? Go for it!

For open-ended blintzes, fry both sides of the crepe. Add filling and roll it up, then add topping.

For those interested in a less sugary experience, 3 Tbsp agave syrup may be substituted for each quarter cup of sugar. Agave has a much lower glycemic index than granulated sugar.

Acknowledgements

My deep and abiding thanks to everyone who bore with me and assisted me as I researched and crafted this story. This includes but is not limited to: Jeanie Reed; Eric James; Bob Turner; Karen MacIvor; Becca Welck; Dilsey Welck; Lorie and her dog, Bones; the Columbia River Maritime Museum; the City of Manzanita; Nehalem Bay State Park; and the Nehalem Valley Historical Society. Any errors are mine, as usual.

Also by Morgan C. Talbot

Caching Out
First to Find
Death Will Attend
Nine Feet Under

Moorehaven Mysteries
Smugglers & Scones
Burglars & Blintzes

Standalone
The Caching Out Omnibus

About the Author

USA Today Bestselling Author Morgan Talbot is an outdoorsy girl with a deep and abiding love for the natural sciences. Her degrees involve English and jujitsu. She enjoys hiking, camping, and wandering in the woods looking for the trail to the car, but there isn't enough chocolate on the planet to bribe her into rock climbing.When she's not writing, she can be found making puzzles, getting lost on the way to geocaches, reading stories to her children, or taking far too many pictures of the same tree or rock.Morgan is a member of Sisters in Crime and Mystery Writers of America and served as a panelist at Left Coast Crime 2015: Crimelandia. She lives in Eastern Washington with her family.